WARFACE
Weird Custer

A Novel

By William Sumrall

WARFACE
Weird Custer

Shanti Publishing
PO Box 6252
Pine Mountain Club, CA 93222

www.ShantiPublishing.com

Chapter One
Wagon Train!

THE SUMMER DAY WAS as hot as it was treacherous. Deceptive imagery blurred in the hazy distance, shimmering like a chimera in the undulating, translucent heat waves. Even from far off, the noisome clattering of the cumbersome, creaking wagons heralded yet another Euro-American bayonet thrust into the firm, strong midsection of the Great Plains.

The massive, ponderous wagon train stretched for two tortuous miles. The wagons – some two hundred of them, were lumbering canvas covered affairs. Many stood out, such as the heavier Conestoga types with the rear wheels larger than the front. These were pulled by multiple pairs of oxen, their heads held low to the yoke. All of the wagons were overladen. The gear wasn't tied down as it should have been; it appeared to have been thrown on quickly, as though the pioneers were refugees who were *fleeing from something*.

Shuddering and groaning along were the lumbering freight wagons which were pulled by teams of up to a dozen massive oxen that strained against the wooden bow yokes that held them in pairs – their massive scarred necks rubbed raw and girded in the U-shaped oxbows. A pair of horses were attached behind the oxen and immediately in front of the wagon. Men rode these horses, lashing the oxen that were in front of them with bull whips that often extended out to ten feet in length.

A discerning observer would take note that this was not the normal flotsam of human debris that washed westward in the irresistible tide that so often composed the Westward Expansion.

Before the winding, serpentine wagon train lay a vast expanse of grassland – the portal into the Great Plains. As the buzzard glides, this region was a highland of monotonously flat terrain, broken intermittently with graveled streams that gurgled over shallow creek beds and became silent as the water deepened. Flung intermittently here and there, more often than not laying unseen – were treacherous, wheel shattering, eroded gullies.

Mangy, horse fly covered American bison, prong horned antelope saturated in ticks, black tailed prairie dogs scratching at fleas, and mite infested prairie chickens – with the thrumming noise that they make, all were thickly represented in the mix of lush grasses.

The verdant, waving seas of grass conveyed a surreal impression of tranquility, vibrant with life; this was a veneer which concealed the desperate, merciless struggle for survival that was waged within those thick, lush, verdant savannas - between hunter and hunted.

The lumbering and jostling of the wagon train combined with other sounds of the great trek; the mooing of the great herd of fat dairy and beef cattle, the curses and profanities hurled at the straining draft animals and the cracks of whips – all of these things combined into a cacophony of sounds which suffocated all other auditory distraction. Among those sonances that were muted were those of the closely following horde of murderous, ruthless, heavily armed Cheyenne and Comanche.

Against the dazzlingly blue sky overhead circled a lone buzzard, its violent assents upwards were caused by heat thermals floating lazily up from the parched ground below. These perturbations in the buzzard's altitude were not noticed by the four tiny figures far beneath it; figures who cared not to look into the blinding intensity of the sun that broiled like molten gold. This was a sun that hovered in an orb of yellow-white - like a golden coin of Apollo glowing in its mold.

The charismatic leader of the wagon train rode at the head of the convoy; on either side of him were his subordinate commanders, dressed in Spartan, utilitarian cowboy regalia. The dust of the trail stuck to their filthy, sweat drenched clothing that reeked of perspiration.

His name was Jedediah Sumrall and like his three companions he was dressed in iconic, practical western wear; from the broiling felt cowboy hat and muslin shirt with vest, to his tan duck britches and black leather cowboy boots - pointed at the toe to facilitate entry into the stirrup. He wore an unkempt black beard, filthy, and blasted with grey.

Hoping that he had found a secure place to set up camp for the evening, Jedediah ordered his subordinates to circle the wagons and prepare to unhitch the exhausted animals in order to let them feed on the thick, dehydrated, grass.

"This looks to be about the best defensive area I've seen that's big enough to handle the camp. Damn that we gotta set it up," stated Jedediah, there was worry in the hard, brown eyes - eyes from which crow's feet radiated to either side of the haggard face. Wrinkles from years in the unforgiving sun and dry, unrelenting wind etched the saturnine visage.

The sagging skin formed bags under the eyes of Jedediah with the weight of responsibility; concern for the safety of the twelve hundred fugitives from the town of Philistine, Kansas under his charge. Jedediah looked with worry toward the low rolling hills from which the following covered wagons were emerging. He wished that they moved more quickly.

"Jubal, you an' Adam get with them team leaders and have 'em circle them hot-damned wagons out here, do it the same as we did yesterday. Keep 'em to this side of the creek. I want sentries quadrupled," continued Jedediah Sumrall, his sixth sense warning him of peril lurking hidden in the somber, grey hills. The fingers, wrists and elbows of his arms tingled with a throbbing sensation of adrenalin fueled prescience.

"I sense it too," commented Aaron Jones – second in command of the journey and engaged to Jedediah's twenty-year-old daughter, Beverly. Aaron was dressed like his elder, but his beard was ungreyed. "The Indians, I feel their presence."

"At the first sign of them, shoot," ordered Jedediah. "Don't be deceived by their treachery, they will at first appear with open hands, expressing friendship. Don't fall for it."

Forty wagons had entered the valley and were guiding to the right before swinging left in the initial arcing phase of the caravan's defensive circle. Once all two hundred wagons had tied into each other, the impression conveyed would be that of an entire village, or town having stopped in transit across the rolling prairie.

Suddenly the reports of rifle, shotgun and pistol began ringing out as the rear column of wagons came under attack. The fury of the tempo increased as the attack consumed its way up the length of the wagon train like a gigantic serpent swallowing a smaller snake.

The bulk of the wagon train was still flanked by low slung, hilly ridgelines on either side. The hills were covered with dry grass, and dotted with trees of medium height - arboreal survivors from years of drought and range fires. Within those deciduous trees, snakes raided bird's nests of their young. The reptiles were seized with their own predatory instincts and did not pay mind to the human hunters that seized upon their prey in the valley beneath them.

At first the shots could be distinguished individually, but within moments the rifle fire had emerged into a continuous, unbroken maelstrom of popping. The sound of the gunfire was amplified and echoed, rebounding through the hills as the column of the wagon train was cut off at the nape of its neck.

The forty odd Conestoga wagons which had rolled out onto the grassy plain lurched and rocked drunkenly as they desperately rushed to complete the defensive circle.

Lean, rangy occupants armed with Spencer repeating rifles were cursing as they leapt from the wagons and ran alongside them, like infantry, through the knee high buffalo grass.

The drivers with their tanned, thickly muscled arms urged on the animals with alacrity as they applied the ten-foot-long rawhide bullwhips mercilessly. The teamed, sweating draft animals sensed the fear in their masters' shouting; it was a contagion that animals intuitively responded to.

The balance of the train – consisting of an odd assortment of one hundred sixty wagons was halted and had to fight it out in an uncoordinated, individualistic, every family for themselves manner. They lacked the coordination inherent in a consolidated position, rendering them unable to concentrate and guide a defensive fire.

It was a different situation with the circled and outnumbered wagons, however. The draft animals were within the perimeter and tethered to the large, spoked wheels of the Conestogas. The men and boys piled rucksacks, blankets, saddles – whatever they could underneath the wagons as wives and mothers handed the articles to them. The defenders placed their rifles across the rapidly improving embrasures and looked through the open sights as they cursed, spitting tobacco juice between stained, rotted teeth.

No time was wasted as they sought to consolidate and improve their firing positions from the prone position. Men bearing picks and shovels hurtled themselves into the excavation of rifle pits where spacing between wagons allowed engineering work. Dirt, often held together with matted grass roots was heaved up in front of the rifle pits to a depth of fifteen inches. Steamer chests, saddles, bedrolls – whatever was available was placed in front of these.

Many of these frantically digging men had blood on their hands. They had blood not only from burst blisters, but also from beating back Confederate human wave attacks at places with names like Antietam, Chickamauga, and Gettysburg. These men knew how to dig.

"Get a move on there!" shouted Jedediah. "Let's see some hustle! Move with a purpose! When you're done, start setting your sights to a hundred yards!"

Overhead, the turkey buzzard that gazed upon a growing meal with its cerulean blue eyes was incognizant of the golden eagle that plunged downward upon him at one hundred miles per hour. The dark explosion of feathers remained for a moment in the form of a brown blot against the azul, turquoise sky. The eagle made off with its stunned quarry that struggled vainly in the iron, flesh piercing grip of the eagle's talons.

"I'm going in there!" shouted Jedediah, grabbing the reigns with one hand and the saddle horn with the other prior to mounting his black stallion, Castor. "The rest of you stay put!"

"Hold your horses, there, Jed!" shouted one of the teamsters, a burly, barrel chested man with bad teeth and a protruding swag belly. "You've got to stay here with us, with you here at least we have a chance!"

"My wife is back there; don't nobody try to stop me! Swing that hitch and let me through!" commanded Jedediah, his stallion was champing at the bit and stamping at the hoof. It caracoled and pranced sideways as several men shifted the heavy trailer hitch and began to swing it outward, to allow the commander of the wagon train passage from out of the defensive perimeter. "I said open that son of a bitch up and let me through!"

"You're not leaving without me!" shouted the future son in law, Aaron Jones. Together, the duo rode at break neck speed toward the disaster enveloping the doomed wagon train. Their figures vanished into the smoke that billowed from the burning canvas of the wagons, smoke that creeped across the veldt like an ominous white fog as the wind caught and carried it. On the wind was carried the shouts and screams of attacker and attacked alike mixed in the rifle fire, as sparks carried on a hot gust of wind portended an inferno.

Within the main body of the wagon train, paralyzed into linear position, a suppressive fire was being laid down from either side of the abutting hills. Flame arrows were being fired into the canvas topped wagons from the hillsides, the shafts were not fired upward to gain arc, but were shot downward into the targets at an almost flat trajectory.

Above the tumult of battle, the keen eye of a peregrine falcon espied the grasses through the openings of smoke, alert to any sign of movement. Nosing downward and tucking in its wings, it fell like a bullet toward a brown, furry muskrat, and opening its wings to brake its fall, it seized the writhing, squeaking creature in its talons.

From above the conflagration atop a hill stood two white men, they wore buckskin trousers, cavalry boots, and the ragged, sweat and dust stained shirts of the Union Army. One of the men, a short, stocky blond bearded ruffian watched the butchery through a telescopic spy glass. It was a single draw brass telescope with the main tube wrapped in black horse hair braid.

"Go ahead and sound the charge, Lester!" the blond haired hoodlum shouted above the din of the shooting. His was a dirty blond hair, unwashed and greasy. It was combed back, yet still partially obscured his cerumen plugged ears. His worn, ragged clothes stank with sweat and filth. "Pretty damned coordinated! They doin' us proud, Lester! Doin' us proud, ain't they, Lester boy???!"

The short, blond man continued to watch through the extended spy glass as his companion placed a dented brass artillery bugle to his cracked, chapped lips and blasted the G notes of the attack signal. The metallic notes carried from the double coiled instrument, trumpeting above the cracking and popping of gun fire.

Instantly waves of howling, painted Cheyenne, Sioux and Comanche warriors exploded from behind every boulder, every dip in the ground, and from holes dug and covered with grass panels. From every conceivable place they emerged, war whooping, running at the defenders full paced - overtaken with the killing lust.

Jedediah and Aaron attained the mouth of the small valley as the bugle call pealed the urgent plea to attack.

"Is that the cavalry coming to help save us?" shouted Aaron to Jedediah.

"No! No way in hell! It's those Galvanized Yankees I've told you about! They're in league with Roman Nose!" cursed Jedediah.

The Galvanized Yankees had been a special attack unit consisting of renegade Confederate prisoners of war. These turncoats volunteered to fight Indians in exchange for being freed from Union prisoner of war camps. Many of these treacherous turncoats had deserted the Union Army and had joined the hostile tribes that they were sworn to attack. After the end of the Civil War, some had no homes to return to and simply remained with their adopted Indian allies. A few were able to coordinate the actions of the hard to control Native American bands of Cheyenne, Sioux, and Comanche. This coordination could be seen as the Cheyenne were using both a base of fire and a maneuver element which was clearly uncharacteristic for them.

The two verminous white men released control to the incensed bonnet wearing war chiefs at the base of the hills. The loathsome, unwashed duo watched the baneful fruits of their months of training and rehearsals culminate into a blood orgy of murder and plunder. They paid no attention to the two newcomers who had arrived on the scene below.

Newcomers who searched with urgency for one lone white woman in a frothing sea of Cheyenne, Sioux and Comanche who were whipped into a distemper-like convulsion of deranged lust.

"Come on, Aaron! We've got to find her!" shouted Jedediah.

The white, acrid smoke was a nauseating mixture of spent black gun powder, reminiscent of rotten eggs and burning turpentine. The turpentine was used to waterproof the canvas of the wagons which unfortunately also added combustibility to the heavy cloth, making it ignite like a torch and incinerate the occupants who fired furiously through openings in the wagons.

The pair entered the melee as dozens of painted and tattooed Cheyenne swarmed them, grabbing the horses by the reins and manes of stiff hair. With few exceptions, all of the Cheyenne were tall. One painted brute – a man with one eye - aimed a flintlock trade musket at Jedediah. The explosion blinded the wagon train leader even as he was dragged from his McClellan saddle, bludgeoned and scalped.

"Jed! Jedediah!" shouted Aaron as he was carried like a writhing log by four heavily muscled braves near the wheel of a wagon. The Conestoga, of which the canvas tarp had been set ablaze and the wood planks of the wagon itself were now burning, took on the appearance of a funeral pyre.

The one eyed Cheyenne's head was shaven smooth but for a scalp lock that thrust from the center of his forehead and ran to the back of his thick neck. This scalp lock was augmented with a fierce roach made of porcupine and deer guard hair, it ran the length of the scalp lock and bristled a foot high. The roach – colored gray-black was secured to the man's scalp lock by means of a series of leather laces and a roach spreader hewn from the bone of a human femur.

The single right eye beamed with exhilaration as the pupil fixed itself on Aaron's revolver. The empty socket of the left eye swarmed with gnats that were drawn to the mucous discharge of the inflamed, seeping membrane.

The Polyphemus shouted in exhilaration and ripped the heavy revolver from the holster of the younger white man. The euphoric brave expostulated a stream of high pitched, nasal toned invectives and began enthusiastically pistol whipping the distraught, exasperated youth.

Aaron was being brutally scalped as he was held by two of the muscly painted killers one to either side of him as he lurched, leaning forward as he tried to pull away.

The smoke that issued from the blazing wagon train was growing substantially in density as ammunition began detonating as a result of the intense heat and flew thousands of feet in all directions. Some exploding ammunition landed hundreds of yards away in the meadow that opened up at the yawning mouth of the range of hills, starting grass fires and stampeding the snorting, bellowing cattle that had accompanied the train.

The panicked defenders were leaping from their wagons, clothing and hair on fire. They ran shrieking at the top of their lungs like human torches past the superstitious braves who dodged aside and let them pass. Other refugees from the town of Philistine ran up the slopes of the hills; they ran with the added impetus of knowing their lives depended on the strength of their legs. The men were gunned down in their tracks; the women and children were pursued with enthusiasm.

"They've set fire to the range! They're gonna burn us out!" shouted Jubal to Adam. Both men were of average height and they ran bent at the waist, surveying the growing defenses of the perimeter within the circled conclave of wagons. They both carried Henrys in one hand loosely at their side as they ran shouting out orders at the top of their lungs. They moved about continuously and maintained a dire air of authority over the rapidly escalating situation.

"We'll fight fire with fire," responded Adam. "Grab every other man and let's burn a ring around the wagons!"

"Ring around the rosies!" spat Jubal. "Pocket full of posies!"

The sweet, acrid scent of the blinding smoke presaged the roaring grass fire that rushed like a searing flood into the outer edge of the charred ring, the fire split and went around the Conestogas like an enormous scarlet wave breaking on an islet. Unable to advance into the perimeter, the inferno went around the island of circled wagons and joined with itself. Whipped by gusts of hot wind, the fire gained strength and raged further on, as uneven tongues of orange red flames waved like banners one hundred feet into the smoke filled air.

"What about the herd!?" shouted Ezra, a short, stocky, bullnecked cattleman who, like everyone else in the wagon train, was out of Philistine, Kansas. The sleeves of his shirt were pushed up high above his elbows and thick veins stood out on the back of his sun darkened hands and forearms. Beads of sweat glistened on the black hair that covered his upper extremities. The overdeveloped forearms were thickly corded with steel muscle. "I've got four hundred fifty head of cattle out there!" his beige straw hat was pushed back on his head, he was young, in his late twenty's and wore a full dark beard minus the moustache.

"The cattle's gone, forget about the herd!" responded Adam to Ezra. Then Adam began shouting so that everyone, including those under the wagons could hear. "Let the Indians have the cattle, we'll be lucky to get out of this alive!"

"If we survive this – we can't go back! We can't go back to Philistine under *any* circumstances!" Jubal shouted to the group, following up on the statement of Adam to the conglomeration of desperate, frightened refugees.

"Well, we've got to get out of this thing, first!" Adam shouted back, before looking about the dozen men. "You guys are the fire brigade!" said Adam to the filthy, unshaven, seated men. "If they get in here, you will all engage the enemy and destroy them!"

"You heard the man! They get in here; you get 'em! I wanna see some kill! Kill! Kill! Now function check yore weapons, 'specially them pistols! Be shore them caps is well seated!" interjected Jubal, who, stoop shouldered and long armed appeared to be ape-like. He had the neck of a bullock, and the heavy, muscle knotted arms of a blacksmith.

"They get in here," Jubal thought, "we're all dead."

The two renegade white men wearing Union Army shirts passed the spy glass from one to the other. They sat atop mustangs as several hundred warriors drew up alongside them, the warriors' horses were lathered with sweat and their ears would peel back as they snorted and flashed their teeth. The traitor whites had descended from the hill and sagely ridden to just out of rifle range of the circled wagons.

"I don't like it," muttered Lester.

"Nope! Me neither," responded Jimmy Carl. "Suicide, to attack that position out here in the open. We could wait till dark, but there's no way this mob is going to stay put long enough for that to happen."

The shooting had all but stopped behind them at the remnants of the wagon train. Hundreds of female and children survivors had been taken prisoner and were being bartered like slave chattel among the euphoric victors.

In the short time that the two Galvanized Yankees had been talking, thousands more warriors had ridden up. They were passionate, rowdy men fueled on too much killing and they spoke rapidly. Adrenaline added impetus to the urgent, high toned nasal diatribe that was shouted in staccato bursts. They motioned with their hands furiously in sign language to fill in gaps for the deficit of nouns and verbs that existed between the Siouan, Uto-Aztecan and Algonquian languages.

White Bull rode a sorrel gelding, a big horse - one of those taken from a cavalry patrol of Buffalo Soldiers that had been ambushed two days before. The medicine man was wearing his long black hair unbraided; it was brushed straight down and was held in place by virtue of a headband made of sagebrush wreath.

Wearing a cavalry shirt that bore the shoulder epaulettes of a US Army captain, White Bull rode along the entire front of the uneven line of shouting, gesticulating warriors, many of whom were ready to go after the circled wagons without pre-meditation. The Medicine Man regarded the situation with unease. The warriors were impatient; they sensed that, like gamblers on a winning streak, they were on a roll and were keen to rake in the rest of the pot.

White Bull, seeking to mitigate the danger, rode in front of the formation, shouting; "Magic broken!

Roman Nose enter wagon at same time white woman give birth!"

There were exclamations of surprise and resignation, as White Bull continued:

"Not fight these wagons, get cattle!"

"Saved by the bell," Lester uttered to Jimmy Carl.

"Yep!" responded Jimmy Carl. "Superstition saved them this time, but not common sense."

Suddenly Mad Wolf, a brightly painted Comanche chief who wore a magnificent single trailer war bonnet of at least sixty immature golden eagle feathers, rode forward and began gesticulating wildly with his hands to White Bull. The copper bracelets of both wrists were adorned with hawk bells and tinkled with bright, liquid sounds as the wrists moved about in sign language.

Mad Wolf, who was not technically subordinate to his Cheyenne hosts, conveyed outrage at the denial of the attack on the circled wagons. After a final frenetic frenzy of sign language in which body movements and facial expressions were used to emplace emphasis, Mad Wolf spat on the ground and swung his beige pony around, facing his cohort, 1400 of them.

White Bull, mounted on the big sorrel gelding, trotted up to Roman Nose who sat on his mount uneasily. His grim, taciturn face revealed no emotion as he saw the Comanche horde launch unevenly into a massive, ragged head-on attack. Then suddenly, as if right on que, the mass of Comanche braves peeled off to the right and left a hundred yards from the circled wagons. The attack formation resembled a circling vortex of swarming hornets.

The thudding of the horses' unshod hooves drove a beautifully patterned prairie rattle snake into the subterranean burrow of a gopher. Two feet in length, the pit viper was adorned with intricate triangular patches of brown fringed with white over a tan, scaly skin. Its safety from the horses' hooves assured, the reptile's fear was replaced by hunger, as it scented the rank urine smell of the rodent inhabiting the winding burrow. The forked tongue flicked outward from the spear shaped head and held for a moment in a quivering motion, before the serpent began inching its way toward its unsuspecting, warm-blooded prey.

While some of the Comanche rode bareback, most did not; they used saddles made of stretched buffalo hide stuffed with straw and sewn into a sort of pillow. To this a girth and stirrups were sewn with rawhide. Some used saddles taken from the mounts of slain cattlemen and pioneers. These saddles were often of the drover, Spanish, or McClellan type.

The ponies were painted with specific designs and symbols which the riders believed held marvelous, magical protective power. Also, the images often portrayed past victories in ferocious battle. These symbols often were horse hooves painted on the flank – each connoting a horse stolen in a raid, on the side of the animal would be painted zigzag symbols, indicating great speed and power. Circles were painted around the eyes for keen vision and upward pointing arrows on the shoulders that were certain to guarantee victory.

An emergency reserve of war paint was always carried dried and pulverized in a leather pouch that was often decorated with brightly colored trade beads. The paint was made from an array of whatever was obtainable; red clay, berries, egg yolk, buffalo fat and so on. Water, mixed with urine or saliva would be added to the pigments to form the paint suspension.

Red symbolized combat, power and invincibility. Yellow represented courage and also symbolized death. Black denoted victory in the field.

The Comanche were armed with a miscarriage of assorted modern and stone aged weapons as they orbited the conclave of Conestogas. The horsemen who were armed with Henrys leaned from the side and fired haphazardly from under the horse's neck. Whereas the brave armed with a muzzle loading Enfield held his shot until he could make it count. Many were armed with the Indian short bow, its arrows tipped with deeply penetrating sharpened metal barbets. These were launched at a high rate of fire at an upward angle, the shafts would then plunge downward at almost two hundred miles per hour.

"Let us go to help them," stated Roman Nose to his sage council and magician, White Bull. Roman Nose was not wearing his war bonnet, but instead had left it within its leather parfleche strapped across his broad back.

"If you enter the fight, you will surely die," warned White Bull.

The cloud of dust raised by the vortex of horsemen served to conceal eight hundred footmen who ran full on toward the circled wagons. Those that had repeating rifles wore bandoliers of rifle ammunition slung over their suntanned shoulders and across the twin shield muscles of their broad, sweating pectorals.

This was not a measured, jogging type of pace, but was more akin to the mile run at full speed that is practiced by track and field athletes. The war paint streaked and ran down their faces and into their eyes; eyes that were focused into slits of concentration as they struggled to breathe and not fall back.

Bullets smacked into the saw milled oak planks of the Conestogas and ripped through the canvas tarps covering the prairie schooners, speeding through and imbedding into the wooden frames of the wagons on the other side of the perimeter. But these shots were fired wildly, and only sheer luck would see them to a human target.

Sheer luck, however, was not on the side of the unfortunate oxen, mules, and horses tethered to the massive wagon wheels. The oxen bellowed furiously as hot lead entered their heads, chests, and abdomens. Horses neighed and whinnied, baring their teeth and pulling back with all their might as they were struck. Bloody froth flew from their mouths and flaring nostrils as they shook their heads and broke free, running in circles within the perimeter and bolting over the wagon hitches.

Jubal watched as the deadly vortex grew nearer - he did not see the eight hundred footmen who rapidly approached from behind the cloud of dust.

At the first fusillade of defensive fire, fifty braves were unseated from their saddles. Two dozen more had their horses shot out from under them, and dozens were pinned under their mounts in this heinous manner. Several more mounts raced madly out of control, dragging their writhing, twisting riders by the stirrup over the charred, blackened ground. The braves screamed at the top of their lungs as their backs left trails in the ash while their painted ponies drug them out of the killing zone.

Within two minutes the situation for the mounted braves had become super critical. That is when the foot men emerged coughing and wheezing through the suffocating ash colored cloud of dust. Almost three hundred doubled over and fell forward cursing and screaming as they were hit low in the abdomen by the desperately firing refugees from the town of Philistine.

Like a phalanx, the rear elements stampeded over their fallen comrades and hit the heavily defended circular fortress head on, with the surviving warriors swinging their axes like maddened lumberjacks at the wagon hitches that frustrated their ingress.

"Fire brigade! Fall in!!! Two ranks! First rank kneel! Fire on my command!!!" shouted Jubal.

"Steady, rock steady now, boys," said Adam to no one in particular as he focused on the scene unfolding in front of him. He was aiming his Henry at a big Comanche – a brute of a man wearing a magnificent bear claw necklace who was swinging his axe like an enraged Paul Bunyan into the wagon hitch. The claw necklace seemed to heave and lift from the warrior's sun browned skin in slow motion with each succeeding swing of the axe.

"First rank expend all ammunition!!!" shouted Jubal, "Second rank pick yore targets! They're coming in!!! They're breakin' right through!!!"

Adam fired from the standing off hand position, his right cheek was melded into the rifle stock, his cheek weld was sound. He squeezed the trigger just as the big brave with the axe locked eyes with him. The widely spaced onyx eyes stung with sweat as the eyelids of the brave, plucked of eyelashes, narrowed into slits to focus his vision onto the image of Adam deliberately aiming his rifle at him. He noticed Adam, really for the first time, as his mind registered what was about to happen.

The heavy .44 caliber slug from the big repeating rifle entered the forehead of the Comanche whose hair was parted down the middle; jet black hair that had been braided into two pony tails secured by rawhide and colored cloth. A single, large eagle feather - the top half dyed red was secured into the hair at a jaunty angle. The forehead was sloped back over a pair of obsidian eyes that stared with incredulity at the muzzle flash of the Henry.

The warrior's scarred, calloused hands flew to the dime sized hole in his forehead even as his brains flew in a fatty globular red spray into the faces of those behind him. He continued to stand, holding his hands to his forehead until he was brusquely knocked aside as those behind rushed into the open area within the perimeter – falling to the earth, doubled in agony as they were shot immediately upon entry.

"Second rank, fire!!! First rank reload, fire at will!!!" shouted Jubal as multiple rounds plowed into steak slabbed chests and ripped into lithe, heaving abdomens, causing the rectus abdominis to tauten at the moment of impact before sending the warrior down, twisting and shouting.

"They're in! They're in the perimeter!" shouted Adam, who was aiming as he fired from the shoulder. He moved the big repeater in short increments, from side to side as he emptied the magazine with the rapidity of a Gatling gun.

"Adam!" shouted Jubal. "Take charge in here! Make them keep firing! I'm keeping everybody under the wagons until the last minute, or else they'll come in through there, too!"

Many of the Comanche warriors had dismounted and were running toward the breach in the circled wagons, stumbling over the top their fallen comrades and hurtling headlong into the hornet's nest that awaited them within the hive of death.

The marksmen beneath the wagons were littering the fields of fire with human detritus as massive bullets splattered painted skulls and ripped off tattooed arms, the taloned fingers opening and closing spasmodically, pulling the appendage through the charcoal dust of the burnt grass.

Despite the murderous fire from beneath the wagons, scores of swarthy, shouting Comanche had entered the perimeter and were overwhelming the dozen mobile defenders that comprised the fire brigade. Jubal's Henry ran out of ammunition as a horrific Comanche wearing a single trailer war bonnet ran at him screaming and wielding an axe.

Jubal had to act before he could think. He reflexively lifted his rifle using both hands over his head as the single edged axe, the type used for splitting logs, crashed down in a deadly arc onto the brass receiver cover and smashed it in at the junction of where the tubular magazine joined the cover.

The impact of the heavy, wedge shaped axe stung Jubal's hands as stumbled backward and tripped over the fallen teamster Ezra, who was shot through both lungs and gurgled frantically for oxygen. His lips were blue tinged, and he coughed a frothy champagne of oxygen saturated red, bloody sputum.

"Breathe through your nose and out your mouth!" laughed the big Comanche at the drowning man as he approached Jubal.

Jubal's hands were too numbed from the axe blow to draw his revolver. He watched the big chief loom over him with the axe poised to deliver the killing strike. Jubal noticed, as in a slow motion nightmare - the magnificent war bonnet.

The bonnet flared out symmetrically from the broad forehead. The immature golden eagle feathers were sewn into the crown of a felt hat – almost hidden by the thick firecracker-like red and white wrappings at the base of each eagle feather. The tips of the feathers had gold colored horse hair attached and at the point of attachment were small fluffs of feathers dyed purple. Sewn onto the front of the felt hat crown was an ornate brow band made of beads sewn in intricate patterns of teepees and mountains. Half a dozen metal hawk bells sewn into the brow band jingled with the sudden movements of the warrior's head, chiming with those that he wore on copper bracelets around each wrist.

"Heathen!!!" shouted Jubal as the axe descended downward, the force of the blow was given impetus by the latissimus muscles of the chief's broad back which formed an enormous V. The distinctive trailer of the war bonnet failed to ensconce the play of the sweat glistening flared back. The rippling effect of the broad back muscles was highlighted by the shadows of the late afternoon sun.

"Arrrrrrgggghhhhhhh!!!" croaked Jubal, who grabbed the smooth hickory handle of the axe with both hands, despite his skull having been split from the crown of his head down to his jaw.

Suddenly the chief looked to his right although he didn't know why.

"Wish you hadn't done that, Chief. He was my best friend," stated Adam, in an aberrant, nonchalant tone.

Despite the chaos that defined the situation all around him, the big Comanche did not attack the younger man who stood ten feet from him. Adam struck a match on the heel of his boot and lit a cigarette. The act was so incongruous with the see-saw melee, that the big Comanche smiled, revealing strong, straight, tobacco stained teeth. The gum lines of the smiling Comanche chief were receded, making the teeth appear even longer than they really were.

"Gonna havta' kill ya' over that one, Chief," continued Adam and drawing his empty revolver, dropped it on the ground. "I don't have no more chicken shit bullets, an' I ain't usin' no knife." Adam threw the butt of the cigarette on the ground and stabbed it out viciously with his heel, grinding it savagely into the hard earth beneath the thick grass before stepping forward.

"Don't need no axe," responded the Comanche. The axe dropped onto the ground as he released it, the thud it made as it hit the ground was obfuscated by the din of gunfire. The Comanche chief Mad Wolf extended his muscle knotted arms away from either side, and said invitingly, "Come on! Come on, boy!" His ham like hands were open, ready to grab. He stood at a crouch, ready to spring like a timber wolf.

The gunpowder blackened defenders from beneath the wagons began emerging and added their weight to the fight, causing Mad Wolf to reassess the direness of his situation. The chief grabbed the buffalo horn that was suspended from a leather cord about his bull neck. He raised it to his lip and sent forth a high pitched peal urging his warriors to fall back, what few there were that remained.

"I get you next time, Man Who Smokes. I skin you alive!" promised Mad Wolf, his macabre smile implying horrific intention.

Chapter Two
General Sheridan's Plan

GENERAL SHERIDAN PACED the oak floor of the large stone block house – the only truly defensive structure of Fort Hays, Kansas. The fort was in reality without walls and spread out much like any other town in the frontier west. He stopped to look at the map – an atlas that covered the greater part of an entire wood planked wall. The wall, made of heavily knotted yellow pine, shone with linseed oil. On his desk lay the telegraphed message of yet another massacre of westward bound pioneers. This time it was some bizarre religious sect fleeing a frontier town named Philistine. The reasoning behind their hasty exodus remained unclear.

"Forsyth, I'm sending you after Roman Nose, Custer would go with you and lead this expedition if he was available. As it is, officially he is still at Leavenworth with his wife, Elizabeth. However," General Sheridan paused, before adding, "unofficially, they are actually both here at the moment on excursion. I am certain to reinstate him soon and have it on good word that this is assured."

General Philip Sheridan continued, "This time the Cheyenne under Roman Nose wiped out all but forty wagons of a caravan consisting of nearly two hundred prairie schooners. More than a thousand settlers were killed; hundreds were taken captive, the children being adopted as Cheyenne and the women being subjected to indescribable degradation. I say settlers, for lack of a better term, because apparently they were on the move in an attempt to escape something."

That little runt, thought Major Forsyth, *fancies himself still Commander of the Cavalry Corps of the Army of the Potomac.* Major "Sandy" George Forsyth studied the general before him; General "Little Phil" Sheridan was a small man, standing barely four feet, eleven inches in height. And that was in special boots with an elevated insole.

"There's no Army left after the disbandment following the surrender of Lee," Forsyth complained to Sheridan. "What little there remains, is scattered throughout Dixie in Reconstruction duty."

Sheridan's diminutive, stunted appearance reminded Forsyth of Shakespeare's "dwarf in giant's clothing," the unimposing physical appearance of President Johnson's Head of the Department of the Missouri was amplified by the oversized Union double breasted frock coat, the sleeves of which extended over the knuckles of the gnome-like hands. Hands that depended from arms of abnormally long length, reaching almost to the short, bow-legged knees; knees made bow-legged from years in the saddle on campaign in the Civil War and Indian Wars.

"We can't catch him," continued Forsyth. "Roman Nose is illusive, diaphanous - a Will o' the Wisp."

The black, slate colored pupils of Sheridan regarded Forsyth for a moment, they sparkled with insight. Although Sheridan's parents had both immigrated from Ireland, he bore little resemblance to an Irishman. He appeared more like a mixed blood American of Indian descent, with his dark hair and epicanthic folds over his eyes.

The face was oval and the nose, short and straight. A thick moustache resided over prominent lips and grew down to below either side of the small, pleasant mouth, stopping at the jaw near the non-prominent chin. The facial expression conveyed the impression of a kind, gentle man with great patience. The head was set upon a thick, bull neck.

Despite the benign appearance of his superior officer, Forsyth knew that Sheridan was ruthless, and would kill anybody who got in his way. Sheridan had not hesitated to send tens of thousands to their death during the final phases of the recent Civil War. Life, death, these things meant little to Sheridan, Forsyth knew. Forsyth also knew that "Little Phil" Sheridan was about to send him on a suicidal mission to kill the renegade Cheyenne war leader Roman Nose, who was setting the frontier on fire.

"Oh, you won't catch him," replied Little Phil. "He'll catch you, and you will kill him."

Sheridan poured a glass of port from a heavy, expensive crystal decanter. The decanter shown with a deep, translucent blue from the dangerously high level of lead content within the glass. The addition of lead made glass easier to work with, and nearly every glass drinking vessel had it. Sheridan handed the glass to Forsyth and then poured one for himself.

"I have decided to approach this problem as I have similar problems in other places," continued Sheridan. "You will be provided with fifty professional gunfighters as scouts, among other things. These men are assassins, expert scouts, hunters, trackers, and all with a score to settle – a score to settle with Roman Nose."

"You've got to be kidding, Phil," expostulated a clearly concerned Forsyth. But the worried officer knew that his superior was not kidding, and that human life meant nothing to him – nothing at all. He swirled the dark, fortified wine in the open mouthed crystal ware and inhaled the aroma, catching a glimpse of his reflection – a reflection that betrayed his worry – before quickly downing the glass. He walked to the partner's desk, a large, polished mahogany double desk that was the dominant feature of the general's office. He poured another glass of port from the expensive decanter without asking. Sheridan didn't seem to notice.

General Sheridan walked bowlegged to the large map covering the knotted pine wall to the left side of the desk; he took a pointer stick and patiently explained the overall situation to Forsyth. His accent betrayed his Irish parentage.

"As you can see," said Sheridan, pointing with the stick at the map. "Roman Nose has literally set fire to the West. It is rumored that through diabolical magic he has managed to unite more than one hundred clans of various tribes of Southern and Northern Cheyenne. Dozens of Sioux and Comanche clans have joined him."

"How on earth did he manage that?" riposted Major Forsyth, his curiosity was unfeigned.

"Largely through the so-called magic of a medicine man that goes by the name of White Bull," answered General Sheridan. "Although he is also known by the name Ice. From what my sources tell me, White Bull has meticulously constructed a bizarre war bonnet. I don't know if it's poor shooting on the part of our soldiers or just plain luck, but Roman Nose never gets shot. A lot of people believe this hokum, Forsyth – but I don't buy into it."

"What the devil is in this port?" interrupted Forsyth.

"An opiate, Sandy," answered Little Phil. "Now, bear with me. Roman Nose has been augmented in his demonic designs by this Cheyenne sorcerer named White Bull. White Bull has created this war bonnet through his arcane mechanizations, the details of which are too horrific to elaborate upon. Whether there is truth to the war bonnet or not is irrelevant at this point. What *is* relevant is that all of the tribes believe it and are flocking to him by the thousands."

"What kind of magic, Phil?" asked Forsyth. "I've got to sit down, I feel like I'm floating. I can't feel my lips."

"I have it on good word that the war bonnet is widely believed to convey the power of invincibility," answered Sheridan as he poured another glass of the heavily opiated port for himself. He filled his large oval shaped red Bordeaux glass almost to the rim. "My spies tell me that the war bonnet makes the wearer and all those around him bullet proof!"

"I don't believe in magic," answered Major Forsyth. "And about these gunslinger frontiersmen, Philip, these men don't follow orders from army officers. They would as soon tell me to go to hell." Forsyth was leaning back into the leather of the overstuffed club chair, his high topped Wellington boots resting on the matching ottoman. His face was covered in perspiration from the opiated elixir. "They won't take orders from anybody."

"They will follow *your* orders, alright," responded General Sheridan. "They are being enlisted into the army as a special attack force. They will be uniformly armed with the same weapons for obvious reasons. The very best that are available.

"President Johnson sent a detachment of special agents tasked with the delivery of these armaments to your special attack force. Your band of hired killers has been familiarizing with these state of the art weapons. They have been on the qualification range from dawn to dusk for the last two weeks, honing their marksmanship skills."

"Um hum," grunted Forsyth, "You intrigue me, Little Phil." Immediately Forsyth regretted the insult as he saw Sheridan wince. "Sorry, Philip, it's the wine, I never would have said that, otherwise."

"When is the last time you witnessed an execution, Sandy?" Sheridan's voice was low, serious and did not betray the enormous amount of opiated port he had imbibed.

"I saw a hanging yesterday, I see them all the time," answered Forsyth, frankly.

"You ever seen a man guillotined?" the tone of Little Phil's voice was unemotional, the opium made it sound surreal and detached, thought Forsyth.

"What in blazes are you talking about? This isn't Europe!" croaked the inebriated officer to his superior.

"Well, how do you think I got all those Rebels to become Galvanized Yankees?" inquired Little Phil, patiently.

"Eh? I'm still not connecting the dots, old friend," responded Forsyth – he felt as though he were speaking in a dream.

"It's really quiet simple," answered General Sheridan. "I had a guillotine brought over from Ireland and set up in the stockade, where all the captured Rebels could see it. So, when I was tasked with the creation of a combat unit consisting of Confederate prisoners of war, I needed volunteers, I *had to have* volunteers, George." Sheridan had approached Major Forsyth and was speaking into his ear, bending forward as he whispered. *"I began guillotining them."*

"Huh? Wuzzat?" expostulated Forsyth, struggling to maintain consciousness.

"Yes!" exclaimed General Sheridan, smacking the closed fist of his right hand into the open palm of his left. He walked sway-back to the large window that faced toward the street of packed earth, badly rutted with wagon and buggy tracks below the two story building; the building from which the two officers discussed the coming campaign. He placed his hands behind him on the small of his back, one hand clasping the wrist.

"Within one day I filled an entire regiment with Rebel scum," continued Sheridan, becoming animated. "Scum who became deserters, and traitors to their cause! They enlisted out of fear into the Union Army! They became ruthless, deadly foes of the countless war parties of Cheyenne, Comanche, and Sioux that ravaged our frontier! All it took was the lopping of a few heads with the guillotine!" Sheridan had become exhilarated as he spun suddenly from the window and faced Forsyth.

"What are you getting at, I still don't get it," mumbled Sandy Forsyth.

"Come here, and look through the window. Here, I'll help you," General Sheridan insisted as he assisted Forsyth to his feet.

What Major Forsyth beheld beggared the imagination. There, below in the middle of the street a guillotine, complete with platform, had been erected. Forsyth shielded his eyes with his hand as the constricted pupils smarted in the sun light from the window. He saw the sun flash from the blade as it crashed down heavily, decapitating the head of a prisoner.

"You see, George my boy, President Johnson pretty much allows me to maintain control by any means I deem necessary. Look! There is the best pathfinder and scout that was ever conceived in the womb of a woman! He shot and killed another man in a poker game. Although he was clearly in the right, I did not intervene in the sentencing because he refused to join our merry band of fifty. He has since reconsidered his decision and volunteered to assist you! But he doesn't know that I have stayed his execution. Now, watch!" Sheridan ordered his subordinate.

A half dozen condemned men had been brought forward for execution. Among these desperate men was Simpson Everett Stillwell; a cat with nine lives who had already lost several.

The nineteen-year-old youth was one of several peculiar anomalies who would be assigned to the expedition; a six-foot three-inch teenaged Hercules.

Stillwell flashed back in his mind to his brush with death that had brought him here, to the scaffold.

Simpson Stillwell had been a skilled poker player imbued with above average luck. The altercation which led to his capital punishment had developed when he caught his opponent cheating. Stillwell remembered this in its entirety as he mounted the wooden steps of the scaffold leading to the massive guillotine.

"Cheater!" Stillwell had shouted at the opposing poker player, who had earlier secreted the Ace of Spades in the sleeve of his shirt, and skillfully added it to what he held through sleight of hand.

"Cur!" responded the exposed cheat, drawing a single barreled, .38 caliber Remington cap and ball derringer from beneath the sleeve of his other wrist. The movement was quick, facilitated by a rubber band attached to the weapon and middle finger of the gun hand. By merely lifting on the ruffled sleeve of the airy, cotton shirt, resistance was terminated and the derringer flew forward into the shooter's palm.

The cheater squeezed the trigger without hesitation, detonating the percussion cap, but not the gunpowder. The man's fate was sealed with the failure of his weapon.

"You cheating son of a bitch! You tried to kill me!" shouted Stillwell, as he stood up abruptly, intentionally flipping the card table backward onto his opponent and drawing a big, outdated and by the standards of the day - primitive Colt Patterson .36 caliber revolver.

The forefather of all revolvers, the Patterson which was marketed widely in 1836 only held five shots. Curiously, the trigger remained folded and hidden within the frame until the hammer was cocked, allowing it to immediately drop down.

"Don't do it!" shouted the cheater; a card shark with thick, black, unruly hair. His black buffalo wool felt hat connoted fine tastes; it was in the Grandee style – with a four-and-a-half-inch tall crown, and a four-inch brim. The hat was canted on the back of his head, above his shoulder blades. It could be suspended from the dark complexioned man's scrawny neck by means of a black braided horsehair stampede string which was adjusted to perfection by means of an expensive gold string-tie slider.

The English spread collar was open at the neck of the cheater's white, long sleeved cotton shirt. The shirt was button-down and the full length of the center was frilled, as were the cuffs. Over the airy shirt was a single-breasted, button-down paisley type black vest in black canvas duck. It was unbuttoned and straight cut across the bottom front. Within the four front pockets of the vest were additional playing cards, secreted there with intentions of dubious integrity.

"I was just tryin' to scare ya!" assured the villain. The high forehead furrowed in consternation above the bushy, black eyebrows. Jet black eyes regarded

Stillwell as the devious mind sought to maneuver its way out of the perilous situation. A finely formed nose, aquiline in shape set the center of a handsome face with moderately pronounced cheekbones. Beneath the nose resided a dark moustache which was neatly trimmed, and detracted from the full lips but not the gap that resided between the two upper front teeth; teeth that were white and belied the true meaning behind the dishonest smile.

"Like this?!" retorted the big kid, shooting the poker player five times in the face and forehead. The man wouldn't seem to die, holding his face with both feminine hands as he screamed and choked on blood.

"What the hell is goin' on here!" roared a walrus-mustached sheriff as he approached Stillwell with gun drawn. His heavy gut hanging over his two tone, brown tooled leather gun belt.

Stillwell snapped back to the present and the new peril that faced him.

"Let go! Let go of me! I'm not going up there! Hang me instead! I'm not stickin' my neck under that thing!" shouted the youth, struggling against the two husky ruffians that manhandled him up the wooden steps of the scaffold.

Atop the scaffold stood a monstrously built man, his loose fitting tunic unable to hide the overdeveloped muscles of his chest, across which he folded his arms-arms of which the biceps easily would have measured twenty inches. The executioner's face was hidden by a black hood, pointed at the top and falling loosely to the broad shoulders. Two holes were cut out of the hood from which glared the dark brown irises of eyes that beamed with horrific anticipation.

"Damn your eyes!" shouted the condemned teenager at the imposing executioner. "You can go to hell before you get me under that thing! You're not cutting off *my head* with that blade! Damn you! Damn all of your hides to hell!"

Stillwell looked up, not noticing the dull gray clouds that scudded across the Kansas sky. Neither did he pay any attention to the scissor tailed fly catchers that snapped up flying insects into their beaks. Instead, his gaze had fixed upon the monstrous blade of the guillotine, a two hundred-pound steel razor which was forged and then cut at a forty-five-degree angle.

Into the angled blade had been drilled five holes, three aligned in a row above two others. Into the holes were inserted large bolts, weighing five pounds apiece, these secured the blade to a lead weight carefully calibrated to the tune of six hundred pounds. A full thirty-six inches of blade extended evilly beneath the lead weight, which was meant to add impetus to the downward motion of the killing machine.

"Hol' dat sumabitch man steady there!" ordered the executioner in a deep Southern drawl. His accent betrayed his low breeding by virtue of the hard to understand white trash vernacular of the Deep South.

The executioner moved with the supple, dangerous ease of a tiger as he approached the doomed convict.

"Hol'im fast! Ah sed! Hol' dis heah miscreant still!" shouted the executioner, trying to place a dark hood made of burlap over the black haired Stillwell. Horse shoe triceps of iron stood out, quivering in bold relief under the sweaty, glistening skin of the muscle knotted arms of the executioner. The tunic, sleeveless, was pulled in tightly at the waist, cinched with an oversized, black leather belt. Stillwell's green, crooked teeth flashed in the sun as he twisted his head back and forth, his neck muscles distended with the efforts of dodging the hood.

The blade of the guillotine was dull gray, the sides of which could clearly be seen the marks of the forge. The cutting edge, however, was as shiny as a mirror. It was suspended ten feet and held in place by a thick hemp rope, well oiled. Sturdy timber comprised the frame into which a channel had been beveled on either side to guide the murderous object in its drive downward.

The condemned would be placed onto a gurney of oak and secured by leather straps, this would be slid forward until it came into contact with a pair of wooden gibbets. The gibbets would then secure about the victim's neck and hold him in place.

"You murderin', rabid dawg! What pard uh Anglish canchu nod unnerstan'?" boomed the executioner's voice, whose scarred, sledge hammer like fist slammed into Stillwell's tightened abdomen, doubling him over and allowing the executioner to emplace the black hood.

"Onto the gurney wit' dat son of a slut!" drawled the executioner in his heavy Mississippi accent.

Jack Stillwell was manhandled onto the gurney by the small crew of seasoned executioners. "Jack" Stillwell was then physically lifted onto the gurney and strapped to it, then slid forward, his head being secured in place by virtue of the gibbets.

The roar of the blood thirsty crowd grew in lusty crescendo as the struggle of the convicted killer had prolonged and whetted the anticipation of the execution. Wives with hourglass waistlines and mothers in touring dresses stood alongside cattle bums in leather chaps with .44 and .45 caliber six shot revolvers holstered in cheap gun leather. Wizened old conjurs gummed black, tar colored plug tobacco with toothless perseverance as the excited crowd of spectators yelled and cheered for the executioner. This adoration seemed to be ignored by the man of the hour as he went about completing the sinister intricacies of his profession.

"Belay that execution!" shouted a clerk of General Sheridan. "His Excellency General Sheridan, Head of the Department of the Missouri, has ordered the man's life reprieved! Stay that blade!"

Suddenly the hood was ripped from Stillwell's head and he looked straight down into the large wicker basket, several bushels in size, located directly beneath his face.

"Son of a bitch!" Stillwell gasped, "Am I seeing into hell? Can this be real?" looking up at the frontiersman was the head of his friend Tim Westwood, whose eyes were alive with recognition and understanding.

Westwood's blue tinged face resided beneath a high forehead crowned with thin, receded black hair. His face was bloated, the bluing capillaries of the pronounced cheeks had swollen to the point of rupture as the vessels sought to constrict and staunch the loss of blood.

"Tim! Are you still alive? Can you hear me?" gasped the six-foot three-inch killer, his blood congealing in horror.

The edematous eyelids of Westwood closed, and then opened, the pupils fixing on those of Stillwell. The mouth was closed, surrounded by a full, thick black beard. The lips pulled back and a croaking noise like that of a large catfish emanated from the hideous orifice.

"If a cat has nine lives, den yo' down to seven!" laughed the executioner. "Gimme a lock of yo' hair, boy - fo' luck!" with that he ripped a handful of Stillwell's thick dark hair from the back of his scalp.

The gibbet was lifted and as the gurney was suddenly jerked back, Stillwell saw Tim Westwood try to speak for the last time; as an obscene croaking issued urgently from the head's gullet.

Suddenly the military band which had been seated on the shaded veranda of the courthouse struck up the lively tune of *Gary Owen*.

Lieutenant Colonel George Armstrong Custer stood with his wife Libbie and sister Margaret on the hard packed earth, watching the event unfold at the scaffold. Elated with the bands rendition of *Gary Owen*, the Yellow Hair then looked up toward the window where Sheridan and Forsyth stood gazing at the spectacle. Sheridan directed his stare to Custer and nodded his head.

"Libbie," said Custer to his wife. "I'm going to talk with Sheridan. I'll be a while. You and Margaret stay and enjoy yourselves with the remaining executions."

"Autie!" hissed Libbie Custer. "With but four of these executions being realized of these loathsome souls condemned to an everlasting hell, Margaret and myself will bear audience to the remaining capital punishments without your presence to invoke the appearance of decency. If Margaret and I are to anticipate your absence at the exhibition of the brass knuckle pugilists as well, then I emphasize the imperative that you accede to the promotion that I so desperately desire."

"Libbie, I can only speculate as to the fruition of your desire, and General Sheridan has intimated that I am assured to the command the Seventh Cavalry," answered Custer. "Sheridan gave me the nod and wants me up there to discuss matters of great importance."

"Your presence should be appreciated there, Autie," replied Libbie. "You are the left hand of Philip Sheridan and without you he is nothing. And furthermore, these people look up to and worship you. Like a martyr I will sacrifice my dignity and endure the embarrassment if Margaret and I are left unattended in the midst of this societal excrement."

"I can't help but empathize with you, Libbie. I am almost certain Sheridan will guarantee me the Seventh Cavalry in a matter of moments," offered the Boy General. "General Sheridan *owes* me," added Custer as he departed from his wife and sister, headed toward the two story stone block house where General Philip Sheridan waited.

"You had best get a Colonelcy, Autie, after all, that's what you intimated this long, dreadful journey was about," reposted Libbie. Elizabeth Custer fumed at the humiliation of being left unattended with her sister among the largely male audience of the executions. On the other hand, she desperately wanted her husband promoted. The potential advancement to colonel would put Custer within reach of being a brigadier general once more.

Custer's military fortunes had risen with the Civil War, becoming the youngest general in the history of American arms at the age of 23. However, his star had fallen with the end of the war.

Elizabeth Custer found herself married to Lt. Colonel Custer, instead of General Custer and it rankled her, bitterly.

Large, ominous dark clouds rolled in, heavily laden with moisture. The ground trembled with the dull rumble of distant thunder. The metallic smell of rain was carried on a strong breeze that had begun to blow in from the south, traveling up the corridor of the Gulf Coastal Plain from the Gulf of Mexico.

Chapter Three
Brass Knuckles and Fair Ladies

THE IMPROMPTU FIGHTING ring was a square shaped enclosure; the ground being covered with a thickly set, closely cropped mat of crab grass. It was twenty-four feet square and enclosed by virtue of eight shoulder height poles supporting two stout ropes made of hemp. A rough scratch had been gouged into the turf demarcating the territorial domain of the contestant on either side.

A violent struggle was in progress deep beneath the cropped blades of grass, as ants fought one another. Small, red ants attacked larger, black ants. Heads were sheared from the smaller ants, even as legs were shorn from the articulated joints of the exoskeletons of their larger, dark adversaries. This deadly war amongst insects went unnoticed by the cowboy boots that stepped on them.

Both of the male contestants had their own seconds, umpires and a mutual referee to monitor the fight for fairness. The combatants were shirtless and wore tightly fitting knee length under-drawers, which were searched for weapons before the brutal pugilistic competition began.

Closely following the London Prize Ring Rules for brass knuckle fist fighting, the contestants were forbidden from attacking an opponent when he was down. Gouging of the eyes and biting was also prohibited.

Both fighters were armed with lethal brass knuckles – the type of which were provided with murderous, sharp, nail-like one-inch-long projections. The combatants wore the perfectly legal fighting boots as well, with three inch knife-like blades protruding evilly from the toe of the high laced leather boots.

A warm, driving rain had begun to come down in thick, transparent curtains, accompanied by forked sheet lightning and rolling thunder which caused the ground to shake and the horses to shy.

"Margaret, if the sun were to recrudesce, I could but adore it as though I were an Aztec paying obeisance to her deity. This is going to be the most abominable of weather! Had not the other officers' wives spoke of this championship with such lofty regard, I do not speculate for a moment that we could endure such an unremitting deluge of precipitation!" complained Elizabeth Custer to her sister-in-law, Margaret.

Both women sat atop side saddles on their horses. Side saddles were common and unique to female equestrians. The origin of the side saddle was a riddle that hinted to speculations of great antiquity. These side saddles were of the more recent, two pommel kind. One pommel, about ten inches tall stood nearly straight and was off centered at the front of the saddle. The rider's right leg went around the fixed pommel which served to secure the right thigh, and the left leg hooked around the second pommel. The second pommel was smaller than the first. This pommel was adjustable and the rider would place the left foot into the single stirrup.

While the origins of the side saddle disappeared into prehistory, the introduction of the second pommel or "leaping horn" as it was also known completely changed the side saddle. It morphed into a secure riding implement and allowed the female rider to be anchored firmly onto the mount and to ride at a full gallop.

Libbie and Margie had chosen to attend the pugilistic exhibition mounted atop their horses. This was to better afford vantage of view to the savage spectacle about to unfold. Others sat atop horses as well, including the garrison's officers and their wives, who Libbie greeted graciously as they began to aggregate about her and Margaret. Custer on the other hand lay prostrate on the steer hide leather settee of General Sheridan – the torrential downpour having begun to exacerbate his asthmatic symptoms.

"Oh Margaret," continued Libbie. "Will this incessant deluge but relent for a moment? How are we to observe and take note of the intricacies of this martial concourse if the finer points of their art are obfuscated by these driving torrents of rain!"

Margaret's lightly constructed black and gray colored marquis (tilting) parasol whipped violently to the right in a sudden wind gust. The sheet of rain drove down in a torrent between the cleavage of her breasts which were pushed boldly upward by the tightly fitting corset underneath her dark riding habit. Both women wore the black, austere, uniform-like riding habits common to proper ladies. They had the jacket style high necked bodice with long basque and peplums.

"Libbie, would that we could call it a day, I worry for you in those wet clothes!" Margaret responded, adding, "I am of an inclination that we excuse ourselves. I don't see the need for you to risk your health in wretched, drenched attire."

"Bless your heart, Margie! I concur emphatically with your altruistic motivations. After the brass knuckle pugilists are finished pommeling each other, I fully intend to step out of these wet, sodden garments before I take a cold!" ejaculated Libbie.

The two contestants sat on short, three legged wooden stools at their corners. These stools were the type that dairymen sit upon to milk cows. The fighters sat low to the ground on these stools as their seconds and umpires massaged the thick trapezius muscles of their broad shoulders and inundated them with pointers and advice. The umpires checked the placement of the brass knuckles on the hands of their fighters, and double checked the tightness of the boot lacings of their fighting boots.

Suddenly a bolt of multiple forked lightning struck one of the few trees nearby - an ancient cottonwood already long dead from numerous such electrical strikes. A dull rolling rumble erupted into a loud clap of thunder which followed several seconds later. The thunder bolt shook the ground and caused the horses to startle. Quickly, Libbie firmly grabbed the reins of Margaret's large bay mare and spoke to the eight hundred-pound beast soothingly, lest it spook.

The Southern drawl shouted by the referee was audible above the downpour, but individual words could not be understood. Like nearly all of the men he wore a large straw or buffalo felt cowboy hat, his was darkly dyed, and a tan duster; a heavy rain slicker that doubled as a dust coat in dry weather. The women by contrast relied on umbrellas and parasols to shield themselves from the driving sheets of rain.

"Libbie, are they going to fight, or simply wait out the rain?" asked Margaret, growing impatient and clearly miserable.

"Look, Margie!" assured Elizabeth Custer. "They are about to fight!"

"The things that I have to do to keep this garrison entertained," complained Little Phil Sheridan to the prostrate Custer, who lay wheezing and short of breath on the settee.

The Yellow Hair had managed to roust himself from the long, high backed, brass studded leather couch and try to attend the brass knuckle match but found he could not. His rapid hyperventilation seemed to provide no relief to the air hunger that had temporarily incapacitated him.

"Damned rain, always causes my lungs to close up," replied Custer, adding, "yes, but the people seem content, that's a good thing this far out."

"I'm giving you the Seventh Cavalry, Autie," stated Little Phil. "Grant's blocking your promotion to colonel. I warned you about him."

"Grant – sure – holds – a – grudge..." gasped the Yellow Hair between breaths, wheezing.

Sheridan stood at the paned window, looking through the blue tinged, lead impregnated glass down at the event unfolding below. He studied the two shirtless men as they approached each other in the square shaped ring; men who were diametrically opposite of each other in every means of appearance.

Out of the left corner approached a gigantic Negro, a six-foot eight-inch mixed blood colossus whose skin shone like polished amber in the summer rain. He was called the Mexican, but no one knew his real name. He made his living going from one sun blasted frontier town or post, to the next, winning large purses in vicious bare and brass knuckle competitions.

The Mexican had a fighting weight of three hundred pounds and a reach of ninety-eight-inches. The Mexican's enormous physique conveyed the false impression of slowness, suggested by his deliberate, languorous stride to the center of the ring. But in combat, he moved with the deadly speed of a Bengal tiger. Massive muscles played and rippled under the gleaming skin. His skull shattering blows could fell a full grown ox. Many times a single sweeping blow with the cruel, spiked brass knuckles had ripped the face from a dodging, ducking competitor, leaving nothing but a gaping, screaming, toothless maw.

The black man's hair was shaven, his facial features were a hybridization of his Negro mother and Mexican father, but his skin was an amber complexion. The face was heavily boned, the forehead proud and the cheeks high set. The nose, broken so many times that it sat flat against the face like a child's deflated balloon, resided over thick, mangled lips. The face, also, was shaven. The darkness of the skin was interrupted in many places with ragged, horizontal and vertical white and red scars earned in the ring. The right ear had years ago been bitten off in a Texas Death Match.

"Looks like my man's going to have a fight on his hands," Sheridan speculated to Custer, as he turned from the window, facing his favorite officer. "There's no way I can allow you to accompany Forsyth. Even as a civilian. You have to let it go, Autie."

"Surely there's a way," intervened Major Forsyth, who struggled out of his opium induced stupor.

Custer had almost forgotten that Forsyth was there, for all appearances – but in reality the Yellow Hair was acutely aware of the major's presence.

"Autie is the best cavalry man in the Army!" Forsyth's earnest enthusiasm for Custer's presence on the expedition belied the jealousy he had for the Yellow Hair, and was purely for show. Custer knew this. Forsyth knew that Custer knew this, and Little Phil Sheridan knew that everyone in the ruggedly furnished room was aware of it.

The booing and catcalls could be heard even behind the glass in the second story room. Despite the driving rain storm, the unpopularity of the black Colossus of Rhodes could be heard.

Cobwebs hung loosely from the corners of the high ceilinged, knotted pine walls. No one in the room paid notice to the fly that struggled to escape the sticky web as the spider reacted to the tugging of its glue like threads.

"I am of an inclination to agree with you, Philip. In my present circumstances I would be a liability to the expedition. I will not allow my selfishness to impede this momentous task," Custer replied, adding, "as soon as this weather improves, I'll be in better health and return with my wife to your home at Leavenworth."

"It won't be long," assured Sheridan. "You will be reinstated in two or three more weeks as the commanding officer of the 7th Cavalry."

"Sandy," placated Custer. "I am sincerely sorry, but it's not in the stars for me this time around."

But the Yellow Hair had other ideas. Secretly, camped five miles away in a Sibley tent was an English anthropologist named Gladstone and an Arikawa scout, his favorite – Bloody Knife.

"Ugggh! Libbie, what a grotesque man! He looks like some demon from a tale inspired to frighten children into obedience!" cried Margaret Custer. She turned her head away from the Mexican, shielding her sight with her parasol hand, allowing more rain to pelt her in the process. She held the reins of her horse with her right.

"What an imbalance in parity!" ejaculated Libbie to her sister-in-law. "I have a premonition that this concourse will be consummated in the twinkling of an eye!"

From the opposite side of the ring approached Sheridan's man – Sergeant Maggot, also known as the "Battalion Stallion;" a popular sergeant among the troops. He also had a reputation as a solid brass knuckle fighter.

Maggot stood at five foot nine inches and weighed two hundred pounds at fighting weight. He had sixteen-inch biceps and a seventy-inch reach. The brown hair of his bullet shaped head was tightly cropped, his closely set eyes were blue and intense as they assessed his monstrous adversary.

As with his ebon opponent, the sergeant's nose was also flattened, the cartilage long ago having been snapped. His ears, like those of so many other pugilists, were cauliflowered. The jaw seemed to meld into the thick, bull neck. Compact and powerfully constructed, Sergeant Maggot advanced warily to the center of the ring, as a bobcat approaches a mountain lion.

A flash of lightning and crash of thunder released another torrent of moisture as the rain pattered on and cascaded off of the referee's cowboy hat.

"OK now!" shouted the referee above the tumult of thunder and waves of rain that pelted his hat. "You guys know the rules! Now I want you two to shake hands!"

The Mexican quickly went through the motion of extending his palm so that he could crush every bone in the smaller man's hand, finish the job, and hurry to the saloon with his winnings.

Sergeant Maggot extended his hand quickly and mischievously slid it under the thin fabric of the regulation under-drawers of the Mexican and seized the giant's penis, grabbing onto the bratwurst sized appendage.

Before the referee could intervene, Maggot had torn the penis from the groin and stepped back quickly, avoiding the dangerous right hook that caught the referee squarely in the jaw, tearing it nearly completely off.

The referee stumbled sideways, his jaw hanging by tendons and ligaments. Blood spurted in numerous fine threads and two thick streams as he sought to maneuver the mandible back into place. He dropped to his knees on the wet ground, screaming incoherently through his fingers as the crowd went livid with applause and laughter.

"Margaret! Did you see that? The sergeant tore off the black man's penis!" shouted Libbie at Margie, grabbing Margaret's wrist in excitement.

"Libbie, you know that the sight of such a vulgar object makes me nauseated!" responded Margaret, who saw the sergeant dance backward, insolently dangling the object in front of the enraged Hercules, who rushed in, swinging blindly – and missing. "I can't hold it back, Libbie! Oh my land! I am going to wretch!!!"

The Mexican continued to swing and miss as Sergeant Maggot ducked and weaved, stepping back when the larger man charged. Suddenly the Mexican grabbed Maggot in a suffocating bear hug and began squeezing until Maggot heard the first of several ribs pop. Simultaneously the Mexican buried his face into the meat slabbed chest of Maggot, rending off a mouthful of toughened flesh and spitting it into the water that had begun to pool in the thick, short grass. Then he buried his face back into the beefy chest and began gnawing into the deep hole that oozed dark, coppery blood.

While Libbie sat on her saddle, transfixed by the event taking place, Margaret was vomiting violently. Several of the fort's countless mongrel dogs began fighting over the slimy, chunk filled emesis, spooking her horse.

"Margaret," reassured Libbie. "You must sustain this vulgar display of masculinity but for a moment longer; it appears as though our gallant Sergeant Maggot is not much longer for this world!"

"Let me take hold of the bridles, Margaret and Libbie, I can't get any more wet than I already am, while yet, you two may still make use of your parasols," announced Beverly, Jedediah's daughter, who appeared unexpectedly through the driving torrents of rain like some sort of apparition.

The rain drops were big – the size of 00 buckshot, and stung any exposed skin that they struck. The lightning and thunder however, had moved further to the north. The storm showed signs of strengthening as it moved farther inland; the sky was hidden with cumulonimbus clouds of deep purple, sporadically illuminated from within by internal lightning. The rumbling of thunder sounded like distant artillery.

"Beverly, that is most kind of you, but you are wet to the bone!" answered Libbie, who appraised Beverly with genuine concern. It was widely known that wet clothes on a woman could lead to the dreaded pneumonia.

"Well what is the difference," laughed Beverly, her jet black hair spun back tightly into a bun and covered with a black Quaker styled full bonnet. "Out on the range I have been drenched in sweat – soaking wet in sweat! For days on end! Haven't taken a cold yet." Her black day dress was the wide pagoda sleeve type with a high neckline and laced collar, and while the dress rested flat over the front of the thighs, it bunched out behind.

"Bless your heart!" interjected Margaret, who wiped the vomit from her mouth with a large, embroidered, white cotton handkerchief, trying to smile out of politeness. "I am so embarrassed. But I saw the most hideous sight at the beginning of this fight – this fight which never seems to end. And it made me violently ill!"

"I like watching my brothers fight," answered Beverly. "But now they're all dead! All of them! The Indians killed all of my family but for my mother and father," Beverly began sobbing hysterically, her tears ran down her cheeks and fell into the mud at her feet. "They – oh, they killed – my fiancé, Aaron, too! My mother – my mother was taken captive!"

The roaring of the crowd caused Beverly to look toward the cause of the commotion, she could not see the contest due to the mob of spectators bunching in droves of rabble around the ring.

"Oh, do sit upon my lap and watch the fighting, Beverly. It shan't last much longer, and let your mind escape from the terrible tragedy that has befallen your family," soothed Margaret.

"Rest assured Beverly, my husband General George Armstrong Custer will make the Cheyenne pay in rivers of blood for what they have done!" seconded Libbie.

"Look, Beverly," cooed Margaret, the Negro is chewing into the sergeant's chest! Men can be such animals. Hideous, hideous, sight to behold, my dear, unfortunate friend." Margaret secured Beverly by means of placing her arm around the hourglass waistline, made thin by the overtight corset.

The twenty-year-old girl looked up, seeing the fight really for the first time. The sergeant wasn't doing too good.

With his arms pinioned to his sides and the enraged eunuch gnawing into his chest, Maggot began kicking madly at the legs of the Mexican. Riverettes of blood streamed down the pillar legs of the larger man, who would not relinquish his hold as the boot knives sliced through veins, muscles and ligaments. Then suddenly the boot blade embedded deeply into the shin bone, causing the Mexican to release his hold and fall to the ground in the fetal position, both arms pulling the injured leg tightly into the abdomen. He lay on his left side in a pool of water, screaming curses as he massaged the shin bone.

"Libbie, I must egress to our room at the hotel. I beg your pardon to leave," apologized Margaret, who, looking past the bonnet of Beverly saw the seconds and umpires halting the fight. Two of the cowboy hatted, rain-slickered hoodlums were pulling back on Maggot, causing one of his kicks to wildly miss as he was jerked violently backward.

"You can't kick a man when he's down!" screamed the new referee, an Irishman in a bowler hat and wearing a ridiculous set of sideburns. He too, was wearing a duster in the driving rainstorm. The count had begun, and the Mexican rose to the occasion. The entire front of his regulation under- drawers was saturated with deep, bright red blood as he advanced on the sergeant, limping like a freshly gelded horse.

"Just stay here with *me* Margie. You know I'll have to get out of these wet clothes after these two reprobates eradicate one another," Libbie cajoled Margaret, adding, "besides, wouldn't you like to see these two hideous beasts finish killing off each other?"

The pugnacious sergeant adopted the classic bare knuckled boxing pose; one arm outstretched, bent upward with hand fisted, the other arm bent similarly, but closer to the face. One foot in front of the other, body turned at an angle to offer a smaller target.

The left hand of the Mexican shot straight forward with lightning speed at the face of Sergeant Maggot in a vicious jab. The needle sharp spikes of the brass knuckles missed the sergeant's face by a fraction of an inch as the smaller man canted his head to the right. Maggot then drove his right hand into the right side of the face of the Mexican - who canted his head to the left, but not in time to avoid the glancing blow.

The sharpened spikes of the brass knuckles caught on and rended off the entire side of the Negro's face. The teeth, lower and upper jaw were revealed in macabre anatomical detail as the crowd roared with assent. Several spectators enthusiastically began shooting rifles and pistols into the air. Rotgut whiskey was passed from hand to hand. Women in mended dresses and faded flower bonnets showed rotted teeth as they laughed.

"Oh, Margie! I think our man has won!" shouted Libbie as she shifted eagerly on the saddle.

"Why do these athletic events seem to draw on and on, Libbie?" retorted Margaret. Margaret's keen desire to leave the brass knuckle contest was overwhelming. Margaret was also intensely aware of the close physical contact of Beverly as she adjusted her position from time to time on Margaret's lap. Margie tightened her arm instinctively around Beverly's waist. The wet clothing of Beverly conducted a damp, comforting warmth to Margie.

"Careful, now. Don't you slip off!" cautioned Margaret.

The strong impetus of the powerhouse glancing blow that had taken off the right side of the Mexican's face had overreached and threw the smaller man off balance. As he lurched forward, the black giant swung downward in a sledgehammer left hook; the brass knuckles crushed through the temporal bones of Maggot's skull like a pile driver would smash through a thin veneer of porous, rotted concrete. The ham sized fist entered into the brain, which extruded from the point of entry around the wrist of the Mexican.

Maggot grabbed the wrist with both hands as he dropped to his knees. Contemptuously the Mexican tore his brass knuckled fist from the brain cavity of Maggot's skull with a sickening, slopping, sucking sound. Large fragments of bone matted with hair pulled loose with it.

"Well, that son of a bitch killed my best sergeant!" exploded Little Phil Sheridan.

Custer studied the lavishly furnished room as he lay wheezing on the settee. His strength had recovered to the point that he thought he could make it to the hotel where his wife and sister would be staying. Away from the window and near a walnut book case containing volumes related to astronomy, Custer saw a fine Alvan Clark refracting telescope. The largest he had ever seen. The objective lens must have been around five inches in diameter, Custer thought.

"That's a mighty fine scope you've got there, Phil," commented the Boy General, sitting up. He did not comment on the outcome of the fight.

"How can you bring up something totally off the wall like that, Autie? I not only lost my best sergeant, I also had bet an enormous amount of money on that underdog. It's going to take a lot of wheeling and dealing, special favors and lucrative land deals against the Indians to cover my losses," retorted Sheridan. He was now seated at his desk, leaning forward, elbows on the desktop as he massaged his temples. "And if things couldn't get any worse, now my head is killing me!"

"Get some minor tribal chief – someone with an axe to grind against the whole Cheyenne Nation – to sign over a few thousand square miles of territory, Phil. That'll cover your losses," interjected Forsyth, who had up to now been in a drugged, semi-conscious state.

"I'd hate to do that, Sandy, but I may have to," answered General Sheridan, who, turning to Custer added:

"Listen, do me a favor and take Jedediah's daughter Beverly under your wing for a while, would you? She's been with Elizabeth and Margaret since the fisticuffs began, and seems to have caught on with Elizabeth and Margaret pretty good anyhow," requested Sheridan. "At least until this mess gets settled with Roman Nose. Her mother was taken prisoner and her fiancé was killed in the wagon train fiasco. Depending on a number of variables, it may be several months before her father can find a suitable husband for her. As it stands, he could prove useful to me and I'd appreciate your help in this."

Chapter Four
General Sheridan's Telescope

THE STORM HAD PASSED and with it any hope of stability to the evening sky. While a moonless night was efficacious to the amateur astronomer, on this night it did not prove so; all of the moisture in the atmosphere was being cajoled by high winds and served to make the stars twinkle and glitter violently, like riflemen firing in the darkness at great distance.

General Sheridan was aware of this as he unlimbered the large refractor, before opening the window to the night sky. He needed time to relax, recompose, and organize his thoughts after the catastrophic gambling losses he took when Maggot crashed like a felled tree to his knees in the soggy grass.

General Philip Sheridan had not bothered to lay his star charts out across the mahogany partner's desk that dominated more than any other piece of furniture the broad expanse of his office. He had already identified all of the Messier objects several thousand times over. What he needed now was to lose himself in time and space. Reluctantly, he opened the decanter and poured another glass of opiated port, and took two large swallows, followed by a smaller one. Smacking his lips, he approached the ultra-modern, state of the art telescope.

"Would that I had my Newtonian, but it is too big to haul around. I could use it to great effect here," reflected Little Phil, remembering his sixteen-inch reflector retrospectively. The amateur astronomer rolled his favorite astronomy chair, a padded captain's chair equipped with wheels, to the Alvan Clark refractor.

General Sheridan's Newtonian reflecting telescope afforded magnificent deep sky views encompassing thousands of countless multihued stars, and in summer months even the darkest and most barren parts of the sky were littered with nebulae. But the Clark offered advantages as well – crisp, well defined images of lunar landscapes and planets. The Cassini Division of the rings of Saturn could easily be discerned with the expensive refractor.

The night had been moonless and there was much wind in the upper atmosphere – conducive to creating a boiling effect at higher magnifications. Not good for star gazing – the seeing, the general thought, was in one word – *terrible*.

The telescope he was using would be the pride of any science department at a major university. The brass tube of the refractor was fifty-six and a half inches in length and was mounted on an overlarge equatorial mount, for precise stability. The lens was tended to carefully.

Disinterested with the poor seeing opportunities, the Head of the Department of the Missouri stood up and slewed the big scope down toward the dim lantern light emanating from one of the rooms in the hotel below, across the street.

Using a low powered eye piece and adjusting the focus knob, Sheridan gently tapped the telescope into position until the light emanating from the bedroom centered into his ocular. The general focused the soft light into sharp clarity using the patience and skill acquired through decades of amateur astronomy. Added to the telescope was a much smaller finder scope, which accelerated the acquisition of celestial objects.

The general continued to make micro adjustments through use of the focusing knob. Although images always appeared upside down, this did not matter in sky gazing. It was, however, a major annoyance when bird watching or observing other terrestrial events, but he had learned to cope with the inconvenience.

"Did I see movement?" the general asked himself, suddenly more alert - the brass barreled refractor homing in on the window. "That's Margaret Custer," Sheridan mumbled, acutely aware of the sense of guilt, the sense of intrusion that he felt. Nevertheless, Little Phil did not turn his telescope to the heavens; he continued to watch.

Margaret was seated on a high backed chair, the heavy, worn out type which accompanied a cheap hotel suite. She had changed into dry attire - a black riding skirt, with a white blouse, her auburn hair appeared to have been toweled dry and was brushed straight. She had her hands behind her neck, fingers interlocked as she leaned into the back of the chair. Suddenly another figure appeared in the room, walking in through the bathroom partition – this was Elizabeth Custer, General Sheridan realized, adjusting the focusing knob to bring the image into sharper focus.

"What is going on in there?" Sheridan asked himself, mesmerized by the sight unfolding before his eyes. Elizabeth was wearing a heavy, white bathrobe, and was facing the mirror which was mounted atop a small dresser. She appeared to pay Margaret, her sister-in-law, no mind, as though she wasn't there. The general could not detect any sign of conversation between the two women.

"Damn my eyes!" Sheridan pressed the ocular into his eyeball to realize the full potential of the optics. "She is about to disrobe herself! With the curtain drawn open and her sister in-law present! Wait! What is this?"

Another figure appeared in the single room, having entered from the hallway. Also a female, this one differed in that she had shiny, black hair, spun tightly into a bun. The woman was short, attractive, and demure. She was dressed in the drab black dress of a woman who worked on a farm, common to many of the women that served in various practical functions of the rugged, pioneering lifestyle of the Western woman. The short statured, heavy breasted brunette woman leaned against the door jamb, having left the door open.

"Beverly Sumrall!" the general's lips mumbled, watching as Libbie Custer contemptuously flung off the bath robe onto the scarred, hardwood floor. She kicked the discarded bath robe aside in a derisory manner and began brushing her hair vigorously. Her apple sized breasts bounced and jiggled violently with the savage strokes of the ivory handled hair brush. She turned her head suddenly toward the dark haired, heavy breasted younger woman at the door, ignoring the gunfire outside on the main street, as ruffians settled scores with each other.

"Shut that door! Men could walk by there!" ordered Elizabeth Custer coldly.

"I'm sorry, Mrs. Custer," offered Beverly, alarmed at her transgression. "That was absent-minded of me. It's been a long day and well... "

"Take this brush, Beverly," stated Libbie, the statement was in the imperative, and in no way implied a request, "and untangle my raveled mane! The concourse of the day's events has put me yet once more into the doldrums of an uttermost malaise. Alas, I am left but to speculate, how, my dear Beverly, General Philip Sheridan's favorite lost the brass knuckled fist fighting contest to a Negro wanderer, of all things!" chirped the malcontented and nude Libbie Custer.

Margaret Custer watched how even the slightest movement Libbie made would cause her perfect, apple shaped breasts to quiver as though they were made of shaky pudding. The escalating gunfire between the drunk hoodlums and white trash outside did not persuade her to avert her open staring at her sister-in-law – who was standing completely naked in front of her and Beverly.

"AAAAAHHHHHHHH!!!!" came a high pitched shout from one of the gun-fighting ruffians out on the dirt street. *"I'm hit!!! I'm hit!!!"* The screaming was followed by an even louder, more robust fusillade as the loud clopping of cowboy boots could be heard racing up the stairwell that led onto the hall where the Custers' room was situated.

Elizabeth Custer thrust the large hairbrush at her new companion who had been imposed upon her by General Sheridan. Beverly Sumrall accepted the ornate hairbrush, as she approached uneasily. This was the first time she had seen her new matron angry, and Beverly was unsure in how to act. To react in the wrong way could be perceived as an insult by Custer's wife, and Beverly didn't want to risk being abandoned and thrown out on the street in this rough, frontier town.

Libbie was acutely aware of the awkward discomfort the austere, reserved woman felt toward her nakedness. She seemed to pay her sister-in-law

Margaret no mind, as though she were an invisible spectator.

Turning suddenly toward the mirror, Libbie intentionally stopped in mid-motion. The premeditated, sudden halt in movement made her perky breasts jiggle like gelatin, Margaret thought. Libbie speculated in silence to herself for a moment, as the movement of her breasts quickly subsided. The vivacious eyes of Custer's wife fixated on the worn out, wicker chair in front of the dresser.

Suddenly a frantic pounding on the heavy wooden door interrupted the scene, as Sheridan observed all three women look suddenly toward the doorway.

"Let me in! Please! *I've been shot!!!*"

"Get on out of here! You filthy ne'er do well!" shouted Libbie, padding barefoot across the dirty floor to the door. Although dimpled, her behind was firm, and beneath the doughy, insulating pad of fat, strong gluteal muscles played in the light that was cast from the smoking coal oil lanterns. "Get away from my door and go bleed to death somewhere else!!!" reiterated the irascible Elizabeth.

"She's fit to be tied!" thought Margaret, studying the plump, dimple marked round curvature of her sister-in-law's behind, and focusing her eyes onto the large divide that constituted her surprisingly wide gluteal fold.

Boot steps could be heard rushing up the steps in pursuit of the wounded miscreant, whose own boot steps rebounded down the hallway, away from the door of Libbie Custer.

"Low life, riff raff!" spat Libbie, as she turned around, running both hands through her auburn hair and raising it straight up, high above her head. She leaned back as she did so, arching her back and causing her breasts to lift. "Filthy scumbag men. The world would be so much better off without them."

"Where were we now? Oh, yes! Your hair!" spoke up Beverly, seizing the initiative to ingratiate herself into the safety of the Custer clan.

Completely ignoring the eruption of gunfire at the other end of the hall, Elizabeth became exasperated, speaking rapidly and energetically.

"I have an idea, Beverly Sumrall! Why don't I just turn that chair around one hundred eighty degrees, and voila! I can rest my arms across the top of it and plant my chin on them while you brush my hair!" cried the exuberant Libbie, fully cognizant of the vulgar display that her jutting, naked behind would present to the uncomfortable Beverly.

"I don't know what you mean by one hundred eighty degrees, Mrs. Custer," answered Beverly, honestly. The full, red lips betrayed no emotion beneath the petite, slightly flared nose. With mental alacrity the mind behind the dark, liquid eyes sought to maneuver safely through this treacherous minefield.

"Well! It goes something like this!" Libbie turned the chair about and sat leaning forward into the back rest. Libbie's back was to the twenty-year-old woman, her chin rested on the top of her forearms, which crossed one another on top of the chair's backrest. Her bare behind was thrust obscenely toward Jedediah Sumrall's daughter, who began brushing her matron's hair.

"In geometry, what I just did is to turn the chair one hundred eighty degrees, completing what is known as a straight angle, Miss Sumrall! Now, get those stubborn tangles out of my hair!" continued Libbie, who added, "I like sitting one - eighty, I feel that it's good for a young lady's posture!"

General Sheridan sat transfixed, he had swapped out the captain's chair for a higher sitting stool. The eye piece was welded to his eye socket. Yet a fourth figure entered the scene playing out before his keen, dark eye. It was the figure of a man. The man was bareheaded, blond with a receding hairline, and wore a ridiculous walrus moustache beneath his Gallic nose. He was wearing the uniform of an Army officer – it was Custer!

The Head of the Department of the Missouri saw a flurry of violent action; first, Libbie flew out of the chair, knocking the ivory handled hairbrush from the hand of Beverly Sumrall. Little Phil watched as Libbie viciously slapped Lieutenant Colonel Custer across the face – hard. He turned his face with the slap and when he looked back at her she slapped him again, across the other side of his face.

The general watched Margaret Custer's reaction through telescopic vision, seeing how she ogled the swinging breasts of her sister-in-law as she continued slapping her older brother, "Autie" Custer – who just stood there taking it.

"Shut those curtains, Beverly!" shouted Elizabeth Custer at her new, erstwhile companion. Her face had transformed from angelic into a visage of pure hatred. General Sheridan saw blood fly from the nose of Custer with the next vicious slap, a strand of blood struck the window pane in the form of a red necklace, the shape reminding Sheridan of the constellation of the Pleaides before running down the glass. Suddenly the curtains closed and darkness reigned over the night of Fort Hays, Kansas once more.

Chapter Five
The Special Attack Force

IN THE WIDE OPEN courtyard facing the blockhouse that comprised General Sheridan's headquarters stood a group of fifty white men. Although most had an Indian grandmother or great grandmother and they reflected the darker hair and skin of the Indian, they did not consider themselves as such. They listened somberly to the general who addressed them. They were with exceptions, mostly younger men under the age of thirty, lean and muscular. Not an ounce of fat on them.

They were professional gunfighters, rangers, and scouts. Most of them were hunters and paid killers who had fought in the Civil War, on one side or the other. Many had fought in blood feuds for various cattle barons or the local family aristocracies indigenous to every frontier town.

They were ostracized by their inability to fit in with civilized ways and many had struck out on their own, raising families in far flung reaches where no cavalry patrol dared to go. These men had lost their families to marauding bands of Comanche, Cheyenne, Sioux and Arapaho. All they had left was an unremitting desire for vengeance.

All wore wide brimmed hats in the cowboy style – some were made of buffalo felt, most were made of straw. While some were dressed as cowhands and gun slingers, others wore the leather shirts and buckskin breeches of their hated enemies. Some wore the heavy leather work shoes that laced up, while others wore moccasins, Wellingtons, or pointed toed cowboy boots.

All were heavily armed with uniform lethality; Spencer repeating rifles, and a Colt Army Model 1860 revolver. Heavy hunting or butcher knives hung in scabbards that depended from belts on trim waists. Most carried a derringer for suicide, if it came to that. But suicide was not the only purpose of the small, .38 caliber double barreled pistol. It could fit in the palm of a man's hand and in a disparate contest where no other weapon was available, the ubiquitous derringer could be a decisive game changer.

"In one of the biggest massacres in the history of the United States of America," General Sheridan shouted, as he stood atop a hundred-gallon oak water barrel to make him appear taller, "Roman Nose attacked a wagon train of settlers, killing over a thousand of these intrepid pioneers in their trek toward Utah! Many prisoners were taken – the children are being raised as Cheyenne! The women are subjugated in the most demeaning ways imaginable! All adult men were killed on the spot without mercy!"

A tall, gaunt figure dressed all in black stood beside the general. His head was bowed, his beard moved as he prayed silently. Not wearing a hat, the suture lines of the skull were barely visible beneath a heavy layer of unguent, the edges of the flesh were reddened and wept a clear, serosanguinous fluid from the horrific scalping wound.

On cue, Jedediah Sumrall lifted his head to give a searing account of what had happened, but instead began rending the hair from his disheveled, gray streaked beard, screaming:

"Kill! Kill them! Kill them all! Murdering bastards! There is no place deep enough in hell to send their souls! Kill! By the name of my father I will kill them all myself! My wife! My wife is among them at this very moment! By the Lord that is my master I will attend to this...Kill them!" ranted Jedediah, who had gone quiet insane. He dropped to his knees, his face bleeding from where he had ripped loose handfuls of beard, yanking away from the face loose folds of skin with the tearing motions. He began cursing and ranting incoherently.

"You will proceed to the scene of the massacre!" General Sheridan shouted above the raving Jedediah. "Where Roman Nose inflicted this travesty! Jedediah will take you directly there, where you will pick up the trail and follow Roman Nose to the ends of the earth if it so be!!!"

Within ten hours the mounted column led by Forsyth and Beecher had left Fort Hays behind. Ahead lay Fort Wallace. It stood almost by itself; an icon of Afro-American military power embodied in the all black Tenth Cavalry Regiment. There were one or two small enclaves situated miles from it, making it one of the last outposts of civilization on the vast frontier. Between them and Fort Hays lay a vast array of ghost towns and abandoned homesteads as they made for the headwaters of the Solomon River.

The air was fresh and the sky gun barrel blue. The column passed through herds of tens of thousands of horsefly blown buffalo which continued foraging, not lifting their mangy heads. The column was circled by huge groups of antelope which warily eyed a large pack of grey wolves that hung to the edge of the herd. Thousands of prairie dogs lunged into their filthy, urine saturated holes at the approach of the apocalyptic riders.

The hazy, foggy mist rising from the Smoky Hill River signaled that the separation from the final vestiges of civilization lay far to the rear. Ahead, awaited a land abandoned by whites during the Civil War, as Indian war parties burned out the settlements. The country that the column was entering was one which had quickly reverted to its primordial state.

They crossed the Saline River and the south fork of the Solomon and located Beaver Creek, at the point where Short Nose Creek flowed into it. They moved up along Beaver Creek, through heavy timber and made track directly for the last vestige of Euro-

American civilization – Fort Wallace. They arrived during darkness on the night of September fifth, 1868.

Major Forsyth was granted audience to Colonel Bankhead, the commanding officer of Fort Wallace. Bankhead commanded a garrison of Buffalo Soldiers; ruthless, merciless, Negro soldiers who lived to fight hostile, renegade Indians. These ebony killing machines were looked to in desperation by the isolated, besieged settlers and pioneers who faced constant attack from Roman Nose.

"The town of Sheridan, thirteen miles east of us has come under Indian attack," stated Bankhead. "A mule freight train headed to Sheridan was obliterated at the terminus of the Kansas Pacific Railroad, of which all construction has halted owing to the frequent attacks led by Roman Nose. An estimated fifteen hundred warriors of predominantly Cheyenne along with a sizeable clan of Sioux killed two hundred of the teamsters and mule skinners, and took dozens of mule teams with them upon departing the scene of the atrocity. I didn't say *upon fleeing the scene of the atrocity*, because they didn't; they simply sauntered away at their own pace, as if *daring* someone to challenge them."

"I see," said Forsyth, who along with Lieutenant Beecher sat on rocking chairs that faced the bureau of the commanding officer of the fort. "I have a couple of men who are down and need to convalesce, but otherwise we will be rested and depart at first light, Colonel."

"There is more to it," added Bankhead. "I was saving the worst for last," Colonel Bankhead stood up from the oak captain's chair, sliding it back on the rough-hewn wood planked floor. It made a rough, high-pitched squeaking sound against the coarse wood. "Roman Nose destroyed the entire town of Sheridan, he killed every male over the age of twelve. Then he set fire to the town, reducing it to ashes before taking the women and children as hostages."

"Damn my soul!" remarked Beecher.

"Beecher," Forsyth addressed him in a professional, courteous manner; belying the rage that welled up inside of him. "We will have the men fall into formation in an hour's time. Mainly to tell them what has happened before bedding down for the night. I will confer with you shortly before I issue orders."

"General Sheridan telegraphed me before the line was cut," resumed Colonel Bankhead, "saying that you only have fifty or so men under your charge. Although they are highly skilled in Indian craft and are in the main – professional killers."

"I can travel fast with this number," replied Forsyth. "We are heavily armed, and have the fire power of an infantry regiment." Major Forsyth then added, "And yes – they are for the most part gunfighters; psychopathic killers. They can shoot a fly off the side of a barn at a hundred yards."

"Interesting. Well, I don't doubt you," responded Bankhead. "Little Phil is a born killer and when I read the telegram, I knew he would send someone like you."

"Thank you, sir," responded Forsyth to what he correctly perceived to be a compliment.

"Anything you need, you shall have it," continued Bankhead, "just tell me, I don't care what it is. If I can't come up with it, there are grateful civilians who will. Horses, mules, ammunition, chewing tobacco, coffee – name it."

Chapter Six
Lieutenant Beecher and
Major Forsyth

LIEUTENANT BEECHER and Sharp Grover scouted the trail of the enormous war party. They recognized that the party was breaking up into smaller bands of warriors and splitting off from the main body. Grover was an older frontiersman, in his mid-forty's. He stood five feet and ten inches in height, and weighed a hundred and fifty pounds.

The off-tan colored Stetson cast a shadow over his forehead and closely set, weasel-like eyes. It was a large wool felt cowboy hat, with a hand tooled leather hat band with a three-piece buckle set. The crown was in the popular "cattleman" shape and it had a generous four-and-a-half-inch brim. The leather stampede string hung loosely from the hat and rested on Grover's muslin pullover lace up shirt with leather draw strings.

The low slung Western style gun belt that resembled the popular Buscadero, which it predated, was chocolate brown hand tooled leather and featured beautiful floral designs. The Colt 1860 was secured in the holster by means of a thumb loop over the hammer spur and the utilitarian holster was secured to Grover's right thigh by means of a thin leather thong tie down.

Grover's Livingston styled black brushed-cotton trousers were supported by means of suspenders. On his steer hide, pointed toe cowboy boots were black, steel Mexican style spurs; the bands were one-inch-wide and had two-inch, five point rowels.

His entire body was rock hard. His swarthy complexion reflected his Cherokee grandmother. He was an expert tracker, hunter and marksman. He spoke Sioux, had friends among them, and had been shot in the back by them. His countenance was saturnine and he spoke little. Grover was a legend in his own time, on par with Jim Bridger, Buffalo Bill and Dick Parr.

The hunter-killer band was organized along the lines of an Army cavalry unit, and had a chain of command reflecting that. Most of the members were Civil War veterans who fought on either side, not out of patriotism, but rather, for the sheer love of killing.

Five days later the special attack force tracked a particularly large group of what appeared to be a party of several hundred braves. The Forsythe group crossed onto the north bank of the Republican River and came upon a conglomeration of wikie-ups. These were simple, temporary shelters and had been constructed by bending saplings over, tying them together and then covering them with rushes of grasses. There were close to a hundred of these.

The mounted group cautiously followed the meandering, rustic trail for several miles. Eventually the large, beaten path fed into a larger trail that led to where the Republican River forked. The trail stopped at the river's cat-tail lined edge and reappeared on the north side of the Republican. Crossing the river, the group continued to follow the trail which grew in size as other, smaller trails fed into it. By now the trail was a full sized road of beaten earth. The stench of death assaulted their nostrils.

"Smells like a battlefield," commented Beecher.

"Could be only one thing," replied Forsyth, "the wagon train, out of Philistine - brace yourself."

As the special attack force approached the scene of the ambushed wagon train, hundreds of thousands of turkey buzzards, crows, and birds of prey took flight. There was literally a concussion wave generated by the flapping of wings on the heavy, stench laden air.

There were very few trees; range fires and grazing buffalo having prevented new growth for over a generation. The few trees that remained were predominantly cotton wood, oak and Osage. Some were very large. These were blackened with the number of turkey buzzards that covered their branches, watching the approaching band of professional killers impatiently, through aqua-blue colored eyes.

Thousands of feral dogs that followed the bands of nomadic Native American tribesmen feasted on the carnage. The dogs, which were endemic to every Indian village did not resemble the domesticated breeds of the European American immigrants. They were much larger and resembled the gray timber wolves of the North, from which the displaced tribes had brought them.

Only within the last generation had the horse supplanted dogs as an animal used for the pulling of travois during the massive relocations that occurred nearly every season – often related directly to the migration of the titanic buffalo herds that blackened the Great Plains. The utility of the dog had transcended from that of laborer to that of a basic food staple.

Included among them were wolves, coyotes and foxes. The latter three classes of canine fled at the approach of the column of men, who began spreading out in a military, linear formation. The wild dogs, unafraid of humans, remained. They growled at the rangers as they passed, showing their teeth. All showed signs of heavy mange infestation, and large ticks swollen with blood filled their ears.

The line of exhausted frontiersmen stopped, one man in four taking bridles as the main body dismounted. To either side of the small valley riders rode up the steep hills in threes to scout for threats, and to see what lay beyond the low set hillocks.

Beyond the hills an endless plain of short, grassy meadow unfolded, as far as the eye could see. The blackened scars of the range fire nearly having been expunged by shoots of young grasses. Here and there were stand-alone tree lines which indicated a watercourse.

In one of these riparian tree lines life and death swam its course as a cotton mouth water moccasin struck a plump, medium sized bullhead catfish. The bullhead thrust its venomous pectoral spines forward, locking them in place and puncturing through the thick, scaly serpentine skin - sealing both their fates while being engulfed by the unhinging jaws of the reptile. The water moccasin tried in vain to regurgitate the bullhead, whose spines had forever impaled it in the snake's gullet.

The green, healing land that lay directly in front of them was of a gently rolling nature, beyond that it flattened out. The green edge of the most distant reaches of prairie vanished about seven miles out, with the curvature of the earth.

Hundreds upon hundreds of naked bodies were found, filled with arrows and bullet holes. The heads of most of the bodies appeared to have been beaten in with war clubs. The skulls were often fractured in several places, allowing the brain to extrude onto the ground as it swelled. Many of the dead had been dismembered, no quarter had been given. But of the women, children, and infants – there were few of these.

The stench was overpowering and blue bottle flies swarmed the corpses, their open mouths and eyeless sockets writhing with balls of maggots.

Dead mules, horses, and oxen lay along the entire road where the ransacked, burned out wagons stood motionless. Clothing, eating utensils, and pioneering utensils lay strewn in the vicinity of each wagon.

The outriders galloped in and reported to Forsyth, who accepted the reports, nodding sagely.

"Go ahead and take what you need, men. They don't have use for it any more. If you come across flour, bacon or canned goods, stick it all in your bags," ordered Major Forsyth. "Once you're up, we're getting out of here!"

"What about the dead, Major? We can't just leave them like this," postulated Lieutenant Frederick H. Beecher, Forsyth's second in command, the twenty-eight-year-old veteran Civil War officer and nephew of Harriet Beecher Stowe.

Lieutenant Beecher was dressed in a cavalry officer's uniform, at the insistence of Major Forsyth. Beecher was vested in the garb of an Army lieutenant, with a wide brimmed slouch hat pushed far back. Dark, brown sweat matted hair strung over his high, broad forehead from underneath the four inch brimmed buffalo felt hat.

The lieutenant had a Spencer repeating rifle sheathed in a leather saddle scabbard next to his right leg. He wore a Colt model 1860 Army revolver his right hip, the handle was occulted by the flap of the regulation Army holster which depended from a black Army issued gun leather belt. Regulation suspenders supported the sky blue colored wool cavalry trousers. A black stripe ran down the seam of the trousers on the outside of each leg.

"There're more than a thousand bodies here, that's too many to inter. I mean to latch onto the trail of these renegades and track these killers. We will make contact and wipe them off the face of the earth. Take what you have to have and be quick about it. We ride in one hour," Forsyth stated in an emotionless tone to the lieutenant, who, he knew, was a seasoned killer and not often given to such moments of emotional outbursts.

Beecher breathed through his yellow bandana, to lessen the heinous smell. The stench from the badly decomposing bodies was nearly overpowering. He regarded the man before him, as he swept flies from his sweaty face with his left hand. He held the reins of his brown cavalry gelding with his right. The sound of flies was so loud as to be confused with the hum of thousands of bee hives, so many there were.

Forsyth was also dressed in cavalry attire; an odd decision. It would seem that to have worn the uniform of an Army major would have drawn too much fire during a gun fight with hostiles, and why Major Forsyth chose to do so can only be explained by the need to maintain command. It would have obviously singled the two officers out.

Forsyth wore a wide, blue slouch hat – the type that was regulation issue to Buffalo Soldiers. It had a massive five-inch brim, bent down at a sharp angle in the front to shield his eyes from the sun when it was low on the horizon.

Beneath the stifling felt hat, sweat matted, greasy, sour smelling gray streaked black hair grew thickly. The forehead, high and proportional to the face, was shielded by the low brow of the massive hat.

Underneath Forsyth's bushy, grey eyebrows, the dark, scrutinizing eyes resembled those of a wolf. The nose was long, straight and had never been broken. Hair from the nose grew untrimmed into and joined with the large, gray brown moustache that he always wore.

The face was rectangular in general shape and form, and the jawline square shaped. The well-formed head sat atop a neck that was neither scrawny nor great, the shoulders were narrow and stooped. He also wore a regulation belt and flap holster for his Colt.

"One hour, and we git," reiterated Major Forsyth.

"What you say makes sense," agreed Beecher. "I just haven't seen something like this in a couple of years now, and while I knew what to expect, it still hit me. And another thing, while we're still here, I'm glad you decided not to bring Jedediah."

"I had nothing to do with that," answered Forsyth. "The man lost his mind and was going to be committed to an insane asylum after we left."

"Just a damned tragedy," returned Beecher, "Good looking daughter, too. I'm needing a wife."

"Get your mind off of it, Beecher. She's from Philistine, they say there's something odd about that place and the people who lived there. You're Army. The two won't mix," answered the commanding officer, who leaned back and reached into a saddlebag. Forsyth drew a kerchiefed brick of black tarry chewing tobacco. He cut off a corner with a small knife suited to the purpose and handed it to Beecher. "Almost time to go," he said.

Chapter Seven
The Golden Bullet

SHADOWS FLITTED ABOUT like specters on the gray canvas walls within the Sibley tent. Shadows made overlarge by the flickering of struggling candlelight that illuminated the two figures gesticulating patiently to each other in sign language. Neither of these animated characters paid any attention at all to the magnificent gypsy moth that flew into the flame, its wings singed as its body made a single, subdued popping sound. One of these men was the Arikawa, Bloody Knife; sworn enemy to the Sioux, and a faithful friend to the man who faced him, George Armstrong Custer.

One other man also moved about within in the tent, a strange looking white man whose presence seemed incongruous with the rustic setting. This strange man sat cross legged, mumbling Latin words intelligible only to himself as he drew curious images with a stick in a bed of coals.

Outside, not far from the tent, was a sentient being who was lurking surreptitiously in the darkness. The man appeared as a painted devil whose insidious intention was to listen for sounds that could betray the number of men within the tent.

The second white man within the Sibley tent continued mumbling incantations. Before him lay the bed of coals, glowing a dull red within a hole scooped from the earth.

To his right side on a rabbit skin, lay a one-ounce twenty-dollar golden Double Eagle, first minted in 1849, it contained ninety percent gold. Next to this lay a bullet mold. The strange man took a long handled lead dipper and placed the coin inside it, then set the dipper onto the coal bed. Sparks flew as the mumbling man adjusted the dipper to rest evenly on the bed.

He took the molten gold, and carefully poured it into the bullet mold and allowed it to cool. He continued to utter the incantations as he did so. He spoke the incantations in the Latin language. Later, the golden bullet would be pressed into a .56-56 rim fire copper cartridge and kept separately from all other ammunition.

The golden bullet was to be fired from a peculiar rifle. A specialized hunting version of the Spencer was fitted with a Berdan type sharp shooter scope – one of those made by William Malcom, of Syracuse, New York. The black steel telescopic sight tube ran practically the entire length of the barrel and had an elevation and deflection knob at the rear end, which helped to anchor the optical tube to the rifle. The twenty-power sight enjoyed the clarity offered by the use of achromatic lenses, which limited color refraction. This sight made the Spencer repeating rifle accurate out to eight hundred yards in the hands of a skilled rifleman.

The modifications added to this weapon were augmented with the increasingly hard to come by, higher quality gun powder that Custer had procured from sources in Augusta, Georgia. Although it had been closed down in April, 1865, the Confederate Powder Works had produced gunpowder of exceptional quality and dwindling stock piles could still be found – at a price.

The conversation between Bloody Knife and Custer transitioned from sign language to that of spoken, the more important things having already been gesticulated.

"Understand, Boy General like big hunt, big hunt man. Why General, why you hunt Roman Nose? Very danger, to Boy General," the Arikawa scout maintained a stoic expression as he warned Custer plainly of the danger.

"I have to have his war bonnet, Bloody Knife," answered the Yellow Hair frankly. Custer enjoyed his close friendship with the Arikawa, and had a long working relationship with the tribe of Bloody Knife as a whole. "Stipulations," Custer paused as he thought of words his friend might understand.

"Needs, certain needs must be met, so that I may use the war bonnet to further my personal ambition."

These words were lost on the Arikawa scout, who speculated only that Custer wanted to bag Roman Nose and secure the war bonnet as some sort of trophy.

Bloody Knife had always regarded the Yellow Hair in awe, and exhibited an almost slavish devotion to the volatile, unpredictable man who sat facing him on the folding field chair. The Boy General, Bloody Knife observed, was relaxed and clearly enjoyed this hunting expedition and escape from civilization. The Arikawa studied the blonde haired man before him, without the man appearing to know so.

The dark blond hair was effeminately long and wavy, falling almost languorously to the shoulders. Custer looked younger than his twenty-eight years thought Bloody Knife; the high forehead, shielded constantly from the sun by wide brimmed, flamboyant cowboy styled hats was unlined. Dark blond eyebrows rested above intelligent blue eyes, very blue. These were keen sighted and often betrayed a bizarre, sick sense of humor.

The handsome face was to some degree thin and rectangular, with a strong jawline set beneath high cheek bones which were not overly pronounced. The otherwise perfect features were marred by a large, Gallic nose under which resided a ridiculous and disgusting walrus moustache.

This moustache completely covered the upper lip but was trimmed to allow a full, pouting lower lip to be revealed. Beneath the lower lip grew a tightly trimmed vertical goatee, very thin in width. The chin melded into the jaw symmetrically and added to the natural good looking features of the man. If not for the long, hooking nose, Custer could have had the face of a deity, thought Bloody Knife. Custer's head was set on a thick, athletic neck. But not so thick as to be considered "bull necked."

Without warning, Bloody Knife blew out the candle, leaving the interior of the roomy Sibley tent faintly illuminated by the coals tended by the praying votary.

"Injun come!" whispered Bloody Knife to Custer. "Bloody Knife kill! Boy General wait in tent while Bloody Knife kill bad Injun!"

"I'm going to ease out of the tent with you, Bloody Knife. You stay here, Gladstone," said Custer to the seated man, who did not halt in his incantations. The soft glow of the coal bed cast an orange illumination on the moving lips of the enchanter.

Outside of the Sibley, the moon had not yet arisen, the stars stood out against a singular black background without the milk of Hera spilled across the heavenly vaults. Jupiter and Saturn glowed brightly high on the eastern horizon, as did Mars, with its angry red eye, as it preceded the former two across the ecliptic, high above.

A light wind was rustling out of the south, agitating the leaves of the trees. Sound carried a great distance on the soft, persistent breeze that occasionally gusted.

Hundreds of packs of mange ridden coyotes howled, the individuals numbered in the many thousands and sounded quiet close. Great horned owls hooted, both near and far away. Their calls were answered by other species of owls, culminating in a disquieting symphony to the night when suddenly a thrashing in the bushes and a gurgling sound stole audience from the nocturnal orchestra.

Bloody Knife stepped forward out of the brush holding a warrior in front of him. He had his hand clutching the long hair and had cut the throat, almost from ear to ear. The dying man was urged forward in his impetus by virtue of the short bladed skinning knife pressed against the right kidney of his lower back.

"Only one, buck out lookin' for scalp," spat Bloody Knife, releasing the man. The interloper dropped heavily to his knees, clutching his throat with both hands. His trachea had been cut through and he struggled to breathe through the laceration as hot blood sprayed the ground. The escaping blood sounded like rain pelting the dried leaves.

"What is he?" inquired Custer, stepping closer to see in the faint starlight.

"Can't tell," answered Bloody Knife. "He only one. He lookin' for scalp."

"Drag him into the tent," ordered Custer. "We've got to know what he is. Let's cast some light on the subject."

The three men kneeled beside the fallen gasping warrior, while the sounds of the night remained outside the tent, pregnant with pregnant with the intimations of movement. They heard these, but they were the rustlings of raccoons, opossums and other nocturnal creatures that tread cautiously through the dry leaves and grass. These were animals which exercised great care in everything they did - and were frequently killed when they did not.

Igniting the wick of the candle by placing it against the coal and blowing on it, Gladstone cast the flickering glow over the bleeding man, who had ceased to breathe.

"Bad Injun," exclaimed Bloody Knife. "He Northern Cheyenne."

Custer examined the dead brave closely in meticulous detail, taking into account everything about the warrior that lay before him. The Yellow Hair's blue eyes narrowed into slits to better focus the dim, unsteady light of the struggling candle.

Long, thin, black unbraided hair extended to the slain warrior's abdomen. It was parted in the middle of a head which sloped sharply back. Black, obsidian pupils stared into lifeless eternity from eyes that were overhung with heavy epicanthic folds. The cheekbones were set high, and were the dominant features of the face.

The nose was of average length but had been broken long ago, the cartilage having been separated and pushed in. The upper palate extended into an over bite that detracted from the weakly defined jaw. The well-formed, pronounced lips were pulled back in a post mortem grin.

The front teeth had all been pulled except for the canines. The entire face had been war painted in white, then two vertical black lines ran down from the forehead to either side of the face, touching either corner of the grinning mouth. The other painted lines extended vertically to the midline of the jaw.

"Young one, out for his first kill," mumbled the Boy General, lifting the double hair pipe breast plate and looking at the freshly healed scars on the warrior's chest. "Looks like he had his Sun Dance last summer but he isn't wearing a feather yet."

Looking over the rest of the brave, Custer noted the knee length breech clout, and fringed buckskin leggings. The moccasins were beaded in the Cheyenne design and the soles reinforced with rawhide.

"Get him out of here," said Custer, who looking at Bloody Knife added, "the three of us will pick up his trail at daybreak. We'll break camp and follow the signs he left for us."

Gladstone and Bloody Knife each grabbed a hand of the fallen warrior as they prepared to drag him out of the Sibley.

"Wait!" postulated Gladstone, pulling a short bladed boning knife with a deer antler handle affixed to the tang. Quickly, he made an incision beneath the brave's sternum, then Gladstone inserted both hands and located the still faintly quivering heart.

"Don't do that in here," said Custer, his voice was impatient. "Take him outside and do whatever you wish with him."

"It's important, General. If this man's heart yet beats, the power that it will impart to the golden bullet cannot be overstated," the strange white man replied to the Boy General. The tall, thin Caucasian man was red haired, his face was light complexioned and partially covered with a mutton chop beard, leaving the chin exposed.

He was dressed in a bibbed, calico checkered muslin long sleeved shirt tucked into a pair of gray, high backed riding trousers with black inseam. A narrow waist belt served to hold up the high backed trousers and over the small belt was a much larger gun belt of nut brown horse hide leather. The holster had bronco tooling designs pressed into the leather and a thumb loop over the hammer to keep the Remington New Model 1858 Army revolver secure in the holster. At the base of the holster rig was a leather thong tied around the magician's thigh. It was a right handed holster rig.

He wore pointed toe horse hide cowboy boots and his wide brimmed tan felt cowboy hat dangled from its stampede string on the single tent pole in the center of the Sibley. He was in his late twenties and spoke with a heavy British accent.

"By inserting the golden bullet into the living heart and uttering the words as exactly as I tell them to you, the bullet will find its mark. There are limitations certainly," continued Gladstone, adding, "you must be the one to insert and withdraw the bullet from the cardiac womb. Repeat what I say exactly. Do you understand, General?"

"Yes, Gladstone. Let's do this right – no short cuts about it," answered the Yellow Hair.

The Boy General, heeding the sage advice of his council, a rare event, did as he was told, and withdrew the blood covered golden bullet from the quivering cardiac double pump as he repeated the words uttered by Gladstone.

"If it takes magic to gain magic, then I'll do whatever it takes to get that war bonnet," the Boy General stated to the magician. "A golden bullet to kill Roman Nose, blood on the bullet from a beating heart to make its flight true. I may burn in hell for this, but I will have that war bonnet, and I will become President of the United States. Bloody Knife, you will figure prominently in the Bureau of Indian Affairs; you will have land, money, power and any woman you want. Professor Gladstone, I swear you shall be the curator to the Smithsonian Institution."

"That would provide to me the most arcane and closely guarded secrets of the occult that are available on the continent," the Englishman responded to Custer.

The candle light reflected in the eyes of the Englishman that seemed like schist; deep, abysmal and steeped in horrific knowledge. Custer shuddered with incertitude at the services he was employing, at the powers that would be invoked and the debt that would be owed.

"It's a bargain between us and your master. Now, for Pete's sake, let's get that poor devil out of here!" added the Yellow Hair, changing the subject as he rubbed dirt over his hands and fingers, removing the blood from his hands as he did so prior to pouring canteen water over them.

"We take it all with us," advised Bloody Knife. "tent fold down small, not slow us down."

"We might cache the Sibley when we near our objective," returned Custer, adding "and pick it up on the way back."

Bloody Knife's expression remained impassive, but inwardly he smiled; for he knew well the former general's love for camping and for this particular tent. He knew also, that the Boy General would never cache the Sibley, that he would take it with them wherever they went.

"Me gonna find trail, I come back by time Boy General has tent packed on mule," responded Bloody Knife.

The eastern sky was colored with savage orange-red paintbrush strokes which presaged the coming of dawn as the two white men tore down the tent and carefully packed everything onto their horses and mule. The camp fire was dowsed with coffee and all traces of the camp were carefully expunged.

The body of the slain warrior was carefully prepared to be weighed down and submerged in a small creek. The intestines had been eviscerated and the abdominal cavity filled with heavy stones prior to submerging the cadaver in the cool, flowing waters. Quickly, dozens, then hundreds of small silvery perch and bream swarmed the gaping, stone filled cavity of the slain Cheyenne.

Ahead of them lay a long ride following a circuitous, rustic trail that became steadily easier to follow as the hours consumed the march.

The three men, all diametrically opposed to each other in appearance, had ridden at a pace that consumed many miles throughout the late summer day.

The insides of their thighs were chafed raw from the relentless pursuit of the elusive Indians, and when the trio stopped to relieve themselves on the trail, they would salve the insides of their thighs with bear grease.

Attention was not lost on the mule, which carried the heavy Sibley tent. The straps and harness were readjusted and the mule's back was greased with the salve.

"Horse dung!" advised Bloody Knife, alerting the two white men to the nearness of their quarry. "Bad Injuns maybe one - two hours from us." "Let's stop here – we're close to the river. Let's have a look around," said Custer. Although the ride had been exhausting, the Yellow Hair seemed fresh, vibrant, and full of energy.

Custer and Bloody Knife began scouting ahead, leaving the mysterious Englishman with the horses and mule. They entered a thicket of wild plum brush and pushed through rushes of young willow trees that grew seven feet high in places. Spider web glued to their faces and hair causing them to halt occasionally, as mosquitos swarmed any exposed part of the body.

"No like," said Bloody Knife in a low voice. "No sound, no birds talk."

"I concur. Let's get back to the professor, too quiet in here. Something isn't right," responded the Boy General, looking cautiously from right to left, Custer was also scanning high in the surrounding tree's branches as he did so. The vista was an insane, overgrown conglomeration of willows, sycamore, elm, oak and eastern red cedar. Mosquitos swarmed Custer's face with the high pitched, urgent hum as they lit on his neck and the back of his hands which were shiny with sweat. The humidity was stifling. Chiggers and seed ticks covered his sweat drenched clothing, seeking any way possible to get beneath the rancid, reeking clothing.

He listened with intensity, but all that he could hear were the mosquitos and the ringing in his ears; tinnitus, from years of shooting without hearing protection. The ringing was chronic and he was so used to it that he often paid it no mind – except in times like these.

Custer and Bloody Knife were beginning their return to the waiting Englishman when suddenly they were halted in their tracks by the loud crack of a dry tree branch being stepped on. Taking cover behind the trunk of a large, fallen sycamore tree - uprooted during a tornado two years before, they held their breath as a small hunting party of Cheyenne stealthily approached.

Emerging from the overgrown thicket of mixed vegetation, the point man of the hunting party of about ten warriors advanced cautiously, trying to make no sound. The head was shaven entirely except for a scalp lock in back, to which two tail feathers from a mature bald eagle were attached. The effect of the coif imbued the cruel, hatchet-like face of the point man with an even more sinister affect.

The closely set, coal black, ferret-like eyes darted shiftily this way and that as the brave halted and looked all around him before stealthily moving forward. The ears were pierced in many places and decorations of beads and dentalium shells swung from them. The nose was unbroken, of medium length and hooked evilly downward. The septum of the nose had been pierced and a golden earing depended from it.

The warrior was shirtless but for a magnificent triple hair pipe war vest. A dark blue loin clout was held in place with a belt taken from a dead soldier. From this belt hung a black leather flap holster with a Colt 1860, along with a large bone handled hunting knife, and an Army issue canteen. The brave wore leather breeks held in place with a separate, smaller belt; the breeks were favored by many who traversed through thorny underbrush. He wore high topped moccasins that extended halfway up the leg and which were heavily reinforced at the soles.

Behind him followed a column of tall, powerfully built warriors, who looked from right to left, their dark, keen eyes penetrating deeply into the steamy green walls that surrounded them. All carried either a repeating rifle or an Enfield rifled musket in one hand, while using their other hand to move the low hanging branches of trees and undergrowth aside. Other than the initial sound of the tree branch cracking, they were silent as they prowled the riverside forest, hunting for game. Their progress would frequently halt, as they stood motionless, listening for the sounds that would betray a deer or wild pig.

They had resumed their trek toward the river when without warning, the rearmost man in the column froze, the tendons of his neck standing out suddenly as he turned his head and stared directly at the fallen tree from which Custer and Bloody Knife lay hidden. He was horrifically tattooed on the face, arms and chest. The face was reminiscent of a man of Middle Eastern origin, and it was tattooed with vertical and horizontal lines made of black ink consisting of coal, muscadine and Devil's Club.

Black, vertical lines with circles between them were tattooed the length of both arms, as well as his back, chest and abdomen. The man was a heavily muscled brute of above average height, like so many of the Cheyenne.

He wore no shirt, and across the heavy pectoral muscles of his chest was slung a broad leather strap from which a hardened leather cartridge box rode on the left side of his hip. This box was filled with carefully prepared paper cartridges for the Model 1852 Lee Enfield muzzle loading rifle that he carried in his right hand. A choker collar-necklace of human teeth was attached loosely around his thick, ox-like neck.

Custer watched with unease as the overdeveloped biceps of the warrior strained against the primitive beaten copper arm bands that barely contained them. A belt of rawhide held up a loin clout of red cloth that extended past the trunk-like, tattooed thighs and down to the warrior's knees. Attached onto the belt was a leather scabbard containing a hefty butcher knife.

While obviously Northern Cheyenne, he had Hittite facial features and wore large, hoop earrings of gold; stolen no doubt from an ambush of a wagon train. Few settler women could afford such baubles and the previous owner had obviously been a woman of some importance, probably headed to California from the East.

He stood crouched while searching the length of the fallen sycamore for an inordinate length of time, and then advanced toward where Custer and Bloody Knife lay hidden. His rifle was held with both hands at waist height, muzzle pointing forward as he drew nearer the fallen sycamore. Custer and Bloody Knife heard the audible click as the hammer was cocked back.

The sound of a rifle shot caused him to stop and suddenly look in the direction of his comrades, his golden earrings swung with the motion. He paused for a moment, uncertain as to whether or not to investigate what lay behind the fallen tree or to join his friends.

Suddenly, a skillful imitation of a dove cooing caused him to look toward where his comrades had trekked. He saw one of his companions; a man who wore a buffalo skin skull cap with a polished horn jutting upward from either side of the temples. From beneath this fur cap extended shoulder length black hair, cut square mane. This man intimated that the curious brave should choose the latter.

The rearmost man glanced furtively several times back over his shoulder at where Custer and Bloody Knife lay hidden, as he disappeared into the verdure of the riparian forest.

Chapter Eight
Tenth Cavalry Enters the Fight

THE SIX-HUNDRED-MILE Smoky Hill Trail was a stretch of pitted, rutted dirt road used by stage coach lines and extended from Atchison, Kansas to Aspen, Colorado. The stage coach relay stations were suffering relentless attacks from Cheyenne, Sioux, Arapaho, and Comanche. Only the very few that had multiple Gatling guns emplaced behind embrasures of hewn logs or earthworks stood a chance.

While the relay stations provided an opportunity to stretch, quickly down a cold meal or maybe afford a sponge bath, their purpose was mainly to change out the mules and get a new team hitched up – as fast as possible. The stage relay was to be ready in less than sixty minutes. Survival from pursuing mounted warriors depended on having fresh mules and plenty of them. Mules were preferred by the stage lines over horses, not necessarily for speed, but on account of their strength, sure footedness on the unimproved road and stamina.

Increasingly, the Butterfield Overland Dispatch was running up to a dozen coaches at a time in tightly bunched groups for mutual protection. This time it was would be different; in escort was an unusually large contingent of Buffalo Soldiers from the Tenth Cavalry Regiment. Five companies of grim faced, dangerous Negro cavalry on the prowl and looking for a fight. There were a total of five hundred fifty of them.

The Tenth Cavalry Regiment was formed in 1866 and rushed immediately into Kansas where it saw nearly continual combat. The Buffalo Soldiers patrolled against the volatile, ruthless Plains Indians, who hated, feared, and attacked them at every opportunity. As the situation with the stage coach routes became untenable, the elite unit was assigned to protect the vulnerable stage coach lines from attack. The élan of the Tenth Cavalry Regiment was reflected in the lowest desertion rate of any Army unit during a time when soldiers abandoned their units at a rate of fifty percent.

The stage coaches that the Buffalo Soldiers were assigned to protect were the light, kidney-bursting celerity types designed for speed. They were fast because they needed to be.

The twelve stage coaches had set off from their point of departure at the same time. The muleskinners were laying the lash to the backs of the long eared hybrids. Each celerity was pulled frantically by two matched pairs of large, powerful mules – often weighing between fifteen hundred and two thousand pounds.

The companies of heavily armed African American Tenth Cavalry rode split up into platoons. The platoons were allocated proportionately to the front, sides and rear. Those in the rear had it really bad, inhaling the fine, alkaline dust which rose into the air, visible from miles away. The Buffalo Soldiers wore brightly colored bandanas over their faces to staunch the talcum like, choking dust. Their inflamed eyes were rubbed raw by the miniscule gritty particles that had a sandpaper rubbing effect on the eyeball.

The dirty brown billowing dust clouds generated by the desperately racing stage coaches and their large, formidable, dangerous escort were visible to the Cheyenne war leader who finalized his preparations. The gigantic Cheyenne fully intended to respond to the cloud of dust that rose like the harbinger of a great buffalo hunt.

Roman Nose carefully performed the ritual inherent prior to donning the war bonnet. He took his magnificent head dress out of its hardened container made of buffalo rawhide known as a parfleche. The parfleche was in the shape of a truncated cone. The bonnet could be folded in on itself and slid into the leather cylinder which was decorated in earth pigment and had a long, handsome fringe of buckskin.

Roman Nose carefully held the war bonnet over a coal bed onto which sacred powder was poured. He then thrust it upward, first to the south, then to the west, followed by the north, and finally to the east. Only then did Roman Nose place the war bonnet on his head. Instantly he stood as if electrified, as a powerful current of energy surged through his sinews, beginning at the scalp.

He took his escutcheon from a scrawny adolescent boy who had not yet undergone the Sun Dance, and dipped it toward the ground and shook it four times. He looked up, holding the sacred shield toward the sun of molten gold, and shook it four times. The horseshoe triceps of his muscle knotted arm flexing like the arm of a circus strong man each time he shook the rawhide shield. Then Roman Nose ran his left arm through the leather straps inside the shield; the first strap held the shield to his forearm, the second strap he grasped with his hand. On the outside of the escutcheon was painted a circle, and within it a square containing images that represented the four cardinal directions.

The war bonnet of Roman Nose was the only one of its kind ever made. This war bonnet had a single buffalo horn protruding from the front of the forehead, above the beaded head band. It had two long trailers that nearly touched the ground when the warrior was mounted. Eagle feathers had been set along the entire lengths of two strips of buffalo hide. The first four feathers were red, then the next four feathers were black, then the next ones red in an alternating rhythm. The two trailers contained eighty golden eagle feathers each. Each feather in the stunning bonnet connoted a valorous deed.

The medicine man White Bull had meticulously constructed the war bonnet far to the north, in the Rocky Mountains, near the Cave of Silk, where no man dared approach, save those who were steeped in the darkest arts of black magic.

No cloth, thread, or metal had been used in its construction. Nothing was used that had come from the white eyes. This bonnet was very sacred and required much ceremony and strict adherence to certain guidelines.

Only after the war bonnet was donned, did Roman Nose apply the sacred war paint. Indian yellow was painted entirely over the forehead, red across the massive nose. While the rest of the face, including the dimpled chin, was painted in black.

A strict, arcane set of rules had to be followed unerringly; Roman Nose was forbidden to eat certain things, he couldn't enter a dwelling where a child had been born until four days had passed, and there were many other rules. But above all, cautioned White Bull:

"You must eat nothing that has been touched of metal."

Many braves ate with sticks, or their fingers, believing that to eat from metal would attract a bullet.

Roman Nose had a symmetrical forehead which was of average height, neither high nor short; it did not slope back. However, the forehead was defined by a very pronounced vee shaped supraorbital brow ridge which descended abruptly at the center. The thick protruding brow ridge that angled downward in the middle conveyed the impression of anger, which was not in fact true. The head was narrow and the face proportional.

The cheek bones were fleshy and high set, but did not dominate the sun lined, leathery face. That distinction was reserved for the enormous, cartilaginous nose; the overdeveloped ethmoid bone that separated the two obsidian eyes extended prominently into the orbits of the skull. The greater alar cartilage of the nasal septum extended forward at a descending angle, conveying the impression of an enormous, exaggerated, "Roman nose."

Thin lips resided over a slightly jutting chin, which was dimpled in the center. The jawline was well set, and seemed to meld into a thick, ox-like neck, from which powerful trapezius muscles conveyed the picture of a man with a short, thick, trunk-like neck supporting his head.

Raising his rifle above his head, this time a Spencer - for he had several, including four Colt Navy model revolvers slid into his belt - he thrust the rifle toward the speeding stagecoaches in a stabbing motion. He yelled loudly as he did so – the sinuses of the massive nose added a sonorous, bell-like tonal quality to his war whooping.

Roman Nose led the braves down the hillside in a ragged, uneven linear formation. The approach of the

Cheyenne horde was not lost on the armed sentries mounted atop the stage coaches. The primary weapon of the coachmen was a full length Belgian double barrel ten-gauge shotgun designed by the French inventor Louis Flobert, made famous for his design of parlor guns for indoor shooting.

Four men rode atop each of the canvas topped coaches, armed with the devastating Flobert shotguns. These shotguns were made more lethal by the state of the art cartridge that they were loaded with – pinfire shotgun shells. Pinfire shotgun shells were self-contained; the wadding, buckshot and gunpowder being contained in a thickened paper cylinder. A short, brass base attached to the charge, a pin extruded from top of the brass, and was driven downward by the impact of the mule eared hammer when the trigger was pulled, igniting the propellant. The shotgun broke open downward at the breech, facilitating quick and effortless reloading.

The coachmen atop the thick, canvas topped celerity wagons waved their shotguns in warning at the two companies of Buffalo Soldiers following them from fifty yards behind. One of the cavalry lieutenants, a white man who was so covered in orange dust that he could not be distinguished from the Colored troops he commanded, gave the arm signal for his bugler to sound the signal to wheel their horses about.

What they saw to their consternation was a horde of rapidly approaching tribesmen numbering over three thousand, hurtling toward them like an unstoppable, gigantic, steam locomotive.

Immediately both sides began exchanging fire. To the alarm of the Buffalo Soldiers firing at a range so near that it was impossible to miss, none of the warriors were hit. They were led by an unusually large man mounted atop a huge white mare. He stood apart from the rest not only because of his physical stature and beautiful white mare, but also by virtue of his magnificent war bonnet.

The gunfire inspired the coach drivers to apply the lash murderously to the backs of the mules, which were sweating profusely from their necks and backs. A fine mist of sweat-spray flew into the faces of the driver and shotgun wielding co-driver with each application of the lash. These were large mules, weighing more than half a ton. Some, the types bred from large quarter horse mares to large donkey jacks. The truly large mules could attain two-thousand pounds in weight and seventeen hands in height.

As a rule, the often stubborn mules were treated harshly compared to horses, and their shoulders and necks often were worn raw from the sweaty, grimy collars. Their rumps were scarred from the cruel lash of the whip.

The whip was ten feet long and made of braided leather. A strip of raw hide comprised the final fourteen inches of the whip. The handle was about three inches in diameter and it tapered downward in thickness to about one inch at the end.

All stage coach drivers had chronically red, inflamed eyes from the dust and mud that the hooves of the mules flung into their faces.

The stage coach mules had it better than their counterparts in other areas where the mule was employed as a draft animal. When the teams were swapped out at the relay stations the mules were rested after being unharnessed, rubbed down and fed.

In practice, mule drivers were jealous of each other, and they considered themselves superior to one another. But this was different, this was no act of bravado or professional jealousy; this was an act of survival. An act of survival that was motivated by fear, selfishness, and placing one's life in front of everyone else's – no matter the repercussions.

Mules were the animals of choice for draft animals, they retained the favorable traits of their dam; size, strength and endurance were the traits inherited from the mare. The sire was a male donkey.

Alerted to the gunfire, the two lateral wings of cavalry swung around at the urgently repeated calls from the brass bugles of the two rear companies. They rode furiously to assist their beleaguered rear element almost at the moment that it was being overwhelmed. The lead company, in front of the stage coaches was led by a white captain who signaled for his unit to drop back. They formed a loosely organized swarm around the racing celerity wagons as the four other companies fought a delaying action with the Cheyenne who outnumbered them almost six to one.

The Cheyenne charged into the mounted Buffalo Soldiers with blood fury fueled by the animosity toward the Black man, whom they saw as yet another alien race – brought by the hated whites to serve as their killers and to displace them from their hereditary lands. A few of the younger muscular Cheyenne warriors were armed with nothing but fighting knives and a few farm implements, such as pitch forks, and axes, as well as stone aged weapons.

Many of the warriors still carried bows made of locust, hickory, bois de arc and ash. They were for the most part made of one solid piece of wood and were designed to bend through the handle. Many were reinforced with sinew. The arrow shafts had an average length of thirty inches and were made of juniper, also referred to as cedar.

The arrowheads were for the most part made of sharpened metal in the form of barbets. The fletchings were made of turkey feathers, chicken feathers, or the feathers of birds of prey. The quivers were often made of beaver, foxes and coyotes to facilitate the launch of an arrow every two to three seconds.

Approximately one half of the Tenth Cavalry Regiment was committed to the defense of the dozen stage coaches and all were armed with Spencer repeating rifles and Colt Model 1860s. Most rode the large, brown geldings of the Army, there were some whites and blacks added to the browns, but all of the horses had been gelded.

The castration of young male horses was necessary to inhibit the aggressive, uncontrolled rage that plagued nearly all stallions, making them bite, kick and attack other horses, as well as the rider. When in the proximity of a mare in estrus, the stallion would be ruled by its passion and simply become unrideable.

Likewise, mares were avoided in Army procreation of riding stock. The reason being, when the mares came into estrus, their temperament changed, they spooked easily, shied from the saddle, and fought with other mares. The Army only purchased geldings.

Some geldings were unaffected by the castration, and retained the undesirable masculine traits of the stud horse. Geldings that displayed this peculiar aberration were called "proud cut," and were destroyed.

The Buffalo Soldiers mounted on their huge, grain fed geldings were enveloped and swallowed into the seething mass of Cheyenne and Sioux, like a flood sweeping around a sandbar and then washing over it.

Captain Alvord saw his Company M was beginning to disintegrate into chaos. Company M was also known as the Calico Company, on account that it contained horses of many different colors. These could be distinguished in the melee from the Indian ponies by their larger size.

"Bugler! Bugler to me! Where the hell is the bugler!?" yelled Alvord to the desperately firing Afro-American cavalrymen, who were being unseated from their mounts with terrifying frequency. Yet, no braves had begun to fall, despite having been fired on from point blank range.

"We've got to sound retreat!" shouted Captain George Armes, of Company F. "Alvord! Do something!"

"Sound retreat!" yelled Alvord to the bugler, a thin, wiry black man who approached the captain, his legs were pinioned to his horse with barbed, feathered shafts, and his back and chest were porcupined with arrows. He placed the brass instrument to his lips. Immediately the bugle was shot from his right hand and flew into the air, spiraling and then disappearing into the swirling, milling combat of men on horses. The bugle was stepped on and trampled by the horses.

Suddenly Captain Armes's horse went down on top of him. Many cavalrymen now fought on foot, their horses having been shot out from under them. A tall, musclebound Cheyenne saw Captain Armes pinned beneath the nearly two-thousand-pound horse. The huge Cheyenne, with his body covered in war paint depicting circles and arrows ran toward the fallen officer.

The running warrior's black hair was pulled back tightly into a braided ponytail which was secured inside a leather stocking. He was armed with a Lee

Enfield rifled musket, attached to the end of the rifle was a lethal Pattern 1853 bayonet.

The brave had fired his one round, and then mounted the nearly two-foot-long, semi-triangular shaped blade which tapered to a diamond pointed tip at the end. He had slipped the bayonet over the muzzle of the weapon and twisted it into the locked position by virtue of the mortise slot and locking ring.

The screaming warrior ran toward the captain with the rifle held at waist level, the bayonet was pointing at the chest of the trapped Captain Armes. The warrior's meat slabbed chest was bare except for the strap of the leather Confederate cartridge belt that crossed it.

The solidly built brave was mouth breathing as he ran. His buckskin breeches clung to the skin of his thick thighs as they rose and fell like pistons. His biceps bulged beneath the red linen arm bands as he raised the rifle butt to his shoulder. His impetus carried him forward as he leaned into the rifle to drive the bayonet home.

"Help!" cried Armes, who drew his Colt Model 1860 and fired into the brave's face, the black powder smoke obscuring it. To the captain's horror, the brave was not hit. The Cheyenne, the top half of his face painted in red and the lower painted in black, drove the bayonet deeply into the officer's chest. He leaned forward and rose on the balls of his feet after he did so, enlarging the puncture wound that extended all the way through Armes's torso and thrusted like the horrific beak of a gigantic, grotesque mosquito out of his back.

"Break contact! Break contact!" shouted Captain Alvord, suddenly the wind was knocked from his lungs as a lance drove through the erector spinae back muscles and exploded from the cartilaginous xiphoid process, at the base of the sternum.

Alvord grabbed the haft of the Clovis tipped weapon and twisted back and forth violently in the seat of his McClellan saddle. He gargled on his own blood as he screamed. He saw uncomprehendingly a tall, very black sergeant run past him. The man was literally skewered with arrows – a living porcupine. The sergeant showed no fear as he continued to fire his revolver ineffectively into the seething red mass of humanity that was engulfing the Buffalo Soldiers.

The back and chest of the sergeant's single breasted navy blue shell jacket with yellow piping were bristling with arrows. The thirteen button shell jacket was halfway unbuttoned. The sky blue trousers of the sergeant had a reinforced seat and were lined with yellow side stripes. He was wearing ankle high lace up shoes called brogans. The piston-like motion of the sergeant's thick, hammy thighs reflected from Alvord's dilating pupils.

Within minutes four hundred and fifty Buffalo Soldiers lost their chain of command and had devolved into an uncoordinated body of a panic stricken mass of Africana-Americana, firing back with everything they had, fighting like a blinded

Samson against the wave of Native Americans who had plenty of old grudges to settle with the Negro fighting men.

Dozens of mounted African American cavalrymen broke out of the red hurricane of Sioux and Cheyenne. These few escapees fled in all directions, there was not a horse which wasn't arrowed. Many of the riders were bristling with the vicious, cruelly barbed arrows. Behind them, the rest of four companies lay dead, wounded, or clustered in small groups.

The youngest of the Cheyenne warriors were wielding coup sticks as they advanced on these groups of survivors. They needed coups, the young men did, to attain status within the community of warriors.

Sergeant Tipton, an olive complexioned man was nearly too large to be a cavalryman. He controlled one of the larger of these small islands of frantically firing survivors. The sergeant saw a hundred or more braves advancing toward his group on foot, with coup sticks at the ready. Some of the braves held the staff-like clubs two handed as they approached warily. They held them like baseball bats. Others held them with one hand, slapping it against the open palm of the other hand as they approached, anticipating and unafraid.

"Let'um have it!" shouted Tipton. "Give'em everything you've got! But save the last bullet for yourselves!" Sergeant Tipton's blue felt, five inch brimmed slouch hat had been shot from his high, rounded forehead. His tightly coiled, coal black hair was closely cropped for reasons of personal hygiene and to reduce the effects of the late summer sun. The sergeant's slate colored eyes were widely set in interorbital distance from one another and were bloodshot from the dust and gun smoke. He paid no attention to the ringing in his ears.

The perimeter of the beleaguered force was clouded with the rotten egg smell of black powder as a thunderous explosion of gunfire erupted from it. As the wind cleared the smoke, the Buffalo Soldiers saw that none of the braves had been hit.

They saw also, the image of a large man, a figure in a majestic war bonnet, of which the double trailer drug on the ground as he walked leisurely toward them. Tipton fired squarely into the man's chest with his service revolver, but missed.

"Roman Nose!" shouted Sergeant Tipton. The nostrils of his low set nose flaring in blood lust at the sight of his mortal enemy. Tipton's full lips narrowed in on themselves as they tightened in anger.

"Shut mouth!" retorted the big Cheyenne, turning his head to spit tobacco juice. Looking back to face the Buffalo Soldier, Roman Nose smiled, revealing large, straight, tobacco stained megadontic teeth. "You die first, Sergeant!"

Roman Nose was a big man – even by Cheyenne standards; standing six-foot six-inches tall, he weighed a strapping three hundred pounds of solid muscle. The aristocratic head was emphasized, rather than detracted from by the magnificent war bonnet. Two pair of white ermine tubes hung bilaterally as side drops which were sewn into the human skin skull cap, taken from a fallen Shoshone medicine man. The head band of the bonnet was decorated with beads sewn in curious patterns.

The huge feathers of mature golden eagles were widely spaced in the flared design, which was broad, and swept back imparting an even larger than life impression of Roman Nose. The base of the feathers was secured to the brow of the bonnet with red wool quill wraps, known as "firecrackers," around these were white spiral wraps of sinew. A single, polished buffalo horn extended from just above the decorated bead band, unicorn like.

"Red lives matter!" shouted Roman Nose, the deep, bell like voice made was made stentorious owing to the cavernous nasal cavities that the exaggerated nares augmented.

Immediately, scores of young warriors fell upon the handful of Buffalo Soldiers, swinging the coup sticks. None of these warriors wore an eagle feather in their hair, but after *counting coup* on the doomed Buffalo Soldiers, they would be awarded the rite to wear the prestigious eagle feather.

The coup stick in and of itself was no formidable weapon, often it was a sapling dried in the form of a shepherd's walking staff. The intent was to strike an armed enemy with it, thereby achieving a *coup*.

Chapter Nine
Beecher's Island

ON THE SIXTEENTH OF September, 1868 Forsyth, Beecher, and the special attack force were clinging tenaciously to an enormous Indian trail that followed the curve of the Arikaree River. At around sixteen hundred hours the attack force passed through a washed out gorge. During the passage it espied a grassy valley that was about two miles wide and the same in length.

"I think we ought to set up camp here," Forsyth said to Beecher. "I don't like camping in an area like this that is prone to flood, though. When you don't expect a rain is often when you'll receive a deluge."

"We are out of food, about all we have left is salt and coffee," returned Beecher. "Besides, it's a good place to rest and graze the horses while we set up camp and send out a hunting party."

"I'm of the same mind, Lieutenant," responded Forsyth, who saw the lieutenant rubbing his left knee. The major knew that the knee gave the junior officer constant agony, but Beecher never complained of it. Forsyth liked the way Beecher kept his mouth shut about the chronic pain and respected him for it.

Lieutenant Beecher had taken a Minié bullet through the knee at Gettysburg. The Minié ball, developed by Claude Minié was a cone shaped, cylindrical bullet made of soft lead and had a hollow cavity at its base. The base would expand upon detonation of the propellant and swell the base of the bullet into the rifling of the barrel, and impart a tight spin to the missile's trajectory.

The bullet had entered Beecher's left knee, shattering the knee cap and passing through it. The result was that due to destroyed nerves and blood vessels, the foot was constantly swollen and void any sensation other than throbbing pain. The lieutenant walked with a stiff leg, but avoided using a cane out of willful pride and arrogance, the major knew that. Major Forsyth had seen Beecher crash to the ground on occasion and refuse all assistance to help him regain his feet. Forsyth respected men like this.

"Looky there," stated Forsyth to Beecher.

Seventy yards away the major saw a feature of arresting beauty that lay in the center of the river; it was an island made of orange tinged sand and river gravel. The water was low, crystal clear and flanked the island on either side. The river, which flowed around the sandbar island, was split into two streams; each measuring fifteen feet in width.

The island, Forsyth noted, rose to about a foot above the water's surface. The elevation of the ground sloped to the water's level at the tapered end of the sandbar. The river's depth did not exceed five inches. In general, the island was about ninety feet wide at its head, and a hundred and twenty feet long, in the approximate shape of a tear drop as seen from above.

At the head of the island grew sage grass to knee height. In the center of the sandbar-island was a thicket of five-foot-tall willow and alder, which had been permanently bent over from the rushing of water during the wet season. A twenty-foot-tall cottonwood tree stood at the end of this thicket, it too, leaned in the direction of downstream.

The attack force dismounted and began to prepare camp on the river bank opposite the sandbar island.

"Beecher, have the section leaders see to it the horses are hobbled this evening, and that the lariats are perfectly knotted before bedding down. I will personally see to the placement of sentries," the meticulous, justifiably overcautious Forsyth told Beecher.

"I'll see to it that the picket pins are firmly driven in, and that in case of attack, each man grabs his lariat along with his rifle," replied Beecher. "By no means must the Indians be allowed to stampede the horses."

"They are here," responded Forsyth, alluding to the Indians. "I can feel them."

"Yes," answered Lieutenant Beecher. "I sense their presence too. We are being watched. I feel it in my skin."

That night, Major Forsyth slept little; he patrolled the encampment, checking the sentries to ensure that they were alert, and safe – that they weren't lying face down with their throat cut and scalped lifted. The coming of dawn found Major Forsyth standing beside a sentry, they were looking to the skyline of the ground which inclined sharply further upstream.

"I see signs of movement," the sentry said to the major.

"Get ready," replied Forsyth, unshouldering his rifle. "Let's have a shot at them."

The major and the sentry cocked back the hammers of their Spencer repeating rifles at the same time, the sound was made loud in the quiet penumbral moments of dawn.

The feathers of three mounted warriors betrayed the stealthy appearance of a trio of painted faces above the rise. The dull, thudding sound of unshod horses heralded the arrival of hundreds more.

The simultaneous report of the two carefully aimed rifles was answered concurrently with two distinct eruptions of red spray, mixed with gray brain matter and white skull fragments. Hair clung to the latter as the welter of gore issued fifty-five feet into the air in a gruesome kaleidoscope of red, gray, white and black. The feathers floated lazily down, and caught by the edge of a breeze, drifted uncertainly out of sight beyond the weed covered ridgeline.

"Indians!" shouted Forsyth to the command. "Turn out! Turn out!"

Instantly the camp came alive, men armed with Spencers rushed to their horses as hundreds of mounted braves appeared on the high, rocky ground, pausing for a moment as more rode up in large hordes to join them. The special attack force stood to, with the lariats of their mounts wrapped around their left arms, and their Spencers carefully aimed at the mounted braves.

The Indians were a conglomeration of Cheyenne and Sioux. They goaded their war painted ponies down the slope. These were men who came on without fear and at a full gallop. They shook dried animal hides with confidence and beat on drums, some rang cattle bells madly to frighten the white men's horses.

There was no order given to fire; there was not time. The uncoordinated defensive fire unseated seventy-five of the dusky warriors and wounded a score more, some of them fell back with horrific wounds; sides of faces shot off, arms blown off at the elbows and intestines pooled in their laps as they wheeled their ponies around briskly. The arms lay on the ground, the taloned fingers of the hands opening and closing spasmodically.

The brave's horses faired as badly, some spooked when they were hit, throwing the rider from his mount and neighing madly as they galloped away, some trailing intestines and dragging their writhing, screaming rider whose foot was twisted and hung in the stirrup.

Forsyth turned his head suddenly to his right, the tendons of his neck standing out boldly against the shadow effect of the early morning sun. The dawn sun appeared as a molten, yellow gold coin over the hill. Instantly sweat formed on Forsyth's face as the rays of the morning sun made contact with the squinting countenance.

Major Forsyth's eyes were outraged at the site of the surviving band of Indians making off with two of the company's mules. Even more infuriating to Forsyth, was the spectacle of two unsecured horses being taken; this flew in the face of his direct orders.

"I'll have their ass for that," the major thought to himself as he shouted. "Mount up! Mount up! Saddle up quickly!"

The two men whose horses had not been properly secured took off on foot after them, alarmed by the potential of corporal punishment for having disobeyed orders.

"Get your asses back here!" shouted the major. "Stand to horse!"

One of the other scouts was a wild looking man named Sutter - a lean, hawk-faced Alabaman who had fought for both sides in the Civil War, he placed his hand on the major's shoulder.

"Look at the Indians!" shouted Sutter to Major Forsyth.

Forsyth assayed the situation before him with near disbelief, and cold calculation. Indians were appearing from everywhere, running toward them on foot, galloping on horseback, emerging from blackberry brambles and cane breaks, from ditches, trees and from further up and down stream. From all four cardinal directions they came running, war whooping and firing repeating rifles from the hip. Leaping like panthers from the lush, verdant rushes of cattails and buffalo grasses.

The Cheyenne and Sioux, scantily clad in the late summer came sprinting at an all-out run, their black hair was braided into tight, swinging pony tails and most wore one or two eagle feathers secured into the back of the coif. Their faces were covered in war paint of horrific designs that streaked as sweat ran down their faces. All were heavily muscled, and most wore breech clouts of various colors secured by a belt.

"Stand by! Mark your target, aim – fire!" commanded Major Forsyth, "Readeeeeeeee, aim – fire! Fire at will!"

The effect on the indigenous force was catastrophic; the boiling torrent of red humanity wavered in its attack and fell back, cursing. Others were left writhing like snakes in the grass, screaming incoherently as they clapped calloused hands to dime sized holes in their steak slabbed chests. Spitting blood, some regained their footing and rushed forward again, only to have fist sized holes blasted out of their backs as hot lead plunged like heat reddened pokers into their thoracic cavities.

"Beecher! Take Grover and McCall and Sutter! Maintain a suppressive fire and keep them off us as we make for the island!" shouted Major Forsyth.

"Everybody else to the island! Secure the mounts, form a circle and start digging in!" commanded the major. Spit flew from his cracked, chapped lips as he screamed orders to the animated men, who moved with alacrity.

Despite the thundering gun fire, protests could be heard from several of the difficult to manage gunfighters:

"I didn't come here to run, unless I'm goin' to run *at* them."

"What're we diggin' in for!?" shouted another. "Let's be at them!"

Barely within rifle range of only the best shots, rode the mounted chiefs. They rode in front of the swelling masses of enraged braves, urging them to charge on the defenders before they could consolidate their defense.

The chiefs, all big sun tanned men in flowing war bonnets rode shirtless on Appaloosas, their faces were masked in war paint. Their deep chests were emblazoned with geometric circles and images of hail stones. They wore leather chaps and girdled loin clouts of bold colors. They cursed their men and called them women.

Suddenly, from all sides the maddened aboriginals exploded from their sanctuary of distance and rushed the defenders of the island, who were digging into the sand with such fury that the sand fairly flew in an orange haze about the sandbar.

Mounted braves leapt from ponies that had circles painted around their eyes, and arrows painted on their flanks. These men ran like demons, arms pumping up and down with weapons in their hands as they joined the thousands of other footmen in the attack. Some of the Sioux wore waist length, buckskin war shirts that did little to hide the hard outline of their muscles. The pockets were filled with ammunition and those who were armed with Henrys fired from the hip as they ran. Many were shooting wildly and struck their fellow warriors in front of them.

The human wave attack was being shot to pieces as it crashed into the parapets, exploding against the wall of lead like a tsunami colliding against an impregnable breakwater. The survivors fell back to the tall reeds and cattails that lined both banks of the river, ducking into the tall grasses to reload as they cursed and hurled profanities at the defenders. From both banks of the Arikaree River there began to emerge a sustained barrage of accurate rifle fire.

The special attack force was taking casualties, especially among the horses tethered to the brush and small trees within the inside of the defensive perimeter. They neighed and whinnied when they got hit, pulling at their tethers as they tried to rear back. Bloody spume flew from their mouths as their lungs filled with blood.

"Let's attack them at the river bank!" one of the men cried.

"I'm with you!" seconded another.

"Stay at your posts!" commanded Forsyth, adding, "any man who tries to attack on their own, I'll kill'em!"

Forsyth stood near the center of the perimeter, holding his Colt 1860, his situation was desperate, already several of his men had been shot and all of the horses were down. His pupils were dilated from adrenalin as he paced the island like a lion held at bay within its lair.

"Anybody tries to go after them on their own, I'll blow their head off!" reiterated the major. He was shouting, saliva flew from his mouth as he shouted to be heard above the raging gunfire.

"I will too," yelled McCall, "any kill-happy bastard goes it on his own, he's dead!"

"What's gotten in to you all!?" shouted Beecher, who raised his rifle even as he shouted. He aimed carefully at a movement in the tall reeds, and fired. His effort was rewarded with the appearance of a brave who stood up, screaming.

The wounded warrior's head was shaven except for a thick scalp lock that ran full length of the center of it. An enormous black horsehair roach was tied to the scalp lock. The piranha face was painted in red and black, and lifted upward to the lead colored sky as it screamed expletives.

He tore at the small hole in his upper abdomen and a small, grey-red protuberance of intestine appeared at the entry point. The brave attempted to press the gut back in through the hole, but the intestine resisted and extruded around his fingers, suddenly boiling out of the hole in a bunch. He staggered back as he held a bucket full of intestines in his hands. He went down as he was hit by several dozen more bullets.

"Steady men! Keep those shots low! Make every shot count! Don't waste any ammo!" Forsyth yelled at the top of his lungs, he was barely heard above the thunder of the gunfire. His voice was hoarse, and sounded gritty and was growing raspy.

"Get to it, men! Get to your work, shoot like you're at Sailor's Creek, Virginia!" shouted Lieutenant Beecher, "McCall, Grover! Pick those targets!"

The fight had been going only twenty minutes, but casualties among the Indians were horrific. The fire discipline of the special attack force was like the mechanical operation of some murderous calliope which whistled shrilly as the bullets streamed from the death instrument's traction engine in macabre chromatic scale.

The red wave had hit the island, broke around it and having been repelled backward – receded like the ebbing of some grotesque crimson tide - leaving scores of dead and wounded.

The sides of the riverbank were seething with thousands of warriors hunkering in the willows and cat tails, trying to get a shot. On the high bluffs, the wailing of women and children could be heard interspersed with the increasing gunfire of the Cheyenne and Sioux who were arriving by the thousands from more distant villages. The sound of gunfire served as a magnet, drawing the iron willed warriors into the metal storm.

Despite the deluge of incoming fire, the encircled frontiersmen had resumed excavating rifle pits. They used butcher knives – the most common field knife to be found among them, and tin plates to excavate the soft, gravelly sand. Within minutes they had rifle pits dug that measured two feet deep and six feet in length. The excavated soil had been heaped in front of the parapets to a height of sixteen inches, with a thickness of two feet.

The men all lay in their pits, with their rifles resting atop the parapet in front of them. Major Forsyth walked the perimeter stealthily, at a crouch, from one firing position to the next, checking his men.

"Get down, get down!" they urged the major.

"I mean to do just that!" responded Forsyth, finally taking cover in a shallow depression of the ground. It was at that moment he took a bullet to the front of his right thigh, blinding him in pain.

"Arrrrrrrrghhhhhhh!!!" yelled Major Forsyth, clutching his right thigh with both arms and pulling it in tight into his abdomen as he rolled onto his side.

"He's hit! He's hit!" shouted several of the men, aghast at the ominous significance of what the loss of their commanding officer portended.

"It's OK, it's not serious!" lied the major through clenched teeth, who took a full minute to allay the worry of his command, who remained behind their parapets as the deadly fire continued from close distance.

Twenty-five or thirty braves had managed by a series of rushes protected by covering fire to infiltrate the lower end of the island and were targeting individual members of the special attack force.

"Farley, Gannt, and Burke!" shouted Lieutenant Beecher. "Go back there and kill them!"

Farley, the older of the trio looked to Gannt and Burke, shielding his face and eyes from sand that kicked up suddenly from a bullet impact inches from his face.

Unbeknownst to the combatants that fought with rifles and revolvers, other adversaries fought battles no less fierce in the sand, hidden from desperate, furtive glances. Two female stag beetles, whose smaller mandibles rendered them more formidable than those of the massive males, fought a battle of no quarter over a nesting site. Seizing advantage, the smaller of the two clipped off the legs of its larger opponent, leaving it to open and close its mandibles impotently in the moist sand. Victory and defeat were both rendered mute in the spray of sand that a bullet impact hurled over the insect combatants, burying them.

"Get loaded up," said Farley. "Make sure your revolvers aren't fouled with sand." Bullets continued to impact the dirt all around them. "Now let's go!" he shouted, running toward the hidden Sioux and Cheyenne. The other two followed instinctively slightly behind, and to either side of him.

Like everyone else on the island, these three were imbued with the lust for killing, and never had a second thought about following such a suicidal order. It never crossed their mind that they would probably be killed, they had volunteered for the special attack force simply for an opportunity to kill someone. It really didn't matter who.

They ran up on a dozen braves who weren't expecting them. Three were lying in the prone position taking shots while the other nine had clustered in a group, talking rapidly. Further back were a dozen more. They were cleaning the fouled barrels of an assortment of rifles. The spent black powder was causing back pressure to dangerously build up in the barrels and catastrophic failure had to be avoided.

They talked in hushed, urgent voices as they rammed the cleaning rods through the bore of the rifles, dislodging the black powder and soft lead residue that clogged the rifling. The three prone warriors turned their heads as the trio of killers entered into their midst.

The first and second warrior rolled to their side, awkwardly trying to get a shot as the pointed toed cowboy boots kicked in their eye sockets, causing the vitreous aqueous of the eyeballs to burst through the sclera. The third brave rose to a knee and had the wind knocked from him as Gannt shot him point blank in the chest.

The other nine warriors rushed the three assassins - all of them raising their rifles to their shoulders as Gannt, Farley and Burke shot rapidly into them. The braves shot wildly in the direction of the three frontier scouts. Behind them, the other twelve warriors rose to the occasion.

"Too far, no can hit," said the Arikawa to the blond haired man who peered through the Berdan type rifle scope.

Custer did not answer, but concentrated on the sight picture, controlling his breathing, watching the huge rise and fall of the target in the crosshairs of the telescopic sight as he breathed. All the while he slowly applied pressure to the trigger. His cheek was welded to the rifle stock. The detonation of the propellant surprised the Boy General as much as it did the brave whose head exploded.

"Luck," grunted Bloody Knife.

The Yellow Hair ejected the spent cartridge and reloaded another one, using the lever of the rifle. He then thumb-cocked the hammer back, hearing a click as it locked into place. He did not reply to Bloody Knife. Custer was one with the rifle, it was an extension of himself, the barrel rose and fell imperceptibly with each controlled breath the former general took. The barely discernable rise and fall were magnified enormously within the rifle's telescopic sight.

The remaining eleven braves looked about, scanning the tree line and reeds for the gunfighter they assumed to be close by. They were enraged that someone would be drawing a bead on them. Another sharp thud announced the impact of a bullet; this time the strike of the round was low, skewering a brave through the right front pelvis and exploding from the coccyx in a maelstrom of blood and shattered bone. The brave collapsed with his tail bone shattered and shards of bone showing through the obscene, gaping orifice.

The warriors began firing wildly into the foliage that lined the river banks on either side, hitting some of their own men. These in response began shooting back, mistaking the fire for that of the frontiersmen. Within a moment a full blown fire fight developed as the Indians delivered murderous fire into each other.

The group of Indians confronting the three assassins who were sent to kill them retreated to join their comrades behind them. These braves were forced to join in the gunfight against their counterparts that lined either side of the river.

The three psychopathic killers low crawled toward the frantically firing Indians. One of the kneeling braves had just shot another brave on the other side of the river. He turned his head instinctively toward the three frontiersmen who approached the drastically reduced number of infiltrators. His twin ponytails, secured in socks of sweat stained linen swung in slow motion with his instinctive head movement. His movement was fluid as he swung his body around to face the three aggressors. He remained kneeling as he lifted his eight-pound Henry repeating rifle to his shoulder to get a shot.

The blond haired man a mile away had been slowly exerting pressure on the trigger as he aimed at the brave's head through the telescopic sight. The detonation of the high grade gun powder caught Custer off guard again, and as a result the Boy General pulled his shot slightly, causing the bullet to drop in its trajectory.

"Damn!" expostulated the Yellow Hair.

"Good shoot, Boy General," replied Bloody Knife. "Hit low, bullet go through shoulder."

The Henry dropped onto the sand as the Cheyenne bolted upright into the standing position. The veins stood out on his temples and neck as he raised his war painted face toward the gun metal gray sky and shrieked in agony. The warrior's scream seemed to sustain itself for an inordinate duration of time. The bullet had plunged into his right deltoid, plowing through the shoulder socket and exiting out the other. He ran from his position, both arms hanging limply at his sides. He ran penguin like through the water of the Arikaree River and into the reeds and cattails on the opposite bank of the shallow waterway. He continued to run screaming as bullets skipped across the water like pebbles thrown by a red headed bully with freckles.

"Listen, Forsyth!" shouted Dr. Mooers, "I'm digging out my pit – making it bigger! I'm going to drag you over here and get you out of the open!"

Dr. Mooers was a rifle expert, a keen marksman who could shoot the head off a pond turtle at a hundred yards. All of these men could. Several men rushed at a low crouch to assist the doctor in enlarging the hole.

Major Forsyth raised his wounded right thigh to get a look at the wound and in doing so was immediately hit in the left leg – with devastating results. The bullet passed through the tibia, shattering the shin bone half way in between the knee and the ankle.

Major Forsythe screamed like a hyena as the white hot pain blinded him.

"Help me get him the hell in here!" shouted Mooers to the two men helping him deepen the excavation. "He's been hit again!" Sand stuck to the sweat glistening neck and face of Dr. Mooers as he shouted the orders at the top of his lungs – struggling to be heard above the gunfire.

The marksmen were two to a rifle pit, taking only shots that held promise. The semi-circular defensive perimeter was comprised of the rifle pits dug about six feet from one another. Parapets had been erected on the rear of the rifle pits as well, due to the rifle fire coming in from all directions. Forsyth and Surgeon Mooers were at the southern end of the fortification.

Many of the scout-frontiersmen had suffered bullet grazes across their heads and wore bandages. They were no less adroit in their senses and actions as their counterparts; they willingly exposed themselves for an opportunity to kill. Many of them counted this as the finest moment of their lives, with targets appearing all over the place.

The Native Americans were heavily armed; Spencers, Henrys, Springfield muzzle loaders that had been converted into breech loaders, and Remingtons – all composed a panoply of deadly armament.

With the coming of night, hostilities slackened and the special attack force resumed reinforcing their earthworks and dug holes several feet into the ground for drinking water. Guards were picketed throughout the sandbar to prevent barely controlled, psychotic members from exiting individually or in small groups to attack the huge Indian encampment.

Chapter Ten
Wannertushi Makes Them Fight

THE TWENTY-FOOT-TALL human skin tepee was illuminated eerily by the subdued, dull glow of coals. The shaman White Bull had labored all through the night working magic to reverse the damage Roman Nose had inflicted upon himself. A captured Buffalo Soldier lay staked to the ground, the hands and feet were charred relics of the appendages that smoldered in glowing coal beds.

"Now," said the medicine man, White Bull. "The final part of the Spell of Undoing."

The Buffalo Soldier's head lifted up and empty eye sockets gazed unseeingly at the man who uttered the incantations.

Within the previous forty-eight hours Roman Nose had been at a festival of a neighboring village and had eaten meat drawn from fire using a metal fork. He was advised of the sacrilege soon after.

"What!?" It cannot be!" expostulated the alarmed Roman Nose, mortified at the implications of the war bonnet's loss of protective power. "Who has done this thing!?"

"It was no accident, the wife of Lame Bull pulled the meat from the fire with the metal fork," answered White Bull. "She sought to further her husband's position within the Tribal Council, by depriving you of the protective powers of the war bonnet, and seeing you fall in battle."

"Then I shall have her as my own, I have always wanted that slut!" shouted the enraged Roman Nose, he could hear his pulse pounding even above the tinnitus that rang in his ears.

"That means a challenge to Lame Bull. Lame Bull is a mighty warrior, and held in high esteem by his council," countered White Bull, concerned with the possibility of a schism with the neighboring village.

"It makes nought to me if he is a Grand Sachem! The woman shall be mine!" retorted the six-foot six-inch Roman Nose, who suddenly stood up – flexing his enormous biceps.

The impromptu fight was arranged hastily by go-betweens and witnessed by the entirety of both villages; that of Roman Nose and that of Lame Bull. Watching also, was the insolent wife of Lame Bull, who had secretly coveted the leadership position for her husband. Lame Bull would stand to gain much in stature were Roman Nose to die in combat. So she had intentionally withdrawn the meat from the fire using the metallic fork.

A prominent circle had been gouged into the earth within the center of Lame Bull's village. The circle was fifty feet in circumference and if a contender was forced from it, he would be thrust back into the perimeter.

Both men entered the perimeter of the circle slicked down in bear grease to make their opponent's hold less certain. They wore breech clouts of dark color, to hide the filthy sweat, urine and fecal stains on the reeking articles of clothing. Neither had shaven the hair from their heads to deny purchase of the other, on account of the hastiness of the arrangement. It was within the right of the woman to choose how her contenders would be armed.

"How you want'em fight, Wannertushi? Knife? Tomahawk?" asked White Bull.

Wannertushi looked at the two men about to fight for her. They regarded each other with pure hatred. They did not take their eyes from one another as they stretched and limbered up their knotty muscles.

"No knife, no tomahawk," answered Wannertushi in a cold, emotionless voice. "Fight hand to hand. No knife!" The high toned, nasal words came from the small, cruel mouth in monosyllables – like those of a small child.

Lame Bull had no illusions about his chances in the ring with Roman Nose. He'd had no previous knowledge of his wife's pretenses to furthering her social status within the tribe by undermining the power of the war bonnet and catapulting him into a higher rank among the Tribal Council. But to accede to the demand of Roman Nose to take his wife would have been an unforgiveable insult.

The six-foot six-inch-tall Roman Nose towered over his six-foot-tall opponent. But Lame Bull was no stranger to fighting bare-handed, whereas Roman Nose was a skilled gun fighter.

"Fight!" shouted White Bull.

Both men approached each other warily, at a crouch, with their hands opening and closing. Lame Bull dropped to the ground, seizing the knees of Roman Nose and like a young bullock driving himself forward into his opponent's legs, hugging them together and causing Roman Nose to topple, like a felled tree onto his back. A hushed gasp issued from the throng of spectators that massed along the boundary of the circle. Quickly, without wasting a moment Lame Bull mounted Roman Nose and rubbed his cayenne pepper saturated hands into Roman Nose's eyes.

"Ha!" shouted Roman Nose, cuffing his opponent across the right ear open handed, bursting his eardrum, "My eyes! Son of a whore!"

The pain from the burst eardrum seared through Lame Bull's brain like a white hot poker in the hands of a widow. Reacting reflexively, he threw both hands to his right ear as Roman Nose delivered a straight forward jab blindly, hitting Lame Bull squarely in the face, knocking him backwards and causing him to surrender his advantage of position.

Lame Bull leapt to his feet at the same time Roman Nose did. The eyes of Roman Nose were slits of hate that issued tears freely. The big Cheyenne struggled to focus his watery, burning eyes despite the searing pain of the inflamed conjunctiva. Both men seized each other powerfully by the throat using death grips and began throttling each other with both hands, digging their filthy thumb nails underneath the skin and into each other's tracheas.

The flaps of the loin clouts swung as they fought to the death for the same woman. Wannertushi watched the savage combat, uncertain of who the victor would be. As the two braves strangled each other with superhuman strength, Wannertushi began to doubt the wisdom of what she had done. They grunted and gasped for air as they twisted their muscular necks and while writhing, twisted like contortionists in each other's grasp.

Lame Bull slipped out of the grip with a twisting, torqueing motion. Blood oozed from thumbnail gouges in the numerous welts on his bull neck. His jet black hair was pulled back tightly and woven into a double braid. These swung crazily back and forth as he retreated, shaking his head to restore circulation.

Lame Bull's noble Mediterranean features were contorted into an expression of utter antipathy as he regarded Roman Nose and bared his sharpened teeth

– filed to points. He lunged at his larger opponent and caterwauled like a large cat as he ran at him.

Roman Nose seized the man by the shoulders but he could not grip his greased opponent. Clasping both hands together, Lame Bull heaved upward, knocking the hands of Roman Nose aside and then crashed his mallet sized fist like a pile driver into the bulbous nose of his opponent.

The stunned Roman Nose reeled backwards, as Lame Bull leapt on him screaming like a mountain lion. The bear grease that Roman Nose had applied to himself caused Lame Bull to slip and Roman Nose took a further step back, holding both hands to his grotesquely overdeveloped olfactory organ which was bleeding profusely.

Instinctively realizing that this was the moment to press his advantage, Lame Bull rushed the dazed Roman Nose again. Wannertushi, who watched the combat with the alacrity of one who has much to gain or lose hedged her bet on her husband as he ran full on toward Roman Nose.

Wannertushi's shiny hair was raven black and brushed straight down over her shoulders. Her face was aquiline and finely constructed. Close set stygian eyes watched the death struggle from above a small, downward hooking nose that resembled the beak of a peregrine falcon. The petite, sneering mouth was accentuated by the thin lips which were pressed tightly together.

The vivacious instigator of the death match swatted gnats from her face as she watched them fight for her. The loose doe skin dress she wore was pulled in tightly at the waist with a woman's belt taken from a stage coach ambush. She wore nothing underneath, and her hardened nipples were outlined against the soft doe skin.

Roman Nose stepped deftly aside as a torero would dodge a charging bull, and in doing so grabbed one of the pony tails of Lame Bull with both hands, his biceps bunched up and stood out like ostrich eggs as he yanked the braided pony tail back with all of his strength.

The entire half of the scalp tore off of Lame Bull with the slick sucking sound of skin being stripped from a chicken. It tore off unevenly; a ragged tear which extended to the face and ear. Lame Bull roared at the top of his lungs in reaction to the searing, molten pain as Roman Nose swung the scalp lock like a belt. It retained a large skin flap containing the right ear and part of the face.

The shock of the trauma belayed immediate bleeding as the capillaries reflexively constricted. Nevertheless, everyone present could see the plainly visible suture lines of the right side of the skull as the enraged Lame Bull charged Roman Nose again. Roman Nose held the scalp lock by its pony tail braid and swung it viciously at the face of his wounded opponent. The force of the blows struck Lame Bull's face with the stinging, smacking force of a thick, short length whip. The scalp whip made loud, wet, slapping sounds as it smacked into the face of Lame Bull.

Roman Nose tripped Lame Bull on the next bull like assault, causing him to fall forward to the earth. Sand and grass stuck in the horrific wound as Roman Nose mounted Lame Bull from behind and began choking him with the rope-like hair braid. The steel corded biceps stood out like balloons and the triceps flexed into steel horseshoes as he exerted all of his might in strangling Lame Bull with the pony tail.

Lame Bull's head was lifted upward and his pointed, filed teeth were exposed as the lips were pulled back in air hunger over the blackened gums. Roman Nose pulled on the hair rope with all of his might, driving his knee into Lame Bull's back as he did so.

After several minutes of holding Lame Bull in this static position of non-movement, Roman Nose placed both ham-like hands on the head of his incapacitated adversary and twisted it violently to the left, pulling upward as he did so. A repugnant, dull quadruple snapping sound was heard.

Instantly the solemnness of the moment was disrupted by a thunderous applause of cheering and rifle shots into the air. The breech clout of the victor had loosened and fallen to the ground as he stood in triumph over his fallen adversary. Roman Nose and Wannertushi approached each other, Wannertushi saw sweat dribble and fall from the uncircumcised appendage of Roman Nose as it swung with each foot step. Wannertushi embraced the victor, pressing bodily into her new lover, as he cupped and squeezed her firm, rounded behind.

"Take me to your tepee," said Roman Nose, between breaths, adding, "and minister to my needs."

Much had occurred within the forty-eight hours since the victory of Roman Nose over Lame Bull. White Bull had worked feverishly since the incident of the metallic fork two days before. The Cheyenne medicine man had labored exhaustively to restore the power of the war bonnet. Meanwhile, pressure was mounting for Roman Nose to take charge and lead an attack on the island fortress – with, or without the war bonnet.

"This coal, taken from the Sacred Fire of Eternity will restore the protective power to the war bonnet. But only after it has touched the heart of an enemy. Using his bare hand, White Bull lifted the orange coal, the size of an eagle egg, and sat it on the Buffalo Soldier's chest, over the heart. The garbled screams from the tongueless maw of the soldier caused the medicine man to smile.

"It is complete," stated White Bull. "The incantations have been spoken and the prayer offerings made. A word, carried by a waif through starlit gulfs over bottomless lakes has intimated this to me."

"Then, assist me as I don the war bonnet!" commanded Roman Nose. "Summon the chiefs, the braves, and any of the uninitiated who would be a warrior this day! No bullet shall touch me nor those who are with me!"

"No bullet will touch you nor those who are with you," reaffirmed White Bull.

"Then I will stop the slaughter of my braves, I will tan the skin of my enemies and use them for the tepees of the summer."

"Fly, Roman Nose!" shouted White Bull. "Fly into the face of the sun! Fly, son of my people! Cleanse this stain of the white vermin from the land!"

"It shall be!" shouted Roman Nose, removing the war bonnet from its container and beginning the rituals involved before donning it.

"The power of the war bonnet, it is as if it lives," remarked Roman Nose to White Bull.

"Yes, Son of my People," answered White Bull. "It conveys more than the power of protection, much more. It has the power to unite all of the far flung tribes, it gives the wearer the ability to speak in all tongues. With this war bonnet, you shall rid the land of this pestilence that plagues us."

Chapter Eleven
Bath Time for Libbie

THE EXHAUSTED LIBBIE, Margaret and Beverly dismounted the Concord stage coach at Monroe, Michigan. At last they had completed their monotonous journey from Fort Hayes, Kansas. Their clothing was stained with dust that adhered to the oily sweat and was permeated with the pungent smell of body odor, reminiscent of skillet fried pork sausage. Sheridan's offer to stay in his luxurious quarters at Fort Leavenworth had been graciously, and carefully declined.

Custer had told General Sheridan that his family would return to the home of Libbie's father – which fortuitously she had inherited. Naturally, Little Phil Sheridan had inferred that the Yellow Hair would accompany them. But the unpredictable Boy General had his own itinerary. It was also an itinerary that would nearly cost him his life.

Judge Bacon's house was a white, rectangular two story frame salt box style house. It had been constructed conveniently next to the rutted, quagmire-like mud road that served as the main street of Monroe. The house was maintained during the Custers' absence by their adored Negress maid, who had figuratively adopted George and Libbie when they were newlyweds. The modest frame home was lavishly furnished and had been left to Libbie Custer upon her father's death. The Custers' maid, Eliza stayed in the house and oversaw it for the young Custer couple.

The women's equilibrium was unsteady after the long, grueling stage coach ride. The leaf spring suspension of the Concord stage coach acted in such a way as to rotate from side to side, rather than bounce up and down. As the three women mounted the steps of the wide front porch, their legs swayed from having traveled days in the coach. The sensation was that of having debarked from a ship that had ridden heavy seas.

"Eliza!" shouted Elizabeth for her colored maid servant. "Eliza! Are you here? We're home!"

"I'm dead," complained Margaret, dropping her bags and collapsing on the deep leather sofa. "I feel as though I'm still on that stage coach, the way the room is moving around."

"Please tell me how I can be of help, Elizabeth," offered Beverly. "I am so grateful to you for taking me in while my father is committed in the insane asylum."

"Margaret, go across the street to Rhonda Bean's house," ordered Libbie, "and see if she knows the whereabouts of Eliza. Offer to buy some eggs and bacon from her. Beverly, get the stove going, I'm starving and I'm going to need some hot water for a bath!"

Although Margaret was still suffering from the motion sickness of riding the stage coach, she rose quickly at the idea of Libbie taking a bath. She was tired and filthy from the non-stop journey and stank.

The stage coach was called so because it ran in stages, the passengers would stop briefly at a relay station while the mules were changed out and then speed to the next stage in the overland trip. The intention was to travel quickly, without ever stopping for more than an hour.

"There's still a coal bed in the stove, I put another load in and the water will be steaming soon, but there's hardly any food in the pantry," reported Beverly to Elizabeth Custer.

Beverly was dressed in yet another monotonous, stifling hot black work dress. It was a very basic style of attire. The bottom of the dress was small by the standards of the day, not large enough to accommodate hoops. But it could be worn with a petticoat to give it a fuller look. Her hair was done up tightly in an oily, greasy bun.

"Let's inaugurate our arrival at my father's house with the opening of all of the windows to facilitate the ingress of a merciful, late afternoon breeze! By ensuring all of the windows are fully ascended, it will enhance the fullest dissemination of respirable air in here," stated Libbie. "I'm going to my father's bedroom to denudate myself of these feculent habiliments, they reek of malfeasance!"

"Oh, Libbie!" responded Beverly. "You have such a way with words!"

Libbie stood in front of the eight drawer cherry wood Shaker dresser, looking at her reflection in the tarnished mirror that was mounted atop it. Already she felt the tense excitement that came when she flaunted her nudity in front of another woman.

Although she enjoyed Margaret's audience, she had become used to undressing in front of her sister-in-law. Years of frank, uninhibited exhibitionism in front of Margaret had become routine, and unexciting.

Already Libbie had undressed openly in front of Beverly several times. She sensed the younger woman's timidity and unease. She felt an exhilaration in flaunting her nakedness in front of her younger, captive female audience.

"Beverly, I need a hand!" shouted Elizabeth, she tried to hide the building tension from her voice. "It's my corset; I can't get it unlaced!"

"I'm pouring water into the tub, I'll be there in a moment," responded Beverly. "Is there a rain barrel outside?"

"Yes!" responded Libbie. "Just outside the back door, but do hurry!"

Beverly refilled the bucket from the five-hundred-gallon stone rain barrel and set it on the stove to heat. Thousands of mosquito larvae writhed and contorted in the heating water.

Exhausted from the long stage coach ride, Beverly did not pause to think before entering the bedroom of Elizabeth Custer. Libbie stood with her back facing Beverly, wearing nothing but a white, dingy, sweat stained corset. Although a strong, wood smoke scented breeze lifted the curtains, the room was still hot, humid and Libbie's dimpled behind was shiny with sweat.

"Help me off with this," snapped Libbie, fidgeting with the corset lace, realizing she had to control her impulses. "I have to divest myself of this sudor sodden corset. It is simply putrid! It is exigent that I allow my skin some time in which to respire and compulsory that you collaborate in this most urgent of Samaritan endeavors."

Once the lacing was loosened, Libbie turned and faced Beverly in the same motion as she was lifting the corset over her head. She began violently twisting her torso as she did so in order to facilitate the removal of the garment. Libbie was acutely aware that Beverly was observing her perky, apple sized breasts swing and bounce – there was no way that Beverly could avoid seeing them.

"There!" ejaculated Libbie. The tone of her voice conveyed the exuberance that she felt. "That was a tussle!" she threw the foul smelling undergarment - soured with sweat onto the floor contemptuously, kicking it aside viciously.

"Why Miss Libbie!" shouted Eliza, the Custer's longtime maid servant; a former slave who had cared for the newly wed Custers in 1864, during the Civil War. "There you is! Naked as a jay bird, jus' like always!"

"Eliza!" returned Libbie, "Oh my land, you cannot imagine the doldrums through which I have but barely managed to endure. And to set eyes upon you, after so long a tedious journey is to behold a friend most dear to my heart!"

Libbie brushed by Beverly as though she were not there anymore and grabbed Eliza, embracing her fully nude; her breasts flattening as they pressed into the apron of Eliza's flower decorated working dress.

"Now you go on 'bout cho' chores, Miss Libbie, an' I'll getchu' some hot supper cookin' an' have the bath all ready for you in no time!" soothed Eliza. "Why, my po' po' child, ridin' on that stage coach all the way from Fort Hays, Kansas!"

"Oh, do forgive me!" apologized Libbie. "Beverly, this is Eliza, one of my most dear friends, and Eliza, this is

Beverly, she is staying with us for several months, and is almost like a sister to me."

"And to me," joined in Margaret, returning from across the street. She did not try to avert her eyes from her sister-in-law's nudity. Libbie warmed to the way that Margaret openly looked at her and she also enjoyed the discomfort that she sensed Beverly felt toward her brazen nakedness.

"I'd like to go to my ablution now," Libbie stated matter of factly. "Eliza, please procure for me a towel, and Beverly, I shall require assistance with my hair."

Eliza walked carelessly to the hallway closet, fetching the heavy bath towel and took it to the moderately sized bathroom, setting it on the small table that stood beside the large tin, corrugated bath tub. When Eliza passed through the living room she happened to look up at the portrait of Judge Bacon, whose visage scowled down malevolently from above the fireplace.

"Mmmmm, hmmmph!" Eliza expressed to herself. "Dat po' ol' Judge Bacon! Miss Libbie *knew* he had a bad heart. An' her runnin' roun' the house naked all the time! Almos' like she *knew* her daddy would keel over dead from a heart attack one of them days, but she jus' kept it up anyhow! An' now she done got the ol' judge's house!"

Eliza remembered too, the day it had happened. Judge Bacon had been a highly respected circuit judge known for his stern, autocratic decisions. Eliza smiled as she remembered how Judge Bacon would always take his daughter to the numerous hangings he had rendered in his final judgements on the convicted.

"Oh, please daddy!" Eliza remembered Elizabeth pleading. "Please take me to the hangings!" Hangings which Eliza surmised were possibly mandated by the Judge to satisfy the insatiable blood lust of his daughter.

"Alright, Libbie," the Judge had responded to his exuberant daughter. "The venue today will send a stern message to the miscreants and villains that plague my jurisdiction. There will be three public hangings from the scaffold – a triple decker! Now, for Pete's sake, young Lady, do get some clothes on!"

Eliza had been preparing a chicken dumpling inside the large, coal fired oven, and watched carefully from the kitchen as the event took place. Custer, as usual, was attending to military matters and his wife would often return to her childhood home when not in the company of the former general.

"Oh, daddy!" shouted the ecstatic Libbie, her breasts bounced and behind jiggled as she ran across the oak hardwood floor of the living room toward the seated Judge Bacon, who was lighting a cheroot with a sulfur tipped match. "A triple decker! A what the hecker! Please don't weight their feet, daddy! I want to watch them kick like the Devil!"

The exuberant Libbie plopped on the old Judge's lap, completely naked, Eliza remembered, shaking her head.

"Libbie!" croaked the venerable Judge, "I must insist that you dress yourself! The hangings occur in two hours and – oh! *My chest!!!*"

The chest pain radiated up Judge Bacon's neck and into his left jaw. The searing pain shot down the entire length of his left arm. There was an explosion of blinding pain each time the Judge gasped for breath.

"*Daddy!!!*" shrieked Elizabeth, grabbing his face by the whiskers as she leaned into him, burying his face between her small, firm bosoms. "Eliza! Fetch the heart pills, *"Daddy's having a heart attack!!!"*

Eliza remembered uncomfortably the following events. She had run barefoot to the Judge's medicine cabinet where the pills were nearest. They were kept also at Judge Bacon's bedside table, but the medicine cabinet was closer.

"Here, Miss Libbie!" Eliza had shouted as she thrust the small tin of pills to Libbie.

The Judge was turning blue in the face, his breaths coming in ragged gasps as he clawed at his chest. The silver gray clam shell buttons had flown from the white, formal cotton shirt when he'd ripped it open to get at the stabbing chest pain.

Libbie placed her thumbnail under the lid of the medicine tin and flipped the top off, spilling the pills as she did so. It appeared to Eliza that Libbie had *intentionally* spilled the small, white tablets.

Elizabeth straddled the Judge, blocking Eliza's attempt to procure a pill and place it into Judge Bacon's mouth, the muscles of Libbie's back played under the supple skin and her buttocks flexed as she shifted her position in feigned attempts to find the tiny pills.

Suddenly the Judge bolted upright in the large, steer hide overstuffed leather chair, he sat ramrod straight and his blue lips were pulled back from his bad teeth in a hideous grimace. Libbie leapt from Judge Bacon's lap, her breasts bouncing with the suddenness of the movement. The Judge slumped back in his chair, his breathing having slowed to three breaths per minute, and then having stopped.

Libbie placed the heel of her bare foot on the coal of the cheroot and ground it out. Her weight was concentrated on her left leg, flexing the left gluteal muscle while the right hip relaxed. Her arms were folded across her sweating breasts.

"Eliza," stated Elizabeth in an authoritative tone. "Go fetch the doctor. *Daddy is dead!*"

Eliza was brought out of her momentary visit to the death of Judge Bacon by the sound of splashing of water in the tub. "You doin' alright in there, Miss Libbie? I've got more hot water a comin'!"

Margaret watched as Beverly poured steaming water from a basin onto the thick, stringy hair of Elizabeth, who was seated in the tub with her head bent forward.

"Yes, ma'am!" answered Libbie. "Already I am a woman who has been rejuvenated! I feel as though I am a phoenix risen from the ashes!"

Libbie placed her hands on either side of the bath tub and scooted backward, adjusting her position within the galvanized tub of steaming, sassafras scented, water. Beverly heard the blubbery, metallic, staccato sound of air escaping under pressure in a high stream burst of bubbles.

"Oh do forgive me, Beverly! I broke wind in the bath tub!" ejaculated an exuberant Libbie, "and it tickled!"

Eliza entered the bathroom where Margaret stood watching as Beverly sponged Libbie's back. She saw Margaret staring at the puckered nipples from which the bath water mixed with soap suds dripped.

"Didju break wind in dat baff tub Miss Libbie? I gotchu a nice, warm soap suds enema dat help loosen dem ol' bowels up, Honey Child," stated Eliza, thinking to herself; "Land o' Gosha! These white womens is sho' strange in their ways!"

"Well Mrs. Custer," reassured Beverly in a comforting tone as she continued rinsing the shampoo from Elizabeth's hair. "It did make a rather unique sound."

"Stop addressing me by title, and please call me Libbie," Custer's wife responded as she placed her hands on either side of the bath tub and stood up. The liquid sounds of dozens of small water streams ran off the shiny, slippery skin and trickled like streams flowing into the ocean as they fell back into the tub.

"Just set the enema beside the tub, Eliza, I am bathed and fully reconstituted!" replied Libbie to her maid. "I am reincarnated!" Custer's wife exclaimed exuberantly as she stepped over the side of the tub, her left leg first. She bent forward and supported herself by placing her hands on the same side of the tub as she maintained balance. "Procure me a wrap for my hair, as Beverly towels me, please, Eliza."

Elizabeth turned to face Beverly and stopped suddenly. Water droplets flew from the thimble sized nipples with the sudden halting of the motion. They jiggled for a moment more, like gelatin, Margaret thought.

"Towel me," said Libbie to Beverly, who stepped behind her and began drying her back. "No, not my back, Beverly, towel my breasts," Elizabeth was instinctively aware of the horror Beverly felt, and placing her hands behind her head stretched backward felinely. The motion lifted her firm bosom and thrust them at Beverly, who began drying them brusquely.

"Don't be so damned rough, Beverly!" warned Elizabeth.

"Supper 'bout done, Miss Libbie! I'll have yo' plate set at the table here shortly!" shouted Eliza from the kitchen.

"That will be very fine, Eliza! I mean to administer my enema and cleanse my bowels! Then I'll sate my appetite and head straight away for my daddy's bed!

Beverly and Margaret will repose in the rooms of my old bedroom and the adjoining guest room!"

"Yes, ma'am, Miss Libbie! Lemme strip dem ol' dust covers off'en dem beds an dell be all fresh an' nicely made fo' you young ladies!"

The five-foot four-inch-tall Elizabeth padded on bare feet from the bathroom with the towel wrap around her chestnut brown hair. She was wearing a large bathrobe secured with a cloth belt as she exited the back door and traipsed gingerly outside toward the wood framed outhouse, enema bag in hand.

"Well?" said Margaret to Beverly.

"Yes ma'am?" Beverly responded.

"Hurry up and get undressed. I am of a mind to have a bath after you. I can assist with your toiletries but please do not tarry a moment longer," answered Margaret.

"But Margaret, I am very timid. In my family nudity was not permitted," riposted Beverly. Her calm voice belied her rising alarm at this strange family.

"Make it fast, then," soothed Margie, her voice was growing husky, and she had to swallow hard in order to speak clearly. She tried to appear nonchalant, but she was inwardly furious. "I am very tired from the road."

"But the water," protested Beverly, it is filthy with Libbie's sweat and grime. Look at how brown the water is."

Margaret walked toward the open doorway of the bathroom, and stopped, turning around slowly as she responded to Beverly.

"I could drink that water," Margie answered, locking hungry eyes with Beverly.

Although the sun was not fully set, Libbie was already atop her father's bed as Eliza laid out church clothes for the following Sunday morning. The room was still hot, despite the high ceilings and open windows. Libbie lay on her stomach atop the sheets, naked and uncovered.

"You gets cold, later on, Miss Libbie, you jus' cover yo' sweet lil' self up. Jus' ring dat bell atcho' bedside table an' I'll be right down, Miss Libbie," intoned Eliza maternalistically. She cared for this family as though it were her own.

Libbie rolled over on her back, bending her right knee, her right foot was planted on the bed and she crossed her left leg over the upraised knee. She pulled a pillow further under her head, adjusting it for comfort measures.

"Yes, ma'am, Eliza," answered Elizabeth. "I cannot express enough my sincerest gratitude for your Samaritan assistance today. I am debilitated and utterly exhausted from that bromidic stagecoach ride."

"Why bless yo' heart, Miss Libbie! Ain't nothin' but a thang! I is always ready to help my dear Miss Libbie!" replied Eliza, sincerely.

"You know, I never knew my mother very well," responded Libbie, choosing her words carefully. "By the time I was thirteen years of age, my poor mother along with three siblings had all been taken. This left only my distraught father and myself to suffer within a purgatory of utter despondency. My father consigned me to boarding schools in an attempt to assuage the loss of my mother and siblings, and provide the female company that I so cherished.

"My mundane, heartbroken existence has been illuminated with a radiance since you took the general and myself into your kind and merciful heart. I have always considered you as I would my mother. Had I but known her, I am certain that she would have been very much like you."

Eliza smiled, showing straight, snuff stained teeth. Although she was aware of her matron's dependence on her, the statement came as a surprise and deeply moved the former slave.

"I'm puttin' out the light, Miss Libbie," said Eliza. She said the words softly and quickly, in an effort to mask the strange, alien emotions that rocked her down to her very soul. Eliza struggled against the unexpected emotional tidal wave that threatened to make her cry.

Eliza had never cried, not once in her entire life, and thought she was incapable of the sentimental collapse in demeanor. She struggled with all her might to hold back her tears as she moved toward the whale oil lantern. She noticed as she reached for the lantern that Libbie was quiet shaven in her private area.

"These young white ladies," Eliza ruminated to herself, "aint dey jus' the Tom Dickens!" then she put out the light.

Darkness also ruled in the room that Margaret inhabited, but she was not to be found drifting to sleep atop the chicken feather filled bed. Instead, she peered through the keyhole in the doorknob of the wooden door that denied entry into the adjoining bedroom. The bedroom in which Beverly stood naked, vigorously brushing her straight black shoulder length hair. Her plump, fat breasts heaved and swayed with the harsh strokes of the hair brush.

Margaret cupped both hands around the doorknob to focus the dim, barely sufficient light through the keyhole onto her dilated pupil. The areolas were large and pink, the nipples were hardened and jutted from the areolas like sewing thimbles. Margie controlled her breathing with effort, consciously trying to avoid being heard by the object of her curiosity.

Suddenly Beverly turned facing the door behind which Margie knelt, her pendulous breasts swaying with the unanticipated movement. She advanced on the door. Margaret noted the thick, triangular patch of brunette pubic hair even as she pulled away from the door knob reflexively in fear of being discovered. Her heart was pounding in her throat. She heard a brief brushing against the other side of the door, as though an article of clothing had been removed from a clothes hanger.

It was with trepidation that Margaret placed her eye back to the keyhole, uncertain that she was undiscovered in her voyeurism. What she saw was Beverly with her back to the door, three feet away. Her chubby, dimpled buttocks were crevassed by a large intergluteal fold that extended well above the indentions of her upper coccyx. She had a large, red, oblong birth mark on the left cheek of her behind. It was in the shape of a crescent.

"The mark of the Devil!" Margaret thought to herself, in horror.

Beverly began walking toward her bed, the play of her gluteal muscles was accentuated and highlighted by the cast of shadows thrown by the whale oil lamp. As she padded barefoot on the hardwood floor she allowed the thin, cotton night shirt to fall over her shoulders and down to her knees as she climbed onto the four poster bed and extinguished the light.

The following day Eliza escorted Elizabeth and Margaret to morning services where they were received with aplomb. Eliza had gone on to her own church and would be back at Judge Bacon's house in time to cook lunch for the sisters-in-law.

Beverly had dressed, but not yet eaten. She took coffee from the steaming vessel and walked to the living room, surveying the large parlor before sitting down on the leather upholstered sofa. Atop the coffee table facing her she noticed a large photo album. She had not seen it sitting on the coffee table previously.

Carefully, Beverly had told Elizabeth and Margaret that she was skipping church; she was enigmatic and tight lipped in her religious beliefs. The Custer women appeared to be unconcerned that Beverly avoided religious social occasions. Oddly, Beverly thought, there was no animosity among Libbie and Margie when she had carefully lied, saying that she was ill in order to decline the invitation to attend revival.

The coffee was very strong and she crushed the coffee grounds between her crooked, white teeth – crooked from impacted wisdom teeth that were crowding them forward. Beverly placed the cup upon the coffee table and opened up the photo album, it was leather bound and contained many stark, silvery black and white photographs. What she beheld was shocking.

There, in the photographs before her were a half dozen Negro soldiers, dressed in Union Army Civil War era uniforms. They were kneeling, their muzzle loading Lee Enfield rifles, complete with bayonets affixed, were held upright, with the rifle butts planted on the floor.

The photo had been shot in a studio and there was a painted background image behind the kneeling figures. The imagery covered the entire background setting; it was one of murderous bayonet fighting between Rebels and a Colored Regiment.

Standing behind the Negro soldiers was a white woman, completely naked but for a masquerade mask. It was a French Renaissance mask made of black ruffled lace and black braid. It had a large black ostrich plume secured to the right side of the mask. The mask completely covered the upper part of the face.

As Beverly studied the photograph, she was stunned to recognize the white woman as Libbie Custer. Beverly began turning the pages, her shock and surprise were overcome with curiosity. The woman in the photos continued to stand, in various poses that emphasized her beauty and physique, as the Negro soldiers all about her performed lewd acts with one another.

All of the Negro soldiers were heavily endowed with massive male appendages. The masked Libbie looked on, with a Mona Lisa type enigmatic smile radiating from the petite, perfectly formed mouth.

The sound of someone mounting the steps of the front porch prompted Beverly to place the photo album back upon the coffee table, making sure to place it exactly as she had found it – as though she had not touched it.

Chapter Twelve
The Battle for Beecher's Island

"WHY HASN'T ROMAN NOSE led an attack?" asked Custer. There was an edge in the tone of his voice which conveyed nervousness and incertitude. "His braves are being scythed down like wheat."

"Don't know, Boy General," responded Bloody Knife. "Maybe White Bull make Big Magic, maybe something go wrong, don't know."

"Ah!" exclaimed the Yellow Hair. "I think I see him. Bring to me the golden bullet and get it to me quickly!"

"Here! Boy General. Take bullet!" responded Bloody Knife, who studied the Yellow Hair as Custer continued growing more nervous and agitated. He fumbled as he unloaded the big repeating rifle, ejecting one bullet at a time.

"There! There now!" exclaimed Custer. "I'll insert the golden bullet and with luck I'll get a hit on Roman

Nose. He'll be a moving target and over a mile away. At least the wind hasn't kicked up. I'll be shooting at maximum elevation, he's still going to be moving rapidly, and it will be a one in a million lucky shot if I hit him!"

"Just be close in your aim, General," joined in Gladstone, with his British accent, "and the magic will work the rest of it."

"Boy General, if kill Roman Nose, how we get war bonnet?" asked Bloody Knife. "Place heap full bad Injuns!"

"I have to kill him first. One thing at a time, Bloody Knife. I could do it if he wasn't moving, but this is going to be one lucky shot. If I miss, we'll have to start over from scratch," replied Custer, adding, "be quiet now."

Custer had the rifle resting on a sand filled bag, he was lying down, one leg was straight and the other bent. The rifle sling was wrapped tightly around his left upper arm, almost to the point of cutting off circulation.

The large, cream colored straw cowboy hat he wore was pulled down low, to shield the eyepiece of the rifle scope from the late afternoon sun that shone from behind. A horsefly landed on the left side of the former general's face, sweat trickled as the fly drew blood.

Custer remained immobile, motionless, his mind was one with his rifle. The rifle had become an extension of him. His right cheek was melded into the rifle stock, his right eye focused unblinkingly through the scope onto the tall figure mounted on the magnificent white mare; the figure with the war bonnet.

Roman Nose rode back and forth in front of five thousand mounted warriors, they were within rifle range of the special attack force, which fired carefully, yet hit nothing. The mounted braves filled the river canyon, one hundred abreast and fifty ranks deep.

At the crest of the hill abutting the canyon hundreds of young Indian women rode bareback, shouting encouragement to their husbands. Their shiny, raven black hair fell to their waists. Most of these women rode naked in the heat of the day and were small breasted. They were amply hipped and the size of their tanned thighs was exaggerated as they pressed against the horses' flanks.

Suddenly a bugle call sounded and a surprisingly effective suppressive fire erupted from the flanking slope, the rifle fire was carefully aimed and sustained. It was at this time that the mounted warriors rushed forward as a whole, led by Roman Nose.

A metal storm of rifle fire exploded from the sandbar/island as the phalanx of mounted men hurtled forward, untouched by bullets as they neared the water's edge. The shrill yells and war whooping was suffocated by the fusillade of rifle fire that erupted in response.

The rapid motion of the tiny figures visible through the rifle scope was a scene of chaos, as Custer nudged the rifle in minute increments to keep Roman Nose within the sight picture.

"Not going to be a good shot," Custer spoke to himself, as he saw Roman Nose and the first rank of one hundred warriors begin riding through the five-inch shallow water. Spray was thrown high into the air as the unshod ponies kicked up the spume. Still none of the warriors had been hit. The power of the war bonnet mesmerized the Boy General, he knew he had to have it more than anything else in the world.

"They lookin' rat purty good, Jimmy Carl," spat the filthy blond haired man in reeking, unwashed clothes. This man spoke as he watched the action unfold through a telescopic spy glass.

"That's a Roger Slodjer, Lester. Them Cheyennes an' Sioux is fo' sho' lernin' the tricks o' the trade! Why, with that thar suppressive far layin' down on them Yanks, an the magic of that war bonnet that Roman Nose is a wearin', why, we'll have that island in the blink of an eye!" this man held a large, brass artillery bugle at his side. Both men were standing on the ridge overlooking the scene of the attack.

"Sound the cease fire, Jimmy boy. Contact is made," replied the unshaven blond haired man.

The greasy, unbathed white man placed the bugle to his cracked lips and sounded the cease fire. Instantly the suppressive fire was lifted.

"Now looky there! That's what I call fire discipline an' proper response to orders!" shouted Jimmy Carl to Lester. He leaned forward on his McClellan saddle and guffawed, "Yaaaaaaahooooo!!!!"

"Yore hot damn rat it sho' nuff is!" seconded Lester with bombastic aplomb.

"Easy," Custer whispered, applying steadily increasing trigger squeeze, "not going to be a good..." *BAM*! came the report of the rifle. The recoil again startled the Yellow Hair from his deep concentration. Custer carefully tried to reacquire the sight picture through the twenty power telescopic sight. What he saw was Roman Nose clenching his lower right side, near the appendix, he was wheeling his horse around.

The entire front rank of mounted warriors was now being unseated, and the following ranks were being swept by murderous rifle fire. Their horses were tripping over the fallen mounts of the ranks ahead of them and the carnage was piling up.

Custer followed Roman Nose through the telescopic sight and saw a fist sized hole gaping from the right kidney area of Roman Nose's back.

Still, the attack continued. Dismounted Cheyenne and Sioux ran on foot at full pace through the shallow water, some wore loin clouts of varying lengths and colors. But in the heat of the late summer, many had foregone any type of clothing whatsoever, other than moccasins and ammunition bags with wide shoulder straps slung over their broad, sun tanned shoulders. Most of these cartridge cases were military in origin, from both the Union and Confederate Armies.

The Sioux and Cheyenne women watched in horror as their husbands took bullets in wash board stomachs and meat loafed chests. The braves roared like wounded mountain lions in rage as they twisted back and forth furiously, clawing at the bullet holes in their torsos. Their war painted faces were pointing upward toward the sky as they screamed and cursed.

Dozens of tattooed, painted Cheyenne and Sioux had stormed into and were mixed with the defenders. Primitive, savage hand to hand fighting ensued all over the island as the surviving attackers exhausted their ammunition and went after the defenders bare handed, screaming as they ran with their arms in front of them and hands open, in the throttling position. Their faces were contorted into visages of the utmost antipathy, made more hideous by the war paint that smeared their acrimonious features.

High above on the ridges sweat ran down lithe, tanned backs. The salty sweat trickled into the crevasses of the brown, tanned behinds of the women mounted on horseback. The naked women saw the attack disintegrate and the survivors retreat, abandoning the dozens who had penetrated the island and were increasingly having to deal with revolver and rifle fire barehanded.

Lieutenant Beecher found himself facing a murderous opponent, a naked six-foot two-inch-tall Cheyenne who came at him with a butcher knife. Beecher drew his own knife and the two locked in mortal combat. The free hand of either was clenched on the wrist of the other as they stood, straining against each other in a test of strength. Sweat flew from the length of the naked Cheyenne's uncircumcised, swinging penis as his testicles drew in from the exertion of fighting his smaller, determined opponent.

"Hold him, Beecher! I think I've got a shot!" shouted the almost helpless Forsyth. Forsyth held the big Colt with both hands, aiming carefully at the head of the naked man. The hammer was cocked back and he pulled the trigger, hearing a loud "click" that connoted a bad primer cap.

"Damn! Misfire!" shouted Forsyth, pulling back the hammer and rotating the cylinder to the next chamber.

"Shoot him!" shouted the desperately struggling Beecher. "He has the better of me!"

The brave kicked Beecher solidly in the testicles, doubling the lieutenant over, then, almost in the same motion he violently swung his adversary about, yanking the officer's head back by the hair as he placed the razor sharp edge of the knife to the hairline.

Major Forsyth fired instinctively, not having time to aim properly in the split second available to him. The bullet smashed into the sternum of Lieutenant Beecher, spiraling through and exiting into the steel cabled stomach of the warrior, who let go of Beecher and looked down at the bullet that was partially exposed from his rock hard abdominal wall.

He pulled the hot slug from his muscle and hurled it at Forsyth, striking him in the head and knocking him senseless. Seeing all of his companions fleeing for their lives, the brave spat tobacco juice on the face of the prostrate Lieutenant Beecher and ran for the reeds lining the river bank.

A mile away on higher ground, a different scene was unfolding.

"Got him!" swore Custer. "A bad hit, not a clean shot, but he's not long for this earth."

"Boy General sure?" responded Bloody Knife, "I see man on horse turn aroun', but so far away I can't tell nothing."

"You got him, General!" Gladstone assured. "The golden bullet cannot miss. Did you see how the entire attack faltered the moment that you shot Roman Nose with the golden bullet?"

"He's hit, and he'll head back to his village. He's dying, probably," Custer speculated in a saturnine, withdrawn manner. It appeared to Bloody Knife and Gladstone that the Yellow Hair was deeply troubled by the wound he had inflicted on the brave man.

"What will they do with the war bonnet once he's dead?" asked Custer.

"Bloody Knife not sure. Maybe it stay with Roman Nose, what Cheyenne do," continued Bloody Knife, "is place fallen warrior in tree, wrapped in skins and with all things belong to him."

"Listen," responded Custer. "We can't wait until darkness, we've got to move now; we have to get that war bonnet before it falls into the hands of some other rascal."

"You're bloody well right, General!" seconded Gladstone. "Time is of the essence!"

With Professor Gladstone's bold exclamation, the two white men and Arikawa were frantically making final preparations to embark on a quest to secure the war bonnet of Roman Nose.

"We have to get the war bonnet fast, before Hanwi rests and the moon wanes," explained Professor Gladstone to the Boy General.

"So," responded Custer, "if by the last night of the full moon we don't have the war bonnet, the magic will be lost?"

The response was not lost on the Englishman, as the Yellow Hair fell back to packing his gear onto his horse and mule.

"Yes, General," agreed the magician and Professor of Anthropology, "but only for a period of time. Unless we can procure it immediately, you will have to commune with the Sioux deity, Hanwi. Goddess of the Moon.

"You have to be joking," responded Custer, his voice was acidic, he said this as he was securing his rifle in the broad leather scabbard, made unusually wide to accommodate the Berdan telescopic sight.

The Englishman stopped what he was doing and approached the Boy General, his pale skin beneath his red beard stubble reddened under the intense effort to control his temper.

"Now, you listen to me, you pompous ass! I am a magician, yes! But I also have a doctorate degree in the study of your Native American nations and tribes, their cultures, their histories, their languages and their religions! If it were not for me, we would not have made it this close to getting what we want. I never joke, General!"

"When Roman Nose die, we must find his tree, before Hanwi sleep," interrupted Bloody Knife.

"Always it comes back to Hanwi!" responded Custer. "You have mentioned Hanwi twice."

"Hanwi is Goddess of the Moon, Sioux Goddess. Hanwi the Accursed," replied Bloody Knife. "She Sioux, but Cheyenne fear her."

The blowing of human bone whistles and pounding of war drums, accompanied by the wailing of women sounded the ominous fate of Roman Nose to the two white men and Arikawa.

"Wish I could have got him with a clean shot," the Boy General said, it came off sounding apologetic, and sincere.

The Yellow Hair mounted his horse, removing his hat and inserting an eagle feather into his hair to make him appear as an Indian at distance. His companions did the same.

At the besieged island in the middle of the river, other events were unfolding.

Chapter Thirteen
Escape from Beecher's Island

THE BADLY WOUNDED Major Forsyth assayed the situation grimly before him. Thankfully, he thought, no one had seen him accidentally shoot Lieutenant Beecher, who slipped in and out of consciousness. If word got out, he knew it could ruin his career. Beecher had powerful family connections back East, and his aunt, the famous novelist Harriet Beecher Stowe would see to it that Forsyth paid with his career for the callous act of manslaughter.

"I need a volunteer!" shouted Forsyth suddenly, then he added; "I need two! I need two men to head back to Colonel Bankhead at Fort Wallace and lead the Buffalo Soldiers to us!"

"That's impossible," postulated Gannt. "This whole country is swarming with Cheyenne and Sioux. And now that Roman Nose has been hit, they are going to be thicker than flies on shit!"

"Who is the bastard that shot Roman Nose, anyway?" asked the wounded Major Forsyth through clenched, uneven snaggled teeth, stained to a rich, dark brown from a lifetime of chewing tobacco.

Instantly a chorus of "I did! I did!" rebounded through the camp.

"Well, we'll take a vote on it later. Or maybe draw straws. Anyhow," continued Sandy Forsyth, to the two volunteers who had appeared in the darkness, "you two have to backtrack one hundred miles to Fort Wallace and lead Colonel Bankhead's Buffalo Soldiers back out here to help us kill off the rest of them! Not only that! This horse flesh is going rancid. I've got a dozen bucket loads of it buried in the gravel to keep it cooled off, but it's still not fit for consumption. Despite that, the horse flesh is almost all that we have to eat. Take this letter with you."

A young man, Jack Stillwell, was accompanied by a much older, frontier veteran who went by the name Pierre Trudeau. They removed their boots and placed them in their ruck sacks. The duo left the island surreptitiously in the darkness, using stealth. It was surmised that the removal of the boots would imply that the two adventurers were Indian by virtue of the foot prints.

Hours later in early dawn and miles away from the island fortress, Stillwell glanced furtively from side to side, he looked slowly, taking in everything and discounting nothing. He resumed low crawling through the knee-deep buffalo grass to the edge of a sparse wood line, then peered through the thorny branches of wild rose bushes that grew opportunistically beneath cottonwood and post oak trees alongside a seasonal creek.

The creek had gone dry some time ago. Sage brush interspersed with the occasional juniper also grew a small distance from the periodic source of water. Many of these junipers stood skeletally, having been scorched during lightening induced range fires.

Nineteen-year-old Jack Stillwell had lost contact with the older man, the sixty-year-old Pete Trudeau, whom he'd chosen to take with him on the desperate hundred-mile escape back into Kansas. The goal was to reach Fort Wallace and guide the reinforcement element of Buffalo Soldiers back to the understrength Forsyth survivors. Then the combined force could annihilate the thousands of hostile aboriginals that threatened to overrun the besieged island fortress. That was the plan, be it as it may.

It was the gunfire that had drawn the attention of Stillwell, who peered through the concealment of the viciously thorned wild rose bushes.

Clouds of white smoke billowed into the atmosphere from the out of control stage coach fires in front of him. Stillwell watched impotently, unwilling to intervene in the butchery taking place. A dozen stage coaches were burning, the mules which pulled them having been taken by the Cheyenne.

Some of the coaches lay on their sides, the wheels facing the sky were continuing to spin lazily. Other stage coaches of the light celerity fast fliers lay on their bellies – their wheels having flown off as they cartwheeled out of control, spewing passengers and luggage all over the immediate terrain.

The nineteen-year-old scout watched as unmounted braves armed with rifles, shotguns, lances and coup sticks approached a lone stage coach passenger. Adolescent males, out for their first kill, used clubs made of dried saplings and kitchen knives acquired through barter and raids on frontier homesteads. Three dozen youths had circled one of the surviving members of the burning coaches.

They carelessly approached the passenger, eager to swing the clubs, expecting to break outstretched arms that sought to deflect the bludgeons as had the other survivors. Many of the passengers had been badly mangled when the main body of mounted warriors eventually overtook the fleeing stage coaches.

The passenger was one of the few surviving members of the twelve stage coaches that were overtaken when the Cheyenne and Sioux had obliterated the massive escort of Buffalo Soldiers. The defiant traveler pulled a hefty .44 caliber Colt Dragoon Revolver from beneath his vest and began shooting from nearly point blank range, hitting six of the inexperienced braves in the chest and causing the others to back away, like wolves who have a ram at bay, but fear to go in for the kill. They stood as a menacing threat from a safer distance, their lithe abdomens taught, their chests rising and falling in anticipation.

The Colt Model 1848 Percussion Army Revolver was a relic from the post Mexican War era, heavier and less wieldy than the newer generation Colt Model 1860 that the Dragoon had preceded in development. Nevertheless, the obsolete but effective Model 1848 continued to be widely popular and maintained a devoted following.

The doomed survivor was wearing the apparel of a man of means. He appeared to be dressed as a river boat dandy, like some sort of Diamond Jim. Standing of medium height and of stocky build, his tailored clothes gave him the appearance of a river boat gambler. His face, shadowed by a large planter's sun hat, belied the soft living style implied by the clothing; a long dueling scar ran at a downward angle from the forehead above the left eye and across the right side of the face. Even without the disfiguring facial scar, the passenger's face bore a sinister appearance. The tailored clothing clung tightly to the man's skin, emphasizing rather hiding his hard, muscular build.

The miscast dandy holstered the spent revolver but did not relinquish his glaring, threatening stare at his antagonists. The besieged passenger tore off his white silk shirt and wrapped it around his right forearm, then using the wrapped arm he pulled a murderous Bowie knife from the outboard side of his Wellington black leather boot. Keeping the overturned stage coach to his back, the passenger made feinting, thrusting motions with the Bowie knife at his hesitant foes, who would advance, and step back with each thrust of the heavy fighting knife.

Here and there the report of a revolver signaled a passenger's preemptive move to deny the hordes of Cheyenne boys who were barely into their teens from the object of their passion. Stillwell saw one passenger leap up and begin running, only to be brought down by the blast of a muzzle loading Brown Bess musket loaded with birdshot. This far west, the Brown Bess was sold to the Indians by Mexican traders, and it was plentiful.

The British Brown Bess had been introduced by the Mexicans to the Comanches, who traded them to the Cheyenne. It was one of those weapons that was built on a proven design and had staying power. The Mexican Army under Santa Anna had overwhelmed the defenders of the Alamo and were armed with the Brown Bess musket when they did it. By 1838 all of the Brown Bess muskets were being produced with a modern percussion cap ignition system. The large, seventy-five caliber smooth bore was conducive to firing buck shot and bird shot, as well as ball. Furthermore, the Brown Bess was far more accurate out to a hundred yards than aficionados of rifles would let on.

Dozens of young teens, overseen by their mounted adult supervisors were on the wounded man before he could cut his wrists. Easing further back into the dense green sage brush and clusters of plains prickly pear cactus, Stillwell began inching away from the slaughter.

Stillwell remembered in the flash of a moment the events preceding his and Trudeau's escape attempt from the sandbar/island on which Lieutenant Beecher had died.

"I've gotta have me two runners, to get back to Ft. Wallace and get Bankhead's Buffalo Soldiers out here!" Major Forsyth had stated emphatically, as the hastily defended camp site had been nearly overwhelmed by thousands of Comanche and Cheyenne warriors. The teenaged Stillwell was the first one of the besieged members of the special attack force to volunteer to make a run for the only fort in the region, Fort Wallace, a hundred miles away.

Stillwell had been urged by Forsyth to choose an additional scout to go with him. Without hesitation, Stillwell had replied:

"Trudeau! Let me have Trudeau!"

Pierre Trudeau had been captured during the Civil War five years previously during the Battle of Sabine Pass, when the Union gunboat he was guiding as a scout was badly damaged and forced to run aground and surrender. Pierre 'Old Pete" Trudeau was sent to the Confederate prisoner of war camp at Galveston Island, Texas to sit out the remainder of the war.

Galveston Island was twenty-seven miles long and no more than three miles wide; an unusually stable barrier island which at its closest point to the mainland reached to about a mile off of the Texas coast. At its highest point, it was only twenty feet above sea level. Sand dunes were the dominant feature surrounding the prison camp. Sea purslane, morning glory and panicum were the dominant, low growing species that took root in the nutrient poor soil. The taller growing coastal scrub and groves of evergreen live oak with their low hanging branches were numerous further away from the stockade.

The seasonal foul weather and occasional bombardment from hurricanes affected the shape of the island and it was swept by strong currents. Treacherous rip tides made access to the mainland problematical, and escape was extremely dangerous. Some had tried, their screams carried back to the island on subtropical wind as hammerhead sharks fed lazily.

Yet the adventurer – at fifty-five years of age had managed to escape, and if nothing more than an adventuresome Gulliver in his other pursuits, he was, nonetheless an expert when it came to evading the greedy, jealous, snapping jaws of death.

The unsettled Trudeau – old by the standards of the day, remembered the barking of the Bordeaux dogs when they caught the scent of the trail of him and his companions. Two dozen or so of the one-hundred-twenty-pound fighting dogs had been set to the trail by their Rebel handlers – lithe sinewy men who wore beige straw planter's hats, and billowy, loose fitting white long sleeved shirts.

These airy shirts had suspenders straining against them which supported grey, woven cloth trousers. The shirts were plastered with sweat to the backs of the dog handlers. The handlers ran barefooted as they were pulled by their leashed, barking dogs. They were armed with muzzle loading twelve-gauge double barrel shotguns.

Further behind the dog handlers came the riflemen, hundreds of them. Spread out abreast, in two ranks, they were not dressed uniformly and many wore the clothing of farmers and share croppers. They were armed with Pattern 1853 Lee Enfield rifled muskets; a state of the art muzzle loading weapon produced in England.

The Lee Enfield was the mainstay of both armies throughout the Civil War. A British blockade runner had, several months before delivered thousands of these to the Confederate Port Authorities in Houston.

The barking, growling, and difficult to control dogs closed the distance rapidly toward the dozen escapees. One of the inmates had badly twisted his ankle and was in danger of being left behind by the fleeing group of prisoners.

"My ankle! I think it's broke!" screamed Reynolds, a psychopathic killer. Reynolds was a Union deserter who, through some miscarriage of justice, had ended up on Galveston Island instead of where he belonged – at the end of a rope.

"It is not broken," assured Culbertson, a captured Union doctor and medical quack who had carelessly been caught smothering his patients with a wet towel. "It is but a sprain, albeit a sprain that's pretty bad," after a moment's pause the doctor added, "and propitious!" Alarmed at the closing proximity of the baying mastiffs, Culbertson studied the swollen ankle with appreciation.

"What are we going to do? The dogs, they are drawing near!" shouted the agitated Reynolds, wrapping a swathe torn from his shirt around the lower extremity, swollen five times its normal size. "They are almost upon us!"

"No! The question is what are *you* going to do?!" rebutted John Warner. "*We* are getting out of here!"

"The man has a point!" chided Culbertson at the distraught Reynolds. *"You are dog food!* By the time they finish rending and tearing you to pieces, we will be to the other end of the island!

Now, let's get away from him before the dogs overtake us all!" shouted Culbertson to Warner and the others.

Trudeau cursed that the Rebels did not use the same dogs as most civilized white men did. He remembered the owner of the dogs of Galveston Island, remembered the Frenchman who had taken the pack of fighting dogs from his Louisiana plantation when he fled the Union occupation of the state.

The Dogue de Bordeaux was an ancient breed, having its origins in the war dogs that accompanied all of the

Roman Legions. With its small eyes widely spaced in its monstrous skull, the oversized, over-toothed lower jaw protruded past the upper plate giving it the power to crush through flesh and bone alike.

The skin hung loosely from the face and the fur was short and fawn in color. The neck was very thick and powerful, and the shoulders broad. The muscles rippled under the loose skin of the dogs as they closed with their prey. They growled and barked incessantly as they ran, panting. Loose strands of slobber flew several feet from the overdeveloped mouths in the humid air as the fighting dogs salivated while chasing their quarry.

The abandoned fugitive, the others knew, would halt the dogs for thirty minutes or so as they devoured him alive. But this was not the intent of the abandoned Reynolds, who by means of grabbing onto the trunks of small trees and other sub-tropical vegetation managed to hobble along, favoring the non-injured ankle heavily.

"Hey! Wait for me! I can make it! Slow down, you can't just leave me here!" shouted the Union deserter, murderer and sexual deviant.

"We have to put as much distance between us and that cripple as we can!" panted the only German in the group, a notorious Union turncoat thief and cut-throat; a miscreant named Barbie.

"That son of a bitch won't stop his yelling and is going to bring the mastiffs upon us!" added Trudeau, looking behind him, over his left shoulder and seeing the stumbling Reynolds literally hopping on one leg while trying to keep up.

Suddenly a dog burst through thick undergrowth without warning, seizing Reynolds by the calf of his crippled leg, and held onto it tenaciously, growling and digging his teeth into hard flesh as he shook his massive head viciously.

"That will slow him down!" ejaculated Warner, while shouting, "Split up and run for it! Every man for himself!" as the last words flew from his lips three more of the massive dogs leaped upon the desperately struggling Reynolds, who was fighting the first mastiff like a madman. The huge dogs knocked him face forward into the sandy soil which for a split second muffled his screams.

But now the aging adventurer of dubious birth was in a different world far removed from any subtropical island prison he had ever escaped.

The grasslands of the Great Plains were enormous, kept in check by gigantic bison herds and numerous range fires. Bison were not all that shared these ranges; grouse, ground squirrel, mule and white-tailed deer, antelope and wolves in particular were in abundance. The territory got its name from the Spanish noun "Colorado," meaning "colored, or red."

In the distance peaked mountains arose, and the grasslands were divided by the red colored waters of the Colorado River. Although the Rocky Mountain range seemed but a day's ride away, judging distances could be problematical in the Great American Desert.

Colorado was a huge territory; the Rocky Mountains leaped to over fourteen thousand feet toward the sky from the entire western one third of the territory, and several smaller chains were dangled across the region culminating in magnificent mountain ranges. The temperature ranged from below zero in the winter, to over a hundred degrees in the summer. Rainfall was unpredictable, and could vary widely, between too much to too little.

Suddenly Trudeau's senses had been electrified to keen perception by the thrashing sound behind him. Rolling from his stomach onto his back, he maneuvered the big Spencer repeating rifle in the same fluid motion, sitting up and aiming into the direction of the commotion that emanated from the thicket in front of his straining eyes.

A black cavalryman stepped forth, one of the few survivors of the scores of Buffalo Soldiers that had been the escort of the doomed stagecoach convoy when the other four-hundred-fifty cavalrymen had turned about to face the pursuing Cheyenne and Sioux. The Buffalo Soldier was holding both hands to his neck. Blood was streaming onto his flannel long handle shirt; he took two strides and stumbled onto the ground, breaking his fall with his knees and left hand. He looked up at Trudeau without recognition and his voice was a gurgle that hissed cat like from a massive knife slash across his neck-from ear to ear.

The Buffalo Soldier was one of the lucky few who had made it without being caught until the last minute, he was one of the thousands of courageous, ebony cavalrymen who without questioning orders sacrificed his life in the service of his country. He, like so many of his African American fellow soldiers had been a member of the Tenth Cavalry Regiment which was nearly constantly in the field.

The Buffalo Soldiers comprised the elite Tenth Cavalry Regiment of Negro soldiers; specialists who were regarded with superstitious fear and hated by the Native American tribes of the plains. Although the Buffalo Soldiers and the Native Americans respected each other, this respect was based on mutual fear and caution of one another. Mercy and compassion did not exist in their vocabulary.

Trudeau quickly and silently slid into a slight dip in the ground and watched with consternation as a monstrosity of a man stepped out of the undergrowth and peered cautiously from side to side, bending a post oak tree branch away from his face and releasing it as he cautiously stepped forward. He then directed his gaze to the miserable heap that lay before him.

The frontiersman watched in motionless silence as the Brule Sioux, naked but for a loin cloth, kneeled behind the man and savagely yanked his head back by the thick, curly black hair; there was yet life left in the fading color of the brown eyes as the Sioux put the edge of the short skinning knife to the base of the soldier's full hairline. The brave pulled back even harder on the hair and after making a small incision, pulled the scalp violently back - tearing the scalp-lock loose with a slick, wet sucking sound. The sound could be compared to ripping the skin with great force from a slain rabbit.

The Brule Sioux was a big man, standing at nearly seven feet. His head was shaven but for a single large scalp lock that formed near the top, and off center to the back of his head. This was tightly woven into a braid and reinforced with brightly colored strips of cloth. Stuck into the braid were two feathers of a golden eagle, the lower half of each feather was dyed red, signifying he had taken wounds twice while delivering blows to enemies with a coup stick.

Although his skin was darkly pigmented, the hue was further aggrandized by long exposure to the sun while on horseback. His face was painted solid ochre above the hooked nose, and alabaster down to the thick neck, from which the trapezius muscles extended onto the shoulders in bold relief. His eyebrows were shaven and the eyelashes plucked.

Oversized hoop earrings made of gold adorned either earlobe and they swayed with the motion of his head as he looked about again, and then licked the coppery tasting blood from the knife blade. The great swell of pectoral muscles played under the white painted circles that adorned the warrior's chest as he went to work, dismembering the feet from the ankles of the still living man, who groped through the thick grass and clawed into the hard earth, trying to pull himself toward sixty-year-old Pierre Trudeau. The enlisted scout tried not to breathe - so intense was his determination to remain unobserved.

From further back in the darkness that obscured the still grasses, the sound of clumsy crashing through the vegetation startled the big brave. The unanticipated pandemonium alerted and caused him to wheel about-face with lightning speed into a crouch. He half stood, crouching, bent at the waist and knees with his knife held far forward in front of him at chest level. His braided ponytail swung violently with the suddenness of the movement. The gigantic man hissed like a large lizard between his filed teeth as his passion was interrupted - just as he prepared to disjoint an arm at the shoulder of the dying soldier.

Trudeau saw the play of powerful back muscles underneath the magical designs painted on the Brule's back, and saw the Goliath-like warrior step like a mountain goat into the foliage with a pronounced limp. On the right foot the brave wore a leather moccasin adorned with a design of beads, but in the place of a left foot there was, Trudeau discerned, not an entire foot, but a vestigial remnant of a foot, as though the brave had lost part of the appendage through accident. That's what he hoped he saw; the darkness, he thought, distorted the image of the foot and made it appear as though it were a cloven hoof.

Trudeau was preparing to retreat further from the location when suddenly two more Buffalo Soldiers – more survivors from the disastrous stage coach escort, blundered through a prickly pear cactus thicket and began cursing as the barbed needles embedded through clothing and into skin. They chanced into the area where the mutilated soldier lay.

"I've got to stop!" panted one of the Buffalo Soldiers, a short, thin man of perhaps twenty-five years, he was hatless and his thick black hair was covered with cockle burrs. "I've got to catch my breath!" he gasped.

His companion, a soldier of medium height stopped uncertainly, his breath coming in ragged inhalations and expirations, he was wheezing loudly and leaned forward, placing his hands above his knees as he caught his breath.

"We can't tarry long, Philip," expostulated the wheezing soldier, they are scouring the range; they are everywhere! Look! There's Burris! What the hell happened to him?"

Without warning, the Brule sprung like a goat onto the two unarmed soldiers, ripping murderously with the skinning knife, its diminutive size belying its lethality. Quickly the ensconced Trudeau took advantage of the distraction to carefully make his egress from the melee.

"Which is worse?" Trudeau thought as he began to increase his distance, jogging now at a slow pace, "Galveston Island or this place of demons!" The veteran frontiersman froze at the sound of the hammer of a rifle making a distinctive click-like sound as it was cocked back.

The distinctive click of the hammer of a Spencer repeating rifle locking into the firing position warned the seasoned Indian fighter. He dove to the ground like a rifleman and saw a figure aiming the rifle almost directly at him. It was gloomy in the penumbral light, but Trudeau glimpsed an angry, unshaven face behind the rifle sight.

"Don't shoot!" hissed Trudeau through clenched, unbrushed teeth as loudly as he dared to. He ran the risk of alerting the keen ears that listened for any sound of fugitive soldiers throughout the darkening haunts of the eerie prairie.

The flash of black powder propellant temporarily blinded the old frontiersman as he heard a heinous cry from behind him and wheeling about saw the half-footed man standing with both hands to his shattered face; a long, mournful moan issued from the bloody orifice.

Before the gigantic Sioux warrior could recover his senses, Stillwell had recklessly dropped the rifle to the ground and drawn a long, murderous Arkansas Toothpick; in reality a dirk reminiscent of the secondary weapons carried by medieval fighting men.

This dirk was made of an alloy containing a large percentage of sterling silver. Intent on delivering the disemboweling thrust, Stillwell lunged at the formidable interloper, who avoided the thrust with a twisting motion of his muscular torso.

"Gonna get at you!" cried Stillwell, unconsciously abandoning all pretense of maintaining silence.

The dirk narrowly missed the vital organs and skidded in a grating movement along the rib cage, opening up a heinous gash. When the gigantic, half footed man reached to staunch the fine threads of blood, Stillwell severed the arm from the shoulder, with an arcing motion of the Arkansas Toothpick. The Brule knocked Stillwell senseless with a swiping motion of his remaining hand, causing the nineteen-year-old to drop his dagger as he reeled backwards and fell. Jack Stillwell rebounded and using the arm as a bludgeon, desperately tried to beat the warrior to the ground with it. He swung the severed, spasoming arm repeatedly across the mangled face, his knuckles whitening from the iron grip that he exerted on the pulseless wrist.

"Arrrrrrrrrgggggghhhhhh!" shouted the towering Sioux warrior as the frontier scout felt the humerus arm bone splinter into a compound fracture when he swung the amputated upper extremity into the warrior's skull.

The xenomorph seized the youth by the Adam's apple of his ox-like neck using his remaining hand, and as he opened his ruined mouth he yelled loudly once more in an effort to alert others to his whereabouts.

It was a mistake he realized too late as the older man with a Spencer shoved the muzzle of the barrel into his gaping mouth. Trudeau pulled the trigger, initiating a muffled detonation that spewed skull fragments and brain matter in a red spray forty feet into the night air and across the surrounding vegetation.

"Die!" shouted Pierre Trudeau, who extracted the spent cartridge from the breech of the Spencer with the motion of the lever and reloaded another round in the same motion, and with the thumb of his right hand cocked back the hammer.

The Sioux with the half foot continued to stubbornly stand, his hand feeling blindly before him, opening and closing mindlessly as it reflexively sought purchase. He took two steps forward and his legs gave out from under him. As the baleful bleating continued from his throat, the jaw was all that remained of the head. The bleating devolved into a gurgle as blood was sucked into the lungs with each autonomic inhalation.

Stillwell stood over the felled warrior, listening with tense expectancy. Behind the convulsing man-thing he could hear the scuff of moccasined feet on the dried grass some distance out – he could not be sure how far in the purple gloom. The fugitive discerned branches and dry brush being snapped underfoot, and these intimations of sound to his ringing ears insinuated that this was a death trap. He half drew the big Colt from the leather holster at his side, then slid it back in as he faced his newly found companion.

Trudeau flashed back in a synopsis of memory to his escape from Galveston Island; to how the mastiffs did not all remain with the abandoned Reynolds, but fully half of them continued in pursuit of the escaped fugitives even as Reynolds had screamed at the top of his lungs for help as he was torn to pieces alive.

Pierre Trudeau had clung doggedly behind the fleeing Corporal Barbie as the big German tore through the live oak branches, bleeding freely as they lacerated his skin which was dearth of protective clothing in the suffocating subtropical heat. The sweat mixed with blood ran down the German's acne scarred back. The private saw too, how the sweat glistened on the back of the scalp of Barbie as he fled headlong through the skin ripping foliage; his hair was closely shorn.

That was not all he remembered; he reflected in a flash of memory that he stopped for a moment to pick up a large coral rock and smash it with all of his strength into the back of Barbie's head. Trudeau knocked Barbie unconscious in the pinnacle act of self-preservation.

"To the Devil with you, Barbie!" cried Trudeau as he stepped around the prostate figure of his former companion. "You told me once yourself, never to trust anyone!" with that treacherous proclamation the Union Army scout made for the raft which waited at the aqueous, darkened shoreline. His escape was almost guaranteed by the sacrifice of the big German, who regained his senses as the mastiffs leapt upon him.

The cries of Barbie as he fought a dozen of the dogs added impetus to the adrenaline fueled efforts of

Trudeau. The fifty-five-year old's breath came in wheezing gasps as he waded, making sloshing sounds into the warm, saline water. Pierre Trudeau leaned into, and pushed the diminutive raft constructed of flotsam into the tide. Slowly the water deepened and as it reached his abdomen he thrust himself aboard.

"Wait for me!" shouted Culbertson, wading into the water as rifle shots rang out in the distance and screams could be heard. Using a wooden plank as a paddle, the determined Pierre Trudeau made distance between himself and the following Culbertson. Trudeau was assisted in his endeavor by the favorable tide.

Suddenly a tall, black dorsal fin knifed past his raft, the sail shaped fin made a rippling sound as it cut a vee through the water which remained as a phosphorescent trail. It was followed by the protuberance of the tip of the tail fin, which barely broke the surface. The shark was headed straight for the power stroking Culbertson, who was swimming like a man possessed and had almost made it to the makeshift raft.

"Lend me your hand!" shouted the Union soldier, extending his arm desperately outward.

"Take this!" retorted the wiry old Union frontiersman and guide, swinging the oar like a bat, and breaking Culbertson's outstretched hand. "Get away from me! Can't you see you're drawing sharks!? Go on! Git!"

Suddenly Culbertson was jerked violently under the oily, agitated surface. Pierre thought he had seen the last of him when suddenly Culbertson reappeared like a cork twenty yards to the left, coughing while gasping frantically for air.

"Help me!" cried the escapee, a pool of blood had begun to add heavily to the inkiness of the dark water. "Help me! *HELP!!!*" pleaded the doctor as he was jerked violently under again, not to resurface for perhaps two minutes. When he came up it was much further away and for the final time, his shouts for help were abruptly cut off in mid-scream as he was dragged under the surface for the final time.

The old survivor Trudeau considered the sacrifices he had made of his friends in order to save his own skin, and he studied the much younger frontiersman standing before him, introspectively masking the speculations of potential treachery from his benign countenance.

"Let's make distance from this accursed field!" urged Trudeau, arriving at his altruistic decision. The tone of his voice betrayed the fear that flowed through his veins like the icy waters of a river fed by snow melt.

Together, they hurried through the ocean of buffalo grass, brush, and prickly pear, half ducking to avoid the thorny branch of an occasional bois de arc tree which sought to snag their clothing. Low flying screech owls swiped at their faces, drawing blood, and grabbed onto folds of clothing, not wanting to let go. Blackberry thorns ripped through trousers as the fugitives made like juggernauts through the surreal, ghostly prairie.

Chapter Fourteen
Custer Steals the War Bonnet

THE DEAFENING QUIETNESS common at the late twilight moments of fading dusk settled like a heavy, suffocating saddle blanket over the hills. Ridges and riparian valleys of the prairie faded into purple penumbra. Succor was not to be found underneath the obscuring gloom which served to occult the myriad plants and stunted trees that survived in the drought punished expanses.

Many of these plants were armed with sharp spines and barbs. Cockle burrs clung tenaciously to the legs and stomachs of the horses and mule, as well as the heavy cloth woven trousers worn by Custer, Gladstone and Bloody Knife.

The trio halted a hundred yards from the village, beneath a knoll covered with juniper trees. Custer remained mounted as he held the reins of his horse, Vic. He was thinking as he looked over to Bloody Knife, then to Gladstone; The Yellow Hair was dubious and uncertain of his next act in the play about to commence.

To the left, off in the distance a desultory fire was maintained on the island. Custer paid that scant mind. His focus was on the Indian village and the location of Roman Nose with the war bonnet.

"You must do exactly as I have explained," reiterated Gladstone. "You will be guided to the tepee in which reposes Roman Nose. Even now his medicine man, White Bull, struggles to retrieve him from hell. Roman Nose yet wears the war bonnet and you must slay him again."

"Are you certain I will not be recognized?" asked Custer. "How will I know my guide?"

"You will be seen, but no notice will be given you. As to your guide," continued Gladstone, "*you will know.*"

Bloody Knife remained silent. His impassive, emotionless expression remained enigmatic and wooden as a cigar store Indian in the ghostly, blanched light of the moon.

"When I take the war bonnet, I don it and I become bullet proof," stated Custer with uncertainty, his statement was pregnant with worry, and with doubt. "You've been correct so far, Gladstone."

"You *must* do as I have instructed, verbatim," reiterated Gladstone. "Bloody Knife and I aren't going anywhere until you return."

The bombination of hundreds of drums carried through the campfire lit night. At times the resonating drum rolls were almost eclipsed by the high pitched shrilling of war flutes fashioned from human thigh bone. The awareness of the pounding drums dominated the auditory sense of the Boy General who was even conscious of the beating of his heart.

The loud clopping step of a metal shod hoof was a perturbation unique to the horses of white men. The clopping would ring out distinctly, and the former general hoped the sound would be blended to some degree into the thundering of Indian war drums which were being answered by drums from Indian camps further away.

Every fiber of his being was alive with adrenaline as his massive war horse, with an innate sense of direction, approached the source of the thrumming war drums. Custer had the alertness which is incumbent upon every adventurer who risks scalp in crossing the Arikaree River.

The Indian village was set up in several large, concentric circles. They were separated according to tribe and nation. The size of the tepees ranged from ten to twenty feet tall. There were thousands of them. They all seemed alike in the pale, anemic wash of the moon.

Custer wore an owl feather in his golden mane of hair, his face was war painted in curious designs very different from those of the American Indians. His horse also wore the esoteric pigment in arcane illustrations all over its massive body.

The former general, atop his massive thousand-pound gelding slowly glided through a thin, low hanging mist of fog and wood smoke that seemed to catch and glow from the rays of the moon. The wisp of fog was thin, and appeared as a dull green nebulosity. As Custer entered the huge village it seemed as though he and his mount were specters out of a Greek tragedy.

All about him braves shiny with sweat danced in the unsteady light of roaring bonfires. The yellow red flames, blue in the center, illuminated a ghastly scene of carnage. Hundreds of horrifically wounded warriors lay on blankets writhing in pain, blood and excrement. Dogs, hundreds of them of all sizes drawn by the scent, sniffed around the blood and lapped it up. They were kicked and struck with sticks by family members.

Despite the sensory bombardment of extraneous stimuli, the Yellow Hair was startled by the close proximity of a small dog barking. Custer looked toward the emanation of the insistent barking, which seemed urgent in its persistence. He looked down to the bare ground at his right, and saw a small dog that was incongruous with the loose packs of large, half wolf dogs that ran about the tepees. The other dogs either seemed not to notice him, or avoided him intentionally, despite their larger size.

"Rosco! Is it you? It can't be!" exclaimed the Boy General, looking upon a little terrier mix. The terrier waved its tail violently in recognition. "So, Gladstone brought you up from hell to be my guide," said the former general, shaken at the sight of his long dead childhood pet.

"Then lead on, Rosco. Discharge your filial duty to me, and when this is done, stay with me, *don't go back.* You will stay with me, Rosco, that is a direct order," reiterated Custer.

The Boy General and the little terrier entered into a small circular area of ground packed hard and void of vegetation, owing to the heavy toll of foot traffic that led to a huge tepee in the center. The large tepee was painted in geometric designs and surrounded by a conglomeration of smaller tepees of varying sizes. These were difficult to differentiate in the ghostly, diaphanous moonlight. The little dog stopped at the entrance to the abode, standing on three legs, the right front leg was lifted and the tail stood straight out.

Custer was playing this risky endeavor one move at a time, and although uncertain of his next move, he dismounted Vic in a fluid motion. He sensed, without knowing why, that the horse would remain. He knelt and petted Rosco, the first time he had done so since he had buried the small rat terrier mix twenty years before.

The dog responded by licking the former general's hands and wagging its tail fiercely, then returning its attention to the faint light; the disperse light that was spilling from the flap of the entrance to the dome shaped, human skinned tent. The Yellow Hair was uncertain what would happen next - unsure if the magical spell incanted by Gladstone could sustain his imperceptibility.

Although he was nervous and uncertain; the cavalry officer was no coward. Risking his life came as naturally to Custer as throwing the dice in a seedy riverfront casino full of cut-throats and thieves in New Orleans. That he was risking his life now, of this he was certain.

Custer knelt as he entered the gigantic tepee. Once inside he stood up and was startled to find himself looking into the contorted, demonic face of a medicine man. The shaman was standing directly in front of him, muttering in an arcane, sibilant language incomprehensible to the Boy General. The Yellow Hair's gaze was held by that of the shaman, who continued the incantations while making motions with his hands and fingers, as though he were drawing an invisible image.

The shaman's lips seemed to move out of synchronization with the words that reached his ears. The former general felt himself held in place by the onyx eyes that bored into his, entering into and pulling at something *deep* within him. Custer could *feel* something elemental being pulled from his body.

The trance was broken by the snarling and growling of Rosco, who ran up and attacked the witch doctor!

The pugnacious little dog leapt twice his body length, grabbing the medicine man's upper extremity and suspending himself as he swung from the shaman's right forearm. Rosco held onto the muscular forearm of White Bull with the obstinate grip of a terrier.

With the trance broken, Custer rushed past the shaman toward the supine figure that lay on a buffalo skin rug, wearing the war bonnet; it was Roman Nose. The chest rose and fell powerfully as the head bearing the massive nose turned to face the Yellow Hair.

The horrific, gaping wound at the lower right side of Roman Nose had completely healed. Custer lunged for the war bonnet as White Bull fought the terrier that continued to swing from his forearm, growling through clenched teeth.

The dog growled savagely each time the big medicine man struck it. Suddenly White Bull grabbed Rosco with his free hand, noticing that the small white dog had a black spot over its left eye. The warlock grasped the writhing, contorting little dog with both hands and drove the dog into his face. The howling of Rosco caused the Yellow Hair to turn his head suddenly to the scene of his terrier being devoured.

White Bull was quickly stuffing the dog into his mouth, and as he did so his face distended as though he had cheek pouches like those of a rodent. The screaming dog continued to vanish into the sachem's gullet before the Boy General's eyes.

"No!" cried the Yellow Hair.

Roman Nose sat upright, straight - like a rifle bolt placed onto a table top and balanced on its end. His movements were mechanical, almost robotic. The big Cheyenne was moving with jerking motions as life flooded back into him.

"I'll have that war bonnet!" shouted the former general, seizing it from the Cheyenne's head and placing it on his own in a single, sweeping motion. The eagle feathers made a papery, rustling sound.

Custer spun around to face White Bull and saw Rosco as the little dog's head vanished into the obscene orifice of the medicine man, whose jaws had detached and distended like that of a snake. Before the Boy General could act to save the terrier, he was stunned as though struck by a bolt of lightning. The war bonnet was imparting tremendous, electrifying vitality into the Yellow Hair. Electricity flowed through him in a terrific surge of energy, imparting an aura – a barely perceptible angelic glow about him. Suddenly he could see in the dimly lit tent as though it were illuminated by broad daylight.

"Rosco!" shouted Lieutenant Colonel Custer, advancing on the medicine man and seizing him by the throat with his left hand. The youthful face of the former general was contorted into a visage of primordial fury as the hand closed on the trachea of White Bull, crushing it. The trachea made a grating, crunching sound akin to that of two walnuts being crushed against each other as it was pulverized.

Custer flung the mortally wounded holy man to the ground as his wife would fling off an undergarment in front of another woman. White Bull grasped at his throat with both hands as he struggled to breathe, and managed by coughing and exerting diaphragmatic pressure to spit out the dying Rosco, his detachable jaws distending obscenely as the dog slid back out. The terrier was covered with a thick, white, translucent mucosal slime.

"Rosco! Don't go from me again Rosco! I told you to stay!!! You know what that means, boy! Stay! Stay! *STAY*!"

Rosco whimpered and tried to lick the former general's hands as he caressed him. Custer had lost any pretense of fleeing or survival. His thoughts were only for his dog.

The powerful hands of Roman Nose seized the former general by the shoulders of his buckskin jacket from behind, but no effort was needed to lift the Boy General; he was only too willing to do that himself.

Custer leapt to his feet, whirling about-face like a dervish to face his new opponent. The cavalry officer looked ridiculous in the double trailered war bonnet, but any ironic humor was not to be appreciated by the completely recuperated Roman Nose – desperate to retrieve the war bonnet.

"Give back war bonnet!" demanded Roman Nose, reaching for the bonnet before he had completed the command imperative.

The ensuing struggle reflected in the dimming eyes of the little terrier as it left this world for the final time, knowing it had helped its master in the death fight. It remembered, as its vision blurred, the little blond haired boy who had held it once before, many years ago...

"Pray to your gods he does not die!!!" shouted Custer, his voice was choked with rage and emotion. Custer deflected the arms of the big Cheyenne and picked up Roman Nose, lifting him over his head like a sack of horse feed and slamming him to the ground. The great warrior lay stunned, with the breath knocked from him.

George Armstrong Custer turned to the dying Rosco, and held him like a baby. The former general could see recognition in the terrier's glazing eyes as it licked his face feebly once more, ceased breathing and went still. The body was hot and limp.

Once more Custer was attacked brusquely from behind by the even more determined Roman Nose, his heart set on regaining the war bonnet. He was more determined than ever to retrieve the war bonnet.

"Yellow Hair die!" roared the sonorous, nasal voice of Roman Nose as a Colt revolver fired point blank into Custer's back and head. The bullets somehow missed the Boy General, who was vaguely aware of the fact as he held his childhood pet in his arms. The big Cheyenne continued shooting into the former general, holding the .44 cap and ball with both hands as he thumbed back the hammer, aimed, and then squeezed the trigger. Smoke from the burnt black powder filled the tent, obfuscating the vision of Roman Nose, but not that of Custer. Lieutenant Colonel Custer quickly set the dog down to the ground and turning around, approached Roman Nose.

Custer growled doglike as he slammed his closed fist into the chest of Roman Nose. The balled fist crashed through the warrior's sternum like a cannon ball shot from an artillery piece and made a loud, thud-like popping sound. The Boy General's face was contorted into the epitome of antipathy; the visage was like that of a snarling cougar.

"LET ME SEE YOUR WARFACE!" shouted Custer at Roman Nose, as he grasped the pounding heart of the six-foot six-inch Cheyenne and pulled it out of his chest with a violent, twisting motion. The heart, quivering and pumping, tore out of the chest with a thick, sucking sound. The wet sound was punctuated with several loud pops as the great cardiac veins and vessels relinquished their hold of the venous and arterial systems.

Roman Nose stood, staring with an incredulous expression as Custer held the yet beating heart.

"WARFACE!" shouted the Boy General, the magnificent war bonnet made him appear taller than his five feet, ten inches of height. *"SHOW ME SOME OF THAT WARFACE!"*

Roman Nose lunged at Custer, who shoved the beating heart into the man's face, muffling his enraged shout.

Roman Nose collapsed and ceased breathing as he crashed to the ground like a wet sack of feed.

Custer moaned as he picked up the lifeless body of the small terrier. He remained stoic. For the first time in Custer's adult life he was emotionally shaken.

"When the bushes move," Custer's father had told him, "Shoot!" and so he had. Hitting poor Rosco while on a rabbit hunt.

The Boy General was rocked with emotions that had been restrained from that distant day, intentionally stowed in the back of his mind with a cache of other memories he purposely repressed.

His effort at subduing the raw impulse to weep was realized by a primordial strength that manifested itself in a low timbered growl akin to that of a circus strong man attempting a feat of strength.

Then, as in a dream, the substance of the little dog began to waver, and was in a state of fluctuation. Rosco became intangible, diaphanous, and slowly vanished back into hell, from whence he had been summoned to the aide of his master. Custer heard a faint barking, as though far away, and then it too, vanished.

Hundreds of warriors, children, old men and women had crowded about the tent to investigate the commotion. As Lieutenant Colonel Custer exited the tepee, he did not seem to draw attention, it was as though he was not noticed. The Yellow Hair walked as though hypnotized to Vic, and mounted him without thought. He egressed from the village the way he had come, but without the help from his little guide.

"We've got to get out of here!" warned the twenty-eight-year-old former general. Custer was breathing hard from the exertion of not only fighting for his life, but losing his childhood pet – again. "Did you know who my guide would be?" Custer asked Gladstone.

"No, General," responded Professor Gladstone, adding, "I only knew that you would know the guide, nothing more. We must leave this place quickly; my magic weakens. We must escape to a place where I may repose."

In the tepee, White Bull struggled mightily to get the moonstone from his pouch of talismans and apply it to his crushed trachea, his lips forming the silent words to heal the injury; this would take hours. Any hope of restoring Roman Nose to the land of the living would be lost.

"I've done all I can to save him," thought White Bull. "It will be nothing short of miraculous if I can save myself."

"Horrid. Everything I've heard about Roman Nose's medicine man are true," stated Lieutenant Colonel Custer, with an effort to keep his voice low. "I had to take the war bonnet from Roman Nose, White Bull had brought him back to life."

Chapter Fifteen
Stillwell and Trudeau

STILLWELL DREW THE lethal weapon from its scabbard, and plunged twenty inches of the gore covered blade into the ground all of the way up to its brass hilt, and pulling the blade from the earth, cleaned it of blood and gristle using the flap of his shirt.

"It's a real beauty, isn't it?" asked Stillwell.

It was not really a question, Pierre Trudeau knew, but a frank assessment of a utilitarian weapon style that had carried over from the Bronze Age.

The Kansas misfit seemed to be mumbling to himself, thought Pierre Trudeau; one of the true signs of a killer. Pierre looked into the grayish gleam of the straight, pointed, double edged blade as Stillwell continued speaking softly, so that his words would not alert the ears of those who prowled cactus strewn fields in the moonlit night. He was talking to the murderous weapon like it was a partner in crime, a co-conspirator.

"Almost, to be sure, you're a reincarnation of the Roman gladius, used to such effect to the applause of thousands in the gladiator arenas," cooed the big Kansas native son.

"Those are right pretty hard to come by, it looks like it can always come in real handy – like a damn Jim Dandy!" responded Trudeau, who studied the dirk in the dim light. In truth, Pierre yearned for the dagger and craved it for himself. But he needed Stillwell too much to risk killing him over the coveted Arkansas Toothpick.

Stillwell had been fascinated by the enigmatic, older man who crouched in the shadows. Although sixty years of age, Trudeau could pass for a man in his late thirties were it not for the shock of white hair. The gray hair and beard were untraced by any dark hair at all, but the skin of the face was unlined and tight. No slop or jowl depended from the powerful, athletic neck.

Trudeau's physique reminded Stillwell of that which many lumberjacks displayed. Pierre stood at medium height, and had thick wide shoulders. The old man - a penniless adventurer who was gifted with robust health and keen eyesight was broad chested, with a lean waist and thick legs.

"Listen!" whispered Jack Stillwell. "I hear sounds of movement back in the direction from whence we came, I fear for the worse; I suspect them to be onto our trail!"

"They'll have their hands full trying to track us in the dark," responded Pierre Trudeau, directing his vision to the direction from which they had just fled.

Trudeau's statement in point of fact was true. Those who followed in pursuit were not having an easy time of staying on the trail in the hours of darkness.

Chapter Sixteen
Journey to the Cave of Silk

VARIOUS ABSTRUSE, esoteric incantations could not be properly intoned during the incomplete Act of Healing, owing to the crushed larynx of White Bull. The medicine man could only speak incomplete sentences in a halting, rasping voice. His ability to swallow had been badly affected as well. His throat had swollen from the trauma of being crushed and appeared as though he was suffering from an advanced stage of goiter.

White Bull had walked zombie-like outside from his teepee as if in a trance-like state, to the center of a macabre spectacle of young men dangling from poles, tethered and suspended from thongs made of rawhide. He raised his arms to the midday sun, his lips moving but no distinctive, easily understood words issuing from them.

"Cut flesh, for *You*," the words came in a hoarse, rasping voice.

Turning around, White Bull approached the Sacred Fire that burned outside his sweat lodge. He then drew a sacramental knife made of flint and began cutting slivers of flesh from his arms, abdomen and thighs, casting each one into the Fire That Burns. As the skin and fat burned, it curled in on itself and made a popping, hissing sound like that of bacon in an iron skillet.

"I see the Dog Soldiers who sleep!" rasped the great Holy Man. "Dozens of them! I will awaken the ones who sleep!" then he added in a grating, unintelligible voice discernable only to himself, "and they will seize the war bonnet from the Yellow Hair."

The Indian village had become enlivened in recent days with animation enhanced by an unusually spectacular Sun Dance.

White Bull, along with subordinate, tenebrous medicine men presided over this particular Sun Dance collusion between the Sioux and Northern and Southern Cheyenne. This was a loose confederation mainly between the remnants of the still powerful Northern Cheyenne and the plentiful Sioux tribes. The Sioux and Cheyenne had long been allied although the languages of the two cultures differed profoundly in linguistic origins.

"We go now to my inipi," White Bull whispered hoarsely, his voice was barely audible to those few Cheyenne who were brave enough – or deadly enough in the arcane arts of the Native American Occult, to comprise his inner circle.

The Cheyenne were a proud shadow of their former selves. A disastrous series of measles epidemics had been obliterating the very young of the Cheyenne for years, and then an epidemic of cholera had wiped out half of the population of Southern Cheyenne in 1849.

The cholera was a great mystery to the Cheyenne, whose skin turned blue as the diarrhea emptied their bodies of electrolytes. Often they defecated up to five gallons of putrid, fish smelling water daily. Their eyes sunk into the back of their heads and the only means they had to combat this invisible enemy was to drink more water, though most of the infected did not know this.

The repercussions on the Southern Cheyenne were phenomenal; marriage within clans, long frowned upon, was permitted in a desperate effort to save the Nation from extinction. Enemies, sometimes kept as slaves, but rarely being accepted as equals within the Cheyenne tribes were being treated differently now; white children taken in raids were openly adopted into families in an effort to get the Cheyenne numbers up.

Adult captive white women – not treated any better than sex slaves, were fecund and could bear over a dozen children to the muscular braves, and the children born of the captive women had a much lower infant mortality rate; the offspring having inherited immunity to many of the diseases that devastated and wiped out entire Native American populations. But no less importantly, the cholera led indirectly to the birth of a fanatical warrior religious cult.

While the Northern and Southern Cheyenne populations for the most part had for several generations remained distinct, they often traveled together and shared a common language. They also assisted each other in war. With the incapacitation of the Southern Cheyenne, the numbers of the Cheyenne to the south were effectively halved, subordinating them to their brothers in the north – the Northern Cheyenne.

The Sun Dance was comprised of songs inherited through many generations and of music played to the thrumming of a sacral drum. Specialized, hallowed meals were prepared over a consecrated fire which was presided over and maintained by a specially designated Fire Keeper. The Fire Keeper never allowed the fire to stifle and held a great magical role.

Inipi – dome shaped sweat lodges constructed in stoic silence and with intricate attention to detail fringed the margins of where the Sun Dance was held. Each lodge had its own designated leader who was versed in the complex prayers and rituals involved in the sweat ceremonies. This role was taken no less seriously than that of the Fire Keeper; an apprenticeship of four to six years often being required by the Sweat Lodge Leader. The door of each lodge faced the sacred fire tended by the Fire Keeper.

Within one inipi, a serious episode was playing out:

"The Deceptive One who is among us will soon reveal himself," mumbled White Bull, as he cast sacred water on the superheated rocks that filled an indentation in the ground of the inipi. The inipi that contained the ceremony being conducted was a small affair by Cheyenne standards; holding only half a dozen braves.

Unlike the other domed structures, larger in size and covered with buffalo skins or heavy blankets, this one was sheathed in the ancient, preserved hide of mammoth. This bore demonic, esoteric designs on the inside, painted in the blood of saber tooth tigers, long extinct, which had plagued the Cheyenne in their trek out of Siberia and along the coast of Alaska well into the northeastern midsection of the continent. Although this had occurred through the mists of their distant past, the experience remained in the form of vestigial memories and horror tales of the big saber tooth cats were told at night to frighten small children into obedience.

The six votaries had been sitting in the structure for nigh unto four hours. A dim light was able to infiltrate the superheated structure from underneath the base of the inipi.

"I can no longer withstand the heat!" cried Two Face Man. "I go outside lest I collapse, I am short of breath!' he stood uncertainly, his equilibrium compromised by dehydration and nearness to losing consciousness owing to electrolyte imbalance.

"Seize him!" commanded White Bull, his harsh rasping voice was edged with the grating tone of authority.

Four muscular painted killers roughly pinned Two Face Man to the floor of the inipi, face up. Each brawny man firmly held a muscular arm or leg in place. Two Face Man shouted expletives while he twisted and writhed. White Bull took a large pair of rusted hoof trimmers and slammed them down into the mouth of Two Face Man with the force of a pile-driver, shattering all of his front teeth in the process.

Working by feel in the near total darkness of the suffocating sweat lodge, White Bull grasped the tongue of Two Face Man with the hoof trimmers and pressed the two lever handles together, neatly shearing off the tongue of the victim.

Speaking in one of the nearly extinct Cro-Magnon dialects, known to but a handful of medicine men, White Bull invoked a spell through incantation, in which he summoned forth a demon to speak through the tongue-less mouth. He sat astraddle the man, his hands holding either side of the head of Two Face Man.

"Traitor!" hissed White Bull. The Gods told me that the Rite of Purification would reveal you! You who tell our secrets to the Army, for trash reward! Now another will speak through your mouth! Speak to me, oh Demon of Tongues!"

A deep, sonorous voice responded from the gaping, tongue-less maw;

"Enter the funnel, the Spinner's home
In rainments of silk
She is waiting for thee!
The Stone of the Moon
Through which you see
Place to the Brave Ones
To set them free!"

"Prepare him!" commanded White Bull, "Chastise him, fill his mouth with rags and bind his arms!"

White Bull entered the open area where the young men swung, tethered to poles. The wind blew from the west, cooling his body as he massaged liniment into his self-inflicted wounds and faced toward the sun, raising his muscle corded arms.

All about him young men hung suspended, sometimes up to ten feet off the ground tethered by two leather thongs to a pole. Wooden dowels had been inserted through incisions made that perforated into and out of the deep, massive pectoral muscles to which the leather thongs had been fastened. There was no shade and the men were in open air. There were hundreds of them. Most were in a deep state of catharsis, manifested by a semi-comatose state. Flies swarmed their eyes and faces.

Historically the Sun Dance was held in the vernal months and kinship played an important factor for those who attended the ritual. This was a ritual in which young men were sacramentally incised through their chests and rawhide thongs were affixed. The inductees swung and danced liked

Dervishes when they were first bound to a pole. Famishing themselves for days prior to the four-day long ritual, the votaries invested great personal commitment.

White Bull surveyed the hundreds of dangling braves that surrounded him and approved of how they hung limply, suspended above the cracked, moisture starved, sunbaked ground. In instances where the wooden dowels had torn through the pectoral muscles, the young man would plunge to the earth and the dowels would be reinserted.

If the skin and muscles of the chest no longer maintained enough turgor to sustain the dead weight of the warrior's body, he would be pierced through the back, the dowels reinserted and the initiate hoisted dutifully back up into the air.

The skin would distend into the shape of a pair of cones, giving the impression that it would tear at any moment. Friends and relatives sat about the suspended figures, praying and offering encouragement.

Many dozens of the initiates stood barefooted, tethered to a pole by the strong rawhide thongs, too exhausted to dance. Some of these men leaned back away from the pole, the skin of their chests pulling outward as they did so, while an unfortunate few did not survive this initiation.

Years of circumspection and rehearsal of young men had gone into the annual gestation of this ultimate of all Mischianzas, this promenade which was one of the final stepping stones into manhood.

"Lame White Man, come with me," ordered White Bull. "A demon has spoken sage advice to me, and now we must go into the Cave of Silk."

"How may I be of assist to the greatest of all Cheyenne medicine men?" asked Lame White Man.

"There is one there who is like yourself; a Cheyenne war chief," answered White Bull. "You will intercede between he and I, if necessary. I don't know for certain what lies within the Cave of Silk, but only that it is there and something *horrific* resides within the vaults. If I am to reacquire the war bonnet, we must do this thing."

"I have two thousand two hundred and fifty braves even now searching out the Yellow Hair," responded Lame White Man.

"It is for nought," replied White Bull. "Custer is protected by the war bonnet. Your men will never find him. *But there are others who can*."

The import of that solemn statement chilled the blood of Lame White Man with its ramifications. In truth, Lame White man did not wish to accompany White Bull into the distant mountains, their gray, ragged, snow - capped peaks visible in the hazy distance. The Cheyenne war chief ensconced his reluctance through the use of a saturnine countenance to follow the order of the feared and respected medicine man.

White Bull looked back over his shoulder upon the Sun Dance ritual as he and the Cheyenne war chief, Lame White Man departed for the Cave of Silk; a day's ride into the highlands through darkened gorges and shadow cast defiles where horses could not be surefooted. Two Face Man followed on foot, tethered to the saddle of White Bull. He staggered in his walk, often falling down and being drug some length before regaining his feet.

In the distance could be seen the austere, ragged skylines of the mountain range, the higher peaks of which vanished into thick white cloud banks. There, White Bull knew, watched goblin like specters that haunted the shattered ravines. Very few hunting parties ever drew near to the mist shrouded boulders and crevasses. Where the soil thinned out, stunted trees clung tenaciously with roots that sought hold desperately in every nook and cranny.

"Whoa!" shouted Lame White Man as his horse, a prized Appaloosa reared back on its hind legs, whinnying and pawing the air with the black, knife edged hooves of its front legs. So great was its terror that it threatened to fall backwards on its rider who leaned forward in his attempt to remain mounted in the saddle.

"The horse can see what men cannot!" warned White Bull, his own mare snorting and frothing at the bit as he dismounted her.

The Sioux medicine man and the Cheyenne war chief were entering a narrow path that inclined sharply upward, to their right the face of the mountain trail sheared off into a ravine that plunged many hundreds of feet into a darkened, seemingly bottomless descent.

"I untie you from horse. You run, you die." White Bull warned Two Face Man, his words came out sounding rasp, with pauses in between.

"We stay dismounted and we walk the horses from this point on," stated Lame White Man. The statement was matter of fact, unnecessary and White Bull had already dismounted long before Lame White Man said it.

"Just runnin' mouth to hear himself talk," White Bull thought as he kicked Two Face Man sharply in the back of the leg, and commanded "Get movin' dog!"

Suddenly the Appaloosa of Lame White Man neighed and reared once more, the cone shaped biceps of the big Cheyenne jumped into life as he tried to control his panicked mount. This time the loose scree that littered the trail caused the horse to lose its footing and it slid sideways off the path. With ears pulled back and teeth showing, it whinnied as it sought purchase with its front hooves.

"My horse! Shouted Lame White Man. "I cannot save it!" with that fateful exclamation, the reins were torn from the iron grip of the war chief as the prized pony plunged in slow motion to its demise into the bottomless ravine, somersaulting lazily. The Appaloosa's whinnying echoed along the walls and cliffs until all was that was heard was the snorting and neighing of White Bull's nervous mount.

"Cut the saddle straps! Quickly!" yelled White Bull as he fought to restrain his own horse, a diminutive black pony with a captured McClellan US Cavalry saddle.

Not only did the saddle have the rifle scabbard attached to it, but the saddle bags were loaded with ammunition and magical talismans, captured Army water canteens and food. The big Cheyenne vied with all of his strength against the fear maddened pony, which neighed and reared frantically, froth flew from its mouth as it shook its head violently and pawed the air, showing its huge front teeth. Its sharp hooves came dangerously close to the grimacing face of White Bull; his face contorted into a straining visage of determination.

White Bull sometimes did not use the rein on this particular horse, owing to the luxurious mane which extended from the poll to the withers. The mane was jet black, and as long as a woman's tresses. He often preferred to guide the horse by pulling on its mane to one direction or the other, although the rein was always present.

"There!" shouted Lame White Man.

Acting quickly, Lame White Man had cut the saddle straps from the girth of the pony allowing the McClellan to fall free, along with the indispensable saddle bags.

"We have the saddle!" shouted the big Cheyenne as the horse reared once more on the loose, treacherous scree.

White Bull's twin headed biceps muscles were knotted into quivering dynamos of power as he fought to control his mount. Large veins stood out on his corded forearms with the effort, and his lips were pulled tightly back from his tobacco rotted teeth. His darkly pigmented face, heavily lined from unprotected sun exposure was contorted into a grimace of consternation as he sought to bend the rearing, neighing horse to his will. As the black mare reared back this time, large clumps of the thick, coarse mane hair pulled loose into the scarred, calloused hands of White Bull.

White Bull stared incredulously, both hands holding fistfuls of wiry, rough, black hair torn loose from the mane as the horse leaped intentionally from the trail and into the abyss; a bottomless descent that faded to black in the gloomy depths where the sun was denied entry.

"Demons haunt these craggy knolls!" declared White Bull, picking up the saddlebags and shouldering one on the either side of his beefy neck, while thrusting the other gear onto the shoulders of Two Face Man. He was wearing a buckskin war-shirt made in the fashion of a leather jerkin like those worn under the chainmail of medieval fighting men of Europe. "There is no time to waste, and we must hasten to our objective."

Lame White Man shouldered the heavy coil of rope and shoved Two Face Man viciously ahead of him, making the prisoner stumble and almost fall.

The trio progressed up the winding, tortuous mountain trail. Massive walls of holocrystalline, coarse grained granite fissured with deep cracks and vaults containing untold mysteries rose drunkenly upward, disappearing into the fog shrouded heights.

In the distance could occasionally be discerned the vague U shapes of glacier formed valleys lined with treacherous ice age debris.

The Sawatch Mountain Range was really an extension of the Rocky Mountains that lay in the center of the Colorado Territory. It was a high, alpine range, and included nearly half of the twenty highest peaks in the entire Rocky Mountain system. Fifteen of the peaks exceeded fourteen thousand feet in altitude.

It was sprinkled with couloirs filled with snow, packed down with granular ice that remained through the repetitions of thaws and freezes. These never melted and were punctuated with nunataks; protrusions of rock above the surface. Here and there treacherous cornice type ledges laden with snow threatened to slide loose with the heating of the midday.

The fourteen thousand-foot-tall peaks were abominably eroded in places and made treacherous with profuse distributions of talus and scree. Rich in fossils and crumbling rock formations of dazzling colors, this was an ancient range - thrusting like an arsenal of rusting bayonets upward from the supine body of the High Plains.

Rocky Mountain juniper along with limber pine adorned the lower elevations, while large swathes of Douglas fir thickly bristled the upper reaches, often to an altitude of nine thousand feet.

Golden eagles oversaw numerous mule deer and pronghorn sheep as they scoured the rocky outcrops; outcrops in which resided hidden death embodied in the thick bodied, five-foot-long prairie rattlesnakes and timber rattlers.

An older mule deer, ostracized from the main herd by younger males strode cautiously beneath the overhang of an ancient granite boulder, oblivious to the motionless mountain lion that remained as still as the rock from which he waited in ambush, muscles tensed like steel springs and ready to leap.

The trail ended treacherously in front of the two men with their captive. In the darkness of night it would have led to certain death thousands of feet below. Seeking and finding the chiseled hand holes, White Bull turned to his friend and explained the situation in a series of halting, raspy sentences.

"From here we must climb," White Bull stated. Then he cautioned, "But on no account lose your grip, for death is certain."

"What?" expostulated Lame White Man. "You mean we must climb the face of the mountain?"

White Bull hesitated before replying, as he studied the situation in contemplation.

"Yes. We must climb the face of the rock using finger holds on edges and in the niches carved by the Old Ones. It is unwise to look down," added White Bull, his face was stoic. "Two Face Man will stay here. Bind his feet to his hands, and tie the end of the rope about his chest." Reaching into his saddlebag, White Bull pulled forth a powdery substance and poured enough on his palm to form a small mound. He cupped his other hand over it to protect it from the wind.

"Breathe this through your nostrils, Two Face Man!" commanded White Bull, as Lame White Man roughly kicked the prisoner to alertness.

"Soon he will sleep the Sleep of the Undead. Then you and I must climb."

They ascended the headwall; a sheer wall of rotted granite, which disappeared into a thin mist one hundred feet above them. Steadily they made progress through the use of the gouged hand hold niches, protrusions of the rocks, and foot work. Sometimes they were compelled to insert a hand into a fissure and form a fist, in order to climb to the next niche.

"My hands are bleeding," complained the Cheyenne, Lame White Man.

"Cursed hard work this is," mumbled White Bull as the two continued their ascent of the cyclopean escarpments.

Shattered schist that glittered with flakes of mica showered the two struggling Alpinists. Metamorphic, foliated, fractured gneiss also pummeled them as they climbed to, and inched over another protrusion in their perilous ascent. They came to a thin, dangerous ledge that disappeared suddenly behind a curvature of the rocky wall and reappeared further on, where another bend brought it into view again before it vanished into the ebbing, swirling mists.

The wind made a mournful, wailing sound as it passed through the alpine canyons, its baleful sound augmented by the channeling effect of the cliff walls. The sweat saturated clothing of the climbers was chilled by the monotonous, unnerving wind.

The two climbing figures were ensconced by the swirling mist which had begun to form a thin layer of slippery verglas on the face of the sheer rock wall in the biting cold and high altitude. This made the climb all the more treacherous, but White Bull reached the flat promontory that was formed by a massive ledge. White Bull assisted Lame White Man up, and over the precipice.

"Do you seriously think they would have survived all of these years up here, in this foreboding wilderness?" asked Lame White Man. White Bull did not answer, because he had heard whispered by demons in wells what had happened to the Dog Soldiers, and knew what he had to do to bring them back. He did not relate this to Lame White Man. White Bull knew that most of the Sioux and Cheyenne were deeply superstitious. While Lame White Man was no coward of any mortal threat, he would petrify in fear at the description of what waited in the cave.

Lame White Man belied the appearance of a Cheyenne His hair was long and braided into a single thick pony tail - tightly wrapped with colored cloth and a single rawhide thong. Into this braid were thrust two eagle feathers at a jaunty angle, but the hair itself was not the raven black color of that of his cohort, White Bull. Instead, the hair was an off colored brown, and the atypical appearance of Lame White Man to the Cheyenne as a whole did not end there; the Caucasoid features of his captive white mother dominated his appearance.

The forehead was high, pronounced, and dolichocephalic, beneath this forehead resided a pair of hazel eyes; soft hazel eyes that glanced uncertainly to the right and downward as he sought to avoid falling into the purple depths of the gorge. The nose was straight, short, and canted upward at its end, beneath it and resting atop thin lips was a thin, tightly manicured moustache.

Given the proper clothing, Lame White Man could easily have been mistaken for an investor or a banker on Wall Street – were it not for the massive physique of the Chief; blocky, knotted muscles bulged like those of the statue of some insane Michael Angelo. For such a big, heavily muscled man, Lame White Man could move fast, and was renowned for his murderous knife fighting ability.

As the duo circumnavigated the tortuous path, their ears continued to be serenaded by the dirge-like howling of the wind through the craggy, winding, gray mountain passes.

The wind carried with it the howling of wolves, although faint and far away. The sound of the wolves evoked an awareness at a primordial level and added another grim factor to the equation as they forged ahead.

"We're here," stated White Bull. "See that cave?"

"No," answered Lame White Man. "Unless you mean that shadow area underneath the ledge of rock," he said this as he peered from a distance into the shadowy orifice over which hung a weathered arête composed of ancient, crumbling granite. About the orifice lay shattered the talus of a collapsed cliff. The rocks and boulders were of varying color, size and shape.

The mouth of the cave was barely visible in the lateness of the day – even less so at any other time. The evening rays of the dying sun shone into the cave as though through a prism. The cave entrance was a yard wide and twice that tall, it was a bent, crooked, and ungainly entrance.

About the mouth of this twisted cavern were stunted post oak trees. An observant wayfarer may have puzzled at the numerous ghostly gray cobwebs that billowed phantom-like with the wind gusts that whispered among the branches.

"What unseemly place is this, White Bull?" asked Lame White Man, the tone of his voice conveyed the uneasiness that he felt. "I sense that there is more to the narrow entrance of the fissure in the granite wall than what meets the eye."

"This is the home of Porcupine Bear, and dozens of his best warriors," answered White Bull, who added, "Dog Soldiers!"

"That cannot be," countered Lame White Man, "The last of Porcupine Bear and his band of Dog Soldiers vanished nearly ten years ago. Porcupine Bear has been gone from us for many seasons."

Lame White Man was suspicious, and did not want to enter the cave. That Porcupine Bear and more than forty Dog Soldiers could be residing within the narrow confines of the walls of this cavern seemed to him incomprehensible. Furthermore, as Lame White Man knew, the Dog Soldiers were a rebellious warrior sect of Cheyenne who took orders from no other Cheyenne except within their own religious cult.

The Dog Soldiers were renegade outlaws, so uncontrollable that even the noncompliant tribes of Cheyenne who had refused submission to the invading Euro-Americans had spurned them. But the Dog Soldiers excelled in the art of war, and in times of emergency, their misbehavior was tolerated so that their abilities in combat could be utilized by the Cheyenne Nation as a whole.

The possibility that Porcupine Bear was potentially alive filled Lame White Man with speculation and with worry.

"We pull Two Face Man up the face of the cliff using the rope, then we must take him with us into the cave, where *She* awaits," stated White Bull, who was rubbing fine, talc like dust onto his hands. "We must be quick, and on our lives we must not tarry. Let not the sun set with us still in there."

Muffled grunts and moans issued from the rag filled mouth of Two Face Man hundreds of feet below. Neither of his captors could hear him as they hoisted him roughly up the mountain wall.

The cobwebs increased as the three entered the fracture in the mountain wall that was the cave's entrance. Soon cobwebs threatened to cover the cave's floor, lending to an impression of a funnel. Here and there bare rock was exposed on the walls on which was painted what appeared to be an ancient, hieroglyphical story.

As they entered the ceilinged vault, White Bull looked up and saw dozens of shapes hanging in suspended animation in the heavily shadowed light. The eerie silence was broken by a female voice, one of beauty which cried in a pathetic, heartbreaking, melancholy tenor. The voice was one of a woman weeping in despair.

"Oh Spinstress, Weaver of Nightmares, your humble servant brings to you an offering!" chanted White

Bull, thrusting the bound Two Face Man in front of him.

Immediately the crying ceased and a flurry of activity ensued as Two Face Man was jerked upward with sudden violence and began spinning, as though he were an empty spool on which thread was being bobbed. His muffled screams continued even as he was cocooned in white filament reminiscent of silk threading.

Looking about him, White Bull spoke to Lame White Man, there was urgency in his voice:

"Look about you, do you see them?"

Looking about him, Lame White Man reeled in terror, stepping back and falling onto the web covered floor of loose gravel stone. He broke his fall with his beefy hands, which were cut in places from the knife sharp schist that lay ensconced beneath the cob webs on the floor of granite, rotted with passage of countless eons.

The cob webs rose and fell lazily with the perturbations of Lame White Man, who panicked and became glued to the spider webbing as he fought frantically to free himself.

"Look about you, do you see them?" asked White Bull, cognizant of but paying little heed to the plight of Lame White Man.

"No! I see only that I am trapped and HA! What's this! See to me, White Bull! The dam has a litter!" shouted

Lame White Man, his voice echoed eerily down the winding, yawning cavern vaults.

Dozens of small spiders the size of twenty-dollar double eagle gold coins had converged on Lame White Man.

White Bull pulled the moonstone from his satchel of talismans and invoking the name of Hanwi the Accursed, Goddess of the Moon, became the vicar of the lunar Deity; "In the name of Hanwi the Accursed! Call off your minions, Arachne! Call them off lest I unleash hell upon thee!"

Almost as a single entity the arachnid horde dissipated and skittled away in sundry directions, their presence in the nooks and crannies of the cave walls betrayed by the scintillate reflections of waning light on their multiple eyes. Eyes which watched hungrily...

White Bull saw a separate group of cocooned forms dangling from the far part of the cave, "Could that be them?" he asked aloud as he saw to freeing Lame White Man from the sticky, gum like webbing that carpeted the cavern floor. The web didn't stop at the floor; it extended up the walls and depended from the ceiling, forming a sort of silken funnel.

"Almost certainly! We must cut one down to see," responded Lame White Man. "If that group is them, then we must make haste."

Pulling one of the cocoons down and pulling back the old dust covered silken web, which had lost much of its adhesiveness, the pair saw a darkened, preserved face bearing the war paint of a Dog Soldier.

"They were cursed," explained White Bull, "for disregarding the ancient ways and turning their backs on the Old Ones. They became consumed with the lust for gold, as is the white man. But I was told by a demon speaking from the mouth of Two Face Man of their whereabouts. A demon named the Tongueless One."

"But have we time to bring them into the day?" riposted Lame White Man, who eyed the enormous spider that was spinning Two Face Man into a thick, white cocoon. The arachnid's exoskeleton was impressive; the legs – over five times the body's length, were uneven in span; the front jointed limbs being the longest. These spun the hapless Two Face Man with dizzying speed, as his muffled pleas for help drew a smile from the lips of White Bull.

The arthropod's black, shiny body was larger in size than a mighty fighting man and the glossy, black ventrum was adorned with a large, red, hourglass image. The enormous, rotund abdomen was bent at the small, cylindrical pedicel, allowing the chelicerate to quickly dip the taloned forefoot of the two front legs to the web producing spinneret.

The eight eyes mounted in pairs atop the carapace of the cephalothorax scintillated like red rubies in the weak sunlight that snuck its way into the cave surreptitiously, like a Nicodemus into the vault.

The long, shiny black fangs were folded back into a beardlike filter and were attached to oversized venom bags within the underside of the carapace. The fangs occasionally would extrude, revealing themselves in all their horror before folding back in as the arachnid attempted to restrain its hunger.

"There is no time to waste, let us move with haste. We must secure as many of them as we can while there is light," responded White Bull.

"Kneel!" commanded White Bull to Lame White Man, "I'll mount your shoulders, then you will advance to the first one dangling over there. I will pull him down by his ankles from the silken bond that secures him to the ceiling of this cave."

"But have we *time*?" responded Lame White Man.

"Time will tell!" responded White Bull.

The pair rhythmically detached the cocooned Dog Soldiers and without premeditation began hauling them out of the eroded cave; Lame White Man carrying the Dog Soldier by the upper body while White Bull supported the lighter, lower extremities.

Darkness had all but set in, and the muffled screams of Two Face Man had subsided into a series of groans, then whimpers – then stopped.

"We can't get the last one out!" shouted Lame White Man to White Bull; the darkness that surrounded and extended into the mouth of the cave was an event horizon surrounding a hellish black hole. A black hole that led to a horrific eight legged demon and further unfathomed horrors deeper in its winding, tortuous vaults - vaults that led into some nameless hell...

Although he was no coward, the fear of the unknown held Lame White Man at bay, preventing him from rescuing the final Dog Soldier.

"Free him from the silken bondage, and let him fend for himself while we carry this one out!" responded White Bull, his voice was defined by exhaustion, but there was an edge added to it. An edge of worry – of fear. Fear of being caught in the cave in total darkness.

Panting with exhaustion, their breath was exhaled in wafts of steam in the icy air as they dropped their load unceremoniously to the unforgiving, rocky ground.

"Are we going back for the last of them?" asked Lame White Man.

"No, we leave him for Arachne," responded White Bull. Lame White Man thought he could perceive a faint smile on the older sachem's lips as the next scream rang out from the mouth of the cave, this scream was longer and more hideous in duration.

Having been moved outside the cave entrance, the countenances of forty dark, waxy cadavers stared blankly to the night sky that had temporarily cleared of cloud and fog. About them lay the swathes of spider webbing; silken garb that had clothed them for ten years.

"Do they live?" asked Lame White Man, looking uncertainly toward the mouth of the cave and back to White Bull.

"They will," answered White Bull, softly. He reached into his sachet of talismans and brought forth his moonstone, and began uttering, "Hanwi, Hanwi, Hanwi..." over and over again.

"You call upon Hanwi the Accursed!" expostulated Lame White Man, he trembled with fear and uncertainty. "She is not one of our Deities! Hanwi is the Sioux Goddess of the Moon! This was forbidden by the Sacred Council generations ago!"

Lame White Man was confused, his ethos was tormented by a dilemma in which he fleetingly thought of slaying the great medicine man, but cooler reasoning prevailed in the hybrid mind of the big Cheyenne War Chief.

In the silvery wash of the moon, the images of the forty fighting men lay motionless on the rocky ground near the cave entrance. The quicksilver light of the moon shone on the men, revealing ghostly features.

They were warriors of above average height; their ebon hair had been tightly braided into two pony tails. Some of the braids were secured with rawhide thongs, while others were sheathed in socks made of otter or beaver skin. White, translucent spider web partially netted the coiffures. The faces appeared waxen, the eye lids were closed, and the noses hooked evilly downward. All wore knee length war shirts made of buckskin and like-wise breeches. The clothing failed to ensconce the hard, muscular lines of their limbs.

The wooden faces took on life as the luminescence of the moon unveiled their sullen features. Suddenly, the rib cage of one of them heaved powerfully into life as the lungs filled with air...

Chapter Seventeen
Custer Flees with the War Bonnet

THE TWO WHITE MEN and Arikawa scout had ridden desperately throughout the moonlit night, while Custer wore the massive war bonnet. The twenty-five hundred Cheyenne and Sioux warriors who searched ruthlessly for the evasive trio had failed to pick up the spoor of the former general and his two cohorts. But, there were others who had. Others, who were not of the main stream of warriors.

With the onset of day, the threesome had hidden within copses of deciduous trees that fringed large ravines. In order to reduce the chances of being seen by discerning eyes from afar, they would carefully scan the distance before emerging and increasing the lead over their relentless pursuers.

Now, with the setting of the sun, one by one the appearance of the planets heralded the closing of the day. The trio entered into another wooded copse like a group of fugitives. Custer was exuberant, as was

Gladstone. Bloody Knife was hard to phantom, seldom smiling and rarely expressing into words what he felt. Bloody Knife showed his emotions in other ways; primarily through passionate, unrestrained violence.

"There's not too much danger in setting up the Sibley tonight," opined the Yellow Hair.

"I concur," agreed Gladstone, adding, "they can't be anywhere near our trail."

"We'll take turns standing watch during the night," said Custer, swatting at gnats and mosquitos. "Gladstone, you take first watch, Bloody Knife you take second. Wake me up at 2300 sharp and I'll man the third watch."

Placing the war bonnet in its parfleche, the former general settled into an immediate sleep on a folding cot. He had removed his boots, but otherwise remained fully clothed. He slept with his right hand on the handle of his revolver; he always slept with the gun belt and holster on. It was a cross draw holster which the Yellow Hair favored. Not only because he knew it looked good in photographs, but also because he could sleep with his hand on it in a comfortable, natural position.

The flaps of the tent were open to air and faced to the south, from whence the wind came, in small occasional gusts through the trees – mostly hardwood with some pine and juniper intermixed. The sweet smelling tree line was young, not more than thirty years; one of those that sprung up after a devastating summer range fire caused by heat lightning.

The nightmare was anticipated and welcome. The Boy General always relished the nightmares and would record them in a special diary reserved especially for the nocturnal adventures. Custer was one of those men who believed in dreams, especially nightmares – and he took his very seriously.

This dream began oddly; immediately Lieutenant Colonel Custer did not like the subliminal mirage and began trying to wake himself from it – but was unable to.

A small dog was barking somewhere up ahead of him, in the dark, tenebrous woods that were shrouded in a purple mantle of gloom. By using averted vision, the Yellow Hair could barely discern the shape of some vaguely defined tree line. There was no moon, there were no stars, but the tree line was inexplicably discernable.

The Boy General headed in the direction of the barking dog, which grew closer from somewhere within the haunted forest. The funereal wood line lay stretched out before him like the morose setting of a Grimm fairytale. Without explanation he found himself in a tent – a large tepee that was not congruous with those he had been in before.

The Yellow Hair didn't know what was in the mystifying, oversized tepee, but *something* was. *He could feel it*. Incertitude and apprehension suffused the sapience of the golden haired former general.

While yet an inane, inexplicable curiosity drove the Boy General forward, making him suck in his breath against clenched teeth, teeth that were white and unstained from tobacco.

The blue eyes were set alight with adrenaline and glowed with intelligence. The portals of the Yellow Hair's soul had narrowed into slits of apprehension as the diminutive, almost effeminate fingers of his right hand reached across his abdomen for the handle of the revolver that he always kept on his left side. But the big Colt Army wasn't there.

Nervousness ate at the stomach of George Armstrong Custer; the interior of the tepee had expanded exponentially and he stepped forward, advancing toward an enormous pair of mastodon tusks that formed the frame of a large bed. On this bed lay a body, over which a heavy fur blanket of buffalo skin had been pulled, hiding the face.

Although irrational and delusional, Custer was never found for want of courage. It was a fool's courage that prompted him to carefully place his left hand on the buffalo skin blanket. The Yellow Hair held his breath as he cautiously gripped it, as though he were handling a timber rattlesnake in a moment of morbid curiosity. Then in one violent movement he tore the heavy blanket back and froze in horror at what he had exposed.

On the funeral bed lay Roman Nose, the heart had been rudely shoved back into the gaping hole in his chest. The eyes were closed and the features were waxen, reminding the Boy General of one of his sister Margaret's dolls from childhood that he had played with surreptitiously, out of the sight of others.

Suddenly the eyelids of the waxen figure flew open and locked with those of the former general. Custer saw the lips pull back in a death grin revealing straight, tobacco stained teeth set in blackened gums. The wide nostrils flared with the inhalation of air. The inhalation seemed to suck at his soul – *he could feel it leaving his body.* He looked into the obsidian eyes that held his gaze, willing with all of his might to break the deathlike grip of the hypnotic leer.

"Wake up! Wake up!" muttered the Boy General to himself. Custer had to muster all of his strength merely to speak the words, which were uttered in a slow, lethargic mumbling.

The urgent barking of a small dog caused the Boy General to reflexively break eye contact with the cadaverous Roman Nose. It was Rosco. The little terrier looked up at his master, barking rapidly and incessantly, as small dogs often do.

"You have saved me again, Rosco!" uttered Custer. "I'm lost, Rosco, lead me out of here!"

Suddenly Rosco bared his fangs, his barking had turned to a deep, low, sustained growl. The Yellow Hair turned about face in response and faced Roman Nose, who was sitting upright on the bed, his massive, tree trunk thick thighs dangled from the side of the yellowed mastodon tusk as he sat on it.

"You will not keep the war bonnet," promised Roman Nose, seizing Custer by the shoulders. "It is not meet for white man to use magic of the Old Ones as you intend. You are a blasphemy!"

Oddly, Lieutenant Colonel Custer was no longer in the tepee with Roman Nose. Inexplicably, he was in an Army barracks on a post where he had served early during the war. The barracks was empty, and very quiet. He mounted the stairs that led up to the second floor of the wooden troop barracks, familiar with the setting, he looked about, searching for *someone.*

"Boy! Where you at?" shouted the former general.

"In here!" responded the voice of a small child.

Custer was standing in the hall that divided several rooms, and instinctively executed a left face, entering the wrong room. Toys were strewn about the hardwood floor of the room. The window was open and had no curtains. He noted with familiarity a toy cook stove and dolls lying about the floor. But otherwise the room was strangely empty of furnishings.

"Where you at, boy? Repeated the former general affably, as he heard sounds of a child playing in a room further down the hallway, and to the right.

"In here!" responded the child's voice, prompting the Boy General to walk toward the sound of the tot playing with toys in the way that children do, in their make believe worlds.

Custer entered the room and saw a little boy of about six years of age sitting at a small table – such as those made for children. The boy, he noticed, was angelic in appearance and had shoulder length hair that fell in curls. He recognized the boy immediately as the younger version of himself.

"It's time for us to go now," stated the Yellow Hair paternalistically, genuinely glad to see the little fellow.

"*I've been waiting for you!*" hissed the child, knocking over his play table as he stood suddenly. Before Custer could shield himself, the changeling was upon him like a Pitbull, hurling himself into the Yellow Hair like a mongoose and wrapping around the Boy General's neck like a boa.

Custer threw both hands to his neck as he tried to loosen the furry noose that was *alive* and *tightening its stranglehold*. His pulse was pounding in his ears as he worked his fingers under the ligature and *he felt it tighten like an iron band in response*.

"Wake up! Wake up!" urged Bloody Knife. "It 2300, Boy General say he want wake up!"

Custer lay for a moment on the cot, cushioned by the thick sleeping roll - his eyes wide open and his hands feeling for his throat. He could hear his heart pounding and what sounded like the panting noise of an animal inside of his brain. He could also hear the barking of a little dog, an urgent and insistent barking that faded until he could hear it no more.

"Dog Soldiers!" whispered the Arikawa scout urgently. "Boy General awake? Dog Soldiers come!"

"Shhhh! Listen!" seconded Gladstone.

"It can't be!" They've been reported further to the southeast. No one has seen any of them in this area in nearly a year!" riposted Custer, his blood yet running cold from the nightmare.

"We've gotta do something, General, you are a smart guy, come up with a ruse!" suggested Gladstone, who found the Yellow Hair knowledgeable of Indian ways but was unpredictable in how he would respond.

"Tear down the Sibley and get it on the mule," Custer ordered Bloody Knife. The former general then focused his attention to the anticipating Professor Gladstone.

"Watch me now, and learn, Gladstone," instructed Lieutenant Colonel Custer, who moved a short distance toward the sound of where panting and crashing through vegetation could be heard. The Yellow Hair was still badly shaken from the dream and had to focus himself. The progress of the pursuers was near enough to be heard over the thrumming of war drums that had begun to resonate from a nearby Indian camp. From further away, many miles in fact and from different directions, distant drums rumbled in response.

Watching as Custer walked a small distance, Professor Gladstone did not understand how the Cheyenne had so quickly found them. Born in the

1840s, in Liverpool, England, Professor of Anthropology Dean Gladstone stood five feet eight inches in height and weighed a hundred and forty pounds of lean, hard muscle. A mop of thin, red hair was cut short for reasons of hygiene and to combat the heat of the march.

Beneath the high forehead a pair of keen blue eyes scanned the vegetation from which the alarming sounds of pursuit emanated. Overly large ears, which stuck out sideways from years of wearing the large slouch hats or planter's hats listened with a heightened sense of hearing, focusing and directing the sharpened auditory sense, like radar.

His fair complexion, prone to sunburn, was masked by a dirty layer of smoke and grime, his face was unshaven and the grimy red mutton chop beard served to enhance the primordial appearance of his Celtic features.

Although Gladstone was a technically an authority on North American Indian Culture, that had not prevented him from pursuing the occult to enlist the services of demonic allies. Nor did being a naturalist and magician subtract from the fact that Gladstone was a dangerous, ruthless man; an ambitious man who would do anything to get what he wanted. A first rate killer, Gladstone while appearing bookish and remote, had the face of a snobbish boor and the body of an infantryman.

Custer began unbuttoning his britches and removed the filthy, bacteria laden rag he always wore. He wore rags over his groin to absorb the ever present, disgusting, gonorrheal discharge that he had been plagued with since early in his West Point days.

Lieutenant Colonel Custer laid the saturated, rank cloth on the trail they had intentionally made and then urinated all around it. The urine was thick smelling and made concentrated by dehydration. Although the urine stream was barely enough to wet the grass, the old school cavalryman shook the dark, rancid droplets from his filthy, corrupted member and shoved it back into his cavalry trousers. Then the field savvy former general hurried back to Gladstone and took cover as Bloody Knife hurriedly secured the last of the equipment on the horses and mule.

The Dog Soldiers were onto them; from the yipping and howling, Custer and Gladstone deduced the pack to consist of nearly fifty individuals. The manner in which the men ranged in on them and followed the trail was uncanny. It sounded like there were several point men leading the pack - they would bark and howl as they scented the trail, and be answered by a cacophony of howls and yelping barks, from the main pack further back - with growling interspersed into the chorus.

A long, drawn out wolf yell howled from the deep gloom of the High Plains, very near. It was answered almost immediately by dozens of others further back in the dark, semi desert verdure. Soon a human form emerged faintly into view; he was a tall man, broad shouldered and lean hipped. He was dressed in a sleeveless war shirt which had intricate designs consisting of trade store beads and amulets.

The pockets bulged with ammunition for the Henry repeating rifle he carried at port arms. He looked from right to left, then straight forward. Large, silver hoop earrings swung with the darting head movements as he cautiously advanced.

Piceous eyes peered from a face painted with white horizontal slashes as the Dog Soldier advanced warily, at a crouch. He wore the blue cavalry trousers of some slain trooper, and tightly laced knee length leather moccasins.

The warrior was a Cheyenne, one of the Dog Soldiers - renowned for their keen sense of smell. The long nose was hooked downward at the end, forming a sinister angle - like that of a red tailed hawk. The prominent olfactory organ was set against a Greek like face that bore Mediterranean features as it scented the air, nostrils flaring. Obsidian eyes focused through eyelids narrowed into evil slits of hate. The horribly painted face lifted upward, deftly turning from side to side while the man tried to ascertain the origin of the foul scent assailing his nostrils.

Kneeling down on all fours he sniffed the ground like a hound, his nose pushing aside dead grass and loose earth as he scented to the spot where the Yellow Hair had micturated. The warrior stopped, his face was contorted into a mask of repugnance as it hovered directly over the reeking patch of malfeasant urine.

He stretched flat on the ground, the horse shoe triceps on the back of his thick arms jumping to life powerfully as he supported his upper body, palms to the ground. The Yellow Hair and Gladstone could hear the sniffing sounds of the Dog Soldier quicken and grow agitated as he scented his way over the moon limned grassy floor to the discarded rag.

Suddenly the Dog Soldier leaped up, pushing with his arms, the great muscles of his back played beneath the war shirt like those of a great cat. Clutching the heavy wet rag, saturated with gonorrhea to his horrifically painted face, the Dog Soldier's lips curled back revealing teeth filed to points. The warrior then looked up at the full moon and let out a wretched wolf howl. Dropping the reeking cloth to the ground, he cupped his hands to his mouth, lifting his head toward the harvest moon yet once more. He howled again - this time the howl was more powerful and longer in duration.

Other men began to appear, speaking in hushed tones; a sort of nasal staccato diatribe. They were armed with Henrys and captured Spencers. Nearly all had Remington New Army Model 1858 or the state of the art Colt Model 1860 Army, these were .44 caliber revolvers tucked into the belts which pulled their war shirts in tightly, accentuating their lithe waists.

These Remingtons and Colts had been taken from the dead Buffalo Soldiers that had been assigned to protect the stage coach lines. The overland route taken by the stage coaches had been coming under a series of increasingly numerous attacks. All carried murderous knives either sheathed into belted scabbards or readily available in the tops of boots. Weapons, Custer and Gladstone noted grimly, seemed to adorn the *muscly, painted killers.*

The anthropologist/magician along with the former general took careful aim, Custer with his Spencer and Gladstone with his own, unmodified version. Working fast, the two marksmen shot all seven of the painted Dog Soldiers in the abdomen, hitting in the areas of their stomachs, livers, spleens and intestines. As the mortally wounded Cheyenne Dog Soldiers doubled and writhed, clawing at their stomachs, Custer looked at his friend and said:

"Let's make a run for the horses!" Custer took off without looking back at Gladstone, who was hotly on his track.

"Those seven back there will slow up the main group, and we may have a chance..." panted Custer.

Gladstone's breath came in wretched gasps. Horrified at the specter of being caught alone in these gloomy haunts, Professor Gladstone found his second wind, which was punctuated with copious amounts of blood tinged sputum as his weakened, consumptive lungs sought to clear themselves and deliver more oxygen to the screaming muscles of his thighs and calves.

Within moments, dozens more Dog Soldiers arrived at the scene of the ambush, their wounded brethren were doubled in agony showing the heinous signs of injuries.

Suddenly White Bull exploded from the vegetation, a conglomeration of buffalo grass, five-foot-tall prickly pear hedge, and moisture starved, stunted sage brush which he bent contemptuously out of his way.

Quickly taking stock of what had happened, White Bull advanced past the writhing figures on the ground.

"It can't be! They resist me!" shouted the big medicine man, gesticulating with his left hand the Evil Eye toward the direction Custer and Gladstone had fled, and then spitting through the circle formed by the thumb and forefinger.

"There is more to my magic than meets the eye! While these men yet live, I may heal them. Porcupine Bear, come here!" commanded White Bull.

"Yes, Sachem!" thundered Porcupine Bear. "I am yours to command!"

The image of Porcupine Bear was an unsettling one. Standing a head taller than White Bull, the raven colored hair was unbraided, parted down the middle and fell loosely to the broad shoulders. A single large eagle feather jutted from the back of the coiffure at a downward angle, toward the brave's meaty right shoulder.

The forehead was low set, and sloped back sharply. The supraorbital ridge was unnaturally pronounced. Unlike so many others, Porcupine Bear had retained his eyebrows, which were bushy and thick, joining above a nose which was so large that it was the dominant feature of the man's face. The nose was over formed, arched and savagely hooked at the end. Overdeveloped, prominent nostrils flared on either side of the ostentatious, acne scarred olfactory organ.

To either side of the heinous nose were set two disquieting eyes; large, knowing obsidian pools in which the iris could not be discerned from the pupil. The sclera was heavily blood shot. So bloodshot in fact that it appeared that some of the vessels had ruptured. This appearance was enhanced by the thick, overhanging epicanthic folds that completely ensconced the upper eyelid. The small, thin lipped mouth seemed to always be in the form of a half-smile, and was underslung by a prominent, jutting chin. He was not wearing war paint.

Like the other Dog Soldiers, Porcupine Bear was raw boned and heavily muscled.

"Your fallen will rise to pursue the inferior ones. I need those men who flee – dead or alive! They have the war bonnet! Pursue them, Porcupine Bear, and bring them to me," commanded White Bull.

"Where might I find thee, my Lord?" queried Porcupine Bear.

"I take wing to my tepee now, Porcupine Bear. There is magic to make. Already I have sent two who will guide you, but they will be fleet of foot and will kill the thieves who have taken the war bonnet if they reach them before you do," responded White Bull.

The main body of Dog Soldiers had set off in pursuit of the two fugitives, angrily shouting and gesturing in the direction of the fleeing Custer and Gladstone, who only now reached the waiting Bloody Knife. The Dog Soldiers fanned out with six of the warriors leading the main body, cursing as they crashed heedlessly into prickly pear and swiped through sage brush. Others stayed back with their fallen comrades, as White Bull placed his moonstone on the bullet wounds and began chanting the Sacred Spell of Healing.

Three hours later the three fleeing fugitives were shadowy figures that lurked and shuffled silently through the moon cast shadows, leading their horses and mule on foot. They were unwilling to go much faster in the night and risk getting lost or injured. The trio stopped frequently to crouch, and to look in all directions around them. They listened for any sound that they could discern above the sporadic gun fire taking place far behind them and further still, from other directions. These were sounds which carried a great distance in the night. In the day it would have been out of ear shot.

Two distinct reports of rifle fire could be heard several miles distant. The shots stood out distinctly from the intermittent gunfire originating from the vast distances, and were much closer.

"Ah how sad," whispered Custer. "More scouts from the Tenth Cavalry have been discovered and the rifle fire is signaling for the Cheyenne to come up after them."

"Not a chance they'll get away from those ground sniffers," responded Gladstone as he wiped perspiration from his eyes with the sleeve of his shirt. "There's too many of them. They're everywhere."

"Lots bad Injuns," seconded Bloody Knife. "Better we don't go help no Buffalo Soldier." Bloody Knife added, "ever man for he self."

The red moon shimmered like a hot bloody gut wound in the stifling night air, the atmosphere magnified its proportions as half of it became visible above the ragged mountain ranges to the northeast. Soon the whole orb of the moon was set ablaze with ochre, colored by the smoke of distant range fires which always seemed to burn.

The burned out areas continued to give off orange hues here and there, where coals glowed and small fires struggled to survive on whatever combustible fuel was left to them. Other waves of flame tongued their way along, many miles away.

Ants, beetles, and crickets were devoured by the creeping of those far off flames. Mice and rats along with larger mammals tried to out-pace it, while ground hogs went into their reeking, fetid burrows. The ground trembled perceptibly as a herd of buffalo numbering in the hundreds of thousands fled the relentless encroachment of the hungering, insatiable infernos.

"I haven't begun having second thoughts about the war bonnet, General. Although I don't think they'll stop hunting for us while you've got it on your person, the possession of that bonnet trumps the risk," stated Gladstone honestly. Despite the desperateness of their situation, he could not help but think of his future position as the Curator of the Smithsonian Institution, and the untold secrets it would reveal.

Custer paused before replying, as he sometimes did. He often constructed much of his speech ahead of time, in his mind, before replying. He was prone to speak too fast, and was trying to correct the bad habit. Sometimes, he stammered when he spoke – but not as often anymore.

"We could hide it, and come back later for it," the former general speculated, uncertainly. "Be very quiet," whispered the Yellow Hair. "We are being followed again."

All around them, the sounds of the night were resplendent with life. The haunting sounds of the whip-poor-wills called to each other from the nearby lifeless, burned out trees and from overhead, with their "whip-poor-will!" redundant phrases, repetitively. The numbers of the nightjars seemed to be increasing, exponentially.

High pitched "Whi! Whi! Whi! Whi! Whi!" and "chur! chur! chur! chur!" indicated the presence of many diminutive elf owls. Normally solitary birds of the night, it was odd for so many to be coming together. These also seemed to be aggregating in increasing numbers in close proximity to the three fugitives.

Crickets that inhabited the High Plains sang their tune, and cicadas whirred in darkness. Distantly and nearby, packs of wolves howled at the moon and to each other, while the ubiquitous coyotes yelped and cried, sounding human.

Above all the sounds of the night, however, was the continual thrumming of the war drums; drums which were beaten by the calloused, scarred hands of dusky, taciturn men. Drums beaten in the unsteady light of campfires where Henrys and Enfields were cleaned. Cleaned by fiercely painted men who passed bottled whiskey from one to another.

Added to the penumbral sounds were those of two Buffalo Soldiers who had been marked and cursed, then released from the tent of White Bull. They crashed through the ambuscade of thorny tree branches and stands of cacti, their human intelligence corrupted and augmented with the heightened auditory and olfactory senses endemic to that of the werewolves.

The two wolf-men-soldiers ran bipedally, their uniforms were shredded into tatters from unforgiving bois d'arc thorns. They were hot on the trail of Custer, Gladstone and Bloody Knife. Any vestigial remnants of the human form were relegated to the homo erectus shape only.

Their heads were humanoid; the faces covered not in hair, but in fur. The eyes were cobalt blue, wolf-like and saw through the darkness in shades of quicksilver hues. The teeth were canine, and too numerous for the mouth to accommodate, resulting in a protrusion of the upper palate and lower mandible.

The heavy arms were muscular and gorilla-like, thickly covered in kinky, jet black fur. The hands remained human, albeit oversized and fur covered on the backs. The palms were hairless and retained their palm lines, although the life line was shattered on the Plain of Mars. The leather of the cavalry boots strained to contain the enlarged feet and the cavalry pants had split at the seams due to the swell of the great muscles of the hips and thighs.

"Remain very still" whispered Custer, "and whatever you do, make no sound."

Although Custer, Gladstone and Bloody Knife had heard the nearby rifle shots and correctly surmised the inevitable capture of an advanced element of Buffalo Soldiers, they could not have speculated that days before two other Buffalo Soldiers from the Tenth Cavalry had been captured and made prisoners. These two were the ones that would be sent to execute them.

Soon after the capture of the two Buffalo Soldiers from the Calico Company of the Tenth Cavalry, great magic had been worked to reincarnate them into werewolves, and to send them to aid the Dog Soldiers in the hunt for the fugitives and regain the elusive war bonnet.

The werewolves were the spawn of White Bull, a man versed in unwritten magic save that which was painted on his tepee walls and cave walls deep inside the vaulted caverns that infiltrated the mountains which ranged the Colorado Territory.

The change from homo sapien to homo lupus had not come easily. White Bull had been in an altered state of consciousness, seated on a throne made of dinosaur bone cushioned with heavy buffalo hides. His head was tilted backward, his irises and pupils were rolled back into the orbits of his skull, showing only the white, bloodshot sclera. His respirations had almost ceased, coming at one breath per minute. His skin was cold and covered with a slickened, clammy sweat.

Inside the enormous twenty-foot-tall human leather tepee, the walls of which were covered in magical painted symbols of hellish import, were the two Negro soldiers from the Tenth Cavalry, bound with rawhide leather strips to a pair of roughhewn X shaped crosses.

The semi-comatose medicine man was on an astral plane in communication with malevolent spirits, and was striking bargains with the Old Ones. These were the older, largely forgotten deities which sent demons dancing out from the fires on which dozens of other Buffalo Soldiers smoldered and roasted. The fat from their lean bodies hissing violently when it dripped on the live coals. The queen to which these demons showed obeisance watched with penetrating stygian eyes from the cold, sunlit washes of the moon.

"Hanwi, Hanwi…" repeated White Bull over and over, the words were a barely perceptible mumble to the ears of the Tenth Cavalry soldiers bound to the crosses within the tepee.

"What's he sayin'?" asked Ben, a frail, consumptive corporal who cleared his lungs of a blood tinged mucous plug, and then swallowed it. He was wearing a Union shell jacket over a sweat stained long handle top. His cavalry trousers were tucked into his black, high topped Wellington style cavalry boots.

"Hell if I know," answered Johnson, a tetanus ridden sergeant who could barely move his mouth to eat, drink, or even speak. "I just hope to hell that we get out of this somehow," he said through clenched teeth.

Sergeant Johnson was not the first soldier to have stepped on a rusty nail, nor would he be the last. He rued the morning he had walked to the livery stables to saddle his horse. The lean five-foot eleven-inch cavalryman had not seen the rusty nail protruding from the roughhewn board that had fallen to the floor of the stable when the horse had kicked its stall. The nail had driven through the sole of the boot and emerged through the top of his right foot, puncturing through the leather of the boot.

That one of the Buffalo Soldiers was consumptive and the other plagued with an advanced case of lock-jaw did not dissuade the big medicine man from his diabolical scheme of action for them.

White Bull was the interlocutor - the bridge through which the magic, having similarities to other magic rooted in Paleolithic origins, traversed. There were uncanny similarities shared by all of the Paleolithic magic, despite the vast distances of continents and millenniums. White Bull was deeply steeped in their arcane arts. This magic extended back to the earliest known use of tools, some 2.6 million years.

"Where am I?" asked White Bull, he was standing in what appeared to be a large dried lake bed, which was concave, circular in shape and ringed by a tall, ancient ejecta formed ridgeline. The holy man felt the sensation of intense cold and he noticed that the terrain was strangely white and that he felt a peculiar weightlessness. He also sensed that *he was not alone.*

"I did not grant you the permission to speak, White Bull!" the voice was feminine, high pitched and with the tonal quality of chiming bells. The voice seemed to come from nowhere and everywhere. "Drop to your knees Priest, and bow your head into the ground before my feet!"

"Excellency, I meant no disrespect," spoke the sachem in a supplicating, subordinate manner. He was kneeling forward on both knees, elbows and forearms on the powdery regolith. His face was pressed firmly into the basaltic surface. The calmness of his voice belied the danger of his situation, his heart rate increased to the point he thought it would explode as he fought to control his fear.

"Salute me in the manner you were taught!" countered the icy voice, a voice edged with cruelty and as White Bull knew, whetted with unsurpassable knowledge.

"Forgive me my audacity, Hanwi," whispered White Bull, rising to one knee, looking to the monomineralic surface that was covered in shattered rock and volcanic glass. White Bull thrust out his right arm straight forward in a salute. He did not dare lift his head.

"I did not grant you permission to speak!" shouted the deity.

White Bull felt the blood suddenly rush to his head. His nose, eyes and ears began bleeding profusely, he could not breathe. His hands shot reflexively to his throat in an effort to breath. Still not lifting his head, he remained kneeling and with superhuman effort extended his arm straight forward again, in salute. This time he remained silent.

"Is he dead?" asked Corporal Ben to Sergeant Johnson. "He's hardly breathing at all!"

"Just shut up, Ben!" retorted Johnson. "You shut your damned mouth before you get us killed!" The sergeant had been in many tight squeezes before, but never like this one. The sweat from the pores of his dark skin flowed freely, lending a sheen to his Ivory Coast African features. The perspiration came from fear as much as the stifling heat within the tepee.

White Bull had learned much of his magic from an old shaman who lived in a cave in the gray, ragged and eroded mountains to the north, where the icy snow never melted. This shaman had learned his medicine from a warlock who had been taught by one of the most ancient of wizards. One whose shoulders and neck carried the head of a man which bore traits clearly not typical of the contemporary Cheyenne. This one came of an older Cheyenne line who were in the main of Cro-Magnon stock.

Separated off and held in special status, one of the last of the old thoroughbred Cro-Magnon shamans had been provided for, venerated, and kept alive for one thousand one hundred and twenty-six years.

"Look up, White Bull! Look upon my face!" commanded Hanwi the Accursed, the Sioux Goddess of the Moon.

White Bull remained kneeling, and looked up at the face of the Goddess which stood before him, he continued to hold his salute.

The holy man knew the blinding light would be there, it always was when he spoke with the Old Ones, but nevertheless the sheer incandescence startled him and he involuntarily shielded his face with both of his hands. White Bull peered cautiously through the spaces between his fingers; buying time for his eyes to adjust to the brilliance which he could tell pulsated in an aura all around the deity in malevolent splendor.

Slowly the sachem withdrew his calloused hands from his leathery, sun lined face. Nevertheless, the big Cheyenne still averted his vision until his smarting eyes more fully adjusted to the blinding light. Despite the danger of his predicament, he took note of the blackness of the sky and how it was riddled with stars that did not flicker or wink.

Instead, they reminded him of gems and precious stones of many colors hurled angrily aloft by a slighted Goddess. The constellations shown like scattered necklaces of fine pearls flung about maliciously in an uncontrolled rage throughout the heavenly vaults. There was no sound whatsoever save that of his own breathing and that of the deity.

"Look upon my countenance, High Priest!" commanded Hanwi the Accursed. "Tell me, what do you see? Speak!"

White Bull looked upon a visage of the most stunning beauty; the hair, black as a raven's was not combed straight down or braided in the traditional Sioux manner. The hair was cut square mane, and appeared to be brushed back and over to the left from the high forehead. Some of the brunette coiffure cascaded and tumbled forward, adjacent to and below the left eye, resting against the full fleshed cheek of the face.

The forehead was unlined and the skin shone radiantly, as though freshly scrubbed. The eyebrows appeared to have been carefully plucked into thin ebon ribbons that hooked downward as they terminated. The epicanthic fold above each eyelid was less pronounced than on her earthly subjects. The Stygian eyes of Hanwi the Accursed narrowed into slits and locked with those of White Bull.

"What do you see?" she reiterated, her piceous eyes bored into the obsidian windows of White Bull's soul.

"I see, I see, arrrrrggggghhhh!!!!" screamed the holy man. "You are taking my soul!!!"

The high set cheeks of Hanwi the Accursed became more pronounced as she smiled. The full lips, painted red, pulled back in an off canter smile, akin to a sneer, revealing ivory white, straight teeth. The well-formed nose was not hooked at a downward angle, but appeared Caucasoid, the nostrils flared in favorable reaction to the sachem's agony.

"Yes, High Priest, I am taking your soul, and when I return it to you, you will have the power to command those who worship me from four legs, and howl to me in serenade when I cast my glow and shadow their canyons and ridges with my essence.

"You will look downward through the eyes of those who fly in the night, and eschew even the light of my moon. You will put into your enemies the power of my children to do your bidding. Save your breath, White Bull. Hanwi knows of your needs. It is not meet for one such as you to beg favor of the Gods."

"I cringe before your glory, Hanwi! Take my soul whither thy will desires!" cried White Bull, his voice no longer soft and subordinate, but desperate, pleading, and without pretense.

"Then look upon the One who your line of wizards holds to be their most powerful progenitor," commanded the Goddess of the Moon. Her voice softened. "Look upon the Father of Wizards. Think not, sachem, that I favor the Cheyenne over my children, the Sioux. I smile upon *you*; I smile upon you because you come from a long lineage. Those of your line communed with me before the great migrations split my children into distinct nations."

White Bull suddenly felt himself transported through time and space, the wind rushed past him as the stars blurred into scratches and lines across the astral planes. Suddenly in the blink of an eye, the holy man was looking upon the progenitor. White Bull knew without knowing how, that what he was seeing was a cosmic recording of a man he had only heard about. He stood suspended, it seemed, as he watched the story unfold before his eyes.

When a youth, the progenitor had been robustly and powerfully built; he had been tall and heavily muscled. His forehead was dolichocephalic, with narrow supraorbital brow ridges. Like the race that had descended from his fathers, his face was short and wide and the chin was pronounced.

There was one startling difference between the old wizard and the Cheyenne who sent their medicine men to be steeped in his dark wisdom. The old Cro-Magnon had a larger brain. The magic which was made possible by this significant advantage was passed to the more modern Cheyenne acolytes who were sent to him for tutelage.

White Bull watched as this sorcerer from antiquity taught those whose would become priests. He watched in imposed silence as the foremost magician to ever live taught the darkest arts to disciples who had been selected with great care from the ancient tribes.

The incantations were not of the contemporary variations of the modern Algonquian dialects, but of the ancient root words and verbs to which Algonquian owed much of its origins. The verb was the most important part of Cro-Magnon sentence structure, but any knowledge of the etymology was never more than a vague awareness to the students of these arcane arts.

Thus it was that Custer faced more than rifles and arrows in the wilds of the Colorado Territory; he faced Cro-Magnon Magic. White Bull watched the progenitor as he spoke incantations to the old images painted on the cave walls by previous Cro-Magnon shamans. White Bull had been instructed and had duplicated them on the interior leather walls of his tepee; horrifying imagery of demons and half-man, half-beasts.

He knew the cryptic incantations and sacrifices that were necessary to bring them out of the distant gulfs in which they reigned terror, but his ability was elementary. This would all change now as he descried the progenitor, his knowledge increasing tenfold.

Worship of the demon gods ran rampant within the Paleolithic hunter-gatherer societies, where Cro-Magnon shamans ingressed deeply into the abscesses of winding, twisting mountain caves to paint what they saw on walls of granite, exposed by the dissolution of limestone and gypsum throughout the millennium.

The irregular, winding passages opened into fantastic galleries of titanic boulders strewn crazily about in forests of stalagmites and shattered stalactites which had fallen from ceilings that vanished aloft into darkness. These were things that went unseen until illuminated by the violent, fluctuating light of torches made of five-foot-long staves wrapped at the end with skins and saturated in animal fat. The sputtering, hissing torches were held forward at an angle, so that the bearer would not be burned by the dripping accelerant. To venture deeper into the haunted, meandering vaults would be to court death.

White Bull shuddered in awe as he watched the old sorcerer, dressed completely in the skins of dire wolves, conjure up one of the painted demon-figures from the wall. It came alive and skittled down the rock face, running about spiderlike on the slick grotto floor before growing in size and shape. The figure resolved into a hulking, ape-like shape. This sentient being stood apart distinctly from the man-sized stalagmites that rose like enormous inverted bludgeons from the rocky floor of the cavernous, yawning chamber.

The large torches cast an inconsistent, yet powerful illumination on the surreal cavern, the stalagmites that caught the rushes of yellow light threw horrific shadows across the floor, walls and trailed off into the darkness.

Overhead, Mexican free-tailed bats – medium sized with webbed wings flitted about the candelabra of multihued stalactites that depended from the vaulted ceilings like the swords of giants. The high pitched, ultrasonic squeaking of the furry insectivores bounced from the stalactites back onto hyper sensitized ears as the trogloxenes dodged their way through the cavernous chambers and into the penumbral purple of waning light.

Hundreds of thousands of the bats merged with other colonies to form massive streams of the nocturnal hunters, culminating in spools of millions.

Green tree snakes and rat snakes waited, clinging to stunted trees at the cave's entrance as the furry predators flitted erratically by, often to be seized and then embraced by the coiling, reptilian loops.

The incubus knelt on one knee before the shaman, its face did not look into that of the wizard who had summoned it, but was facing the ground. Its right arm was extended forward at a slight upward angle in obeisance to the man who had summoned him.

The progenitor spoke to it in the Tongue of the Long Forgotten in the high nasal sonorous tones inherent to the prodigious sinus cavities of the Cro-Magnon. The warlock sent the demon to kill the chief of a Shoshone village which had been stealing crops and kidnapping small children.

The progenitor then stopped what he was doing, and seemed to take notice of White Bull for the first time. Moving quickly, the progenitor took a black stone knife made of obsidian and made a cut across the palm of his hand. White Bull stood unable to move as the progenitor advanced on the sachem, walked around to his back and cupped the bleeding hand over the face, pulling the head of White Bull violently backward.

The holy man struggled to pull the hand away as the progenitor's blood entered his mouth, sending him into a violent paroxysm.

White Bull's chest rose and fell rhythmically as his respirations increased to twenty breaths per minute, albeit slowly.

"Ohhhhh! Arrrggghhhh!!!!" cried the unconscious sachem as he struggled back to the world of the living.

The chest, heavy with slab muscle heaved upward with a violent, deep inspiration of air. The sternocleidomastoid muscles of either side of the bull neck stood out suddenly, as the sachem lifted his head from the soil.

This soil bore no congruity to the surrounding hinter lands, but was a bed of discolored reddened earth; a compound of iron oxide soil mixed with the ashes of long dead shamans and holy men, from tens of thousands of years past and from a continent away. This soil was blessed and meticulously cared for, being transported from one camp site to the next.

Two naked maidens fanned the wakening White Bull with shields made of buffalo hide decorated with curious, esoteric designs. The muscles played on their shiny backs as they fanned the big medicine man back to consciousness. Beads of sweat ran between the erector spinae muscles of their dusky backs into the crevasses of their tanned, ham-hock haunches, divided by wide gluteal folds.

The thick, veiny cords of the sternocleidomastoid muscles continued to bulge outward on either side of the robust neck as it lifted a head which reflected a grim countenance. The high forehead was topped with thick, ungreyed black hair. The raven black mane was unfettered; it lay loosely behind the thick neck and massive shoulders, resting atop the sacred ground.

The atramentous complexion of the forehead was further aggrandized through a lifetime of reckless, unshielded exposure to the sun. Creased with deep, horizontal lines, the skin of the forehead resembled the tanned leather of a war drum. The eyebrows and lashes had been plucked smooth, and into the bleary sclera of the eyes were set pupils that always appeared to be dilated. So dilated were the pupils in fact, that the man's eyes seemed to be absent of any suggestion of an iris at all.

The dominant features on the morose visage were defined along horizontal lines, lending to the impression of a gigantic, flat, enigmatic expression. Conspicuous crow's feet extended like claws from the corners of the eyes. The pronounced cartilaginous nose hooked viciously. The corners of the thick, full, lips further defined a mouth which appeared to neither smile nor frown, but maintain a flat expression. The mouth remained closed; the respirations were effected through the flaring nostrils of the beaklike nose.

Awakening from his trance, White Bull inhaled deeply, coughing hoarsely as he sat forward, the smoothness of his abdomen suddenly broken by the pronounced appearance of his rectus abdominis. The rows of lean, hard muscle were divided down the middle, conveying the impression of a washboard. It was a well spring – a reservoir of immense physical strength. He then stood up, his maidens assisting him. Speaking in a dialect of Cro-Magnon, White Bull advanced on the two sequestered Buffalo Soldiers.

"Listen, Chief, we didn't want to come here, Sheridan made us take part in all this. We can help you, we can tell you about all the Army's plans – everything!" said the corporal.

"You speak to no chief!" countered White Bull. "I, White Bull have my own plans. I don't need the plans from no-count Buffalo Trash that come riding in here like stink on shit!"

"I'm a sergeant," interjected Johnson. "I've got pull in the Army. I can make sure you get plenty reward for saving our lives. Listen, Chief..."

"You speak to no chief! I have said this! Shut mouth! I am White Bull! Holy Man! Now, you learn, Buffalo Soldier, what it is to be touched by the Gods!"

Ripping open their shirts and pulling aside their long handle tops, White Bull used a live coal at the end of a stick to draw a symbol onto the chest of each man.

"What are you doing, hey!" shouted the corporal. "That's a live coal you've got there!"

"Scream, cursed man. You are my servant. You kill for me, all the time, get it?" responded the sachem.

"Listen, White Bull! I'll kill anybody you want, you just name'em! There's no need for hot coals, man. We've got a deal, right?"

"Shut mouth," responded White Bull. "Don't wanna hear nothin' you got to say."

Hey! That coal burns!" screamed the corporal. "Stop it, you don't have to do that! I gave you my word I'll kill whoever you want! Hey man! Don't do that!"

The tepee reeked of burning skin, much like the scent of hair scorched in a flame.

The holy man continued drawing on the men's chests, all the time uttering incantations decipherable only to him and the deities upon which he called. Staying in the language passed down to only a few medicine men, the second most powerful wizard on the American continent said the word:

"Predators!"

He looked longingly at the image of the half-man, half-wolf painted in human blood on the tepee walls. Walls made of the supple, tanned hides of cavalry soldiers, prospectors and ambushed members of wagon trains.

"Those were some days," the holy man muttered to himself; remembering one wagon train in particular, which had been loaded with Irish immigrants, headed west for the big land grab. "All of these skins that make my tepee, all of these skins are sheets of magic. Magic that I curse you with today!" the voice rose from introspection into a tenor of anticipation from the Grand Sachem as the coal seared into the ebony, sweating skin.

One naked Cheyenne maiden – a virgin, was rubbing her shining, sweat slickened bosom into the oily back of the high priest and reaching around his chest to massage his meat slabbed pectorals as he uttered the incantations. She bit into the sachem's trapezoid, drawing blood, fueling the fire of the magic. Then reaching down, she found and rubbed the bullet scar above his left hip, and mashed down with the palm of her hand on the whitened scar tissue and rubbed it in a circular motion. She continued to nip and bite at the meaty muscles that rippled in the medicine man's back. She made pantherish, growling sounds from deep in her lithe belly as her straight, white teeth reddened with blood and flashed in the firelight.

The other maiden, also naked, continued fanning the holy man with the buffalo hide escutcheon, which bore the symbol of the Cheyenne Universe – a circle encompassing the Four Directions.

White Bull looked over to the tent drawing that he had completed replicating on the soldiers' chests with the live coal. He gazed approvingly upon its likeness burned into the chests of the soldiers, who no longer cried and begged, but snarled and growled, their canine teeth having tripled in length.

From the snarling mouth of the sweating, glistening face of White Bull issued the low timbre of a deep throated growl, originating deep in the wizard's lean, hard stomach. The wizard's abdomen was pulled in tightly.

The growling of the two soldiers tied to the X shaped crosses made of the felled trunks of Douglas firs receded into a subordinate series of snarls and whimpers, prompting White Bull to cut the rawhide thongs which bound them.

Through the camp the Buffalo Soldiers of the Tenth Cavalry ran, their shirts were ripped open with the swelling of muscles. Instinctively the thousands of Indians in revelry stepped aside creating an avenue for the two werewolves, who quickly vanished into the wood line that abutted the fringe of the temporary, nomadic camp.

Collapsing onto the buffalo quilted throne, White Bull began rubbing the moonstone he always carried in his packet of talismans. The stone was the size of a pheasant egg, and rubbed smooth through years of sorcery. The shining, lustrous feldspar seemed to glow, and the grey, cloudy layers of adularia began to pulsate with the warlock's heartbeat. The medicine man began chanting the name of the Sioux Moon Goddess over and over again. "Hanwi, Hanwi, Hanwi…"

Born a Northern Cheyenne in 1834, White Bull spent many of his days versed in deep magic, and had come to devote himself wholly to Roman Nose, seeing in the man a charismatic leader who truly had the faith and discipline to adhere to the myriad rules set forth in the arcane arts of his magic.

That there was no man of equal stature among the Cheyenne to replace the fallen Roman Nose troubled White Bull, even as he invoked powerful magic to regain the war bonnet. Despite the alliance of the Cheyenne to the Sioux, he preferred that a Cheyenne wear the magical war bonnet.

The tightened jawline of White Bull was stalwart as he continued to utter "Hanwi," and the chin stood out in outstanding profile. The swarthy face was horrifically scarred on the right cheek with an old knife-fighting wound. The high set cheeks settled as the face relaxed. The profound, etched lines from decades of exposure to the elements were more defined in the poor light. His entire facial aspect was scored with these deep, furrowed lines, including his neck. This imparted the likeness to a leather drum skin which had been ripped from its cylindrical shell and wadded into a tightly clenched fist, and then flung open repeatedly.

"Hanwi." The next repetition did not exit the thick, quivering lips; lips that contorted into a sneer as the holy man discerned a movement behind the shadows of the two nude women who attended him. Pulling a .44 Colt Army from underneath a fold in the buffalo rug quilting that overlay the throne, the sachem cocked back the hammer. White Bull advanced boldly on the specter who hid despicably behind the partition of colorful wool blankets.

"Crazy Horse!" shouted the surprised sachem in a voice inflected with surprise and growing anger. "How much of this did you see?!" demanded White Bull, his somber countenance becoming swarthy with the onset of rage.

"Enough to see that you are in league with Hanwi the Accursed!" responded Crazy Horse, who continued, "I go now to report this to the Tribal Council!"

The bear greased hair of Crazy Horse was parted along the crown slightly off center and braided tightly into two pony tails which fell to just above the swell of the twin shield pectorals. The pony tail braids were held intact with rawhide thongs and were each sheathed in a sock made of otter skin. The medium size forehead sloped back slightly and was set atop an aristocratic face akin to that of a Greek or an Italian Nobleman.

The epicanthic folds that partially occulted the upper eyelids added to, rather than detracted from the man's natural good looks.

A single bandolier of ammunition for his Henry crossed the sweating shields of pectoral muscle. These played beneath the suntanned skin with an insolent shrug of the shoulders as Crazy Horse prepared to exit the tepee. A gun belt with its holstered .44 Remington New Army Revolver was slung at an angle low on his right hip. He wore a loin clout of knee length, brightly colored fabric over a set of buckskin leggings, which were tucked into the utilitarian knee high suede boot moccasins. These were fringed at the top and laced with a long rawhide thong. Within these was secured a practical, utilitarian skinning knife.

"Look into my eyes and be damned, you who violate the Sacred Oath of Transgression!" The High Priest of the Northern Cheyenne commanded as he held the young Sioux's gaze and plumbed into the darkest depths of the man's soul, plunging into the most inaccessible wells of vile secrets and heinous deeds that the mortal man sought to ensconce. *"Look into my eyes and see the power that blasts men's souls!"*

White Bull locked both vise-like hands around the ox neck of Crazy Horse, and employing an upward motion, lifted the younger man from the hard packed, soil floor. White Bull lifted him straight into the air and shook him as a Pitbull shakes a small child. The triceps of White Bull stood out on the back of his arms like horseshoes made of Tungsten steel as he throttled the madly flailing Crazy Horse. The younger brave's eyes were rolled into the back of his head and white spittle frothed from lips turned blue.

"Have mercy upon him, my Lord!" pleaded one of the buxom, ebon haired beauties, setting down the shield which she had been fanning the sachem with and hurling herself to the holy man's feet.

White Bull contemptuously hurled the lifeless carcass of Crazy Horse onto the sacred ground that rested within a slight depression excavated into the soil floor of the tepee, near the center, adjacent to the cooking fire. An off colored gray dust flew as the body hit the ground with a dull, heavy thud – like the sound of a heavy sack of horse feed when it is thrown onto a wagon at the feed mill.

White Bull walked up to the dead body of Crazy Horse. White Bull's gait was a haughty swagger - a stride extolling confidence; the confidence of a man who is sure of himself and is a master in his calling.

"Where is thy cockiness now, my young Crazy Horse? You who take the wives of other warriors, of valorous men," White Bull reached into his leather sachet of talismans and pulled forth the moonstone.

The transition from the Cheyenne language into Cro-Magnon was fluid for White Bull, who held the glowing, pulsating moonstone overhead as he looked up and invoked the name of Hanwi the Accursed, Goddess of the Moon.

"Go to him quickly now, black haired beauty! There is no time to waste if he is to come back! Give him suckle! *GIVE HIM LIFE!*" commanded White Bull. The holy man's skin was shining with sweat. The glistening perspiration enhanced the definition of the layers of rippling, knotted muscles. The impressive arms were outstretched toward the hole at the top of the tepee, and in his right hand pulsated the moonstone. His eyes were tightly closed, his lips moved as he invoked the ancient Rite of Resurrection.

The dusky, full bosom warbled over the face of the motionless Crazy Horse, the large areola – twice the size of a twenty-dollar golden Double Eagle was punctuated in the center with a nipple the size of a thimble. This brushed against the stricken warrior's lips. Lips which suddenly parted as the nipple was seized fiercely between strong, crooked, tobacco stained teeth.

Muscular red hands grabbed at the pendulous breasts, smashing them into the face; a face which was alive and emitted harsh, muffled breath sounds as it sought air from the sternal area, in the cleavage that divided the mammary glands.

The expression on the face of Crazy Horse could not be seen – as it was hidden in the sweating, shining, and pigmented bosom of the maiden. Back from the dead, he instinctively took each swollen teat into the mouth, suckling as though he were a starving child, he then absorbed the entire part of the breast containing the areola into his edacious orifice.

The large, battle scarred hands moved along the lithe flanks to the firm buttocks of the maiden, seeking, squeezing until suddenly the command from White Bull arrested further development of the situation.

"Who am I!" shouted White Bull, it was a demand, not a question.

"You are White Bull, my Liege. Lord over all Magic, Seer of What is to Be, The Maker of Rain, The Bringer of Buffalo, Apostolate to the Sun!" was the muffled response of Crazy Horse.

"Who are *you?*" demanded White Bull, the biceps of his arms appeared exaggerated in size as they relaxed and pressed against each other, resting over his steak slab pectorals in the posture of authority.

"I am but your humble dog, my Lord," responded Crazy Horse, who eased the vixen from his waist and knelt, his face toward the ground. His right arm was thrust forward in salute.

"You are much more; you are the stuff of Heroes. Go now, young man. Your deeds will echo into history..."

Chapter Eighteen
The Pursuit of the Werewolves!

THE YELLOW HAIRED former general along with the red coiffured anthropologist remained motionless as their heightened, adrenaline fueled sense of awareness alerted them to the presence of the two werewolves. Bloody Knife held the bridles of the mounts as they snorted, scenting the air. They shied and moved uneasily at the scent of the werewolves; the steel corded biceps of Bloody Knife's arms jumped out in bold response each time the horses and mule strained against them.

All could hear the rapid panting of the two wolf-men despite the chronic, gunfire induced tinnitus in their ears. The placidity of the night abetted their heightened senses of cognizance. Virtually any sound the werewolves made was amplified and carried on the night air through the thickets of prickly pear, wild plum bush, and a panoply of thorny brush interspersed with stunted, scrubby trees.

The winsome calls of the elf owls and night jars increased in number as flocks of the nocturnal birds circled the two white men and their Indian scout, pin pointing their location for the unnatural pursuers. The eerie, loathsome calls of the birds increased in volume exponentially as more of them flocked to the precise location of the three stubbornly elusive fugitives.

In the dim light of the stars the birds appeared as a spiraling whirlpool of flapping wings and darting bodies; a vortex of dark, feathered mass that hovered, circling crazily like a tornado beneath a starlit canopy above them.

"He's onto us!" exclaimed Gladstone, in an urgent whisper. "He's one of those who can control the animals of the air and the field!"

"But what about the war bonnet, it's supposed to protect us from discovery," postulated Custer.

"Not not no good 'gainst White Bull," riposted Bloody Knife.

The werewolves in shredded cavalry uniforms located the source of the scent of the two white men and Arikawa in hiding. They sat doglike on their haunches and exchanged a dialogue of low, visceral growls and whimpers, punctuated with rapid panting, as their tongues lolled out of their slobbering maws. Then they split and diverged, advancing on their quarry stealthily, hunkered down at the waist. Their heavy panting vented off the great body heat generated by the pursuit, and bacteria laden saliva drooled from their smiling jaws, detaching as it caught on undergrowth.

The minutes turned into an hour as the wolf-men narrowed the distance from opposite sides. At this point they were low crawling, cognizant of the need for silence. Mosquitos swarmed the faces of both werewolves, drawn by the saliva drooling from their grinning, toothy mouths. One of them angrily swiped the pests from his eyes, disturbing a fallen tree branch in the act.

Lieutenant Colonel Custer turned his head suddenly in the direction of the sound, a crease formed from his jaw line beneath the earlobe and extended at an angle down his face as he executed the motion.

The sounds were faint, but perceptible as Bloody Knife held the reins of the mounts, trying to keep them from becoming spooked. That both of his hands were tasked with restraining the nervous mounts added to his gnawing sense of unease.

The Yellow Hair was alarmed as he discerned several faint perturbations in the thick grass that carpeted the prairie floor; the sound of rustling movements that began and stopped in short increments. He could hear them above the ringing in his ears. The sounds came from over to his right and left.

Custer silently grabbed Gladstone by the back of his shirt, causing him to turn his head and prop himself on his elbow toward the former general. Gladstone strained to listen to the hushed warning that hissed between the clenched white teeth of the Boy General:

"Two of them!"

"Let's do this with our knives, if we shoot, thousands of them will hear it and come running," continued Custer, who elaborated, "you must grab the one who comes at you by his ankles, and hold onto him, bring him down if you can," instructed the Boy General, his voice was coming in harsh, staccato whispers – like distinct bursts of rifle fire from a distance.

Gladstone did not answer, but for a hushed, "OK."

Suddenly, in a rush of movement the two werewolves were upon the soldier and civilian. Custer drove the heavy, overbuilt blade of his Bowie knife through the bladder of his attacker, thrusting at an upward angle. The single edged blade skewered through the small and large intestines, bisecting the spleen and lacerating the liver. Several inches of the large fighting knife thrusted like an unwelcome guest from out of the beast's back above the left flank as it skewered through the kidney. The tip of the knife remained exposed for a moment, before disappearing back through the hole like the head of a turtle retracting into its shell.

The hybrid mammal which only hours ago was the Buffalo Soldier Ben, lashed out at the blond head of the Boy General with its left hand, as it clutched at the knife hand of George Armstrong Custer with its right.

Gladstone grabbed the two treelike legs of his attacker with both sinewy arms and squeezed them together in a bearlike hug, causing the top-heavy beast to growl and gnash its massive, heavily toothed jaws in fury as it looked down. The homo-lupus tottered as it waved its orangutan-like arms in a desperate attempt to maintain balance. It teetered and raked the Englishman's back with filthy, taloned fingernails, ripping through the Englishman's shirt and long handle top.

The werewolf confronting Custer tried to grab the athletic former general by his greasy, sour smelling blond hair, but the effeminate locks were loose, badly receded at the front and easily pulled out in a handful. Seeking other means of purchase, he grabbed the adventurer by the front of the buckskin shirt and lifted him up, howling in pain as Custer hefted viciously upward on the deer antler handle of the oversized fighting knife.

The blade, heavier near the front and made of high carbon steel, cut through the rectus abdominis of the werewolf like a razor blade. The lacerated tendons withdrew into their points of attachment, helping to eviscerate the abdominal wall which opened up into a yawning hole. The evisceration allowed the entrails of the mortally wounded homo-lupus to spill out onto the parched grass that bedded the prairie floor.

The panting, wheezing former general struggled to breathe as he resisted the onset of an asthmatic attack. The cavalry officer locked his blue eyes with the cobalt eyes of his attacker and recognized the malevolent intelligence that dwelled behind them. The were-soldier and the officer growled in tandem as Custer wrenched brutally upward on the antler sheathed tang of the Bowie knife using both hands.

The sound that the effort produced was akin to that of a ripe watermelon, when a sharp blade is pressed to it and it splits open of its own volition.

The Yellow Hair could feel the knife, honed into a beveled edge, catch on and grate against the ribcage, causing the man-beast to step back, clutching the cavernous cavity of its empty thorax in amazement and horror. It egressed into the woods, turned for a moment to face Custer and then howled like a scalded dog, while its intestines drug behind it. Cockleburs, dry grass and ants clung to the sticky, adhesive mucosal lining of the trailing innards.

The Bowie knife that Custer held at the ready was in truth a murderous fighting weapon, the date of its appearance in the American West could be traced to about 1830. It was a top heavy knife, diverging radically from the other styles of fighting knives. Armed with a two-foot single edged blade, it was broad at the front and narrowed at the hilt. The full length tang gave the Bowie the ability to serve as a utilitarian chopping tool, if it needed to be. It was a balanced, hybridized slashing weapon. The top of the blade curved evilly inward as it culminated into a needle sharp point, which allowed it to be thrust into an opponent.

In several Southern states, the length of the Bowie knife had been restricted in order to reduce its employment in the numerous duels that persisted throughout the Deep South, where it was rumored to have originated with the infamous land speculating, slave dealing duelist, Jim Bowie.

Its true forte lay in its employment as a slashing and chopping weapon, akin to an oversized meat cleaver. Even if wielded in an unskilled hand it could change the outcome of a fight. It was said that the merciless duelist, Jim Bowie had created a prototype of the horrific weapon from the metal of a shooting star that he had witnessed plunging into the earth.

The fact that Custer wielded the Bowie with such great effect went amiss on the cognizance of Gladstone, who had lost his grip on the wolf man's legs. The hybrid man-wolf savagely kicked him in the face over and over, the were-wolf's cavalry boot crushing the fragile nasal bones and snapping the cartilage. The red haired man clutched his shattered face with both hands, oblivious to the danger as pain overwhelmed his common sense.

The panting werewolf sensed with humanlike intuition that his true prey was not the screaming, writhing tawny haired man at his feet, but the yellow haired man. The parfleche containing the war bonnet was in plain view, secured by a rawhide strap to the former general's back. Instinctively the wolf man knew Custer was the primary target. He had been sent with hellish intent to bring back the war bonnet and at least one of the fugitives, dead or alive.

It was also the blood of the European American invaders that White Bull had sent the pair of werewolves after. He needed the blood to coordinate the various forms of magic that he was working. Up to now he had relied exclusively on Native American magic, but he was sketchily versed in the Occult of the

Old World as well, and the blood of a European with high military rank would strengthen his medicine one hundred fold.

"Bring to me the evil one through whose heart rushes the blood of a general!" White Bull had growled and barked at the two hybrid man-wolves before setting them loose. 'Bring to me the Unholy One! The yellow haired blasphemer whom they call Custer!"

The humanoid brain residing within the hybrid mammal instinctively recognized the superior rank of the cavalry officer based on residual memories, and lunged for him. Custer didn't have time to slash or thrust, instead he used the pommel of the Bowie to strike blindly at the misshapen head whose frothing, mal-occluded jaws snapped close with a clacking sound as the teeth meshed unevenly together.

The fetid smelling breath was perilously close to his face. Saliva flew from those terrible, champing jaws; reeking, bacteria laden spume entered the former general's mouth and the conjunctiva of his eyes.

"Get off me!" shouted the struggling Yellow Hair, who swung the murderous fighting knife like the Berserker at the Stamford Bridge swung an axe. "Bloody Knife! Escape with the horses!"

The soldier-wolf lifted the contorting, shouting object of his passion off the ground with hirsute, burly arms and walked quickly to a gnarled, deformed post oak tree. Struggling to adjust his hold on the twisting, flailing officer, the wolf-man slammed the former general against the tree. The branches shook the leaves with the impact and they made an agitated, rustling sound.

The Boy General was pinioned against the post oak, continuing to ram the butt of the Bowie knife against the unyielding skull of the snarling beast. The facial muscles of the wolf-man had tensed on the left side of its face, exposing the elongated teeth on that side of the mouth. This lent to the impression of a sneering expression.

Bloody Knife had his filthy hands full with the panicking beasts of burden; they neighed and reared as he tried to lead them hastily from the fight. He was holding the reins of three horses and the mule as he led them away on foot. At times he had to turn around and walk backwards as he tried to restrain them, the reins were wrapped tightly around his wrists and dug into them.

When Gladstone came to his senses, he was mouth breathing and spitting blood. His crushed nose was releasing a torrent of blood and thick mucus down the back of his throat. Instinctively, in order to avoid choking he spat a mouth full of the sanguinary mucus onto the grass as he propped himself up on his right elbow. Professor Gladstone was taking grasp of the critical situation that he and the cavalry officer were in.

The smell of the oxygen rich blood carried to the hypersensitive sinuses of the man-canine, and the hybrid mammal was temporarily distracted by the odor. But not distracted enough to relinquish his tenacious grip on the knife swinging, shouting Lieutenant Colonel Custer.

With an effort that boasted of immense strength, the werewolf easily shouldered the struggling Yellow Hair and turned to his right, preparing to carry the prisoner back to the Indian camp *alive.*

Custer began driving his Bowie knife into the beast's back. Not truly designed with the purpose of employing either the stabbing or thrusting motion, the Bowie met resistance from the thick muscles that knotted over the ribs of the beast's back.

The dingy, grey, matted fur, festooned with scores of cockle burrs began to well with blood that oozed from the growing number of puncture wounds. Although most were superficial, some penetrated deeply, allowing Custer to force the knife and work the big blade back and forth prior to wrenching it free.

Increasingly, the former general had to maneuver and work loose the knife that had become vised in the contorting mass of muscles that played underneath the shaggy mass of fur each time he drove the blade home. A gory sheen reflected from the torn cavalry shirt that was plastered with blood on the beast's back.

"Gladstone! Stop him! He is making away with me!" shouted the panicked Lieutenant Colonel Custer, who writhed and made wrestler like contortions with his body in an effort to break the werewolf's hold on him.

"Give me the knife!" Gladstone shouted back to the Yellow Hair.

Gladstone ran forward at a crouch and seized his companion's Bowie with his right hand, using his left to staunch the blood that flowed like a torrent from his smashed nose. The university educated anthropologist was sage in the ungentlemanly ways of knife fighting. He had learned this unseemly art in the rougher dives of London. He swung the blade in a wide, sweeping arc, perpendicular to his waist and with the blade pointed downward at a thirty-degree angle. The keen blade sliced effortlessly through the back of the legs of the werewolf, to a depth of an inch.

The incision had been neatly made, as if with a surgical instrument. Above the back of both knees was a deep, gaping cut, which did not at first bleed. The cuts had severed the nerves behind each leg, as well as the tendons binding the hamstring muscles to their joints. The effect was immediate; the beast collapsed onto the grassy flora covering the ground, releasing the combative Boy General. Custer skittled backwards on all fours, like a crab, not taking his eyes from the stricken monster of folklore.

"We must run now! And on your life do not look back!" gasped the Yellow Hair, as he stood up.

Still holding the Bowie knife, Gladstone looked at the werewolf, who was dragging himself into a darkened thicket of pear cactus, using his hands to clutch at the tufts of buffalo grass and other undergrowth as he pulled himself along, one or two agonizing feet at a time.

The moon was an orange red globe, magnified out of proportion by the atmosphere as it settled low on the horizon, its face wavering through the sheens of heat waves that still rose from the smoldering range fires many miles away.

Custer and Gladstone lay in the concealment of thick brush that grew at the base of the cottonwoods that fringed the outer layer of a shallow stream – one of many that sketched spidery lines across the Great Plains.

"Damned thing bit me!" exclaimed Gladstone. The Professor/Magician studied the festering wound on the rended forearm with alarm; he was concerned with his own survival now more than ever. With the flowing creek within sight he felt especially anxious to immerse the throbbing extremity in the cool water and allay the burning that he felt running up his entire arm.

Chapter Nineteen
Stillwell and Trudeau
Reach Fort Wallace

IT WAS THE RIFLE FIRE that alerted the duo to their exact location in the early morning pre-dawn. The exhausted pair of messengers had traveled desperately for days, avoiding hundreds of marauding war parties that sometimes came perilously close to discovering them.

"The hill where Fort Wallace is lies directly ahead, on the other side of that stream. But it's surrounded by thousands of Indians," remarked the keen eyed Trudeau. Stillwell was always impressed by the superb eyesight of the sixty-year-old man.

Stillwell felt an enormous sense of accomplishment in seeing the fort, even though it was under heavy Indian attack. Mumbling to himself aloud as he clawed at hundreds of chigger bug bites, Stillwell remarked:

"We covered a hundred miles, I can't believe we've made it back into Kansas."

Sheet lightning transformed the early morning darkness momentarily to eerie daylight as an unpredictable storm threatened to unleash a torrential downpour over the entire area and dangerously flood the large stream known as Pond Creek.

The reports of rifle fire began to escalate and as the sun was nothing more than an orange, hesitant suggestion on the eastern horizon, the sounds were amplified and echoed crazily throughout the Great Plains. It was as though the sun vied with the moon in a penumbral struggle, as the bright flashes of rifle fire stubbornly remained visible in the waning of twilight.

"We'll stay put right here," croaked Trudeau. The maddening pain of his blistered feet seemed to ebb as the moon disappeared beneath a distant range of high hills.

"It doesn't look like Colonel Bankhead is going to come out of his fort and yield the advantage of his position. Once they've finished messing with Bankhead, they'll probably move on. We'll wait this one out, and then make for the fort at an opportune moment," continued Trudeau, removing his boots cautiously.

"Keep an eye out, I've got to do something about my feet," stated Trudeau. "They feel like someone has taken a meat tenderizer to them." After removing the boots, Pierre carefully removed the stockings, worn with holes, from his tortured feet. The skin of the ruptured blisters adhered to the fabric of the socks, and sloughed loose with their removal.

Trudeau and Stillwell heard a commotion some distance back in the prairie, then three rapid revolver shots from a Colt, followed by two more. A Negro soldier sprang from a thin grove of cottonwoods and ran at an angle directly in front of the two vagabonds.

The two scouts remained motionless as they watched a dozen pursuing Comanche close the distance with the running man. These Comanche were distinct from the besieging hordes of Sioux and Cheyenne that assailed Ft Wallace. These were young braves, out for scalps and had been drawn to the sounds of the gunfire that raged from the beleaguered garrison. As three of the fleetest warriors approached to within arms distance, a shot rang out, and the Buffalo Soldier collapsed onto the thick grass, slippery with dew. Bright red blood spurted madly from a massive hole that formed a gaping mouth at the temple of the man's head; he had saved his last bullet for himself.

The Comanche were a wide ranging Nation, of which the tribes were spread across the Great Plains. They had loose, tenuous alliances with the Sioux and Cheyenne, and often abetted them in their wars against the whites.

These warriors lived to fight, and they immediately began scalping the soldier and cutting the clothing from him. Long range rifle fire from the fort was directed at the Comanche warriors. There was a thud and a perturbation in the grass as a bullet struck the ground near where the Comanche were dressing out their quarry. They were pulling off the soldier's boots before dislocating and dismembering the legs at the knee joint.

It was believed by the superstitious warriors that by mutilating their enemies, their defeated foe would be humiliated and crippled in the afterlife, and also, would be unable to seek retribution by returning in some atavistic form to the world of the living.

As the battle raged on at Ft Wallace barely a rifle shot away, more bullets ripped through the sharp edged buffalo grass, thudding into the earth about the milling Comanche braves. The warriors took notice when some of the bullets whistled closely by as they sped like hornets and smacked into the tree line.

One of the red men took a hit to the torso and went down, twisting and writhing like a snake. He raised his head, causing the muscles on either side of the ox like neck to stand out like steel cables as he screamed like a Wampus cat. He rotated his head from side to side like a man emphasizing denial as his life was ushered from his body in pulsating jets of blood.

Two more swarthy figures went down, flailing wildly and kicking as hot lead seared through and imparted a shock wave within the body tissue, which had the effect of displacing and rupturing vital organs. They rolled and twisted like contortionists in the wet grass.

The remaining nine warriors, tall, muscular men, ran toward the tree line, twenty-five yards away - some wore moccasins, others wore sandals or boots. All were wearing britches made of leather animal hide or the pants of slain cavalry soldiers. Some wore the leather war shirts and others were dressed in an assortment of mismatched apparel, including cavalry shirts or long handle tops.

One of the desperately fleeing braves approached the position where Stillwell and Trudeau lay hidden, holding their breath. Bullets impacted the ground behind and on either side of him with heavy thumping sounds as he ran with determination for his life. He did not run in a straight line, but rather in a zig zagging pattern, in an effort to throw off the soldiers' aim.

Stillwell realized before Trudeau spoke that the big brave was running like a superhuman Pheidippides - directly to where the two fugitives lay ensconced, and that there was no avoiding the calamity which was about to occur.

The Comanche hurtled through the ripping boughs of low hanging branches, stepping on Stillwell as he did so. Immediately he lost his footing and went to the ground. He was brutally seized by Trudeau, who grabbed the surprised man from behind, hand over his mouth. He cut the brave's throat on the right side of the neck, thrusting the three-inch blade of the boning knife up to the hilt and pushing forward with it, severing the jugular vein. Trudeau released the brave, who immediately began to run into the thickets. The brave was cursing as he held both hands to the wound that spurted hot, sticky, coppery smelling blood from between the taloned fingers.

A warrior appeared from a shallow hole in the ground ten feet away - as a thatch cover made of buffalo grass flew to the side, the warrior leaped from the excavation. He ran at Trudeau, dodging from right to left, as the much older man shot at him with his revolver, missing. In two seconds the Comanche was upon the old man.

The muscles in the brave's neck and arms grew in size as they bunched out in knots, bulging in effort as he locked his vein covered, beefy hands around Trudeau's thick neck. It was no match as the superhuman strength rushed into the hands of the grey haired man, who slashed at the brave with such fury that the small knife bit into and through the facial muscles, grating against the facial bones of his opponent's skull.

Using the heel of his left hand, Trudeau rammed the nasal bones of the warrior loose in an upward motion and the two went to ground, with the older man on top. The enraged geriatric cut into the neck with the ubiquitous boning knife and wrenched at the aboriginal's throat with the free hand. The sixty-year-old killer tore out the warrior's throat with a wet, cracking, snapping sound and hurled it against a tree.

"Use your revolver and start shooting, Jack!" shouted Trudeau to Stillwell.

Four Comanche cautiously circled the crouching sixty-year-old, as he wolfishly wheeled about in the center of them, like a mongoose surrounded by cobras. Two of them waved and thrusted knives of various types at him in threatening, provocative feints, while the other two readied for a shot. Trudeau moved inside the ring of warriors catlike – quick on the balls of his feet.

The sixty-year-old man's feral blue eyes were alive with intensity. He laughed as he stepped toward one of the assailants, his knife held low at his side, with his left hand forward at shoulder level and open. He would make feinting motions with the open hand while stepping forward with the knife held low, compelling the braves to reflexively move back.

One of the warriors was a painted man of stoop shouldered physique. He wore arm bands of beaten copper that bit into biceps the size of pork loins. He was wearing a hair pipe breastplate over the twin shield pectorals of his meat slabbed chest. The swell of his thighs stretched the fabric of the stolen blue trousers of a cavalry officer, which had a gold stripe running the length of seam. His full length moccasins were decorated in beaded Comanche floral designs and reinforced with rawhide at the soles.

This man pulled the copper butt plate of the Henry repeating rifle into the full, rounded deltoid of his right shoulder, melding his right cheek into the rifle stock. As he aligned the adjustable rear sight with the front sight blade of the twenty-four inch octangle barrel, Stillwell shot him through the back of the head. Trudeau saw brain matter fly from the man's nose and mouth as the warrior fell forward, convulsing to the ground. The leaves made agitated, rustling noises as the warrior's body seized in a violent series of paroxysms in its death throws.

Another warrior wore a buckskin war shirt of which the sleeves were cut out like a sort of tunic, meant to show off his muscular arms. The leather cavalry belt holding his breech clout was cinched in tightly at the waist, making his arms appear even larger than they already were. He had taken aim with a Henry at Trudeau, who swung around to face him when suddenly twelve inches of Arkansas Toothpick erupted from immediately beneath the brave's sternum.

The Comanche reflexively squeezed the trigger as he arched his back, shooting high and to the left. He coughed blood and used the butt of his rifle to break his fall as he collapsed to his knees, blood issuing in ragged spurts from both the entry and exit wounds. The broad flap of his scarlet breech clout that hung between his legs failed to hide the urine that streamed as he lost control of his bladder.

"Whats'a matter, boy? Can't hold your water?" asked Old Pete, looking thoughtfully at the dying brave, who began retching violently.

The remaining two warriors hesitated, regarding the old man through slitted eyes and then fled, one behind the other.

"Boogey Man gonna getch y'all!" taunted Trudeau at the backs of the vanishing figures, who seemed to be accepted by, and then swallowed into the lush verdure of the thick swathe of deciduous and evergreen trees.

Jack Stillwell wiped the blood from the murderous double edged dirk on the leg of his torn trousers, and sheathed the weapon in its black leather scabbard. The scabbard was made specifically to the fighting knife and hung from the belt. The Arkansas Toothpick was a favorite among the low life White Trash to settle disputes among themselves – although it was less prevalent than the Bowie knife and its variants.

"Git up on my shoulders," growled Stillwell. "We're goin' in, hell for leather!" The ancient frontiersman climbed atop the six-foot three-inch Kansan, mounting his shoulders from behind, and then exclaimed: "OK, go for it!"

Stillwell held the shins of Trudeau's legs with his hands as he stood up and began heading toward the large creek that separated them from Fort Wallace. The fort occupied by the besieged forces of Colonel Bankhead loomed before them like an oasis in a desert of red humanity. At first they moved at a slow jog, the pace increasing to a full run as the younger man with his mounted elderly rider approached the creek and began drawing fire from the besieging Indians. The Native Americans were swarming around Fort Wallace in a roiling, seething mass of painted death.

Fort Wallace was the farthest US Army fort on the frontier, it stood alone; a last sanctuary of safety for settlers, stage coaches, wagon trains, and railroad workers who sought refuge from Cheyenne and Sioux. Beyond Fort Wallace was nearly certain death; painted death thundering like a juggernaut on horseback or crouching stealthily in the seas of waving grass that covered the vast, endless expanse of the Great Plains

Fort Wallace had been constructed at the order of General William Tecumseh Sherman and was a formidable conglomeration of stout wooden structures and solid block houses made of stone which was hewn from a nearby quarry. The granite quarry had remained unutilized for a year, owing to the danger of exposure that working the site would entail.

Stillwell and Trudeau made the creek's edge and took cover behind an escarpment as bullets whizzed overhead; the projectiles made an alarming, high pitched whistling sound. Even more disconcertingly, the sound of dozens of voices alerted their ears; voices in the Sioux vernacular, shouting to one another in nasal tones as they leapt into the water. The braves were dog paddling with their heads above water and knives clenched between their teeth. They fought the current as they swam the deep creek toward the escarpment where Stillwell and Trudeau lay waiting.

Bell shaped, waxy white blossoms of countless yuccas accompanied by clouds of yucca moths comingled with bluestem grass, purple clover, and blazing star along the course of Pond Creek. Juniper and sagebrush were randomly hurled into the mix. The heat and humidity prompted the lush verdure to exude a sweet, cloying smell that clung to the odor of spent gunpowder like a red tailed hawk clings to a muskrat.

Along some of the high hills visible in the background, red oak and slash pine were to be seen. The banks of Pond Creek were often straddled with thick poplar groves, which flourished with an abundance of undergrowth consisting of wild rose, blackberry, honeysuckle and poison ivy. It was visited by the fort inhabitants only in heavily armed contingents. Recently the strength of Fort Wallace had been raised to fifteen hundred fifty Buffalo Soldiers.

Pierre Trudeau gave these facts scant thought as he agonizingly gave instructions through Herculean dint of will. His blistered feet had swollen into a pair of throbbin' robins and a serosanguinous fluid exuded from where the skin had sloughed away with the removal of the rancid, fetid socks.

"You pick off as many as you can while they're in the water," Trudeau grated with superhuman effort, as though trying to give instructions through a bad dream.

"Pete, are you all right?" asked Stillwell, who noted the older man's malady with grave concern.

"Son," answered Trudeau as his feet throbbed. "Can't you see them Injuns comin'? I can't ever tell if you love killin' or if you hate it!"

"Ought not I go back and grab a couple of them Henrys?" queried Jack Stillwell. "We were amiss to leave them rifles back there."

The ancient frontiersman was fighting another inner demon with all of his powerful will; the need to kill. The lust to kill was what had driven him to join the special attack force. Trudeau was a man who had begun killing almost as soon as he was old enough to wield a knife. It didn't matter whether it was right or wrong, all that he knew was that he had always been obsessed by the urge. At times it controlled him.

The pair had run out of bullets for their own rifles days before and they had destroyed their longarms, hiding the parts.

"No! Not enough time!" Pierre responded. It's gonna havta all be revolver work!" After a moment's pause, Trudeau added with an edge of hopeful anticipation in his voice, "Knife work too, more'n likely!"

Stillwell eased around the edge of the escarpment, revolver in hand. He peered past the right side of a large boulder weighing several thousand tons and saw a head pop up out of the cold, pistol-blue water ten feet in front of him. The top of the head was covered by a thick mop of wet, stringy hair which floated to either side and behind it. The forehead was sloped back and the eyes were slated into slits of hate, which locked onto his own eyes, beaming into them with a horrific determination. The water had caused the war paint to streak and run down the warrior's face and into the hideous mouth, which clenched a wood handled hunting knife with a five-inch broken blade between its crowded, uneven teeth.

The big teenager cocked back the hammer and pointed at the head, not taking careful aim but squeezing the trigger instinctively. Immediately the back of the swimmer's head exploded in a welter of bone shrapnel fragments and brain matter, which flew in all directions and landed in a mass atop the sluggish, cobalt water.

The fatty grey globules were immediately attacked by hundreds of small fish and minnows. Simultaneously other heads likewise began popping up like corks from the water, knives clenched fiercely between strong tobacco stained teeth as the swimmers dog paddled with purpose toward Stillwell.

Taking aim and firing quickly, the private shot into five more of the paint streaked faces, detonating the back of their heads and causing the water to roil with silvery perch and blue gill. Thousands of small minnows swarmed into the fatty brain matter that the current carried away in bobbing, floating globules. The bodies disappeared under the slow-moving water immediately when the back of their heads exploded, the autonomic nerve system causing the lungs to inhale the water reflexively.

Desperately Stillwell disassembled the barrel from the frame and removed the cylinder of the Colt revolver and began the insertion of another, previously loaded cylinder. He was reassembling the big revolver as several of the dog paddling warriors emerged dripping wet from the tepid waters, knives at the ready, held low for the disemboweling thrust as they rushed in on him. The tattoos on the shining bodies could be distinguished from the war paint in that the ink didn't streak.

Pete Trudeau lunged onto one of the attacking warriors - a man of about forty years of age, grabbing the knife wielding wrist and dislocating it with a loud popping sound. It made a hollow "pop" like when a child presses the bubble of chewing gum between her teeth. The warrior tilted his head back and howled like a freight train, the tendons standing out on his corded neck and merging into the hunched trapezius muscles that bunched on his shoulders.

Trudeau released the howling aqua man, who plunged back into the water, clutching the flopping forearm and frog kicking away. Three more warriors had writhed out of the river and onto the grass, otter like. They immediately rushed the two frontiersmen, running at a crouch, knives held below the waistline and ready to gut-slash. Dozens more heads popped up from the water, with stained teeth clenching rusty steel.

Trudeau slapped one across the face with a large rock, sending water droplets and shattered teeth flying as his head was turned violently to the right.

The dislocated jaw gave the swimmer a comical expression as he dropped his weapon and grabbed his face with both hands, staggering away.

"Eyes right, son a bitch!" shouted Trudeau at the fleeing figure.

"Kill them! Don't let none of them get away, or we've had it for sure!" screamed Old Pete. As if right on cue, Jack Stillwell began taking deliberate aimed shots with the big Colt. The bobbing heads that were knifing through the water as though they were beavers began exploding like watermelons as the red men urgently tried to paddle to shore.

The gray-haired Trudeau attacked three braves simultaneously. The warriors slashed and jabbed with murderous ardor, and without hesitancy. He tackled the nearest one, grabbing for the drawn in testicles from beneath the drenched flaps of breech cloth. Many Sioux and Cheyenne wore these. The flaps, made of colored cloth were held to the front and back of the man's groin and buttocks by means of a strip of rawhide or more often a belt of utilitarian design.

Trudeau tore lose the scrotum along with the testes and shrunken penis as he rolled away from the kicking, screaming warrior. Even before Pierre had completed the roll, another shiny, wet attacker ran dripping water as he confronted the geriatric's attack. The warrior, wearing a knee length faded breech cloth and holding a butcher knife in his left hand leaped on Trudeau, like a duck on a June bug.

The determined brave was highly motivated and war whooping at the top of his lungs.

The third warrior vacillated in his impetus to join the fray. He watched his fellow warrior struggle with the white-haired man who seemed to be possessed with the savage fighting skills of a demon. Superstitiously he backed away even as he peripherally saw the younger white man taking aim at the exposed head of a dog paddling warrior.

The young red man and the old white man rolled over and over in the lush grass that abutted the water's edge, and fought hand to hand in the shade of a large willow tree – one of scores that edged the creek. They were both armed with razor sharp knives, and each grasped the wrist of the other as they belly rubbed and cavorted in their deadly embrace.

The panting Cheyenne warrior struggled for breath as he looked desperately over his shoulder for his blood brother comrade, but instead of seeing the coming of assistance, he saw his fellow warrior fleeing in the distance. He found himself alone in his struggle with this old man who seemed to possess grim determination, and an insatiable lust for killing. The older man was beginning to overpower him.

The remaining dozen or so warriors in the river had begun to submerge their heads and quickly pop them back up for air as they made for escape, stroking downstream with the current. Often the heads were to be shot clean off as a turtle struggles to escape a boy with a rifle shooting from a pond bank.

The big Northern Cheyenne looked into the eyes of the man who was skillfully overwhelming him with horrifying ease. What he saw were not the eyes of a human, but those of a psychopathic killer. Desperately he began trying to disengage from his intended victim, but the older man was consumed with the need to kill.

The combat between the two frontiersmen and the swimmers had been watched with keen interest by both the Indians and the encircled Buffalo Soldiers of Colonel Bankhead's command. Neither group had fired into the uneven struggle for fear of hitting their own people. Now, they watched as the two frontiersmen emerged from behind several large boulders and quickly submerged into the water of Pond Creek.

Rifle bullets struck the water where they had entered a moment before. While some of the missiles plowed into the water with a twisting, uneven trajectory, others glanced off of the water's surface and sped onward, at an upward angle, over the field and beyond the line of trees.

The depth of the water was about ten feet along this stretch of Pond Creek, and it was approximately fifty feet to the opposite shore. Trudeau quickly made it to the embankment on the opposite side while completely submerged. Stillwell on the other hand, had to surface for air several times and drew a fusillade of rifle fire each time that smacked and plowed into the water in spiraling, erratic trajectories. The last time he came up for air he was nearly to his objective, but a bullet struck him in the head when he had gone under the water again, knocking him senseless. As he lost consciousness he felt the strength of Trudeau pull him up and into the lee of the embankment.

"I thought you bought the farm for a moment, Jack!" exclaimed the hoary man. He had a wild, apostle like appearance that was augmented by an insane look in his eyes. A psychopathic John the Baptist, Stillwell ruminated to himself.

The Kansan felt the big lump on his forehead, "Did the bullet penetrate?" before the geriatric could answer there was a cacophony of rifle fire from the Bankhead position as bullets rained down in a deadly deluge on a small war party sent to skewer the two frontiersmen.

"I think we'll stay here until they skedaddle, and then we make our way to the fort. There's nobody going to get us at this point in the game," said Trudeau as he carefully peered over the rim of the embankment, through a rush of cattails. "It appears that the hostiles are losing their enthusiasm for the game. Soon we can tell Bankhead to send out some reinforcements to Major Forsyth!"

Chapter Twenty
Allen Pinkerton Tries
for the War Bonnet

THE THREE HORSEMEN had ridden hell for leather from Ft Hayes, making quick progress that ate up the endless miles.

They each had an extra horse and they frequently swapped them out in order to maintain steady speed.

"We'll get to the place of the massacre!" a stocky, barrel chested man shouted. "And wait for Custer there!"

Few would have given the shouting man more than a cursive glance, and fewer still would have guessed that this was Allen Pinkerton, former head of Lincoln's Security Service.

President Johnson had given Pinkerton the personal responsibility of securing the war bonnet - even if it meant killing the Boy General.

∞

"Got to head east," said Custer to Bloody Knife and Gladstone. "I'll soon be overdue at Fort Leavenworth. Sheridan will be giving me command of the Seventh Cavalry and I've got to be there." The sun had long since passed its zenith, and was casting long, ominous shadows of the three mounted horsemen across the green grassland. The grass for as far as the eye could see had been flattened by a grazing buffalo herd numbering in the hundreds of thousands. The bison were still present in huge numbers. The pulling of grass by the bison was so loud and pervasive that Custer had to speak loudly to be heard over it.

All day the trio rode east, through the massive herd of buffalo. The prairie was divided by numerous, dry stream beds. In the distance rose a range of high hills, they appeared at first to be clouds that nudged over the horizon.

"Pity we can't kill a few hundred of these magnificent beasts!" lamented the Yellow Hair. The interests of the former general were wide, and the sport of hunting and taxidermy were among the myriad hobbies that he enjoyed.

"Never mind the killing of these stupid beasts," postulated Professor Gladstone. "My arm is killing *me*; the pain is driving me out of my mind! I say set up camp here – I can't go on like this much longer!"

"Maybe get to hills, find good place, set up Sibley!" interjected Bloody Knife, whose close attention to

Gladstone went unnoticed. Ever since the werewolf bite on Gladstone's forearm, the enigmatic Arikawa had been watchful of the man, although he betrayed no such misgivings in his demeanor.

"I beg the General an hour to rest," reiterated Gladstone. "It's my *arm*, it feels as though it is *aflame!*"

"We must continue to the hills, Professor," answered Custer. "We'll find a good, secluded spot that's not out in the open and there we'll set up the Sibley."

Custer knew that Gladstone would not make such a request lightly, and briefly considered a pause in the march. But he knew also that they were making good time and that any halt would jeopardize their arrival at the hills before dark to set up a proper camp site.

"Soon be there, Red Hair," Bloody Knife assured Gladstone. "Bloody Knife tend to wound. I clean it, make better!"

Bloody Knife saw the high ranging hills grow larger in the shimmering heat waves as they drew nearer. They seemed to rise from out of nowhere on the prairie – a narrow range that extended backwards into the distance, rather than horizontally along the front. He recognized them as the hills where the wagon train from Philistine had been ambushed.

"You think that arm's giving you fits, Gladstone?" teased the Boy General, trying to allay the worry of the Englishman. "You ought to try living with the clap for as long as I've had it!"

"Haw haw! Haw haw haw!!!" guffawed the Arikawa, causing the two white men to look at him suddenly. It was the first time any of them had ever known Bloody Knife to laugh.

Bloody Knife wore a cream colored, sweat stained felt cowboy hat over his straight combed, shoulder length, greasy black hair. Sagely, he had doffed his blue cavalry jacket and had it secured to the bedroll that was tied to the back of his McClellan saddle. He was wearing the blue trousers of a cavalry officer and for footgear always preferred moccasins – the only article of Native American dress that he wore.

The trio had entered into the divide that ran the length of the fat, solemn hills. Daylight was fast fading into a penumbral twilight and the Yellow Hair selected a level spot of land within a small cluster of trees in which to set up camp.

"X marks the spot!" exclaimed Custer, who did not seem in the least to be tired. His love of camping and setting up the Sibley tent quickly overcame any suggestion of exhaustion, Bloody Knife knew.

Undulating waves of nausea swept over Gladstone like a late evening tide as he was helped from the saddle and led to the shade of a short, thick trunked Osage orange tree. Professor Gladstone was too consumed with pain to pay any notice of the shrike which had alit on a thorned tree branch to his upper left. The shrike held a grasshopper in its bill. The yellow wings of the grasshopper were fanned open as the small, gray bird impaled it on a tree thorn and watched it struggle through its bright eye.

"Tend to him, Bloody Knife, as I pitch the tent," ordered the former general. Giving orders came naturally to the yellow haired man, and he did so without inciting resentment. Being in charge was as natural to Custer as cutting a throat was to Bloody Knife. Besides, Bloody Knife knew setting up camp was not a chore for the Boy General. The Arikawa smiled inwardly, knowing the Yellow Hair's obsession with camping and especially the Sibley tent, which Custer never failed to carry with him.

Standing twelve feet high and measuring eighteen feet in diameter at the base, the Sibley in no small way resembled a tepee, with its opening at the top and lack of guy lines. However, it was far superior to the animal skinned tents and any similarity to other domed shaped tents vanished when it came to setting up and tearing down the tent.

The Sibley could quickly be erected by one individual through means of a telescoping pole. The base of the pole was set into a broad metallic tripod, directly over the cooking fire within the tent, a cowl over an opening at the top center of the tent allowed for the escape of smoke. The base of the Sibley was anchored to the ground by means of twenty-four pegs and required no guy lines.

Patented in 1856 by Army officer Henry Hopkins Sibley, an ardent outdoors enthusiast who also invented a stove to go along with the tent, the Sibley rapidly gained a devoted following. Although the tent could sleep twelve, Custer never allowed for more than three or four close associates to shelter overnight in the tent. However, he would hold consultations with staff that sometimes exceeded that number in the comfortable tent.

The fact that Major Sibley eventually left the Union and joined the Confederacy was a financial catastrophe for the innovative, camp minded soldier-inventor, who lost his patent on the revolutionary tent design. Custer didn't speculate on this as he hammered the stakes into the loops at the base of the tent prior to entering and erecting the telescopic pole; lifting the tent to its full, erect tepee shape in a matter of seconds.

As Lieutenant Colonel Custer became more absorbed in finalizing the establishment of the tent, Bloody Knife carefully unwrapped the fetid, pus drenched bandage from the suppurating right forearm of Professor Gladstone. The face of Custer's favorite scout remained impassive as he inspected the badly swollen, inflamed extremity.

"My Lord!" exclaimed Gladstone, seeing the arm for the first time since it had been wrapped many hours earlier, "The arm must be taken off!"

"Me get Boy General," replied Bloody Knife. "Him know better what do." Inwardly, Bloody Knife agreed with the professor, but he urgently felt the need for Custer to see the arm with the daylight that remained. Whatever was going to be done about the festering arm, Bloody Knife knew it would have to be done quickly.

"I don't have the surgical instruments to do it," Custer expostulated to the Professor of Anthropology. "Bloody Knife is going to clean it up while I look about the burned out wagons and see if something was discarded by the Indians that may be of use.

"Even if you don't find what you need, General, the arm must come off," reiterated Gladstone.

"Wash that arm out good, Bloody Knife. I'm going to have a look around and see if I can find something," said Custer.

Putrefying flesh clung to the bones of oxen, horses, and mules that were scattered amongst human remains all along the shattered remnants of the wagon train out of Philistine. The Yellow Hair gave up looking for any surgical kit as the shadows deepened with the waning of the day.

"No moon tonight," thought Custer to himself. "A good thing too."

"You've got to take it off," insisted Gladstone, the radius and ulna of the forearm were clearly exposed, having been denuded of muscle tissue by voracious flesh eating bacteria.

"OK," answered Custer. "Before we get started, there is one thing I need of you."

"Name it, but be quick," replied Gladstone through clenched, unbrushed teeth.

"Bloody Knife," said Custer. "Bring Professor Gladstone's satchel here."

The sinewy, muscular Indian brought a black leather case from the saddle bag of Professor Gladstone.

"I need to know," Custer said, "what the future portends for us. Once we conduct the amputation you may not snap out of the shock."

"I understand," replied Gladstone. "Open the satchel and take it out."

Custer removed a soft suede, black bag from the satchel.

"Take it from the bag, and look into it. Don't give up. Sometimes nothing can be seen for a length of time, but I will concentrate all of my will on the ball," instructed Gladstone.

"A shew stone," remarked the former general. "It's heavy."

"There is a base for it, but I left it behind. Sit down and place it in your lap. Stare into it," stated Gladstone, the strain in his voice as he fought to speak was noticeable.

The two white men were inside the tent, Bloody Knife remained outside, unsaddling and tending to the horses and mule.

Custer gazed into the heavy, unusually large, thirty-pound sphere of polished quartz. There was no way of telling its age from looking at it.

"How old is this?" queried the former general, himself an avid rock collector and amateur geologist. He studied the various colors of the crystal, which was polished so smooth he could see far down into its clouded, smoky depths.

The orb was filled with rich impurities. Intergrowths consisting of chalcedony, and polymorphic morganite streaked the deep interior of the crystal ball. Sard, onyx and agate hung suspended in the rose tinted quartz, adding a panoply of iridescent mineral colors that piqued the Boy General's curiosity and conveyed suggested hints of unfathomed mysteries.

Although the light from the flickering flames of the campfire beneath the telescoping tripod burned brightly as they would before settling into coals, that could not explain the origin of all of the light some of which, the former general felt, was originating from deep within the sphere itself.

Custer stared more intensely into the crystal, as deeply as he could see into it, fascinated at the beauty that floated perpetually inside. He thought he saw a slight movement within the perfectly round orb, he peered more strenuously, leaning closely forward.

"Yes," the Yellow Hair whispered. "Movement."

He was seeing images that were blurred, but slowly came into focus. In the master bedroom of the Bacon house, his sister Margie entered the bedroom, holding an envelope. His wife, Elizabeth was removing her blouse, she was not wearing a corset. She wore a black riding habit. The Boy General saw his sister staring at the jiggling breasts of his wife as she violently opened the envelope, not seeming to care if the letter inside was damaged.

The image clouded and came hazily back into focus, he was seeing through the eyes of his wife, Libbie. Lieutenant Colonel Custer saw that the envelope contained a telegram, it was a message from him. "The war bonnet has been taken from me..."

The image faded, and vanished. Sensing intuitively that there would be no further visions within the crystal ball, Custer uncertainly placed it in its bag, and stood up, approaching the prostrate Gladstone.

"What did you see?" asked Professor Gladstone.

"I saw that I am to lose the war bonnet," answered Custer.

"Not necessarily," replied Gladstone, adding, "that was one outcome of events which have not yet come to pass. Take it as an omen, General, to never let the war bonnet leave your person. Keep it with you at all times. Now, down to business; off with my arm! There is no time to lose, for surely they who also seek the war bonnet are not far off."

"We'll take the arm off at the shoulder, Professor. Although the corruption is below the elbow, there is streaking extending all of the way up the arm," stated the Boy General. "It will be painful but fast. I will cut through the flesh and joint of the shoulder socket with my boning knife, and sear the wound closed with the flat of my Bowie, of which the blade rests on the coal bed."

Custer continued, "As you know, I don't drink – ever. But Bloody Knife does, "Bloody Knife! Bring whiskey!"

"Don't got none, Boy General!" lied Bloody Knife, who Custer knew was an inveterate alcoholic. "Ain't had no whiskey in days, drink all long time go," Bloody Knife added, his face expressionless in the telling of the irony.

Not only did Bloody Knife not wish to share his precious commodity with the white magician, he also wanted to see how well the man could endure pain. The better a man bore up to pain, figured Bloody Knife, the more of a man he was. If the professor could endure the pain stoically, the Arikawa would hold him in higher esteem.

"Very well then," uttered Gladstone. "Stop talkin' and start chalkin! Off with it!"

"Bite down hard," said Custer, placing a rifle bullet in the left hand of Gladstone. The professor placed the lead bullet in his mouth and bit down on it. He felt his molars dig into the soft lead, imprinting it.

"Hold his hand and grasp his arm above the elbow," Custer instructed Bloody Knife.

"Boy General gonna cut off arm now?" asked the five-foot seven-inch, one-hundred thirty-pound Bloody Knife, eager to see the magician's reaction.

The Arikawa was an anomaly to everyone who knew him; sired by a Hunkpapa Sioux father and born of an Arikawa mother, he did not wear feathers, jewelry or beads. The Arikawa scout had Hispanic facial features and favored the company of whites – dressing like them in Army regalia and adopting their mannerisms.

The soft brown irises were set in a clear sclera and were made prominent by the total lack of epicanthic folds. The fine facial features were highlighted with well molded cheekbones that while high set, didn't extrude so much as to detract from the Mediterranean features of the man. The aquiline nose sat perched above thin lips surrounding a small mouth. The diminutive lips almost seemed to hint at a smile in anticipation of how well Gladstone would hold up to the torture of having his arm amputated.

Without warning Custer made a circular cut completely around Gladstone's shoulder socket, then in an authoritative command, told Bloody Knife to:

"Dislocate it and pull it off!"

"Arrrrrrrgggggghhhhhh!!!!!" came the gritted shout of Gladstone as the arm came off. Bloody Knife wrenched the upper extremity out of the shoulder socket with a tearing, suction like, loud popping noise. The sound could be compared to the "POP! "of a cork being removed from a bottle of champagne. The thick, coppery smell of blood permeated the air within the Sibley tent as it shot out in a powerful stream, the jet growing and ebbing with the pulsation of the heart.

"Get me the Bowie, quickly!" shouted the Yellow Hair, pressing a filthy rag to the wound to staunch the loss of blood. Custer knew he had to have this man in order to keep the war bonnet from being taken, and he was prepared to do whatever was necessary to keep his magician alive.

Custer removed the rag and in the next motion pressed the flat of the hot knife blade to the open wound, the dull red glow of the blade receded to metallic gray as the wound hissed like a shovel of coal dropped into a bucket of water. The tent filled with blood steam, the stench was like that of hair set ablaze.

Instead of passing out unconscious from the pain, Gladstone issued a visceral, low growl from deep in the core of his abdomen. Custer felt the hairs rise on his arms in primitive fear at the likeness of the growl to that of a wolf.

"Somebody outside, Boy General," warned Bloody Knife.

"What now!" What the hell!" retorted the Yellow Hair, "If things can't get any worse!"

"Don't move, anybody! Hands up in the air!" came a commanding voice in thick Scottish brogue.

A heavy set, square figure of a large boned man of medium height dressed in fashionable Western wear entered the tent, followed by two others. They were armed with Colt and Remington percussion cap revolvers.

"Allen Pinkerton!" ejaculated Lieutenant Colonel Custer, "What brought you here?"

"The same thing that brought *you*, General. Now, if you'll be so kind as to hand me the war bonnet, maybe no one will get shot. *Maybe!*" growled the swag bellied Pinkerton.

"You *want* to see it," stated the Boy General. "I know you do. Here, I'll show it to you."

Custer slowly removed the war bonnet from the parfleche, placing it on his head.

"That's it, all right. Now quit showin' off and hand it over," ordered the head of the United States' Intelligence Service, before adding, "before I havta kill ya!"

"Eat shit and die, you fucking Scottish ass-wipe!" shouted the Yellow Hair, picking up the severed arm of Gladstone and swinging it like a club, striking the White House Security Chief across the left side of the face with it. Pinkerton staggered back a step from the blow, discharging his Remington Model 1858 New Army revolver into Custer as he did so, but oddly missing at such close range.

"You immigrant piece of shit!" shouted Custer. "You did a damned fine job of protecting Lincoln, *didn't you!*"

A deep throated growl issued from the prostrate figure of Gladstone, his facial features had changed radically; his mouth had begun to jut forward to accommodate large, canine teeth. He sat bolt upright, assisting himself with his remaining arm.

"Kill'em!" shouted Pinkerton. "Kill ever damned one of 'em!"

The broad, five-inch rimmed Union Army slouch hat was pulled low over Pinkerton's forehead, shadowing the sinister, coal black eyes of the barrel chested man. The squared face was made broad by the full, black beard, streaked with gray. The cauliflower nose had been broken years before and gave Pinkerton the appearance of a brawler.

Standing five-feet eight-inches and weighing two hundred pounds, the former head of Lincoln's security did not fit the stereotype of one who swam in the circles of the social elite. Dressed in a checker paned cotton bib shirt, brown leather buffed calf leather vest and canvas duck riding trousers, he could easily have passed for a highway man. And often he did; impersonating criminals and infiltrating their clandestine gangs.

His riding trousers were high-waisted, held up by a narrow black belt, over which was strapped a broad gun belt at a jaunty angle with an open holster – the type preferred by gunfighters. Allan Pinkerton thumbed back the trigger on the .44 caliber Remington New Army. The Remington was not as heavy as the earlier cap and ball dragoon types. It was made of better metal and was well balanced. It fit into the hand nicely and the tolerances were tight; there was virtually no play in the cylinder when it locked into place.

"Yore a lucky scoundrel, you are at that Lieutenant Colonel Custer!" shouted Pinkerton, as the two assassins on either side of him poured a deadly barrage of gunfire into the three victims.

Pinkerton took deliberate aim at Custer's chest and fired, again missing. In fact, none of the three had been hit by the fusillade.

"Son of a slut! Low bred Scottish street waif!" growled Gladstone, his British accent still detectable in the bestial growls. "Have at you!"

Lunging like a wolf at the miscast security mogul, Gladstone made a swipe with his remaining arm as Pinkerton stepped back. The two bodyguards stepped in front of the big Scott, placing themselves instinctively between Pinkerton and his attacker.

Gladstone ripped into the man facing him; a dark, hawk faced man of lean but powerful build. This man drew a thick bladed hunting knife with a five-inch single edged blade to meet the threat. He fought with skill and savagery; ripping and thrusting with the bone-handled knife as he was hurled backward and down to the ground by Gladstone. He gurgled, inhaling his own blood as Gladstone leapt atop him and ripped his throat out with his teeth.

The remaining bodyguard went for a single barreled derringer as Bloody Knife drilled him with his Henry. The interior of the Sibley was thick with the smoke of burnt black gun powder, and as the Boy General stood electrified by the war bonnet, his heightened sense of vision discerned that Allen Pinkerton had fled.

Anticipating the Englishman's hatred of his hereditary Scottish enemy, he spoke too late to halt Gladstone's exit from the tent in pursuit of Pinkerton. The metallic clopping of horse shoes could be heard as the Scott fled.

"Gladstone!" shouted the Yellow Hair. "Get back here!" but it was too late; Gladstone had vanished into the night, in pursuit of Allan Pinkerton.

"Quick, Bloody Knife!" shouted the Boy General as he placed the war bonnet into its parfleche. "We have to break camp! You get the mounts ready as I tear down the Sibley! Without Gladstone we are in grave peril!"

Chapter Twenty One
President Andrew Johnson
Wants the War Bonnet

STANDING AT FIVE-FEET ten-inches tall, the robustly built, heavily muscled seventeenth President of the United States stared down at the diminutive, dwarf-like figure standing before him.

"My sources tell me that Custer has the war bonnet," growled the suspicious president, who knew that the man who stood before him was another one of the numerous people he could not count on.

"I spoke with Custer two weeks ago, Mr. President. I was under the impression sir, that he, his wife and sister were returning to Monroe. He was not in good health, but I assured him that he would receive command of the Seventh Cavalry in a short time," responded Little Phil Sheridan.

"I thought Custer was my friend," confided President Andrew Johnson to General Sheridan. President

Johnson paused as he confronted the confusing, paranoid emotions consuming him and then continued, "but he is duplicit in the most base manner."

"Sir, it is true that Lieutenant Colonel Custer is an avid hunter and outdoorsman, a naturalist, an architect and a taxidermist. A geologist, biologist and an amateur scientist, as well as a best-selling author. But to go after Roman Nose alone would be preposterous – even for him," reposted General Sheridan.

"I can't trust anybody. Everyone is against me," responded the president. "Now Custer, the so-called "Boy General," President Johnson paused as his face reddened. "The newspapers call him the *"Boy General!"* shouted the Commander in Chief, then violently Johnson swept ledgers and piles of stationary from the top of his desk, sending papers flying everywhere. "This man who I called *my friend* has deceitfully gone and killed Roman Nose and has taken the damned war bonnet for *himself!!!"*

The president, known for his volatile temper and fits of uncontrollable rage, was trembling with fury. His normally dark features were becoming apple red with anger. The forehead, wide at the top was thick with unruly graying hair that thinned suddenly at the temples, leaving a pronounced widow's peak. Thick, dark, grotesque eyebrows overhung the accusing, distrusting, obsidian eyes that locked with Sheridan's.

President Andrew Johnson's thin upper lip was made nearly unnoticeable by the full, pouting lower lip. The frowning mouth was made more sinister by an overhung, downturned and hawk-like nose. As the man aged, the nose would become cauliflowered from excessive drinking, and frown lines would etch the corners of the mouth.

Ravaged by kidney stones and high blood pressure induced headaches, President Johnson frequently lashed out violently at those he did not like.

"Surely this can't be *totally* true, Mr. President," responded Little Phil, not backing down from President Johnson's accusing gaze.

Little Phil Sheridan dreaded these meetings with the president. He maintained his professional demeanor as he saw the muscles of President Johnson's pronounced, square jaw tighten. Spittle flew from the president's mouth as he raged, some of it ran down the cleft of his proudly defined chin.

"Damn it!" shouted the president. "Damned kidney stones!"

President Johnson arched his torso, reaching behind him with both hands to massage the low of his back, over the kidneys.

Sheridan saw the handle of the Model 1858 Remington New Army revolver extend out of the vest as Johnson leaned back, it was holstered in a brown, expensive, polished leather shoulder rig. It stood out nicely against the suede black Baxter vest.

Johnson was a concealed carry man, and always went armed despite his ample security that was always present. He was a paranoid, suspicious despot. Johnson could never be too sure even about his own security people.

Although the Army had contracted with Colt, Andrew Johnson preferred the Remington due to the top strap that extended over the cylinder, adding enormous strength to the frame. The Colt Model 1860 lacked this feature and the president felt that it was dangerous to load the gun much past thirty grains of black powder.

The volatile president was wearing a white cotton button down shirt, tightly tailored and high necked with a turn over collar. His dark brown necktie was broad, loose, loop tied and secured in place with a stickpin. He was said to make his own clothing and intentionally tailored his clothes to accentuate his powerful build and thereby intimidate others.

The controversial President Johnson was a veritable rags to riches story like out of some kind of twisted Horatio Algiers tale; Andrew Johnson had begun life in abject poverty. He was rumored to be the illegitimate child born of a triste between his wash woman mother and any number of clients she did the laundry for. Indentured at an early age to a tailor, he ran away at fifteen years of age and established himself as a skilled tailor in his own right, growing wealthy and using the proceeds to buy slaves and enter politics.

Eventually Andrew Johnson settled in Tennessee and became a wealthy slave holding plantation owner who had sided with the North. Lincoln chose Johnson as his running mate in 1864 for practical reasons, one of which was the fact that Johnson owned slaves and Honest Abe sought to further splinter Southern allegiance within the Confederacy. But when Honest Abe was assassinated, Johnson was thrust into an office where his acidic, bullying, and uncompromising personality earned him numerous and powerful enemies.

Added to Johnson's confrontational, paranoid demeanor were blinding headaches related to hypertension and stabbing, incapacitating lower back pain caused by the never ending presence of kidney stones.

"Yes! Yes! Yes! It is all totally true! I have it on good word from Allen Pinkerton," the president replied to Sheridan. "And that's not all," Johnson added, as he resumed rubbing the small of his back.

"I wouldn't put too much stock into what Pinkerton has to say, Mr. President," stated Little Phil. "His information was always exaggerated and often erroneous during the war."

President Johnson stopped rubbing the small of his back, and regarded General Sheridan suspiciously, wanting to let him in on a secret, but not sure whether or not to trust the general.

"I want to show you something," said the president, making up his mind and adding, "come with me, and say nothing regarding what you are about to see this day."

Sheridan and the president entered one of the cellars beneath the White House, they were surrounded by nervous Intelligence Agents as they did so. Down in the basement was darkness, and one of the agents lit a powerful torch lantern; the type used on ships. He cast the directed beam about the large, dank room. The beam illuminated a large animal cage, the type used by zoos for the transport of dangerous animals, such as gorillas. The cage was empty and the door had been flung open, its locking mechanism had been sheared as though with great strength.

"We've got to get out of here Mr. President," cautioned a lean, piranha faced White House Security man. He was of medium height, wore a derby and spoke with an Irish accent. Johnson preferred Irishmen, Scotts, but most often Negro soldiers for his personal protection. But he did not trust anyone, truly.

"Nobody's going anywhere," replied the husky Johnson, adding, "*It* is in here, watching us."

Suddenly, a large dark shape rushed from a stack of empty crates and barrels, knocking the lantern from the man holding it. The lantern smashed to the floor, as the whale oil spilled out from it, the fatty liquid ignited, illuminating the room - including the entity that stood before the group of men.

Instinctively the armed detail assigned to protect the president surrounded Johnson. The beast that stood before them was bipedal and heavily built. It was covered in red fur and emitted a low growl, like that of a wolf. The face was humanoid. The creature had recently sustained a horrific injury, reflected in the fact that its right arm was missing at the shoulder.

"Don't shoot it," the president commanded in his thick, southern drawl. "This is the best means we have of getting the war bonnet."

The werewolf leapt on the bodyguard nearest the president, tearing out the man's throat in a second, and before the group could react, the homo-lupus lunged onto President Johnson. The president caught the man-thing in a bear hug and smashed his forehead into the snout, driving the beast back as he released it. The president advanced on the beast, his hands opening and closing in rage.

"No! Mr. President!" shouted General Sheridan. "Don't approach the thing! Tell me if you will, sir, the meaning of this!"

"Very well, General," responded the president. "Leave the thing as he is, but secure the door to the basement and post ten sentries on it," the president directed the security detail.

"What about O'Reilly?" asked one of the bodyguards. "We can't just leave him here."

"Sure we can," replied President Johnson. "The thing needs to eat."

Later, in the Oval Office, the president and his general sat down to talk. They were alone; Johnson felt like he could trust Sheridan enough not to have his security detail present.   Although Johnson never really trusted anyone – always suspecting even close family members of being potential assassins.

"It is well that you stopped me," confided Johnson to Sheridan. "That shows you have my best interests at heart and are indeed a friend. That thing would have torn me to pieces had I lit into it."

"Mr. President, what is going on here? That beast is a werewolf!" responded Little Phil Sheridan, clearly shaken and in need of opium. General Sheridan felt ill at ease in the presence of Johnston, and tried in vain to overcome the discomfort he felt at being around the man.

"That, my good sir, was a man named Gladstone; a Professor of Anthropology and also a skilled magician," answered the president. "I don't know what happened to make him this way. But Allan Pinkerton barely escaped from it with his life. The Pinkerton men set a trap and somehow captured it, losing at least three dozen men in doing so."

"So, what Pinkerton had to say holds merit," replied Sheridan, looking about the office for a concealed whiskey locker. He knew the president was a hard drinker, and rumored to be become violent when inebriated.

"Yes," answered President Johnson. "Pinkerton said he saw the war bonnet and demanded that Custer hand it over. Well, Custer actually put on the war bonnet and an altercation developed. Pinkerton lost two men and ran for his life. He said that neither Custer nor the two men with him – Bloody Knife and Gladstone, could be hit by gunfire even at point blank range."

"So those rumors about Roman Nose and the war bonnet were true," replied Sheridan.

"Undeniably true, General," answered the president. Johnson studied the reaction of Sheridan. If Little Phil was surprised, he managed to dissimulate it. Maybe, Johnson thought, General Sheridan had his mind entirely somewhere else – perhaps conniving an assassination attempt? The president's paranoid delusion was interrupted by the small man sitting in front of him.

"Where is Custer with the war bonnet now?" asked Sheridan.

"Only Gladstone can answer that," replied Johnson, adding, "but he hasn't reverted back to his human form as of yet. I've been looking into this strange phenomenon that afflicts Professor Gladstone, but secrecy is paramount. A situation in which much blood is spilt may in some way or form serve as a catalyst to bring him back."

"What have you got in mind, Mr. President?" prompted General Sheridan.

"Johnson's Island," responded the president, "is a three-hundred-acre island prison three miles from

Sandusky, right off shore in Lake Erie. "Not many people know about this, but several hundred Confederate Prisoners of War remain incarcerated there; all of them are veterans of Picket's Charge at Gettysburg. They are brainwashed, dangerous men incapable of being reintegrated into the New Republic."

"What do you mean to do with them, sir?" asked the surprised General Sheridan in near disbelief.

"Glad you asked, Phil," responded the president. "At Rock Island Prison there an equal number, if not more, of Negro Federal soldiers; highly decorated combat veterans who have been detailed to await there, pending their deployment against Picket's men. I'm going to have the Rebels all sent by rail down to Rock Island where they can mix it up with the Colored Troops in a little bayonet competition. While the two opposing forces are locked in mortal combat, I mean to set Gladstone loose amongst them, even as they fight."

"What the devil!" expostulated General Sheridan, clearly aghast.

"I am the Devil," smiled President Johnson, lacing his fingers between one another behind his head as he leaned back in his swivel chair on the other side of the massive desk of Abraham Lincoln in the Oval Office.

Chapter Twenty-Two
An Uncertain Dawn

THE DAWN WAS TWO hours away as Custer and Bloody Knife distanced themselves from the scene of the wagon train massacre. They rode at a slow, measured pace, to avoid the hidden pitfalls that loomed in the darkness.

Bloody Knife found the man he accompanied to be unpredictable in many ways. He never knew with certainty what the Yellow Hair was going to choose to do next but like a Sancho Panza to his Don Quixote, he followed the Boy General through one perilous adventure after another.

They felt their way through the darkness, trudging further into the barely mapped wastes, staying well off of the wagon trail.

Dawn was an uneven band of orange luminescence on the eastern horizon when the pair approached the heap-like shape of a human body lying face down in the dew drenched grasses; a mix of fescue, little bluestem and buffalo grass. Interspersed were clutches of brightly colored, orange swathes of Indian Paintbrush.

"Keep an eye out," instructed the Boy General as he dismounted Vic. The Yellow Hair approached the cadaver that lay motionless, face ensconced in the grass. The former general was adjusting the position of his gun belt as he walked. Out of habit he placed his hand on the handle of his revolver that was sheathed in its cross draw holster. It felt good to him having his hand on the revolver and walking that way. He knew it looked good to others, too.

The area was punctuated with small groves of large trees, mainly red oaks – a commonly found deciduous tree whose range extended from southern Canada to Georgia and spread westward. The larger acorn filled trees were the ones that survived the frequent grass fires that devoured the saplings. Knee high buffalo grass gradually became the dominant flora of the mixed species and spread out like rolls of waving green carpet between the oak groves.

Custer knelt beside the motionless body, noting an absence of flies or insect scavengers. The Boy General looked around him, at the copses of trees whose shiny, deep green leaves rustled with a light breeze as the rising sun warmed the air.

"Boy General," uttered Bloody Knife. "Something not right."

If Custer heard Bloody Knife, he did not show it. Carefully placing both hands on the left shoulder and torso of the body, apparently a Cheyenne Dog Soldier dressed in a sweat stained buckskin war shirt and US Army Cavalry trousers, he heaved the heavy corpse onto its back.

Instantly the body came to life, both hands seizing the Yellow Hair by the throat with amazing strength. Custer grabbed either side of the warrior's face, painted with bold red and black vertical slashes.

The former general's lips pulled back from his straight, white teeth as he used his thumbs, digging the dirty untrimmed nails into the piceous eyes with great force. The thumbs slid under the eyeballs all the way back into the orbits of the skull before he extracted them in a torqueing, ripping motion. Both eyeballs resisted, bulged, then exited the sockets with a loud popping sound, akin to a boy stepping on a toad.

Immediately Custer leapt up from the cursing, screaming Dog Soldier and reached for the parfleche strapped to his back as he ran. Lieutenant Colonel Custer extracted the war bonnet from the dried, tubular rawhide case and hastily donned it.

The sightless warrior ran erratically toward the Boy General with both hands extended forward. The taloned fingers raked the morning air as the Dog Soldier swept viciously this way and that. The empty eye sockets bore into the blue eyes of the Yellow Hair, blue eyes which regarded the determination of the warrior with respect – and concern – concern at the unnatural determination of his painted adversary.

Bright red blood streamed down and added to the macabre appearance of the Dog Soldier's painted face. He screamed not in pain, but in rage as he ran, tripping and falling, then getting back up and running again to where he assumed the former general to be.

"An eye for an eye, Dog Soldier!" ejaculated the Yellow Hair in a jocular exclamation.

The verdure of the oak trees shook as moccasined feet slid down the tree trunks or leapt from the sturdy branches onto the grass. Six Cheyenne Dog Soldiers raced on foot toward the Yellow Hair and his scout, while two other braves rode up holding rope attached to the brave's horses, bringing them in tandem.

"Dog Soldiers! It's a trap!" shouted the Boy General.

One of the warriors was firing at Custer from the shoulder as he ran, trying to get a hit by pointing the rifle like a shotgun. The brave worked the lever of his repeating rifle as his muscular thighs pumped up and down like the pistons of a steam driven locomotive. He ignored Bloody Knife, who was drawing a bead on him with his own Henry.

The bullets all missed, as did those of another brave who kneeled, taking careful aim at Bloody Knife. The warrior fired at ten feet. He missed but caused Bloody Knife to involuntarily jerk the trigger as he fired on the running man. The errant bullet hit the

Dog Soldier in the far right side of the forehead, causing the left side of his body to go limp. Fatty brain matter oozed out of the back of the warrior's skull as he attempted to drag himself using one foot toward Custer.

"Hold the horses," shouted Custer, drawing the Colt from his left hip with his right hand in a slow motion cross draw movement.

Bloody Knife watched as the Boy General performed the draw; bent at the knees, Custer accomplished the action in a single, fluid maneuver Bloody Knife noted approvingly.

The Boy General held the trigger down and repeatedly struck the hammer spur of his service revolver with the palm of his left hand. The revolver was held at waist level. The shots were fired wildly at close range hitting two of the Dog Soldiers high in the abdomen and knocking the wind from them.

The wounded braves did not drop to their knees as other men would have from such murderous wounds. Instead, they came on. They came on with murderous intent. They raced toward Lieutenant Colonel Custer on moccasined feet like hounds out of Hell.

Custer slid the empty Colt back into its holster and pulled the Smith and Wesson Model 1 from the large right pocket of his buckskin jacket. Aiming the tiny single action revolver with both hands, Custer took aimed face shots at the two Dog Soldiers who rushed at him, closing the distance to an alarming five feet.

The Model 1, firing a .22 caliber short - a rim fire cartridge, stung as they entered the tattooed, painted faces. The warriors dropped their trade store hatchets and threw their hands to their faces as the hot, tiny lead projectiles entered their eyes, mouths and sinuses. The braves spat teeth and hawked blood, hands to faces as they staggered toward the frantically firing former general, who sidestepped the zombie like attack and looked to Bloody Knife quickly as thoughts of survival raced through his mind.

The Smith and Wesson Model 1, .22 caliber short was unique; ahead of its time, it was one of the only revolvers capable of firing a metallic cartridge. Smith and Wesson held the patent on revolver cylinders that could be bored through to accept a metal cartridge. Colt and Remington had to stay with cap and ball, while Smith and Wesson had a virtual monopoly on cartridge firing revolvers for twenty years.

Custer turned his attention to the two remaining Dog Soldiers on horseback as Bloody Knife tried to keep his mounts from panicking. Both warriors released the tethers to the horses of their fallen comrades as they aimed their rifles, one a Henry and the other a Spencer, at the Boy General. They fired as fast as they could get off aimed shots. Custer heard the projectiles whiz like enraged hornets past his face, but oddly, the bullets all missed.

The Yellow Hair ran for the big Spencer in its scabbard on Vic, as the two Dog Soldiers attempted to ride down the Boy General while he raced for his horse. Bloody Knife brought down one of them – a lithe, wiry warrior wearing a buckskin war shirt heavily edged with long fringes and buckskin leggings adorned with knee length beaded bands. He drilled him with a shot through the torso - in through the left side. Bloody Knife aimed the rifle with one hand while holding the tethers to the horses and mule with the other.

Bloody Knife had no love for the Cheyenne, whom he despised on account of their close alliance with the Sioux. Bloody Knife was not wholly Arikawa, being born of an Arikawa mother and a Hunkpapa Sioux father. Living with the Sioux until he was about fifteen years of age, he had been ostracized and viciously bullied by the Sioux, who considered him inferior because of his Arikawa mother.

Two of his brothers had been killed and scalped while accompanying a group of Sioux on a hunting party who left their bodies in the field to be eaten by wolves. Several of the emerging great leaders of the Hunkpapa Sioux had been in on the double-cross of his brothers, including Gall and Sitting Bull.

The remaining Dog Soldier, wearing a buckskin shirt adorned with fringes, ermine tubes, and beadwork leapt at Custer from his saddle, with a butcher knife drawn. But he was deflected to the ground just out of reach of the Boy General by some unseen force emanating from the war bonnet.

Bloody Knife got off another shot, one handed. The bullet entered the warrior's painted right cheek, causing the left jaw to fly off. The jaw bone, complete with filed, pointed teeth flew like a boomerang and circled back, imbedding itself in the hedge apple of an Osage orange tree and knocking it onto the grass. The motion of the hedge apple had barely ceased when blue bottle flies settled upon the jaw that was embedded in the coarse green flesh of the rotund fruit.

The warrior looked menacingly at the Boy General, as he held his hand to his ruined face. The blood was shooting from the horrific face wound in long, pulsating spurts. So much of it covered the grass that it caught the sun and reflected, like sapphires spat in rage from the cursing mouth of a centaur.

"We have to go! We have to get out of here!" Custer yelled to Bloody Knife, whose stoicism was belied by a hidden fear that welled in his soul – a growing fear of these men who seemed incapable of dying. Custer's wide, flamboyant, cream colored straw hat was pushed back far on his head as he shouted, sweat was pouring down the Yellow Hair's face, Bloody Knife absentmindedly observed.

"We not finish'em off?" postulated Bloody Knife, his lust for killing vying with his common sense. He badly wanted to take the scalps of the wounded Dog Soldiers.

"No time for that!" snapped the Yellow Hair. "We've got to get out of here and reload while we're on the move. Besides," Custer added, "that group of wounded braves will slow up the main war party. They are after the war bonnet, I'm sure of it!"

The former general and his Arikawa scout rode the horses hard as they placed distance between themselves and the ambush party. Looking overhead and all around him, Custer could see a great flock of crows following him. Further back, at a great distance, he could see a single dark entity high in the air and silhouetted against the harsh orange-red brushstroke of the morning horizon.

Studded by Poseidon and given birth by Medusa, the blood of the Gods pounded with every heartbeat of the winged horse as it closed the distance to the ravaged ambush party of Dog Soldiers.

A massive warhorse, it would have surpassed in size the horses mounted by the French knights at Agincourt, who were hoisted onto their mounts by grunting, sweating peasants whose arms bulged with muscles as they operated the enormous winches and cranes.

Wings festooned with heavy, knotted muscles extended forty feet from the withers of the solid white stallion, and each stupendous sweep of the wings buffeted a gust of wind that would knock the war bonnet from the mightiest chief.

The diminutive figure of a man was mounted on the broad back, just forward of the massive loin. This was the flying horse of Hanwi the Accursed, Goddess of the Moon. As the magnificent winged equidae approached the scene of the failed ambuscade, the figure became noticeable as White Bull.

Long before, told in legends, horses had ranged the vast sweeps of the North American continent but had been hunted to extinction, and the winged horse of Hanwi stood prominent in folklore.

Some two dozen mounted Dog Soldiers were riding frantically to the area of the wounded braves, the same area to which the snorting, winged beast was breaking its descent. The massive wings angled serving as brakes against the rising air, lifting the shoulder and crest of the ivory colored horse as the hocks and hoofs to the rear lowered in preparation for setting foot upon the ground.

The concussion of air from the flapping wings bent the grass flat and showered the wounded braves with dew as the horse of Hanwi the Accursed landed. Immediately White Bull dismounted the magical steed, shouting, "What has transpired here! Porcupine Bear! What sayest thou!?"

"My Lord, the Yellow Hair has the protection of the war bonnet!" responded Porcupine Bear, his sightless eye sockets swarming with gnats and blue bottle flies.

"I have eyes among many friends," answered White Bull. "Those who fly see for me even now. The blasphemy they call the Yellow Hair is fleeing in the direction of Philistine. I will take the heart of the Boy General and roast it over a bed of coals, in supplication to the Goddess Hanwi the Accursed!"

White Bull was surrounded by mounted Dog Soldiers as he surveyed the ravaged ambush party. His right hand, trembling with rage, withdrew the moonstone from his sachet of talismans as he prepared to begin the Sacred Rite of healing.

"Those crows are his minions! They've seen us and know where we're at! Let's head for Philistine!" shouted the Boy General to his sanguinary friend, Bloody Knife.

Already a day's ride into Kansas, the fugitive former general and his Arikawa scout were by no means near safety. The western half of the state was virtually under Indian control, and many towns had been abandoned, the inhabitants hastily leaving only with what they could store in a single wagon.

One of these such towns was Philistine, a veritable ghost town; feared and shunned by superstitious travelers who gave it wide berth. It was rumored that horrific things had gone on in Philistine before the controversial and ostracized inhabitants fled before the red tidal surge of Cheyenne. Even the Cheyenne, Sioux and other tribes avoided the town of Philistine.

"Boy General," expostulated Bloody Knife. "Me not wanna go close by to Philistine."

"Maybe those who pursue won't wish to go there, either," responded Custer, adding, "it looks like the whole countryside is after the war bonnet. Philistine is the safest, closest place for us to seek sanctum."

As the Boy General and his faithful disciple entered Philistine, the dyad dismounted and walked their horses along the cobble stone main street, overgrown with mixed grasses. The Yellow Hair noted with his architect's eye a grim symmetry about the red brick buildings that lined the stone main street, as the clacking of the metal horse shoes echoed eerily, the sound bouncing along the abandoned edifices.

"Bloody Knife think Philistine bad place. Maybe we leave. What say, Boy General?" Bloody Knife urged the Yellow Hair.

The town had been abandoned very quickly, many items of use had simply remained in place, and were there for the taking.

"Let's water and feed the horses and mule," replied Custer, who added: "We won't be sleeping in the Sibley tonight! Look around, over there is the hotel. We'll head over there and get us a room after tending to the animals. We'll live it up in luxury tonight!"

"Listen!" warned Bloody Knife, who lay down on the grass, placing an ear to the cobble stone. "Bloody Knife hear horses, lots of 'em. Don't have no horse shoes."

"Damn!" cursed the Boy General. "Damn! Damn! Damn!"

"Them bad Injuns comin' into Philistine, Boy General!" warned a clearly alarmed Bloody Knife. The skin of his forehead wrinkled into lines as his eyes narrowed and his face furrowed into a frown.

Custer became agitated and unsure of himself. He pushed his oversized straw cowboy hat to the rear and down the back of his head, allowing it to rest between his shoulder blades, suspended by the rawhide stampede string. He ran his right hand through his greasy mop of yellow hair, pulling it back as he did so and exposing the pronounced widow's peak of his prematurely receded hairline.

"Leave the saddles on the horses and mule, and spook them out of here. If the Indians don't get them, maybe there is some chance that we can retrieve them later," ordered the former general, his voice was coming in staccato bursts. His thoughts came faster than his words, and he repeated himself, stammering as he did so.

Bloody Knife had seen the Yellow Hair do this on numerous occasions when Lieutenant Colonel Custer had been confronted suddenly with overwhelming odds.

"What do now, Boy General?" asked Bloody Knife as the horses and mule fled the town. The beasts had taken to hoof without prompting and Bloody Knife had not needed to spook the animals; they fled on their own, he observed uncomfortably.

"We'll head for the last place that they'll want to go," replied the Yellow Hair. "To the funeral parlor! It's getting dark now, so let's hop to it!"

Chapter Twenty-Three
Bayonet Tag at Rock Island

FIVE COMPANIES OF Colored Troops stood in tight combat formation, resplendent in new Union Army uniforms, replete with the accoutrements endemic to combat units of the field. These soldiers were veterans of dozens of battles in which they had distinguished themselves through bravery and self-sacrifice. Many bore scars on their backs from the lash of former slave masters and relished the opportunity to once again settle old scores with the icons of their former oppressors.

They were motivated by the promise of positive fitness reports and accelerated promotions in the Colored Units of the regular Army if they performed the task at hand – if they survived it.

Their opponents, captured Confederate survivors from the disastrous Picket's Charge at Gettysburg entered the stadium from the darkened cellars beneath the amphitheater, shielding their eyes which were unaccustomed to the blinding light. These men had no hope of parole, and faced certain death – if not today, then eventually. They were emaciated, starving men, dressed in filthy rags and barefooted.

The Rebels rapidly fell into tight combat formations consisting of five companies. Their officers and NCOs shouting as their drummers beat the drum rolls, used as an effective battlefield communication system.

Drummers who had been ten and twelve-year-old boys at Gettysburg and were now in their teens beat furious tattoos with drumsticks that moved in blurring motions. The staccato sound of the snare drums reflected the pedigree of the ancient war drums that they had evolved from, primarily the Tabor – which was often accompanied by the flute.

The concussion of the Confederate Infantry drums carried, echoed, and reverberated in the walled arena of the Union stockade at Rock Island as the sergeants walked along the ranks, checking the gear of their soldiers and reporting to their officers. In the center of the formation of starving men, the torn, ragged remnants of the Confederate battle flag waved and snapped in a sudden gust of wind, threatening to further unravel the banner, which was perforated with scores of bullet holes.

Both formations seemed similarly armed, with Lee Enfield rifled muskets and bayonets sheathed in leather frogs on their cartridge belts. As it was understood by the Confederates, this was to be bayonet fighting only – no ball and powder had been issued to them.

In the stands above the dirt floor of the arena thousands of spectators looked down; guests invited by a special Executive Invitation.

Originally a US Army fort, the conversion of the fort of Rock Island to a prisoner of war camp had begun in 1863. Occupying an island encompassing nearly a thousand acres, the Rock Island Prison Barracks lay in the center of the Mississippi River and technically was a part of the State of Illinois. The stands overlooked a broad field, conducive to the maneuvering of large marching formations. The nucleus of the prison itself was centered in a twelve-acre stockade, at the north end of the island. The twelve-foot-high fence encircled eighty-four frame structures that made up the barracks.

The president, dressed in spectacular form, wore a black frock ensemble and shawl collar vest over a wing tip shirt tucked deeply into dark wool fall front trousers. These trousers were distinct in having a button down bib consisting of two pair of three oyster shell black buttons holding up the bib.

The physically imposing president stood up and began shouting the rules of engagement. His deep baritone voice was difficult to understand with the heavy Carolina/ Tennessee accent. The rules of engagement were monotonous, rambling, and strayed into a political speech. Few people took notice of what was in the gorilla cage at the south end of the work yard.

"When the white handkerchief touches the ground, you may commence fighting!" concluded President Johnson, who turned to a stunningly attractive young lady, and added: "You have the honors, Mrs. Custer!"

"The martial exhibition of the employment of the bayonet will prove to be an excellent display of gymnastic exercise," Libbie replied to President Johnson as she accepted the large white handkerchief, adding, "in addition to being a worthwhile amusement, the combat will imbue in our gallant Free Men of Color an added degree of self-respect and confidence."

President Johnson's wife very seldom left her home in Tennessee; this did not seem to bother the president, who had little difficulty in finding attractive proper female escorts to be present at public events. If women were not attracted to the man himself, they were drawn by the power of his office.

While Johnson had a tenuous, complex friendship with Custer – one of the few figures of national renown who openly endorsed the president's unpopular policies, Johnson had nothing but admiration for Custer's wife, Elizabeth. The entire nation adored Elizabeth Custer, and the hated, ostracized president was grateful to have her at his side.

The president, who could count his friends on the fingers of one hand, remembered the time back in September, 1866, when the Custers had accompanied him on an extensive, circuitous, nearly month long train ride in a public effort to build up support for his post war policies aimed at the South.

The disastrous oratory campaign witnessed the often drunk President Johnson engage with hecklers and compare himself to Jesus. The contentious, vituperative speaking engagements grew increasingly hostile – and dangerous. Hundreds of protesters were killed when the platform they stormed upon gave way and sent them plunging to their deaths in a swampy morass. The presidential train barely escaped with Johnson clutching his trusted Remington revolver.

But it was in Ohio that Johnson saw the extent of loyalty held by the Boy General truly for the first time.

"I was born two miles and a half from here, but I am ashamed of you!" shouted the Yellow Hair at the dozen or so ruffians who cursed at and repeatedly jeered the president.

"Cock sucker!" one of the members of the coarse group yelled at President Johnson.

"I'll have your ass for that insult!" roared Johnson, stepping from the podium. "Get away from me!" warned the besotted Commander in Chief at the Secret Service agents, pushing them aside.

"Which one of you spineless dogs called me a cock sucker!" demanded the president, as he approached the group. Raucous laughter erupted from the growing crowd that had quickly swollen into hundreds that had come to protest as the president spoke.

President Andrew Johnson regarded the laughing, mocking group with antipathy, sizing them up individually.

"*Maybe it was you*!" The president shouted, grabbing the largest man of the inciters by the neck collar and trouser belt. Lifting the six-foot five-inch, three-hundred-pound man over his head like a rag doll, he turned and walked several steps toward the railway track, hurling the writhing, twisting man onto an iron rail.

"My back!" screamed the rabble rouser. "He has broken my back! I can't move my arms or legs!"

"See what that got him?" taunted Johnson, smiling as he approached the hecklers once more.

Suddenly the air was electrified by the rifle shot like cracking of a whip as Custer laid the lash onto the malcontents. They backed away, arms raised, shielding their faces from the tip of the bull whip which seemed to be guided by a mind of its own.

The president grabbed a short, heavy set man dressed in bibbed dungaree overalls who was holding a bleeding, empty eye socket.

"I'm going to beat you like a red-headed stepson!" shouted the out of control President Johnson, showing strong, tobacco stained teeth. Press reporters noted that he was raging like a lunatic.

"Eat this!" the president shouted, slamming his fist into the man's pudgy, unshaven face. The blow was like that of a pile driver, the impact driving the loose, rotten teeth backward into the gullet of the man's throat.

"Back! Back I say!" yelled the Boy General, wielding the whip like a mule skinner. Noses, ears, and flesh flew from faces contorted in fear and hate.

Snapping back to the present, President Johnson looked with appreciation upon the beautiful lady addressing the silent crowd, which was wooed by her charm.

"It is with the utmost honor that I accept the privilege of initiating the hostilities among these two combatant forces!" spoke Elizabeth Custer, trying to raise her voice loud enough to be clearly heard, but not so much as to appear to be shouting.

"Before us stand five companies of Free Men of Color!" Elizabeth Custer continued, unintentionally lifting her voice to be better understood. "...Willing to display their ardor to the New Republic, and to President Johnson – who has granted them this opportunity! Facing these heroes who represent our great nation today are the humiliated, filthy riff-raff that I abhor with the utmost antipathy! Mammon-worshipping, slave-owning rich landowners who lead an ensemble of share-cropping, white trash miscreants, as they did in a battle where they took a licking a scant five years ago!"

A chorus of shouts and "ayes" and "yeas" issued from the spectators, many of which had fought in the recent war and all of which had lost close relatives fighting the starving rabble that stood at rigid attention in the amphitheater.

President Johnson noted the positive reaction of the audience to Libbie Custer and was gratified by it. He recalled, ruefully, the pervasive, redundant lies put out by the press.

"To know me is to hate me!" the president had laughingly admitted shortly after blinding a man in brawl that occurred in Baltimore, Maryland. "That much was true," Johnson thought. President Johnson was known to have been walking the town after hours incognito, when suddenly he was recognized. Always proud of his ascendancy from poverty to the Nation's Oval Office, Johnson saw himself as "The Working Man's Man."

He would sometimes dress in less formal, but always tightly tailored, well maintained clothing and venture out to speak with "his" fellow countrymen. After the blinding occurred, in which the president injured several other detractors, Radical Republicans seized on the opportunity to slander Johnson in national newspapers, accusing the POTUS of dressing like a bum to avoid recognition and beg drinks surreptitiously.

An avid bare-knuckle fist fighting enthusiast who saw his legislation to legalize dueling defeated, Johnson sometimes attended the pugilistic competitions disguised as a spectator. Often, traveling fighters would offer challenges to the audience, expecting an easy victory over the local talent. In one such instance, the five-foot ten-inch, two-hundred-pound president took up the challenge, entering the ring and almost beating the man to death.

The Commander in Chief was jeered and booed for kicking his fallen opponent while he was down. The president's incognito appearances resulted in many assault and battery cases, in which men vaguely resembling the POTUS were attacked openly on the street, being mistaken for the most hated president in American History.

The POTUS was jarred out of his retrospections by the standing ovation that Libbie Custer was receiving. So enthusiastic was the ovation that Libbie had to pause momentarily, unable to be heard above the applause. Spurred by the rare public approval of one of his social contrivances, President Johnson reacted spontaneously, during Libbie Custer's pause.

"This is not all!" shouted the president, standing suddenly and raising both arms. "This is not all! Today I have a great and wonderful surprise for you! A beast only rumored to exist has been captured in the Far North of that vast expanse of the Alaskan Wilderness! Alaska! Which under the supervision of Secretary Seward I directed to purchase for this great nation of mine!"

A chorus of "Ohs!" and "Ahs!" reverberated in the stadium.

Seeking to build upon his ephemeral popularity, the president expanded upon his lie. "Seward caught a werewolf in the Alaskan Wilderness! A beast which cannot control its passions at the sight of violence and blood!"

At this, the crowd began to cheer and shout in a frenzied ardor of excitement and blood lust. Intuitively the president gave Libbie the nod to drop the handkerchief.

Libbie Custer was wearing a black and white touring hat that while ostentatious, effectively shielded her face and neck from the early morning sun. She wore a matching, more subdued black and white high collared pin striped blouse tucked beneath a pinstriped walking skirt. The Edwardian hoop underskirt added a robust fullness. The white corset pulled her diminutive waist tightly in while pushing her bosom up and revealing the cleavage, beginning to shine with perspiration. The tiny waist was emphasized by the broad, black cotton belt.

"Let the contest begin!" shouted Libbie, oblivious as to whether or not shouting would be construed as improper and unladylike.

The Colored troops watched as the handkerchief drifted to the ground, the Rebels on the other hand watched their ebon opponents, and awaited the commands of their officers and NCOs.

"Fix bayonets!" was shouted in both formations as left hands shot to the bayonets, sliding them from the frogs and locking them into the bayonet lugs at the business end of the rifled muskets. The Rebels made their move first.

"Company!" shouted the raggedly clad officers. "Platoon!" shouted the barefoot NCOs, their shell jackets dearth of buttons and shredded trousers held to their waists with lengths of cord. "Forwaaaard, *MARCH*!"

The five companies of Rebels moved forward. The front rank of each company held their bayoneted rifles to their front, at waist level, the triangular, beveled tips of the bayonets pointing toward their opponents. The rear ranks had their rifles shouldered as they advanced behind those ahead of them in short, choppy steps.

"One two! One two! One two!" shouted the non-commissioned officers as the Rebels approached the immobile blue clad soldiers, who remained at attention, showing great discipline.

Then suddenly, without warning the tempo of the Rebel momentum changed.

"DOUBLE TIME – *MARCH!!!*" the Rebels erupted into a heinous, long, mournful yell as they broke ranks into a full run at their stoic opponents. The bayonets were held low, preparatory to the disemboweling thrust.

The Rebel yell sent chills of panic through the spectators, it had the uncanny semblance of a ghost wind blowing through a ravine at high velocity. It started low, reaching higher and higher in pitch until it became an almost shrill, ear drum piercing tenor.

"First rank!" shouted a gigantic Negro with first sergeant chevrons sewn to his blue sleeves. "Ready, aim, fire! Second rank to the front, fire! Third rank to the front, fire! Fourth rank to the front, fire!"

In increments the Colored formations moved inexorably forward. The effect on the charging Rebels was nothing short of catastrophic. Rifles, arms, hands, teeth and skull fragments along with brain matter flew hundreds of feet into the air as their impetus carried them forward over their screaming, clawing comrades. Their élan reflected that of men who knew they were already dead. They desired nothing more than to close with their enemy who had unfair advantage over them.

"Libbie!" shouted Margaret. "I have never seen anything more exciting in my entire life!"

Probably five dozen from the five hundred attackers had survived the fusillade and were now in the ranks of Negro soldiers and working their bayonets. A deficit of command and control was evident within the Colored ranks, while a single Confederate officer seemed to control the tiny group of surviving Rebels with lethal skill. The Rebels moved as a single deadly entity through the seething, milling mob of Union soldiers, leaving a red wake of contorting, writhing carnage in their trail.

"Damn it!" shouted President Johnson. "Somehow I've gotta stop that man!"

The president, an expert shot with a revolver – or any firearm for that matter, drew the big Remington from his shoulder rig. Cocking the hammer back and taking careful aim at the Rebel officer – obviously a man of charisma and great leadership ability – he pulled the trigger and hit the emaciated officer squarely in the back. The Rebel Captain staggered forward three steps and dropped to his knees.

The crowd roared with approval and the president, seeing this, waved acknowledgement to his fair-weather friends. The Free Men of Color seized upon the advantage afforded by the president and fell upon the diminutive group of Picket's men with horrific savagery. The Rebels would parry and thrust at the swarming Negros, many of whom had reloaded and were firing point blank into the shrinking band of gray.

"USA! USA! USA!" chanted the spectators in unison as the Union soldiers ruthlessly pressed their advantage and seized victory. The audience in the stands began stomping their feet to the chant, causing a rumbling, thunder like sound, the reverberations of which shook the ground.

"Now is the time!" shouted President Johnson. "Release the thing!"

The president gave the signal and a single bugle blared the "Attack!" melody. Two men dressed in blue zookeeper's uniforms raced across the bare ground toward the gorilla cage. One was hit by an errant bullet and went down immediately. The crowd roared with laughter as he struggled to get up and collapsed again. His companion tried to extricate the keys from the death grip, and had to kneel, placing the weight of his knee onto the dead man's wrist to obtain them.

The Colored troops - hundreds of them, were applying the bayonet mercilessly to the encircled body of Rebels, which fought back with the ferocity of a dying lion being swarmed by droves of hyenas.

The surviving zookeeper managed to unlock the door to the gorilla cage, but instead of simply leaving the key in place, he tried to extricate it. Gladstone flung the door open with such force that the door caught the zookeeper and slammed him against the grill, exploding his head like a watermelon. The keeper's hands continued to grip the steel bars of the door as he slid to the ground in a heap.

"Oh, look, Margaret! It really is a werewolf!" squealed Beverly, grabbing the sister-in-law of Libbie by the arm.

Margaret watched the one-armed Grendel through the opera glass; it had the human form, and was completely covered in red fur. She moved the glass forward and away from her eyes to try to sharpen the image.

"Don't grab me like that," quipped Margaret. "I'm trying to get a close up view of the wolf man and - oh! He appears to have only one arm!"

"Let me see!" pleaded Beverly, who was wearing a crisp, white cotton gather-sleeved Louisa type summer blouse. It was a full button down blouse. The shirt was unbuttoned halfway and Margaret was transfixed at the near open display of the heavy, pendulous breasts. This was unlike Beverly to be so informal in her normally austere appearance.

"Here," said Margaret. "Take them – but only for a moment!" Margaret offered the opera glass to Beverly, taking the opportunity to ogle the sweaty mams as she handed the primitive binoculars to her.

"That's incredible!" shouted Beverly. "He does have only one arm, and oh! What's he up to? He's picking up something, Margaret!"

"What is it!? What is it!? I want to see!" responded Margaret, trying to ogle the cleavage of Beverly's breasts over the wide brim of the heavy breasted girl's white sun hat. The shirt was stuck to the skin with sweat, and Margaret could see through the thin cotton fabric much better as a result.

"He has something in his hand, Margaret! It looks like a rope – no! It's a chain! Yes, Margaret! It's a heavy length of chain! And he's swinging it like a weapon!" cried the excited Beverly.

The remaining Rebels in the center of the ebony mass of humanity had been driven to the ground and were being repeatedly bayonetted by the victorious Free Men of Color troops. Now the blue clad soldiers turned their attention to the wounded Confederates who lay in heaps by the hundreds where they had been mown down in the initial attack.

Four to five Negro soldiers would circle a fallen Rebel, who often tried to maneuver on his back, kicking at the beveled, twenty-eight inch blades that licked at him.

"Git back!" cried one Confederate, kicking at his attackers as he lay on the red dirt, shot through a lung.

"Come at'im from the other side while I try to stick'im, Roy Lee!" shouted one of the Free Men, jabbing the bayonet at the kicking man, trying to find an opening to the vital organs. Two more Union soldiers rushed in with bayonets to assist with dispatching the downed Rebel.

Overcome with the blood lust that comes with victory and easy killing, the Free Men of Color were oblivious to the threat that approached them from behind. They mistook the rising applause and growing crescendo of roaring approval from the crowd of spectators to be in reaction to the finishing off of the Confederate wounded.

This erroneous inference caused them to go at their work with more zeal, driving cold steel through outstretched hands and into bare ribbed torsos. Bayonets skewered empty stomachs that hadn't known a half ration in years - neither as a soldier in a starving army nor as a Prisoner of War.

The lean, hard abdominal muscles beneath the gray rags seized around the diamond pointed bayonets that plunged through them. The rectus abdominis tightened as the Negro soldiers worked the twenty-eight-inch-long triangular blades, enlarging the wound cavity. The wounded soldiers in gray rags grasped the bayonet shafts with both hands, screaming as they lifted their hips obscenely against the thrusting, twisting of the blades.

The applause of the spectators and the screams of the bayonetted drowned out the commotion from further behind. Some of those who circled the kicking writhing men as they sought entry for their bayonets looked up in the direction of the commotion. They saw dozens of their team mates rushing toward the fiasco with bayonets at the ready. Distinct rifle shots could be heard above the tumult.

"Care to take a look?" President Johnson asked Libbie Custer, handing her the brass barreled Lemaire binoculars.

"Why, thank you, Mr. President!" responded Libbie, quickly searching the area where the new focus seemed to be. "I believe your werewolf is doing a number on our brave soldiers!"

Gladstone saw the menacing forms of Union infantrymen approaching him from all directions, bayonets at the ready. The blue clad soldiers approached cautiously, carefully, they were crouching with their bayonets held far forward as they got closer to him. Sometimes one would fire into him, the impact seemed to sear through him but caused no damage. What did cause damage though, was the five-foot length of chain that he swung in a circular motion above his head. When he canted the angle of the rusted chain, it tore through the soldiers like a scythe.

Hair, eyeballs, jawbones, throats, flew in all directions in response to the propeller type impact of the chain length.

Scores of Free Men of Color lay twitching in heaps with shattered skulls. The blue clad soldiers continued approaching, leaning forward with their bayonets as they neared to contact, carefully, with skill and experience. The Negro Infantry did not react in panic as the murderous rusted chain mowed through them.

The vestigial part of the werewolf's mind that remained human began to feel a sense of concern akin to worry as it saw the noose of Negro troops slowly tightening around it. The Negro Infantry were approaching in short, choppy steps – a sort of shuffle in which their brogans kicked up dust. The Negro riflemen advanced in a forward posture, bent slightly at the waist, shoulder to shoulder with their murderous bayonets now ready to thrust. On all sides they approached in an ever shrinking three-hundred-sixty-degree radius.

Gladstone began to panic, swinging the chain in such a blinding frenzy that the motion caused it to blur, yet the Negro Infantry came on...

"Sound retreat!" laughed the president. "I think my elite Free Men of Color have had enough excitement for one day!"

At the sound of the bugle call to retreat, the Union soldiers reacted as a single entity, backing from the scene of the xenomorph cautiously with bayonets toward the threat as they passed through the gate that led into the building structure in squads and platoons. They paid no mind to their stricken comrades who lay screaming in despair for help on the blood stained earth.

Much later that evening, the president would host festivities in hopes of cementing strategic friendships out of the unprecedented success of his private event on the parade field.

Uniformed soldiers acted as ushers, informing the invited guests that it was time to leave, and that later that evening there would be a gala celebration in the large cafeteria of the complex.

Not everyone left, though; the president remained, along with a large security detachment.

"What about the wounded, Mr. President?" came the question in grotesque Scottish brogue.

"Let's leave them out there for a bit, Allan," responded President Johnson, adding, "if blood and violence can shock Gladstone back into his human form, then this certainly ought to do it. Gladstone is the only one who has the arcane ability to see into a crystal and tell us where to find Custer with the war bonnet."

Gladstone lay atop a pile of Union corpses, his hunger sated. The red fur was matted in human gore as he again attempted to crawl forward among the dead and dying. The effect was drug-like, he felt as though he were a snake about to slip into an unconscious stupor after gorging itself.

The man beast was aware of other people, not only of the carnage that lay all about, but the presence of men who stood near him, uncertainly, talking among themselves. One man stood out in particular, he seemed to be the leader of the others. The reaction was immediate.

"Look out, Mr. President!" shouted one of Pinkerton's men, throwing himself between Gladstone and President Johnson as he had been trained to do. Gladstone raked the man's face with the talons of his left hand, causing the front of the face to slough off and then he lunged at the president.

"Stupid animal!" exclaimed President Johnson, seizing the beast's arm in a firm lock, in which Gladstone's hand and wrist were held firmly in place underneath Johnson's armpit, "Attack me again and I'll kill you barehanded!"

Johnson's right hand was clenched firmly on the broad, powerful neck of the beast, the president tightened the hold on Gladstone's arm - standing on the balls of his feet and leaning back, exerting more pressure on the arm lock. He looked into the deep, aqua blue eyes of the werewolf, which stared back at him.

"You and I," continued the President of the United States, "are going to get to know each other very, very well!"

Chapter Twenty-Four
President Johnson Peers into the
Crystal Ball

TAPERS FLICKERED ON the walls of the dungeon-like cellar beneath the garrison hospital at Rock Island. The sputtering flames generated a yellow, unsteady luminescence. Objects that stood in the path of the light cast enormous, disfigured shadows on the walls and floors. The shadowy, demon-like aberrations danced wickedly in the erratic torch light.

This was the largest building on the island; a huge, two story wood framed, white washed structure that stood next to the mess hall. On the stone paved floor was a pile of hay, atop this lay a red haired man, naked and covered with a blanket.

The quavering orgy of torch light which cast obscene shadows added an even more malevolent aspect to the already grim features of President Johnson, who sat on a wicker chair. Gigantic Negros in Union Army uniforms stood to either side of him, armed to the teeth. They were part of his personal body guard, combat veterans of a dozen battles; dangerous men, ruthless killers. All were Medal of Honor winners - twenty-five of them.

A small table made of polished black walnut was set before the president who relaxed in the wicker chair. On this table sat a full bottle of Tennessee sipping whiskey. The flat sided, pear shaped vessel was made of brown, translucent glass and a featured a bold relief of President Johnson on one side of the bottle - on the other side was a relief of the American Bald Eagle. The bottle was a short quart, or "fifth."

The Commander in Chief broke the seal of the unopened bottle - he tore the cork out with his strong, brown teeth and tilted the bottle bottom side up. Pockets of air entered the bottle as the president swallowed forcefully, making a "bloop, bloop, bloop," sound.

"Ahhhhhhhhh! Now, that hits the spot!" declared President Johnson, as he wiped his mouth with the back of his powerful right forearm. The sleeve was rolled up past the elbow and revealed a forearm thickly corded with well defined, sinewy muscle. There must have been very little subcutaneous fat underneath the skin because the muscle striations stood out distinctly. He sat the half-emptied bottle on the table and regarded the sleeping figure of Gladstone that lay on the bed of hay in front of him.

"Time to rise and shine, Professor Gladstone!" shouted the president in an out of character, convivial, friendly voice.

The armed detail of Medal of Honor Recipients that guarded their Commander in Chief stood at a modified position of parade rest. Their right hand grasping the upper barrel of the Spencer repeating rifle that each one was issued, and thrusting it forward. The butt of each weapon rested on the floor. The left hand was placed at the small of their back, and the feet were spaced ten inches apart. These men would spring like tigers into action at the slightest sign of danger to the president.

"Ohhhh," moaned Gladstone. "I have seen hell."

"I mean to have you see more than that, once you have been cleaned up and dressed in attire fitting a man of your stature," responded President Andrew Johnson. "I mean to have you see into a crystal and tell me the location of Custer and the war bonnet!"

"To whom do I speak," mumbled Gladstone. "The room is spinning; I feel as though I am Lazarus being pulled from the grave."

President Johnson immediately fell into the habit of comparing himself mentally to the Christ, as the powerful Tennessee bourbon eased his inhibitions. That Gladstone had compared himself to Lazarus immediately evoked the recurrent illusions of grandeur, in which Johnson saw himself as a sort of Messiah.

"You speak to the most powerful man on this earth," responded Johnson. "I am the president! President Johnson of the United States of America! And with the war bonnet of Roman Nose, I shall rule the world!"

"The war bonnet holds magic of unsurpassed power," replied Gladstone, as if speaking from a dream. "But even Custer does not know how to exploit it fully."

"We will speak tomorrow, my soldiers will minister to your needs for now," the president paused, then added, "I have a gala event to attend, I must not be late."

President Johnson mounted the stairwell, then hesitated and looked back, as though he wished to say something more, but passing it off continued up the stairs.

The tables of the large prison mess hall had been pushed roughly aside to make room for the impromptu ball. None of the guests had formal attire, but wore the sweaty clothing from earlier in the day. That did not detract from the festivities, and the Army Marching Band was there to provide music of the highest caliber.

"Mr. President! Mr. President!" chorused a panoply of false friends and sycophants as the POTUS hurried to a massive wooden double door, guarded by immaculately dressed Colored troops, resplendent in parade uniforms and bedecked with medals.

"I'll be back in a moment!" shouted the president in an exuberant, affable tone.

"Are they ready, Secretary Seward?" asked President Johnson.

"Yes, Mr. President," answered Seward, seeing the president tilt the nearly empty bottle of bourbon straight up and finish it completely.

"Hey! You, the bartender over there!" shouted Secretary Seward at one of the Colored soldiers tending the bar. The soldier wore dress blues and two rows of medals decorated his broad chest.

"Bring the president another bottle of bourbon!" ordered Secretary Seward, shouting above the orchestral band and ongoing conversations of drunken guests. The sounds of laughter and easy conversation mixed well with the orchestral music to create an atmosphere of joviality and comradery among the revelers. They did not notice the bartender as he hurried past, carrying the bottle to the President of the United States.

"Is *she* in there with them?" croaked Johnson, his voice became husky with the question. The president felt overwhelmed by his macabre lust for the exotic, sensual woman which he *knew* waited beyond the doors.

"Yes, Mr. President," replied Secretary Seward, who lowered his voice, adding, "be careful in there, sir. You must remember to never touch her."

The heavy, oak doors opened inward as the soldiers lay their shoulders into them. President Johnson walked into the high ceilinged room, hearing the massive doors squeak on their hinges and thud closed behind him.

Before the president stood an entire company of the president's personal guard of Colored soldiers, dressed in magnificent Army dress blue uniforms. Around the bull neck of each soldier depended the Medal of Honor, suspended from a blue neck ribbon. The soldiers were standing in four platoons of thirty men each. They stood at the position of attention, their Spencer repeating rifles held at right shoulder arms.

Behind the ranks of one hundred twenty black soldiers stood the lithe, curvaceous figure of a young white woman. She was standing on a wooden platform with her hands covering her face, elbows raised. The right leg was bent slightly at the knee and the left leg was offset at an angle and locked straight. Her left buttocks was firmly flexed while the right side gluteus maximus relaxed. The auburn hair was pulled up in a tightly woven bun, held in place with a diamond inlaid golden brooch.

From to the right, came the hollow beat of a double bongo drum. The motionless white woman came to supple life, moving her right thigh in a back and forth motion while she extended her right arm horizontally from her side. Her left arm remained raised, bent at the elbow as she continued to shield her face with the back of her left hand.

Suddenly she extended her left arm out from her side also, revealing her face for the first time. The upper half of her face was entirely hidden by a masquerade mask. It was a French Renaissance mask made of black ruffled lace and black braid. It had a large black ostrich plume secured to the right side. This was the only article of clothing that the Caucasian woman wore; from the lower half of her face, down – she was entirely nude.

President Johnson tilted the bottle bottom side up, taking a deep pull from the amber vessel that bore his visage. He did not take his eyes off the serpentine woman as he tugged off of the bottle. The tempo of the bongo drum grew in intensity.

The black musician playing the bongo braced the dual percussion instrument tightly between his knees, the twin drums were unequal in size, the larger drum pressed against the inside of the right knee.

The alabaster figure of the naked woman writhed like a cobra to the drum beat as the president took another pull from the bottle. Her hips swayed to the beat of the drum as she bent half way down at her knees and held her arms out to her sides, moving in tandem with the drum. The dancer's movements were liquid, elegant, and serpentine.

"Now," said the president to himself. "That is worth a man's soul!"

The naked woman moved her hands to her firm, apple sized breasts and began mashing them together, then pinched her nipples and pulled upward on them, the president could see the sweaty crease beneath the breasts before she released the nipples, allowing the breasts to bounce back into firm position, jiggling provocatively. The nipples remained distended, as they engorged with blood, the president speculated.

"Bring me a chair, somebody!" President Johnson uttered throatily in a husky voice, a voice that was deeper than it normally was. The words had come with effort as he tilted the bottle again.

"Get me a chair, by Jove! Can't you see I'm having the best of times? Here now! *Move with alacrity!*" shouted President Johnson, as he looked at the swaying, hypnotizing figure.

The impression to an observer may have been that he was shouting at the woman, but that was not the case; *he simply could not take his eyes from her.*

The tempo of the bongo remained steady, as the woman stepped down from the dais in a supple, cat like motion. She walked slowly, in a deliberate, torqueing sway that would place one side of her body to the direction of march, and then the other. She advanced toward the president, passing through the formation of Negro soldiers which stood at attention.

"There now, let's have it!" shouted the Commander in Chief, grabbing the chair from an immaculately dressed Free Man of Color in resplendent dress uniform. "And get me another bottle!" he shouted, as he quaffed the final dregs of Tennessee bourbon.

President Johnson wiped his mouth with the back of his right hand which still held the empty vessel, while his jet black, hungry eyes feasted on the woman like the eyes of a man whose soul had been starved.

"Son of a bitch! What a show!!!" the president shouted, hurling the empty bottle across the room. "Hell yeah!!!" roared the president, feeling himself beginning to truly unwind and relax as the effects of the alcohol assertively began to take strong effect on the two fisted drinker.

The naked woman approached the seated president, then with suddenness of movement faced about, and neared the first rank of Colored troops.

"First rank, kneel!" commanded the president, breaking the seal of the bottle, and working at the mouth of the bottle with his strong, straight tobacco stained teeth to loosen the cork.

The entire first rank of each platoon took to the knee, right hand on the rifle barrel, left on the stock - the butt of the weapon to the floor. President Johnson watched the play of firm muscles in the woman's back and behind as she slinked her way to a soldier kneeling in the center of the second platoon. The president saw the female's haunches flex and tighten as she thrust her shaved mons Venus almost into the face of the kneeling soldier.

The kneeling soldier remained immobile, looking straight forward and not breaking the kneeling position. The woman placed her hands on both sides of the darkly pigmented, shaven face, caressing it. Then without warning she slapped the man viciously.

The tempo of the bongo was increasing in its staccato, hollow beat as she went to the next kneeling soldier and turned her butt to his face. She looked at President Johnson as she placed her hands behind her head and arched her back powerfully. She began thrusting her mons at the piceous eyes of the president, while at the same time shaking her torso, making her breasts gyrate violently to the beat of the bongo.

"Now!" the woman in the masquerade mask shouted.

"Yes!" responded the president.

The thrumming of the bongo drums intensified in their urgency as the Negro soldiers began undressing. The hands of the drummer alternated the strikes of the smaller macho drum on the left with the larger hembra drum on the right, producing a steady ostinato of eighth notes.

Ignoring the talk and banter of the men as they shed their uniforms, the lady in the masquerade mask approached President Johnson, in the slow, swaying motion of the cobra, placing her mons Venus one inch from the president's face.

"Ungggghhh!" groaned President Johnson, dropping the nearly empty bottle of bourbon and clasping the firm buttocks of the woman who stood before him.

"Pig!" hissed the woman in the mask, the sibilance of the insult reminded the president of a hissing kitten, but he still continued to grasp and feel the contours of the woman's derriere.

"Don't – hurt – me, *Mommy*!" gasped the Commander in Chief as the petite, beautifully formed mouth of the woman contorted into a puckered sphincter of hate.

"Filthy beast!" hissed the naked woman, slapping President Johnson full in the face, the sting of the slap smarted enough to shock the president back to his senses, as another slap spun his head.

"Harder, hit me harder, Mommy! *Please*!" groaned the president.

"Look up at me and tell me what I want to hear!" said the naked lady, slapping the president with such force that his nose began bleeding. Her breasts jiggled violently with the motion as a rivulet of perspiration ran between them.

"Black lives matter..." replied Johnson as he looked into the malevolent eyes behind the mask.

"That's right! Now, open your mouth, you accursed, damned swine!" commanded the woman, whose face was directly over his. The masquerade mask added to the mystique of the dancing girl as the president, near to passing out from too much drink, opened his mouth.

"*Bastard!*" she hissed, leaning forward. "Open your filthy mouth!" she reiterated, pinching either side of the president's mouth with the thumb and index finger of her right hand, the finger nails deeply imprinting the shaven face and drawing blood. The pain caused the president to fully open his fetid, reeking orifice.

The naked woman with the masquerade mask hawked, clearing her throat and spat fully into President Johnson's open mouth and stood up straight. She turned about and walked brusquely toward the dais. She passed through the Negro soldiers; the firm, full gluteal muscles of her behind flexing haughtily with every fluid, insolent, barefooted step.

His eyes closed tightly as he lifted his face toward the ceiling and let out a long, deafening train whistle like yell. He held the yell, maintaining it at the top of his lungs until his breath was spent.

"WHOOOOOOOOOOOOOOOOOOUUUUUUUUUUU!!!!!! shouted the president, as the drummer beat increasingly faster on the bongo drums. "WHEWHOOOOOOOOOOOOO!!!!!!"

The percussionist was using both open hands, the motion was so fast the movement seemed blurred. The man's head was shaven, the skin was very black, and the face was narrow, with cheekbones that were high set but not overly pronounced. The forehead was neither high nor sloping.

Sweat beaded the man's face and stung his eyes as he alternated striking the right drum from the left drum. The *bongasero* expertly thrummed the tandem drum held between his knees at a blinding tempo. The man's face was contorted into a pained grimace, the lips were pulled back from the long, straight white teeth and conveyed a snarling expression.

The soldier-musician, his blue regulation uniform blouse removed, wore a white cotton button down shirt. The white shirt was stuck to his back with sweat as he thrummed the striking edge of the drum heads even faster and harder with the fingers and palms of his hands.

"Get me some good pics of that woman amidst the soldiers, Illingworth," mumbled the semi-conscious Johnson, straining through his inebriation to taste the residual saliva of masked woman. "Make sure she gets as many as she wants. That's always part of the deal with her."

"Yes, Mr. President," came the muffled reply from William H. Illingworth, whose head and shoulders were covered by the black cape of the large wet plate camera as he positioned the photographic device atop the enormous tripod.

Sensing the proper moment, he illuminated the scene as the nude white woman in the background posed, and then he shot the plate. Illingworth worked quickly, carefully replacing each plate with another. Already the photographer William Illingworth could see that the photos were masterpieces of art. The upper half of the beautiful face was occulted behind the flamboyant masquerade mask. The beauty was enhanced by the enigmatic, Mona Lisa-like smile.

President Johnson fought the urge to vomit as he began to lose consciousness. His face was cold and clammy. The *bongasero* played the single skinned, open bottom instrument like a madman as the president urgently motioned for a receptacle to regurgitate into.

Chapter Twenty-Five
Escape from Philistine!

THE FOLLOWING DAY saw President Johnson seated once more in the shadowy, torch lit basement. The Commander in Chief was seated on the wicker chair in front of the small table made of black walnut, surrounded by shadows thrown on the wall from the torches, shadows which danced like demons at a warlock's coven. On the table was not a bottle of whiskey but rather, a crystal sphere of deep, translucent beauty. It sat upon a pedestal of ivory, of which the contact surfaces were cushioned with red velvet. This sphere differed in appearance from the one used by Gladstone earlier in the Sibley, with Custer; it was smaller and in a way appeared more plain. However more utilitarian it may have appeared, it nevertheless captured the eye and was an arresting object of singular beauty.

"What can you tell me from looking into that thing, Gladstone?" queried President Johnson.

"Nothing, Mr. President," answered Professor Gladstone, adding, "you need to understand, sir, that it is *you* who will be looking into the ball and seeing images, dreams, or shapes of things related to what you seek. I will assist you by focusing my concentration on the crystal orb."

Half a continent away, Lieutenant Colonel Custer and Bloody Knife urgently sought to hide themselves somewhere within the funeral parlor as the hordes of undisciplined, rampaging Cheyenne and Sioux entered the abandoned town of Philistine.

The fact that Philistine had been hastily evacuated was manifested in the preserved cadaver that lay in the uncovered coffin. The corpse had been there at least since before the town had been abandoned, and was dressed in a tuxedo to which various awards and military decorations of European origin were affixed. The Boy General and his Arikawa ally were nervously exploring the mortuary for a place to hide themselves and had looked at the corpse in passing.

"Lay down on the mortuary table and rest the back of your head on the skull block," instructed Custer. "I'll cover you with the sheet and they won't dare to lift it. As superstitious as they are, I'll wager that they won't venture to set foot in here."

"Me no like," responded Bloody Knife, adding, "bad to hide where white man keep dead folk."

"Hammer meets nail, Bloody Knife! This is the safest place to hide from those muscly, painted killers," the Boy General assured his reluctant friend. "Here, take this," Custer continued, as he handed Bloody Knife the trocar – a metallic, sharpened proboscis-like nozzle akin to a gigantic mosquito beak. The trocar was used for insertion into the thoracic cavity to facilitate draining of body fluids under a high vacuum induced suction.

"If one of them pulls back the sheet," said Custer, "just jab'im with this! Depress the handle and the vacuum from that large suction bottle behind you will pull their vital organs through the hose attached at the base."

"How I jab'em, Boy General?" queried the uneasy, nervous Arikawa.

"By thrusting it forward into their abdomen! Like this!" explained the former general, making thrusting motions with the evil looking instrument before handing it to Bloody Knife.

"I jab'em! By thrustin' it in!" repeated the Arikawa scout. "Then release handle. Then what happen, Boy General?"

On the other side of the continent, President Johnson peered into the aquamarine, green-blue depths of the crystal ball, seeing the vague shape and outline of the funeral parlor begin to take shape deep within the gemstone quality, blue beryl sphere. The president had no control over what he was seeing, as the image of what appeared to be a cadaver floated hazily into view among the impurities and mineral striations that hung suspended in eternity. The image of the cadaver in the funeral parlor for a while remained indistinct, but then sharpened.

The hair was jet black, the full hairline extended down to the low set, sloping forehead and in no place did it recede. The black eyebrows were thick and bushy, joining above the bridge of the medium sized, proportional nose. The eyelids were closed and the full, bulbous lips were painted a deep red, apparently with a lipstick.

The corpse had a pasty blue, alabaster complexion and the neck was hidden by the high collar of a white shirt beneath a lavish, medal bedecked tuxedo. Over this was a black cape made of wool, it was red on the inside. The sleeveless garment was fastened at the neck and open down the middle.

Johnson watched as the image of Custer approached the cadaver and looked over it, as a taxidermist would study the work of a skilled craftsman.

"Where are they?" asked President Johnson, not looking away from the orb which seemed to be faintly illuminated from within.

"They're in one of the abandoned frontier towns within the state of Kansas," answered Gladstone. "You must not talk or the image will be lost."

The president could hear nothing that transpired within the globe; he could only see images. He saw Custer turn and approach the glass paned window of the funeral parlor and disappear from view, as he did so, he saw the parfleche on the former general's back which contained the war bonnet.

The imagery became muddled as though a stone had been dropped into a pool of water. After a moment of intense waiting, the imagery settled smooth once more, and the face of the cadaver materialized into view again. He had, Johnson thought, the appearance of some nobleman or count from Eastern Europe. His presence was incongruous with the Kansas ghost town setting.

President Johnson had his hands cupped to either side of his eyes as he peered into the crystal orb. The meaty outer edges of his palms pressed against the beryl sphere as he struggled to see more clearly.

Andrew Johnson was vaguely aware of the similarity he had experienced as a boy, when trying to peer into the translucent depths of a cistern as the sun lit the waters briefly in its arcing travel across the ecliptic. The face of the cadaver that floated deep within the suspended mineral striations of the crystal ball slowly began to manifest itself.

The Yellow Hair looked through the plate glass at the cobble stone street, which was heavily covered in weed and grass. Tumble weeds rolled along the street like phantoms, pushed by the wind. The Yellow Hair ignored the tumble weeds but focused his keen eyes on the howling mobs of Cheyenne and Sioux, whom he observed with alarm, who were going from building to building ransacking and then setting them ablaze.

Concerned, the Boy General hurried into the parlor where the cadaver lay with the lid of the coffin open. He noticed that the red, lipsticked lips were not sutured closed, the lips were full, flush and almost lifelike. Custer continued toward the back of the mortuary, looking for the door to a cellar or other means of egress.

"What Boy General doin'?" asked Bloody Knife from beneath the white linen sheet, his voice betrayed the fear of the supernatural, and the sheet over his face magnified his concern for his safety – he couldn't see what was going on, but he heard the howling mobs outside, growing nearer.

"I'm looking for a means of escape, should we have to leave this place," replied the Yellow Hair. "There are Cheyenne and Sioux going from building to building, engaged in acts of arson, setting the structures ablaze. I'm hoping they will fear this place of death and avoid it."

"Eh?" the president mumbled silently to himself, cognizant of the need to remain quiet. "Did I hear a sound in there?"

For the first time, President Johnson thought he could actually *hear* a noise inside the crystal; it was faint and vibratory – like the sound of a blade being sharpened on a grinding stone at very high speed.

The president concentrated on the bizarre image of the dead man in the coffin, trying to understand what he was seeing in the crystal ball. Suddenly the eyes of the cadaver flew open and locked with his, the lip stick painted lips pulled back in a hideous, snarling, bestial expression revealing extended, tusk like yellow canine teeth. The dentition struck Johnson as resembling aged, yellowed ivory. The tiger-like, pointed fangs crowded against the smaller frontal incisors, making them appear snaggle-toothed and crooked.

There was, the president thought, the most extreme hatred and malice conveyed in the malevolent expression of the cadaver. The grating sound of metal against stone increased to almost deafening proportions as the cadaver sat suddenly up in the coffin, ramrod straight and reached for Johnson abruptly through the translucent layers of aquamarine. That the POTUS had not anticipated any encounter of this nature rendered him paralyzed and unable to tear himself from the orb. He felt himself suddenly seized by the shoulder...

"Snap out of it, Mr. President!" shouted Professor Gladstone, shaking the president with his left hand.

"Custer is in grave danger!" shouted the visibly shaken President Johnson. "There must be some way of discerning his whereabouts!"

"There are dozens such abandoned towns along the frontier, Mr. President. We can wait a short spell, say an hour, and attempt to reenter the sphere," offered Gladstone.

"Not me!" replied President Johnson. "That thing, whatever it was, *reached for me!*"

Custer stood motionless behind a curtain which was drawn to, concealing various liquid and chemical containing vessels of the mortuary trade, such as formaldehyde, arsenic salts, and alcohol.

Bloody Knife listened with tense expectancy under the linen sheet as he heard the handle of the door jiggle violently and then the shattering of glass as five painted, pantherish men – Dog Soldiers entered the funeral parlor, Henrys and Spencer repeating rifles held at the ready as they advanced cautiously, spreading out and smashing objects with the butt of their weapons.

The light that entered the room from the conflagration outside was augmented by the flaming torch held by one of the braves. The thick, greased hair at the top of his pate had been combed back in a pompadour and the rest of the hair fell over either ear in a braid. The twin braids rested in front of the broad shoulders above the swell of pectoral muscles that flexed with the warrior's arm movements. Around the Dog Soldier's thick, athletic neck depended a six loop necklace of human teeth through which holes had been made, allowing a rawhide cord to be strung through them. The brave held the torch high above his head, thrusting it in sudden, stabbing motions this way and that so as to throw light all about in the strange room.

"Dead man!" grunted one of the brutes, a six-foot dark complexioned man, his skin browned by recent days of overt sun exposure. "Bring light!" The warrior, who appeared to be in his mid-thirties, was shirtless but for a three paneled hair pipe bead breastplate. His thick, greased hair was worn in a double pony tail and the braids were wrapped in purple cloth. Two eagle feathers jutted at a jaunty angle from the black coif and the face was etched with frown lines into a permanent scowling expression. He wore a boldly colored bright red breech clout over a pair of deerskin leggings beaded down the front.

The brave with the torch approached his accomplices, his forehead was low set, and eyebrows plucked smooth. His high, pronounced cheekbones, painted with horizontal white stripes, rested beneath shifting brown irises that never seemed to rest.

"Take scalp!" grunted the voice of the torch wielding Dog Soldier. If the braves felt any apprehension at the odd looking man in the coffin, they did not show it.

The group gathered about the cadaver in the coffin, as others entered the funeral parlor and turned their attention to the human outline beneath the white linen sheet – the figure of Bloody Knife.

"Gonna see what under sheet!" shouted one of the braves.

"What sheet?" responded a tall man with an authoritative voice. This Dog Soldier had a red bandanna wrapped around his eyes, from which dried blood had melded with the war paint – it was none other than Porcupine Bear.

"Take scalp from funny man!" commanded the warrior with the torch to another one of the braves.

His full lips curved downward at either side of a wide set mouth. Although his face betrayed no emotion, the muscles that defined his pronounced, block shaped jaw tightened in anticipation of the scalping.

One of the warriors grasped the luxuriant, combed hair of the waxy, lipstick painted cadaver and placed the blade of a hunting knife at the nape of the thick, low set, oiled hairline. The brave - a tall, lean hipped, thickly muscled Dog Soldier prepared to lift the scalp.

Around the brave's ox-like neck was fastened a pony bead choker with a large mussel shell disk and hair pipe pendant. The Cheyenne, dressed in a tightly fitting breechclout, a buffalo skin cape, and a beaded belt, applied pressure to the razor sharp blade as he began the horizontal incision.

Three of the others busied themselves in the unsteady light, breaking glass objects, knocking books from shelves, tearing costly canvas paintings from walls and smashing them across the top of high backed chairs.

There was movement behind the curtain, one of the warriors noticed. The warrior, an accompanying Hunkpapa Sioux in his early twenties, wore his hair in a modified roach. The hair was long in the back and tied into a knot beside the left ear. He wore an apron made of mountain lion skin which retained its tail in the rear. The edges of the skin were fringed with strips of rawhide.

Not taking any chances, the hatchet faced warrior fired into the location where Custer was rapidly donning the war bonnet. The action of the big Henry .44 caliber rim fire was as smooth as butter as the Cheyenne worked the lever and squeezed the trigger.

At the other side of the room, the wrist of the brave standing over and scalping the cadaver was seized suddenly with terrific force as the eyelids opened and the lip stick painted lips pulled back.

Simultaneously another brave had guided the hand of Porcupine Bear onto the sheet, and the blinded man immediately ripped the linen from Bloody Knife. The Arikawa let out a war whoop and plunged the trocar into the wash board stomach of Porcupine Bear, then released the handle. Immediately a loud suction noise was drowned out by the man's stentorious shouts as he clutched the brass proboscis of the trocar with both hands.

Porcupine Bear, wearing a bear tooth necklace and a George Washington Peace Medal twisted his torso violently, making the medallion swing back and forth as Bloody Knife fought to keep the trocar imbedded. The sculpted rectus abdominis of the struggling Dog Soldier tightened around the proboscis like a vagina.

The Cheyenne's hair was parted precisely down the middle and braided. The braids were held intact with rawhide thongs through which hawk bells had been strung. These jingled urgently as the Dog Soldier cavorted, dancing like a maddened Dervish.

The impaled Chief of the Dog Soldiers continued shouting angrily as he grasped the trocar with scarred, meaty hands. The enraged brave's curses and threats turned to animal-like growls as he fought at the sharpened instrument which was sucking out his intestines, stomach, spleen and liver.

The gutted man pulled suddenly backwards, detaching the hose from the proboscis. Several feet of small intestine rapidly vanished with a violent whipping, flopping motion into the open end of the hose. The eviscerated aboriginal cursed as he pulled the trocar from his abdominal wall and hurled it at Bloody Knife.

The trocar missed as Bloody Knife deftly canted his head to the right. The velocity of the missile was halted suddenly, as it imbedded itself deeply into the lower back of the Hunkpapa Sioux who had been firing into the curtain.

The big Hunkpapa dropped his Henry and grabbed at the front end of the trocar, which had skewered through the right kidney in its impetus and sprouted like the gigantic beak of some hideous, grotesque mosquito just above his appendix.

His lips pulled back in a grimace, showing teeth filed to points as he tilted his head back and screamed at the top of his lungs. The veins stood out on his temples as the wavering light of the torch highlighted the distended tendons of his straining neck.

Across the room, the cadaver bit deeply into his assailant's raw boned wrist, drawing blood before releasing it. He sat bolt upright, and placing both hands on the sides of the coffin, leaped onto the hardwood floor. His cape billowed behind him with the movement, even as he took a fusillade of bullets.

The impact of the heavy, cast lead bullets knocked the thing backward, but he quickly rebounded, hissing – like a large cat. The brave with the torch thrust the flame at him, causing the demonic thing to back away.

Flinging the curtain aside, the Boy General assessed the situation with his keen eye. The Yellow Hair looked at the skewered Hunkpapa grasping the proboscis of the trocar that emerged from above the appendix, and quipped wittily:

"I think you got the point!"

"Stick by me!" Custer ordered Bloody Knife. "Let's head to the back door!"

Yelling and shouting grew as more shooting erupted in the parlor, the air was thick with gun smoke. More armed braves were entering through the front door and as Custer saw to his alarm, warriors approached the rear door, as well.

Some of them were wearing bison heads and their bodies were painted with white and red stripes. The war paint extended around their muscle corded arms and thick thighs. They were armed with rifles and shields, as well as an assortment of stone age weapons, such as spears and bows.

"Look for the cellar door – the door to the basement!" shouted the Yellow Hair. "It may be hidden by a throw-rug!"

"Boy General!" Bloody Knife yelled. "I find door on floor! It have stair!"

"Looks like we've run the fox to ground, Lester!" shouted a white man who entered the funeral parlor. Greasy blond hair and a scruffy, untrimmed beard somewhat masked the inbred features of the moron - a genetic abomination of the copulation of double first cousins so common in the hollows and cane brakes that prevailed in the Deep South.

"Sumabitch gotta be 'roun heah somewhere, Jimmy Carl!" answered Lester, shouting to be heard above the gunfire being directed at the vampire, who not only was holding his own against the increasing number of braves confronting him, but seemed to be gaining the upper hand.

"Why do you hesitate, Running Deer?" the Count was addressing the braves by their given names in their own languages which startled them. "Why do you back away from me, Dancing Bear?"

"Wheah you at boys?!" shouted the vampire in trashy Southern vernacular.

"We headin' down the basement after Custer!" answered Lester, confused by the addition of another English speaker to the fray.

"Well I be on yo ass lak a duck on a June bug!" shouted the European Count in response, ripping into the wavering throng of Cheyenne, tearing the Bowie knife from the hand of one and chopping with the deadly weapon as though it were a meat cleaver.

The torch wielding, thickly muscled tattooed arm of the brave who had first encountered the vampire fell to the floor as the cabinet containing the embalming fluids was pulled away from the wall and down to the rug immediately igniting.

The Dog Soldiers, some of whose faces were contorted in fear, were hurling whatever objects they could to impede the progress of the demon thing that staggered toward them, reeling under the gunfire. Its arms were extended in front with open, taloned hands as it advanced into the withering metal storm.

One of the braves, a tall husky Cheyenne wearing a tunic-like scarlet cloth shirt, knee length moccasins and an indigo muslin robe with braided edges backed away. He was lifting the magazine follower of his Henry and locking it into place, then he desperately fumbled sixteen of the huge .44 caliber copper cased cartridges into the top of the magazine near the muzzle of the repeater, sliding one in after another as they slid down the twenty-four-inch spring loaded magazine tube of the almost four-foot long rifle.

The funeral parlor erupted into a fireball with explosions of alcohol and embalming fluids. Hastily, a handful of surviving braves entered into the dark basement, including the two Galvanized Yankees, who pulled the basement door shut behind them and barred it with a heavy oak plank.

The Count, pulling at the door, at first could not get it to yield. Then with a strength born of rage and blood hunger he ripped the door from its hinges and flung it into the roaring flames that grew in size and intensity within the funeral parlor.

The caped figure of the vampire stood framed above the doorway, highlighted by the roaring inferno that raged all around him before stepping downward onto the stairwell.

"I'm commmmmminnnnnnnngggg!!!" announced the vampire in a thick accent heavy with Rumanian overtones as he stepped deliberately down each of the wooden steps, licking his chops with each foot placement.

Several of the warriors uttered expletives born of superstitious fear at the approach of the cloaked figure. Others crouched hidden behind coffins and caskets, some of which contained the embalmed corpses of Philistine citizenry who had been left unburied owing to the hasty flight of the town's population.

Custer fidgeted with the war bonnet in silence; he felt the sensation of electricity flooding his body, starting at the scalp.

"Follow me," the Yellow Hair instructed Bloody Knife, "we'll make for the stairs once that vampire is occupied with the others in here."

"We go up – into fire? Into that?" expostulated Bloody Knife.

"Yes," responded Custer. "Now standby, and on my mark go!"

Showers of sparks and flaming chunks of wood embedded with glowing coal fell through the basement opening, silhouetting the Count from behind, making his eyes glow like rubies as they peered into the darkness.

Custer felt the glowing, demonic eyes lock with his and before he could blink, the vampire was standing before him, lifting the war bonnet from his head and placing it on his own. The Yellow Hair stood immobile – unable to move his arms as the vampire stole the prized possession. The effect on the Count was immediate; he stood, hands to his temples as the power surged through him.

"Boy General! We make run for it!" urged Bloody Knife, "We go for stairs now!" Bloody Knife shoved Custer roughly past the Count, who seemed frozen in place, as though struck by lightning and did appear not to notice the egression of the Yellow Hair and Arikawa.

The torpor of the vampire; a servant of Satan, was temporary in duration. Feeling the power surge through its limbs, the undead advanced on Jimmy Carl, who moved further back into the shadows, placing several braves in front of him as he tried to reload his Colt Army painstakingly; one cylinder at a time.

As the searching, penetrating cerise eyes of the vampire regarded each man knowingly, the collective group of human prey could not help but feel a primordial fear of the carnivorous, demonic predator confronting them. The eyes of the vampire studied each man in turn and settled on Jimmy Carl.

"Do not live in hope! Young man! Zehr ist no vun to vrescue youuuuuuu!!!!!" laughed the Count in a booming, Eastern European accent at the horrified Jimmy Carl, who fumbled at the cylinder as he tamped down a round ball with the ramming plunger of the revolver.

The admonition of the Count was reciprocated by the sound of more laughter as the heavy lid opened on a mahogany casket and another cadaverous figure bolted upright.

"Shoot'im, Lester!" hollered Jimmy Carl. We're in a whole nest of 'em!" Two braves rushed the Count, who grabbed both by the hair and rammed their heads together, fracturing the skulls utterly. The ruptured, hemorrhaged brains oozed out as a combined mass and slopped onto the paved floor. The Count could not control himself and thrust his face into the neck of one, while releasing his grip on the other.

Six rapid-fire shots from Lester failed to hit the Count who now wore the war bonnet, even though they were fired from less than ten feet away.

Custer ran up the stairs followed by Bloody Knife. They ran through the flames of the parlor as the walls supporting the ceiling threatened to give way and collapse.

Leaping through the broken windows of the front of the burning building, Custer and Bloody Knife ran with their hair and clothing on fire and plunged into a watering trough for the horses.

The moon was gibbous, the main street of Philistine was thickly overgrown with sagebrush and buffalo grass that had sprouted from around and in between the cobble stones. The main street appeared as a wide, dull yellow path illuminated by the burning buildings of the town. Occasionally a brick wall would collapse, falling forward into the street and issuing an explosion of red and orange embers that seemed to reach to the moon's cusp before floating down and settling on the roofs of neighboring buildings.

Remaining in the watering trough, Lieutenant Colonel Custer and Bloody Knife peered cautiously over the edge for a scant moment, before ducking back under the water.

Teams of marauding aboriginals armed with repeating rifles edged around the corners of buildings, while a huge contingent moved along the street. Some were mounted on buffalo, lending a pristine effect to the eerie menagerie that threw monstrous, dancing shadows from the fiery light of flaming buildings.

Lieutenant Colonel Custer's head was above the water, but he would pull it back under as a turtle retracting its nose from the surface if needs be.

Bloody Knife was electrified with adrenaline born of fear. He crouched up to his nose in the fetid water, not daring to risk another glance over the edge. He glanced with worry at the Boy General, whose scorched yellow hair floated in the water that covered his shoulders.

A tremulous orgy of orgasmic colors exploded from the towers of multihued flame and reflected on the water's surface. The reflection caught on and sheened off the wet skin of the former general's face. The fire seemed to be prescient and alive on the surface of the mirror-like water. And it added another dimension to the overall aspect of the Boy General, thought Bloody Knife.

The Arikawa scout was conscious in this particular moment, as he had been at other times, of something strange and surreal about the former general. Custer did not think in the same direct manner as the other white men he had known; he was crazy.

Some people considered the Yellow Hair to be a gifted leader, with the luck that accompanies an accomplished gambler. That Custer himself outwardly did not seem to be aware of this made his persona even more magnetic. This, Bloody Knife knew, was one of the many things that inspired him to follow the man.

Custer and Bloody Knife both sensed the danger before seeing it and ducked their heads beneath the fires that reflected from the surface of the water.

An enormous albino wood bison, mounted by the medicine man White Bull approached the water trough. Weighing 2,800 pounds, the twelve-foot-long nearly seven-foot-tall at the shoulder buffalo plowed its muzzle into the water and began sucking in large volumes of the liquid.

It was joined by five Indian ponies of multiple colors that also began slaking their thirst with long, protracted sounds of suction.

The braves, Dog Soldiers armed with Henrys and Spencers, led by White Bull dismounted and moved stealthily toward the buildings that had not yet been set alight. Two warriors remained with their beasts, watching over them until the others returned.

The lungs of the Boy General began to burn, the water level of the trough had dropped precipitously and he had contorted into the fetal position as he held his breath. He was aware of movement to his right as Bloody Knife shifted and readjusted his position beneath the surface.

One of the braves, a tall, thin, sinewy Cheyenne of about forty years of age became suspicious – he didn't know why. Atop his black, double braided hair he wore an otter fur turban with a beaded rosette headband. His US Army shirt, taken from a slain Buffalo Soldier, had sergeant's chevrons sewn onto the sleeves and was decorated with buttons and beadwork. Two medals – one of them a Medal of Honor from the slain soldier, hung from his thick, trunk-like neck.

Handing the reins of his mounts to his fellow, he bent over the water trough and peered into it, seeing only the reflection of himself and of the fires that raged all around. Then suddenly a violent sequence of large bubbles broke the surface, distorting the mirrored imagery into a series of ripples that flowed outward in a sequel of growing, concentric circles.

Custer was looking up through the water at the face of the Indian who was looking down at him. When he could no longer hold his breath he coughed out his air in a stream of bubbles. The urge to inhale was overcoming the Boy General's iron resolve.

The brave reached into the watering trough, overcome with curiosity as to the origin of the bubbles. He felt something of a physical nature, of what – he could not be certain, as he ran his hand about Custer's upturned face.

The brave holding the reins of the horses and buffalo was distracted by sounds of crashing about that emanated from the burning mortuary directly in front of him.

Suddenly Custer and Bloody Knife exploded from the water simultaneously, Custer facing the brave that had been feeling about him. Water flew in slow motion from the swinging, top heavy blade of the Yellow Hair's Bowie knife as it cleft into the left side of the warrior's neck.

The off balanced blade clove into the sternocleidomastoid muscle of the warrior like a meat cleaver. The heavy fighting knife severed tendons and ligaments, along with the jugular vein and carotid artery. The warrior stepped back, his face a frozen mask of surprise as he thrust both hands to the mortal wound in a useless attempt to staunch the pulsating geyser of blood that jetted from between his fingers.

Bloody Knife tried to lunge from the water at the brave holding the horses and bison, but fell heavily to the ground. Unsure for a moment of whether to release the mounts or engage in combat, the brave chose to shout for help.

"Let's run for it!" shouted the Boy General to his scout.

The roaring of the fires and the crackling of burning timbers mixed with the shouts of the rampaging warriors as they burned the town. Long, wavering sheets of flame towered hundreds of feet above the burning buildings, hurling enormous, dancing black shadows along the main street of Philistine.

"What about..." expostulated Bloody Knife.

"Never mind! Run! We head east! Let's get the hell out of here!" responded Custer.

The Boy General and his Arikawa scout ran first to the church, centered on the right side of the town's main street. The church steeple was emphasized against the roaring oceans of fire in a Dante-like Inferno. Orange red flames that tongued hundreds of feet into the air sent myriad sparks soaring into the night sky, the halo from the conflagration could be seen from hundreds of miles.

"Boy General! Building going to fall, look out!" warned Bloody Knife, noticing too, that dozens of howling warriors were rushing upon them from behind.

"Let's go for it!" shouted the former general, running in front of the church and avoiding the inferno of wooden homes that roared behind it.

All around them the fires burned, human forms, made amorphous by the misguided light of structural fires could be seen darting among the howling structures. An unsteady rain of red hot cinders pelted the Boy General and his cohort as the burning church collapsed on the pursuing braves.

The former general and the Arikawa found their egress defied by a solid sheet of flame; they could barely hear their shouts to each other above the yawning, crackling snaps and rifle shot popping of incinerating timber.

The air was made thick with smoke, and the heat threatened to scorch their lungs. They began to backtrack through the lurid glow, looking for any means of escape.

"At this point, Bloody Knife," Custer was shouting almost into the ear of his friend, "all that matters now is getting out of Philistine! There's got to be a way out of here!"

Suddenly three Northern Cheyenne exploded through the flame of a fallen structure, they rolled on the burnt grass of the main street trying to suffocate the flames of their burning hair and clothing.

"We'll go that way!" shouted Lieutenant Colonel Custer. A one lane street, completely covered by flames on either side was the exit that Custer sought. Without vacillation he and Bloody Knife ran into the raging corridor, deafened by the crashing of floors and roaring of heavy, hardwood structural timbers that were collapsing all around them. Wind fanned the flames, whipping them into firestorms of tornadic intensity.

The Boy General and his Arikawa scout ran bent at the waist, breathing through rags as they stepped on the live coals that covered the street, melting through the soles of their boots and moccasins. The heat singed their hair and eyebrows, the urge to close their eyes against the heat was denied as they hurtled through the roaring hell.

"Boy General!" yelled Bloody Knife. "Your back on fire!" quickly the Arikawa knocked out the flame from Custer's back. Glowing cinders fell like a molten rain on the two escapees. Their hands were badly blistered from constantly brushing coals from their hair and clothing. Often, the coals penetrated completely through the rags they now wore.

The pair choked on black, consuming smoke as they staggered through the whirling eddies of flame on either side of them. The entire sky had become an orange glow from the numerous tornadic vortexes of fire that spiraled upward into the glowing sky.

"By the Gods I think we may survive!" cried the former general, as the pair stumbled into a burnt out area, left completely devoid of any remaining combustible fuel. It was a charred, blackened and smoking landscape illuminated eerily with the glow of hundreds of thousands of glowing coals and embers that continued to rain down.

"Boy General! I see something move up ahead!" warned Bloody Knife.

A dark, furtive figure whirled suddenly at the sound of the Arikawa's voice. The clothing and hair were singed from the humanoid body. Through the smoke the demonic creature that had been the Count saw the Arikawa and lifted its face upward, trying to scent through the smoke. Its yellowed, ivory canines could be discerned as it contemplated what it would do next. The war bonnet, or what remained of it, was burned almost beyond recognition and the creature sought escape in the end, as dawn approached.

Lieutenant Colonel Custer and his ally watched as the vampire vanished like a phantom into the banks of smoke that hovered over the fire blasted landscape like a sea of fog.

"We've got to head straight for Fort Wallace," exclaimed Custer to the Arikawa, "and warn Colonel Bankhead that the entire Native American population has risen in rebellion!"

What the Yellow Hair did not say however, was the urgent need to telegraph his wife, Libbie, that the war bonnet of Roman Nose was lost forever to the flames of Philistine, provided that the telegraph line had not been cut, speculated the Yellow Hair. This would further complicate his tenuous relationship with his wife, who held him accountable for her sterility.

The late summer sun began to rise like a cauldron of molten gold, shimmering through the heatwaves of the burning town of Philistine as Custer and Bloody Knife made their way east, toward Fort Wallace.

About the Author

I'm William (Bill) Sumrall, born in Florida back in 1959.

A biography, such a simple word, but when one is faced with describing his own life it becomes less simple. Complicated is a better word. As a young man I took a BA in Spanish. I was a sergeant in a Marine Rifle Company. Also, I have a wide array of interests and hobbies, the latest being a popular game called "Trivia Crack."

I married at age thirty to my wife Maria and we have two adult children; daughter Kyla in the Navy and son Billy in the Army.

I work in a rural hospital in Oklahoma.

Writing escapist historical fiction has given me a lot of laughs. I hope nobody gets too bent out of shape with my portrayal of the Weird West.

More by William Sumrall:

Metal Storm: Weird Custer

Coming Soon!

Washita! Weird Custer